Walter Besant

The Life and Achievements of Edward Henry Palmer

Late Lord Almoner's professor of Arabic in the University of Cambridge and fellow

of Saint John's college

Walter Besant

The Life and Achievements of Edward Henry Palmer
Late Lord Almoner's professor of Arabic in the University of Cambridge and fellow of Saint John's college

ISBN/EAN: 9783744751582

Printed in Europe, USA, Canada, Australia, Japan

Cover: Foto ©Raphael Reischuk / pixelio.de

More available books at **www.hansebooks.com**

EDWARD HENRY PALMER.

THE

LIFE AND ACHIEVEMENTS

OF

EDWARD HENRY PALMER

LATE LORD ALMONER'S PROFESSOR OF ARABIC
IN THE UNIVERSITY OF CAMBRIDGE AND
FELLOW OF SAINT JOHN'S COLLEGE

BY WALTER BESANT, M.A.

LONDON
JOHN MURRAY, ALBEMARLE STREET
1883

PJ64
P35 B47

PREFACE.

MY OWN ACQUAINTANCE with EDWARD PALMER began in the year 1868 or 1869, when he first went out to the Desert and Peninsula of Sinai, as a member of Captain Wilson's Surveying Expedition. After his return we worked a good deal together on various subjects, chiefly connected with the Holy Land ; and quite naturally, because everybody who worked with Palmer became his friend, our acquaintance ripened into a friendship, which has been to me one of the greatest joys of my life. There are many older friends of his who would, perhaps, have done fuller justice to the man, and produced a better record. The lot, however, fell upon me to write this book. I had to write the history of a life which in many respects was unique. Palmer was a scholar and student most earnest and resolute, yet always with the heart of a boy ; so great a linguist that he stood alone, yet

always modest; full of reliance in himself and his
own powers, yet never vainglorious; always at work,
yet always with time for leisure; the most serious
man in the world when he had a purpose in view, yet
the most delightful and the most mirthful of companions.   It was decreed by fate that this great
Oriental scholar was to become a friend of gipsies,
a conjurer and magician, an intrepid explorer of un-
visited deserts, a writer of leading articles, a translator of the New Testament, a mesmerist, and, among
his friends, a *raconteur* of the first order.   Finally,
it was ordered for him that he should end his days
after an exploit unparalleled, and in a manner
strange, wonderful, and tragic; and that he should
find a resting-place with England's heroes.   To write
this life has been my task.

In one sense it is a compilation.   Everybody
has been anxious to communicate something to make
it complete.   His early history and his undergraduate life have been related to me by his cousin,
Mr. Edward Russell; by his old friends, the Rev.
Alfred Bridgman and the Rev. Joseph Pulliblank;
by Dr. Parkinson, Professor Bonney, Mr. Todhunter,
the Rev. Arthur Calvert, who were tutors and lec-
turers of St. John's in his time; by Professor Cowell,
who examined him in Persian; by Mr. Walter
Pollock, Mr. Gordon Wigan, Mr. Aubrey Stewart,

and others, who were his friends at Cambridge ;
by Mr. Charles Leland, his gipsy 'pal'; by Mr.
Stanley Lane Poole, himself an eminent Arabic
scholar ; by Mr. Robert Wilson, Palmer's colleague
in journalism ; and by a great many others, to
whom I am profoundly indebted.   Above all, I
have to thank the Regius Professor of Arabic in
the University of Oxford, Mr. G. F. Nicholl, for the
learned paper he has placed in my hands on Palmer's
Oriental work.   Such an estimate was absolutely
necessary to complete the life of a man who, though
he worked at many things, and made himself master
of many arts and accomplishments, as the reader will
learn in the chapters which follow, was above all, and
before all, a scholar in Persian, Urdu, and Arabic.

W. B.

United University Club :
May 1883.

CONTENTS.

———◦◦◦———

THE

LIFE AND ACHIEVEMENTS

OF

EDWARD HENRY PALMER.

———•◦•———

CHAPTER I.

THE DAY OF SMALL THINGS.

I HAVE TO RELATE the history of a life beginning
under apparently unfavourable conditions, and showing at first little promise of becoming different from
ordinary lives, which, by a happy accident—or by
Providence—was directed into an unexpected way
of great and exceptional honour, and which, at last,
found an ending as tragic as any recorded by poet or
historian, after an exploit without a parallel in the
heroic deeds of all the ages. To one who considers
at the outset this achievement alone, it seems as if the
whole of the previous life may be regarded as the
preparation for it. So much, indeed, may always be
said of any great and noble deed. But I think that
in this case there is more to justify the opinion than

B

can generally be observed.   The work that Palmer accomplished at last could not have been done save by a man who had lived the life which he lived, step by step, learned the things which he learned, did the things which he did, possessed at first, as he possessed them, and developed, as carefully as he developed them, the same rare and wonderful faculties.

It is the history of a man who was a great scholar, yet never a bookworm ; a great linguist, yet never a pedant ; a man of the schools, yet no mere grammarian ; a man of the pen and the study, yet one who loved to go about, observant, among his fellow-men : a man separated, as all real students must be, from the common struggles and selfish interests of most men, yet one who could sympathise with and understand the better side of those struggles ; one to whom there were no ranks, grades, or distinctions of men at all—a true Republican : to whom men were interesting or dull, curious, attractive, or the reverse, according to their qualities and not their position ; who was prepared to love a prince as much as he might love a pauper, and was ready, on occasion, to esteem a bishop as much as he might esteem a gipsy tramp.   There are startling incidents in his history ; curious and unexpected things happen in it, things such as do not happen to common people.   The subject of the biography is from the beginning strangely unlike other men.   He is a *Wunderkind* ; in the old days he would have been attributed to the fairies in a benevolent mood. He is unlike anybody else : he possesses strange gifts ; all sorts and conditions of men are attracted by him ; the grave college Don thinks it a privilege to look after him, because he is in practical matters helpless ; yet with a misgiving, because he is a new experience and no one knows what may happen with him ; even the Ritualist clergyman, although he knows that Palmer has called him the man dressed in book-markers, regards him with affection.   The gipsy, the German peasant, the English tramp, the Druse, the Syrian, the Arab, the Persian, the Indian Prince, all alike acknowledge the glamour of his presence, obey his bidding, and are ready to follow him, to get up or to sit down at the motion of his finger.   A *Wunderkind* indeed !

Edward Henry Palmer was born on August 7, 1840, in Green Street, Cambridge. His father, also a native of the town, kept a private school. He died when his son was still little more than an infant, and his death was followed by that of the child's mother, whose funeral was one of the earliest things he could remember.

On the maternal side the child was connected with a family named Sword, of New Buckenham, in Norfolk ; and by his grandmother he belonged to the small Highland clan Chisholm, his great-grandfather having been very honourably hanged for his share in the 1745 rebellion. Those who care for show and display might desire a lineage and ancestry more illustrious. The result, however, is more to be considered than the means. And besides, if one considers the means, it must be owned that a ' blend ' in which the sturdy blood of the Highlander, of the Norfolk farmer, and of the stout Fenman are the component parts would seem at the very outset to promise well. Certainly in this case the outcome proved beyond all reasonable expectation.

I have little information about the father except that he was a man of considerable acquirements, with a strong taste for art. Some of his paintings have been preserved, and show great power and feeling. A portrait of himself, now in the possession of his daughter-in-law, is characterised by a certain fineness in expression which was specially noticeable in his son. One is quite sure, from a consideration of this portrait, that there were great thoughts in the man, with possibilities and powers undeveloped ; but consumption, or bronchial asthma, which his son inherited, carried him off before the age of thirty ; so that, outside his own family circle, no one knew much about him, and perhaps, after all, if he had lived a long life, his ambition might have mounted no higher than the successful conduct of a middle-class school, with time and opportunity to paint and read, and to meditate things lofty—an unknown scholar and student among the scholars and students of the great University in which he had no actual share or part.

The child's only inheritance was a tendency to asthma and bronchial disease.   Fortunately he had an aunt, then unmarried, who was able to take him to her own house and there to educate him.   There were two other cousins, about Edward's own age, who were brought up by the same kind and large-hearted woman.   She was, so far as Edward was concerned, a mother indeed; she loved him as her own son, and he, who owed everything to her, never spoke of her in after years without the greatest tenderness and emotion.

The town of Cambridge has furnished a goodly number of eminent scholars for its University, from Jeremy Taylor to Edward Palmer.   A clever and bookish boy cannot fail, indeed, to be attracted by the prizes held forth with hands so lavish by the many noble foundations of the place.   The colleges are always there ; the gownsmen are always in evidence about the streets ; there is, in fact, hardly a family in the place which has not been honourably connected by some member or other with the University.   We should, therefore, have expected that the earliest imagination of a clever Cambridge boy would have been fired by his surroundings.   It would have been, we might think, his natural course, after a career of distinction at the grammar school, to have entered as an . undergraduate, proceeded to take a good degree, and, in due time, to obtain a fellowship.   Also, in the ordinary course, he would have presently taken orders, become college lecturer, college dean, tutor, what not, and finally settled down to the comfortable obscurity of a fat college living. This, which is the history of most lads of promise, might have been Palmer's history. Unfortunately, there was one thing which, at the very outset, rendered this career impossible. It was the simple fact that Palmer did not greatly distinguish himself at school ; he was not a bookworm, nor was he precocious.

His school life began at a private school, conducted by a Mr. Johnson, and was continued at the Perse Grammar School,[1] whose Head Master was then the Rev. Peter Mason. Here he made fairly good progress in Latin and Greek, arriving at the sixth form before he was fifteen. But he always disliked mathematics. Now, many town boys of Cambridge have entered the University from the Perse School, but, so far as I remember, nearly all of them, in and before Palmer's time, were mathematicians. Certainly Palmer's attainments, or promise, did not so far impress his friends as to justify an attempt at fortune—which at Cambridge means a fellowship—through the University.

Those who remember him at that time, and were his schoolfellows, say that he was always small, and apparently weak of frame, yet that he could do things which proved great muscular strength and endur-

---

[1] They are so careful of their history at the Perse School that the present Head Master assures me he can find no record of Palmer having been there at all. Fortunately I have learned the particulars given above from some of his schoolfellows.

ance ; thus he was admirable on the trapeze and the gymnastic bars, and he was a bold and fearless swimmer. He took no part in the cricket field or at football, but he was clever with his fingers and he was constantly making or devising things ; he read a great deal, especially poetry ; and he was greatly caressed and petted by everybody, partly on account of a general belief that he would die very early, partly on account of the singular personal charm which was always his most striking characteristic.

He began to feel his way in languages while still a boy at school, independently of his Latin and Greek. He learned Romany. This is not a language with a grammar, save at those heights of pure Romany to which few of the People attain. It is a vocabulary. The boy learned it by paying travelling tinkers sixpence for a lesson, by haunting the tents, talking to the men, and crossing the women's palms with his pocket money in exchange for a few more words to add to his vocabulary. In this way he gradually made for himself a gipsy dictionary. No one of all those who have been attracted by these picturesque wanderers knew them better, or could more readily enter into their minds, than Palmer—not even his brother in Romany lore, Charles Leland. This acquisition of Romany is the only achievement of his school days in which one can find promise of the later years. There are not, it may be owned, many schoolboys who save up their pocket money in order

to take lessons of tramps and vagabonds in the
gipsy tongue.

Then came the time when thought must be taken
about his future.   Now when a boy belongs to the
middle class, if he has shown no promise at school
of ambition and distinction, as a matter of course
he is destined to remain on the same level in which
he was born.   Therefore, as there was some family
interest in the city of London, the boy was sent up
there, and for three years was a clerk among clerks.
Nothing could have been better for him ; he learned,
in this way, experience, self-reliance, knowledge of
men and of the world.   It was a very good thing
indeed for him to escape for awhile from the semi-
monastic life of the University, and to learn that there
is a wide world outside the colleges.   One need expend no regrets at the apparent waste of time, for, in
fact, there was no wasted time ; the London years
were productive of excellent fruit.   The things he
learned and did while a clerk were of immense value
to him ; he found out, for instance, that if you
ardently desire a thing you can generally get it if
you work hard enough for it (at Cambridge he would
have been taught to get it through the help of a
private tutor) ; that, as regarded his own brains, he
had the power of learning a good deal, certainly as
much as most men have, perhaps more ; that what
other men had done he could try to do : in other
words, he learned self-confidence, a thing in which

most young Englishmen are so sadly deficient. He learned something of his own powers; understood something of what he could do, and trusted himself so far.

The house in which Palmer became a junior clerk was that of Hill and Underwood, of Eastcheap. The work he had to do was, of course, that usually assigned to boys on entering. It is not, it may be presumed, very delightful work; in fact, there can be, one imagines, nothing very delightful in City work until one arrives at sharing the profits. And then the joy of the work must depend on the amount of the profits. Palmer's duties were what is called 'dock business.' As regards his prospects, one does not know exactly which these were; a great many clerks enter the City every year with no prospect at all but to continue in clerkery until the appointed end; a great many also look forward to promotion, to partnership, to ultimate independence. Perhaps Palmer's aunt, who was comparatively wealthy, had it in her mind to buy him a partnership. Most probably no plans at all were formed, or even thought of, beyond the first necessity for business training and the acquisition of the *technique*. Nor need we believe that the boy had conceived as yet any definite ambitions or plans of his own; he was still only a lad, and docile; he did what he was told to do; he performed his allotted tasks with diligence; he studied to please his employers as an honest lad should; so that, though his capacity for business, that is to say, for his own business, afterwards proved to be minute, one is not surprised to hear that when he left the service of the firm the senior partner bade him farewell with the assurance that he was the very best clerk the house had ever had.   This is good to learn, but it must be understood as applying to the duties of a junior clerk only, because in after life there never was any man more unable to look after affairs.   Perhaps, however, the dock department had no connection at all with the financial.   Now, where no money was concerned Palmer could be quite methodical and a mere creature of order.   It is possible, therefore, that in the nice conduct of 'dock business' Palmer may have had no fellow.

The leisure hours of a young City clerk are generally uninteresting to look back upon, even to him who has enjoyed or wasted them.   Those, however, of young Palmer were full of interest and active work.   He was restless ; he could not sit still without occupation ; the day's routine of office did not satisfy his brain.   First and most important of all, he began to learn Italian, working at the language without assistance, and at first by the old-fashioned methods of grammar, syntax exercises, and so forth.   All these appliances he presently threw aside as useless encumbrances.   Most of us, when we learn a new language, want to know it just well enough to read it easily ; but Palmer wanted to know it thoroughly, to speak

it, think in it, make it a part of himself. In those
early days, as afterwards, this was an instinctive
desire with him. He became possessed by an over-
powering ardour to obtain the mastery of Italian.

The method he pursued is instructive. He found
out where Italians might be expected to meet, and
went every evening to sit among them and hear them
talk. Thus, there was in those days a café in Titch-
borne Street frequented by Italian refugees, political
exiles, and republicans. Here Palmer sat and listened and presently began to talk, and so became an
ardent partisan of Italian unity. There was also at
that time—I think many of them have now migrated
to Hammersmith—a great colony of Italian organ-
grinders and sellers of plaster-cast images in and
about Saffron Hill. He went among these worthy
people, sat with them in their restaurants, drank their
sour wine, talked with them and acquired their patois.
He found out Italian waiters at restaurants and talked
with them ; at the Docks he went on board Italian
ships, and talked with the sailors ; and in these ways,
learned the various dialects of Genoa, Naples, Nice,
Livorno, Venice, and Messina. One of his friends at
this time was a well-known Signor Buonocorre, the
so-called 'Fire King,' who used to astonish the multitude nightly at Cremorne Gardens and elsewhere by
his feats. For Palmer was always attracted by people
who run shows, 'do' things, act, pretend, persuade,
deceive, and in fact are interesting for any kind of

cleverness. However, the first result of this perseverance was that he made himself a perfect master of
Italian, that he knew the country speech as well as
the Italian of the schools, and that he could converse
with the Piedmontese, the Venetian, the Roman, the
Sicilian, or the Calabrian, in their own dialects, as
well as with the purest native of Florence.

Also while he was in the City he acquired French
by a similar process. I do not know whether he
carried on his French studies at the same time with
the Italian, but I believe not. It seems certainly
more in accordance with the practice which he
adopted in after life that he should attempt only one
thing at a time. But as with Italian so with French ;
he joined to a knowledge of the pure language a
curious acquaintance with *argot* ; also—which points
to acquaintance made in cafés—he acquired somehow
in those early days a curious knowledge and admiration of the French police and detective system.

The clerk who at the age of eighteen has thoroughly
mastered and made his own, without help or instruction, two foreign languages, not to speak of Romany,
is not common, I believe, in the City. Still less common is the man who has discovered so early the only
true method to the learning of languages, and steadily
follows that road. ' Either you want to learn a language,' he would say, ' or you do not. If you do
not, follow the way of the English schools, and you
will succeed. If, however, you do——'—and here he

would go on to explain how it should first be studied
without the grammar, and with the intention of acquiring, to begin with, the most important part of the actual
vocabulary ; how languages, being in groups, present
vocabularies which, with certain variations, are common property ; how inflections, suffixes, and so forth,
also resemble each other, and therefore come quite
easily to the man who has begun with the words, so
that in learning simply how to read a tongue, without
opening anything more than a dictionary, you acquire
insensibly a vast amount of grammar and a great
quantity of syntax. The true reason, he always insisted,
of the really brilliant failure to teach modern languages
which distinguishes our schools is that we only approach them by the aid of grammars modelled after
the Latin and Greek manner, and that we mistake
the teaching of inflection and syntax for that of
language.   Any intelligent person, Palmer maintained, can learn to read a language in a few weeks,
and to speak it in a few months, unless it be his first
attempt at an Oriental language.   Of course it is
given to few to be able really to master even one
foreign language thoroughly ; but at least we might
try Palmer's method, which undoubtedly succeeded
with him ; we might try whether by its means we
cannot give our boys and girls such a knowledge
of European languages as will enable them to read
their literature with ease and enjoyment, if not to
speak and write them with the correctness of a

pedantic grammarian. It has, however, been decided
by Head Masters that the principal part of such education shall be the writing of exercises in the niceties
of the language; such as—in French, for instance—the
correct use of the past participle, which most Frenchmen do not know, or that of the imperfect subjunc-
tive, which all Frenchmen have long since abandoned;
so that one need hardly wonder why not one boy
in fifty acquires enough French even to read the
newspapers when he is abroad.

During this period one hears nothing at all of
what we should call serious reading. In fact, there was
nothing. Palmer was never, for instance, a student,
in the proper sense of the word, of English literature;
he professed to know nothing of the subject. In his
writings—I mean especially his leading articles and his
later journalistic work—he hardly ever quotes passages
from English authors, and he never labours to show
that intimate familiarity with ancient and modern
writers which it is apparently the sole aim of a small
school in the profession of journalism to display; yet,
on the other hand, if in conversation or reading he
heard or came upon a reference to any English work,
he always recognised it; and he certainly had read
most, if not all, the best authors at some time in his
life. At this time, however, he was too much occupied with other things. For instance, there were first
of all his duties in the City. The hours of the daily
attendance of the young City clerk were then, I be-

lieve, longer than they are now. From nine to five was the ordinary time, but frequently the clerks had to stay till six, and sometimes later. Now, the passion for Italian and French, and this continual quest and search after interesting and conversational foreigners, must have occupied a great many of the few hours left for amusement. The theatre took a good many more, because the drama was always to him the most delightful of amusements; then one supposes that there were some evenings at least, given to society and friends; there were tentative efforts also at photography, but this art soon failed to charm; there was an attempt at wood-carving; and, lastly, there was mesmerism.

When a man begins to mesmerise he opens the door to many wonderful things and to great dangers. The mesmeric power is so strange and incomprehensible a thing that it may lead one on and attract the attention little by little until it excludes all other pursuits: it is, also, so exacting a thing that it weakens, and finally destroys, the nervous power of him who practises it too long; again, it is so subtle a thing that, unless the power be continually exercised, it is apt to be lost.

'Let us,' said Palmer one day to his cousin Mr. Edward Russell, who then lived with him in lodgings, 'let us try to mesmerise each other, and see what will happen.'

This was a sort of formula which he was always

using whenever he touched upon a new thing. 'Let us try, and see what will happen.'

They had been reading together some book upon mesmerism, and they proceeded accordingly to make experiments. It was presently discovered that Palmer possessed the power in a very remarkable degree. He found that he could not only throw a person into the mesmeric trance, but he could make that person do anything he pleased while in the trance. On one occasion he is reported to have used his power in a curiously practical manner. He found a woman lying on a doorstep late at night. She had fallen down, or been knocked over, or met with some other accident, and was in great pain and unable to move. He mesmerised her as she lay, and then went for assistance, and carried her, still unconscious, to the nearest hospital. On another occasion, some years later, at Cambridge, he mesmerised a friend of his, then an undergraduate of Trinity, who was suffering from neuralgia. No one before, I am assured by the patient himself, a man not in the least given to believe in strange powers, had ever succeeded, although many had tried, in throwing him into the mesmeric sleep. When the mesmeric trance ceased the neuralgia was gone. However, of late years Palmer quite ceased to exercise this power, because he found that it caused too great a strain upon his nervous strength.

Little remains to be said about this London time, except that in these years he made the friendship of

Mr. Henry Irving—a friendship which he retained unbroken to the end. It is remarkable indeed that two young men should have been thus thrown together in early life for both of whom was destined a career so honourable and so illustrious. Are there in the City at this moment, one asks, two other friends in youth, one of whom is destined to be the greatest actor of his day and the other the greatest Orientalist?

It was in the year 1859 that Palmer began to be threatened with symptoms of pulmonary disease. These rapidly increased, and became at length so alarming that he was sent to one of the best physicians. He was told that his situation was extremely critical, and that, in fact, unless the disease could be arrested, which was unlikely, he had better put his house in order, because, in a few months at best, he would cease to exist. The poor lad received this dreadful intelligence with resignation. One thing was clear to him : if he was going to die it was no use worrying himself any more with the City. Somebody else, not under immediate sentence, might be found to do the dock business. He, for his part, would go back to Cambridge, and die there as comfortably as possible. Thither he went, thinking that he should see London no more, nor his friends the refugees, conspirators, gipsies, organ-grinders, fire kings, and foreign sailors, and have no more joy in the light of the sun, but should sit expectant, until the end, beneath the shadow of the tomb. And then a very singular thing hap-

C

pened.   I tell it as it was told to me by himself, not once but several times, and as it was certified to me by others who know the story to be true.

There was at that time a certain herbalist living at Cambridge, named Sherringham.   Now the profession of herbalist is one which still exists, and is even extensively, though obscurely, practised, although ordinary people know, as a rule, little about it.   The followers of the craft, in fact, preserve the old traditions concerning the efficacy of certain drugs and herbs, most of which are quite common, and may be gathered in the fields.   There is no disease which they do not profess to cure by the administration of these herbs, and their pharmacopœia is, or used to be before the decay of the profession, very extensive.   I have been assured by a physician that many of the herbs used by herbalists do actually possess the valuable medicinal properties attributed to them, though they have been supplanted by other drugs of more recent discovery and more efficacious action.   There are still, in fact, thousands of people, especially in the great towns, who would not willingly consult any other doctor than the herbalist, and they are strong believers in the powers of marjory, feverfew, dandelion, camomile, and other plants which the old women formerly gathered in the hedges for the curing of the village folk.   The man Sherringham was one of these unlicensed practitioners.   Now, whether Palmer went to consult him, or one of his friends went, or, which is

quite possible, the man himself knew Palmer and
volunteered his experience and skill, I know not : but,
at all events, he did listen to Sherringham, did take
his advice, and did follow the treatment recommended
by him.   It was simple : it consisted of a single very
strong dose of lobelia, a herb which produces, I am
told, effects similar to those of hemlock.   The patient
was first seized with a violent attack of vomiting ;
then a cold chill laid hold of his feet, and slowly
mounted upwards ; it froze his limbs, which he could
no longer move, and struck his heart, which ceased to
beat, and his throat, which ceased to breathe.   They
had sent for a doctor by this time.

'I felt myself,' he said, describing this experience,
'I felt myself dying ; I was being killed by this
dreadful cold spreading all over me.   I was quite
certain that my last moments had arrived.   By the
bedside stood my aunt, poor soul, crying.   I saw the
doctor feeling a pulseless wrist, watch in hand ; the
cold dews of death were on my forehead ; the cold
hand of death was on my limbs.   Up to my lips, but
no higher, I thought I was actually dead, and could
see and hear, but not speak, not even when the doctor
let my hand fall upon the pillow and said solemnly,
" He is gone ! " '

There was no pain, except the feeling of intense
cold, he used to add, nor was he in any concern,
except that he wished he had finished a certain book
he had begun, and he wondered whether in the next

world he would have the chance of finishing it.
' The act of dying,' he would say, ' is nothing to what
people think. I have been dead myself, and ought
to know.'

And then ?

Then he recovered. He recovered suddenly. New
strength came to him ; he not only got the better of
this poison, but the lobelia, or something else, got the
better of his disease.   The consumption was arrested,
and he was no more troubled for the rest of his life,
except on one occasion, with any more anxiety about
his lungs. This strange story is absolutely true, and
is known to all who knew Palmer at that time.

Restored to life, and now convalescent, Palmer,
with the happy *insouciance* of his nature, which
allowed him always to enjoy whatever sunshine there
might be anywhere within reach, proceeded to amuse
himself till the time should arrive when he must
again work. We must remember that up to this
period he had not considered seriously the question
of work at all. In fact, he never, unless he was
obliged, all his life considered the question of work
for money, and the passion for work which afterwards
seized and held him was as yet undeveloped, except
when called into existence for the purpose of learning
French and Italian. He was now an idler: he did not
know what he was going to do ; he hardly thought
about the future ; he must first get strong and well. So
he began, as soon as he could walk again, to amuse him-

self ; he tried writing verses, which is an occupation not
fatiguing to a weak person ; he also began to write
farces, burlesques, plays.   When he grew stronger he
began to act ; he joined an amateur theatrical corps,
and he discovered that he could act better than most
of its members, perhaps better than any.   He also tried,
a second time, wood-engraving, which he again gave
up ; modelling, an art which he always loved ; drawing
and painting.   In the year 1860 he put forth a little
poem in imitation of the Ingoldsby Legends, called
' Ye Hole in ye Wall,' of which all that can be said is,
that for a lad of twenty it is very creditable.   Perhaps
we are not so fond of this style of composition now
as we were twenty years ago.   Such as it was it
pleased the late Mr. Daniel Macmillan, who published
it.   It was illustrated with lithographic sketches drawn
by Palmer himself and a friend.   The following passage will be enough :—

> Oh ! 'tis a glorious thing to stand
> On the shore and gaze on the deep blue sea,
> And feel the innermost soul expand
> With the joyous sense of liberty ;
> But those who never yet have known
> The oppression of a tyrant's sway,
> Nor been in gloomy dungeons thrown,
> Debarred from e'en the light of day,
> Know not the wild, ecstatic glee
> A prisoner feels when he's set free.

He seems, too, at this time to have resumed in a
languid way his old classical reading ; he translated,

for instance, Horace's Epistles, and certain favourite
passages of Homer.   His principal amusement, however, was acting ; he appeared three times on the
stage of the Cambridge Theatre in the year 1860,
once as Timothy, in 'The Soldier's Daughter,' once
in the farce of 'Only a Butterfly,' and once as
Biondello in 'Katharine and Petruchio.'   He also
wrote a farce called 'A Volunteer in Difficulties,'
which was played at Cambridge in October 1860, during the performance of Mr. and Mrs. Charles Kean.
As regards this little play he gave it afterwards to
the Brothers Webb after a performance as the two
Dromios at the Cambridge Theatre, which greatly
pleased him.   On another occasion about the same
time he actually consented to appear at Lynn Regis,
not as an amateur, but as a member of a professional
troupe.   He did not keep his appointment, however,
because he missed his train, and so lost that and any
other chance of becoming an actor.   Had he adopted
the stage as a profession he might have become a
very good actor, but certainly his physique was not
strong enough for the fatigues of an actor's life.
Perhaps there would have been nothing better for him,
had he been an actor, than a little local reputation
and an early grave.   He abandoned, then, the idea
of the stage as a profession, not because he loved
acting less, but because he was rapidly learning to
love something else, of greater importance, much more.
    The period of convalescence closes the first period

of Palmer's life, and begins the second. Hitherto he has been a lad, whose dexterity, brightness, and cleverness, coupled with the best and sweetest disposition, made him beloved by all who knew him. But there has been nothing serious in his pursuits. And there was no one among his Cambridge friends able to guide him into the right way; he had not yet found out himself; nor had he as yet made any influential friends who could advise with him seriously as to his future; nor, again, had he as yet, though already twenty years of age, got any hints or suspicions as to what that future must be. Yet this lad, so fond of things which to many seem merely frivolous, was to become one of the greatest scholars among men. Is there any parallel to this in the whole history of scholarship or literature?

In appearance Palmer was of short stature, a little man, with narrow, sloping shoulders and contracted chest. His figure had, in later years, a slight stoop, caused by continued bending over his desk; his arms were long, and he had remarkable fingers, delicate, long, thin; fingers which belong to the acutely nervous temperament, fingers which seem endowed with a separate individuality. Most men's fingers are dull things, without expression; Palmer's seemed to think and act for themselves, without waiting for orders. His features were clear, his nose straight and finely cut, his forehead high and broad, but somewhat retreating ; it was not the high narrow forehead which goes generally with the theologian, nor was it the broad square forehead of the geometrician.   His hair was brown and silky, and later on he grew a long beard, also brown and silky.   His eyes were curiously large and limpid, and they protruded, as happens to most linguists, so that by all the rules he ought to have been shortsighted.   But the rules in this case were wrong, for his sight was singularly good.   They were also very soft eyes, such as a woman might delight in if he were to love her.

There are two other great linguists upon whom in my pilgrimage I have chanced to light ; one is Signor Lanzone of Turin, the other M. Clermont Ganneau of Paris.   Now both these men are wonderful Arabic scholars, and both have eyes which, although they are not the least like Palmer's, in many points remind one of his.   There is exactly the same *character* in them.   As for his voice, it was soft, and what the French call *caressante.*

One cannot expect that a man who nearly died of consumption should be strong of muscle ; in fact, he was a weak man, unless he was roused.   But then he was full of strength.   It was shown on one occasion while he was still in the City.   He was walking down the Whitechapel Road, when a thief made a snatch at his watch ; Palmer seized him, and they fell together.   The usual crowd gathered round to see the rough-and-tumble which followed.   It was conducted on principles not recognised by the Ring, for, while the thief kicked, Palmer, with the grip of a bulldog, was pounding his man's head and grinding his unlucky nose upon the edge of the curb stone, insomuch that when he had worked his term and came out of prison his own friends failed to recognise that pickpocket. This is the only actual fight which I find recorded of him. It is enough to show that his spirit was great though his arm was weak.

One sees, in fact, in the youth all the characteristics of the man. When he loved his work he poured his whole soul into it. And he was a great lover of amusement as well as of work ; he was always trying some new and ingenious method of amusement ; he made for himself the happiness for which some men pine and feebly grumble ; everything that he admired he tried to do, and he saw no reason why he should not be able to do a thing which other men have done. At all events, to use his frequent form of words, ' Let us try and see what will happen.' He had already tried a good deal, but very little had happened ; he was now about to try another thing, and a great deal was going to happen.

Before we go on to tell what that was let us just remind ourselves once more that Palmer was as yet only twenty years of age, and yet he had already done these things and had these experiences. Not very much, yet how much more than can be related of the ordinary City clerk at twenty-one ! And if he had

been the ordinary clever boy of books at school, with
the usual sequel of a scholarship at Cambridge, and a
fellowship to follow, where would have been the Italian
and French work, with the experiences and acquaintance of strange folk, and the mesmerising, and the
walking about London, and the acting ?   It is always
safest to follow the beaten track ; those men know
least anxiety who tramp along the broad highroads,
but how much more interest is crowded into the
narrow span of life by those who journey—in the
same direction, it is true—through the by-paths and
the winding lanes, where you may easily miss your
way, or even fall into a quag, or into a pit, or down
a hill, or among robbers, but which are full of beauty,
which catch the sunrise and the sunset, the falling
lights and shadows, and are set with dainty flowers,
and lie between leafy hedges, and are very, very much
fresher than the dusty road, and which abound at
every step with Arabs, gipsies, tramps, Hindoos,
authors, Persians, patriots, actors, showmen, poets,
jugglers, acrobats, tinkers, and all kinds of curious,
disreputable, and interesting people !

CHAPTER II.

CAMBRIDGE.

IT was about the close of the year 1860 that Palmer's attention was first directed to the study of Oriental languages. It is worthy of observation that, on examination, none of his personal friends—I mean those of later years—were found to know well how the first steps were taken. Most men assumed that he was born speaking Arabic ; he must have lisped Persian in the cradle : in no other way could his Orientalism have become a part of his nature. When one began to enquire seriously into the origins of things, various stories were advanced with confidence which, on investigation, turned out to be romantic developments of old legends. Some, for instance, stated with boldness that Palmer learned Arabic by talking with sailors at the Docks. This story breaks down when we consider how very few are the Arabic-speaking sailors in the mercantile marine, how much talking it takes to make a linguist, and how scanty are the opportunities of a hard-worked clerk for spending hours

in the daytime with those few sailors. Again, there was
a very pretty story about how he went to Italy, either
in the interests of the firm or else in his own interests
and in order to become the Perfect wine merchant,
finished and rounded ; and how, while so engaged,
he spent six months at Rome, where he learned
Italian—not only pure and literary Italian, but also
the tongue of the people—and how, while there, he
made the acquaintance of two Persians, courtly and
affable, who took a fancy to him and taught him
their own language.   Now it was not until this story
was written down and could be calmly confronted that
it became incredible on the face of it.   For then one
asked whether in the year 1859, or thereabouts, London merchants imported Italian wines, and whether
it was necessary in those days, in order to learn the
mysteries of a London office, to reside in Rome, of
all places in the world ; whether, in fact, this would
not be much as if a young Chicago pig person should
think it necessary, at the outset and commencement
of his glorious career, to become apprentice to a
Parisian *charcutier* : and, further, one asked whether
Rome is really a favourite place of resort for Persians.
Now, as nearly as can be ascertained from the facts
discovered, Palmer's first crossing the Channel took
place in the year 1866, when he went to Paris with
the Nawáb Ikbál-u'd-Dawlah, son of the late King of
Oudh, being then six-and-twenty years of age.   He
may have gone abroad before, but I have not been able

to discover that he did. The uncertainty which surrounded, at first, so simple a question is a curious illustration of the little that one knows about the private
affairs of one's most intimate friends. Unless, indeed,
as generally happens, the life of a man is of the ordinary uninteresting and groove-like character, such as
school first, the University afterwards, and a profession,
with presently creditable success, a wife, children,
length of days, and so on, without adventure, hitch,
false start, or any element of romance whatever, it is
next to impossible to fill up the earlier years without
assistance from all kinds of unexpected people.

Palmer's first introduction to Arabic was effected
in the simplest and most natural manner possible.
He made the acquaintance of Syed Abdullah, when
that able man and teacher of Indian languages came
to Cambridge to read with a class of men who were
going out in the 'Indian civil service. I think that
about the year 1860 his visits to Cambridge were also
connected with a certain readership in Hindustani
which it was proposed to found in the University.
He was the best of the candidates for the post, as
was acknowledged ; but it was known that he was a
Mohammedan, whereupon the orthodoxy of the University, stronger then than now, took fright, and it
was asked how the Thirty-Nine Articles looked in
Hindustani, and Syed Abdullah was promptly rejected. The name of Syed Abdullah is very well
known to many English students of Oriental lan-

guages.   He was a native of Oudh and the son
of Syed Mohammed Khán Bahadur, who held for
a long period of years an important office in the
service of the old Company.   He studied at the
Benares College, and was at first appointed translator
and interpreter to the Board of Administration for
the Affairs of the Punjab.   About the year 1851 he
resigned this appointment, being then twenty-two
years of age, and came to England, where for more
than twenty years he received pupils and lectured on
one or other of the three Oriental languages which
he knew.   He was also a contributor to English
journals.   Latterly his pupils, for some reason or
other, fell off in number, and he returned to India,
where he became a deputy inspector of schools,
and subsequently died of cholera in the year 1879, at
the comparatively early age of fifty.   Syed Abdullah
was a man of great Oriental attainments and much
force of character, who impressed himself on all who
knew him.   Especially he impressed himself upon
Palmer, who always spoke of him in terms of the
highest regard and respect, and maintained a regular
correspondence with him until his death.

One may readily imagine how he would take up
Syed Abdullah's writings out of pure curiosity ; how
the conversation of the able Oriental would attract
him ; how his imagination would be fired ; how, with
that curiosity which made him always look into
everything and try it for himself, he would learn the

Arabic character and presently begin to read it ; and how, stimulated by the help and talk of his friend, his first tentative exploration of the vocabulary would lead him swiftly onwards until he found himself borne along by an irresistible current, a half-idle and languid enquiry having become a passion, so that what at first was sport became the most serious purpose of his life. Syed Abdullah found that he had a pupil not only apt, but with an extraordinary natural genius for Eastern languages. Happiest of all men is he who finds the work for which he was created, and can do that work for the rest of his life ! Palmer had found—himself ; after these experimental years of trying here and there, patiently doing the ' dock business ' all day, playing with Italian and French in the evening, acting, mesmerising, wood-carving, and the other industrious and useless occupations of a restless, unsatisfied brain, he at last obtained the thing which was enough to fully occupy and satisfy his mind for the longest term of life ever granted to man. In finding himself he found more, far more, than he at first imagined ; in becoming an Oriental student he at once stepped upon a higher level ; the old companions could be no longer, in the same sense as before, his friends ; they had their work and place in life, but it was no longer his work nor his place ; he was filled with a higher and more noble resolve than could be theirs ; he was going to be an Oriental scholar ; and somehow or other

—he knew not yet very well how—he would make
of the Asiatic languages, which he had yet to learn,
a profession by which he would live, a ladder by
which he would rise.   Can one imagine a more
splendid change of purpose ?   Eastcheap, the 'dock
business,' the servitude of the desk, the accounts
and the ledger—all this finished and done with for
ever : henceforth, if you please, the holy atmosphere
of a library and the sacred companionship of books,
wise, solemn, sweet, or sad.   He was fated to enjoy this
companionship for twenty years only ; but better ten
years in a library than a hundred at a desk.   In these
days of wealth-worship one is tempted sometimes
to forget the true nobility of the scholar's life ; yet I
think that even the most devoted adorer of the dollar
never ceases in his heart to respect and to envy
(which makes him speak spitefully of his poverty)
the man of books—the man who knows so much
more than himself—the man who can teach.

How long it took Palmer to arrive at this resolution I know not ; but, remembering that he could
not possibly go on at Cambridge doing nothing—
needs must that he should work and earn bread—I
think that it was not long after he began to learn
Arabic.   It was doubtless through Syed Abdullah's
earnest representations that he was allowed to continue
his studies with the avowed purpose of becoming a
Persian and Arabic scholar by profession.   How to
use that profession so as to make it the means of a

livelihood was probably not very seriously discussed. There is always some demand for interpreters ; there are always in London men wanting to learn Persian or Hindustani ; there are always books or Oriental literature to be translated, written, or reviewed ; there is always India, with its colleges and lectureships ; there is continually in this country some work or other for a man who knows Persian, Arabic, or the Indian languages. Therefore the lessons with Syed Abdullah continued, and henceforth there was no more question of the City or of any office work at all.

Palmer settled down to the work of his life with an ardour which knew no abating and an interest which never flagged ; he threw himself into his new pursuit with the same tenacity of purpose which he had displayed in his early Italian studies, but with far more energy, because this was real and the other was only amusement. It has been said of him that he worked during this period no less than eighteen hours a day. The question of how many hours in the day a man can work with profit to himself has been keenly debated. I think that it is chiefly matter of temperament. Many men, even with the greatest pressure, cannot work more than seven or eight hours a day; it has been advanced that in mathematical work more than six hours a day is useless ; but in the case of languages one may admit a good deal more. Whether, however, Palmer worked for eighteen hours a day or less, it is quite certain that he worked with

a zeal and ardour quite unparalleled. At the outset he seems to have had but one adviser besides
his tutor Syed Abdullah. This was the late George
Skinner, formerly tutor of Jesus and at that time
chaplain of King's. Palmer read Hebrew with him,
and perhaps, but I doubt this, some Arabic. He
used to be seen accompanying Mr. Skinner across
the fields to Grantchester, and in those walks they
discoursed on Hebrew grammar which Skinner taught
in this peripatetic manner. Palmer never pretended
to any knowledge of Hebrew, but he probably acquired at this time as much as he wanted for his
own purposes. I am informed by Professor Nicholl
of Oxford that Palmer's case is not an unusual one
among Orientalists ; that is to say, that many Oriental scholars cannot be said to have fairly begun until
the age of twenty or twenty-one. But the extraordinary ardour with which Palmer pursued his studies
and the success which rewarded him are surely unusual. This ardour was uninterrupted for the next
eight years. He found, after a while, many other
masters and advisers besides Syed Abdullah. It is
instructive, as showing his fixed determination to
master his subject, to observe how he took advantage
of every help which offered, and made the most of it.
Thus he was introduced to the Nawáb Ikbál-u'd-Dawlah, son of the late Rajah of Oudh. His Highness,
who is an accomplished Arabic, Persian, and Urdú
scholar, took a very warm interest in Palmer's studies,

CH. II.   *CAMBRIDGE.*   35

allowed him to live in his house when he pleased, and
gave him the assistance of two able munshís, with
whom he read. Sometimes in the Nawáb's house he
would sit up working till three or four in the morning. For three years at least the Nawáb gave him
this generous assistance, and, besides, received, read
and criticised Palmer's Persian compositions.

Next, he was indebted to a Bengalee gentleman
named Bazlu'rrahím, a Mohammedan, with whom he
spent some time, composing incessantly, under his
supervision, in Persian and Urdú. When he returned to
India, Palmer accompanied him as far as Marseilles.
His generous friend gave him on departure a note
for 50*l.* to help him in his studies, and, on arriving in
India, he sent him, in addition, a valuable present of
books and Oriental MSS. There were, besides, three
Moslem students at Cambridge with whom he read
and talked ; there was his friend Hassún the Syrian,
who died, suddenly and mysteriously, in 1878 ; and
there was lastly—though there were many others of
whom I have not heard—Professor Mír Aulád 'Alí
of Trinity College, Dublin, who was constantly his
adviser, critic, teacher, friend, and sympathiser.

There are therefore two points in Palmer's history during these years which appear to be of capital
importance. The first is that Arabic and Persian
did not, as old women say, 'come natural' to him.
Nothing 'comes natural' to any man. This man was
endowed with an extraordinary natural gift for the

acquisition of languages ; no men living, and few men
dead, have had the gift in so generous and ample a
measure ; but without an equal power of industry it
would have been of no avail. Yet genius begets
ardour, and ardour industry. Perhaps such a gift
could not have been wasted.

There is no royal road to knowledge, though some
can learn and some cannot. In Palmer's case.he
arrived at success after labours incessant, ardour in-
extinguishable, and resolution undaunted. As in
the case of his Italian, he got what he wanted, because
he was willing to work for it. Also, what he wanted
was so great, so tremendous a thing, that he was
willing to work for it, night and day, incessantly,
with untiring resolution, patience, and zeal. Nevertheless, as happens to all who can work, he had his
reward.

It follows, from what has gone before, that we
may give up the idea, cherished by some of his friends,
that he was the poor, solitary, and friendless student,
burning midnight gas or petroleum, with a pale face
and resolute eyes, in a lonely study. Nothing of the
kind. He never felt any pressure of poverty : and
he had, almost from the very first, every encouragement, with help and sympathy on all sides. Syed
Abdullah, Mír Aulád-'Alí, the Nawáb and his little
court of scholars, Hassún, Bazlu'rrahím, were all
deeply interested in his work, revising his compositions,
criticising his style, hearing him talk, teaching him

the graces and beauties of Persian, Urdú, and Arabic
literature, helping on the student who promised to
become almost more Oriental than themselves : in
fact, he was always a man of friends, and never, at
any time, without help and encouragement. As regards, however, the University of Cambridge, with
the single exception of Mr. Skinner, he seems to have
remained absolutely unknown for some time. The
Lord Almoner's Professor, Palmer's predecessor, was
Mr. Theodore Preston, and a letter from him, dated
October 28, 1862, thanks Palmer for a copy of 'elegant and idiomatic Arabic verses.' The letter also
conveys his cordial congratulations on the very extraordinary proficiency attained in so difficult a language,
' a proficiency the more remarkable as it is the result
of your own assiduity, unassisted, I believe, by any
native teacher.' Here we know that Professor Preston
was wrong.[1]

It was about the year 1862 that he was first led to
think of entering the University, a step which would
be considered with great care and hesitation, because
what good would it be to him to become a graduate of
Cambridge ? It is a little, only a little, less wonderful
now than it was twenty years ago that a student of
any branch of learning should hesitate about entering
what ought to be the home, and refuge, and *alma*

---

[1] I grieve to say that the death of Mr. Preston in the autumn of last
year prevented me from getting further information from him as to
Palmer's first introduction to him.

mater of universal learning, open alike to scholars in
every department. Palmer had been from boyhood
accustomed to associate the University with classics
and mathematics; nothing else seemed to have a place
there; no solid rewards were offered for anything else,
either by the colleges or by the University. There
were already, to be sure, Triposes in Natural Science,
Morals, Law, and Theology, but few men heeded
them; scholarships and fellowships were not given
for proficiency in any of these things. Therefore,
apart from a certain social consideration, useful to a
scholar, which happily attaches to the possession of a
Cambridge degree, it seemed as if it would be hardly
worth the expense of a three years' course and the
trouble of passing necessary examinations in other subjects. Already Palmer had begun to consider India
as his natural field of work; how could the University
help him in the direction of India? In the end, as
will presently appear, his University refused to help
him at all and left him out in the cold. But there
was one college which had a great deal of help to
give him, and gave it with liberal, bountiful, and
generous hands.

Of all the magnificent foundations for the advancement and encouragement of learning which stand
upon the banks of the Cam and the Isis, there is not
one which has used its endowments more nobly and
more generously for the encouragement of poor and
deserving students than St. John's College, Cambridge:

there is no other college, in either University, which
numbers among its glorious roll of worthies more of
those whose early history has been that of struggle
against adverse circumstances. Palmer was 'discovered' by two of the Fellows of St. John's, the Rev.
Alfred Calvert and Mr. Newbery, the latter of whom is
now dead. They found a young man of two or three
and twenty years of age working with a most wonderful
ardour, and astonishing success, at Arabic, Urdú, and
Persian, with, as yet, few friends to encourage him
except Syed Abdullah and the above-named George
Skinner ; they discovered, further, that he was a person not dull or ill-trained, but possessed of respectable
classical scholarship, and endowed with extraordinary
cleverness, dexterity at all kinds of things, and great
personal charm of manner—in fact, a highly interesting man, and one not commonly met with in any
rank of life. They reported at first this strange
thing to Mr. Todhunter, then Lecturer and one of the
Senior Fellows of St. John's, and recommended that
it should be further enquired into. The result was
that Palmer was invited to call upon Mr. Todhunter.
He came, bearing in his hand a copy of Moore's 'Lalla
Rookh' translated into Arabic. Mr. Todhunter
brought the case formally before the Governing Body
or the Tutors, and it was finally agreed that Palmer
should enter his name at the college, and should stand
for a sizarship in October 1863. Meantime, as it was
necessary to renew the old studies, he began to read,

and read for the rest of his undergraduate career with the Rev. Arthur Calvert, then Fellow and Lecturer in Classics, now Rector of Moreton, Chipping Ongar. Mr. Calvert writes that he found at the outset Palmer well grounded, and that he arrived at the power of writing fairly good Latin prose. It is moderate praise, but then Palmer never professed to be a good scholar of Latin and Greek.

He matriculated, therefore, in October 1863, and obtained a sizarship, which was subsequently followed by a scholarship. We may very well understand that neither was obtained by attainments in classics or mathematics, but that both were conferred upon him solely on account of his linguistic reputation. The Tutor of St. John's at this time was Mr. A. V. Hadley, who resigned in 1865, and was succeeded by the Rev. H. R. Bailey, who in 1867 was in his turn succeeded by Mr. Durell. One of Palmer's best friends during his undergraduate career was the Rev. T. G. Bonney, afterwards Tutor, now Professor of Geology at University College, London, whom he frequently consulted in matters of doubt and difficulty. However, henceforth Palmer had no lack of friends. Then began his undergraduate life, about which a great many stories have been told, as wild as most legends about strange and clever undergraduates. We are gravely told that he made Persian and Arabic take the place of light literature—his only serious study to be considered light literature !—and the old Panurge story about the languages we have heard gravely applied to Palmer, with certain variations. As a matter of fact his undergraduate time was one of continuous and intense labour. It was necessary for him to spend some hours every day over Latin and Greek —in his special case it seemed, though probably it was not, a grievous waste of time; he had college lectures to attend—more waste of time; he generally had one or more pupils reading Arabic with him; he was engaged upon catalogues, first of the Arabic and Persian MSS. in the King's and Trinity College Libraries, and afterwards of those in the University Library;[1] he was corresponding in Urdú with a Lucknow and Agra paper; and he was pursuing his Oriental work with extraordinary vigour and wonderful results. For instance, so early as 1866 Professor Mír Aulád 'Alí writes that he has never, in all his life, met any single European so well versed in Eastern languages as Palmer. In the same year he accompanied the Nawáb Ikbál-u'd-Daulah to Paris as interpreter. The following letter was given him by the ex-Rajah when he came away :—

---

[1] 'No words,' wrote Mr. Bradshaw the Librarian, in September 1867, 'are sufficient to express the mass of confusion which our collection presented, and which has brought down upon us the well-deserved censure of Orientalists. And I do not hesitate to say that without the untiring energy which Mr. Palmer has devoted to the work, coupled with an instinctive knowledge and appreciation of his subject, the University would still be, and might long have remained, without the means of satisfying the most ordinary demands of Oriental scholars.'

I, who am a traveller by land and sea, and have examined mankind in both its good and evil aspects, have seen nothing more wonderful or astonishing than this in the course of my extensive travels (though the wonders I have seen would surpass the capacity of the most astute observer to describe), that I have met a young gentleman of very attractive exterior from the University of Cambridge, a place connected with London, endowed with learning and varied accomplishments. Notwithstanding the fact that he has never visited any Eastern kingdom, or mixed with Oriental nations, he has yet, by his own perseverance, application, and study, acquired such great proficiency, fluency, and eloquence, in speaking and writing three Oriental tongues, to wit, Urdú (Hindoostani), Persian, and Arabic, that one would say he must have associated with Oriental nations and studied for a lengthened period in the Universities of the East.

Whenever he goes to the East, I feel assured that he will soon attain such proficiency and pre-eminence as to have but few equals. In addition to these high acquirements, he is the most honourable and gentlemanly of his race : and is, moreover, of such an extremely gentle, polite, obliging, temperate, and moral disposition that he attracts to himself the love and esteem of all hearts. He may be safely denominated 'dear as one's life,' or rather, 'the amulet of one's life ;' and will be found a most agreeable and trusty companion, and the twin brother of sincerity. Although it is in the nature of mankind to err and fall short, yet his greatest error in the three afore-mentioned languages may be considered as perfection itself ; and we ought to observe with an eye of justice how, without leaving his own home, he has reached the highest pitch of perfection and proficiency entirely through his own talents and application to study. It only proves the truth of the saying that 'the field of knowledge is very extensive, and the rank of a learned person is very lofty in the world.' As Sa'adi says in his ' Chapter of Counsel ' in the (Pandnámah, commonly called Kureema),

' 'Tis not from rank, pomp, or wealth that man attains to eminence, but from knowledge alone.'

In the year 1867 he made an application for the appointment of attaché and interpreter to the Embassy in Persia. It was unsuccessful, for want, I suppose, of some interest ; but it made him apply for, and print, a set of testimonials which are useful now, as showing that even while still an undergraduate, and with a limited acquaintance among Orientals, he had acquired a very marked proficiency. The Persian ambassador says that he speaks and writes perfectly ; Garcin de Tassy, member of the Institute of France, Syed Abdullah himself, and many others declare that they have never met so good an Oriental scholar ; while at Lucknow, where Palmer had long contributed to a native paper, there was a public meeting held in order to testify in the most conclusive way to Palmer's knowledge.[1] India or Persia seemed, at this time, the only field open to him, and, though fate willed otherwise, it was always a subject of deep regret with Palmer that he had never been able to visit those countries.

These incessant labours were carried on at the cost of exercise, because, even for the most industrious, there are only twenty-four hours in the day.

[1] See appendix to this chapter.

Moreover, Palmer was no recluse or solitary student. He loved to burn the midnight oil, but preferred to use it for social and festive purposes rather than for study, and was always ready to sit up half the night, especially if there was any play-acting or pleasant fooling to the fore. As for regular exercise, he detested it; if he 'took the air' it was for choice on the banks of the Granta, with a rod in his hand ; and as for boating, cricket, football, tennis, racquets, fives, or any other game, he never played them. Once he tried to play cricket, and having succeeded in hitting the ball, also managed to swing his bat round and hit as well the wicket-keeper on the head, so that the unfortunate man fell senseless and was carried off the field. Palmer never tried that game any more. Cards he disliked, save as most useful tools for purposes of legerdemain. As for chess, he was once observed playing it with another man, but they had begun by taking each other's kings, and were proceeding to establish rival republics. As for dancing, singing, and music, like other Orientals, he preferred these things to be done for him.

Among the many things which interested him at this time was Spiritualism. He held *séances* in his own rooms, and I am informed that, in those days, he actually believed in the so-called manifestations. I record this evidence because it is given me by one who knew him so well, and was with him so much, that we must accept his testimony. Otherwise I

should have refused to credit or to repeat a statement which no one who only knew him later on
can easily believe. He could, of late years, find no
words to express his boundless contempt for the whole
business, machinery, and pretence of Spiritualism,
which he maintained to be a swindle of the most
palpable and clumsy kind, believed in by credulous
and simple persons, who love to think that the veil
of the grave can be partially drawn aside, and that
they may still exchange greetings, even in faint
whispers, with the dead whom they have never ceased
to love. Very strange things used to happen with
the furniture, the pictures, and the books at these
séances, but Palmer in after years never spoke of
them. Yet they were things so strange that had
they occurred in any other man's rooms he would
most certainly have remembered them. The fact
that he never talked about them is to me curiously
suggestive. I have myself attended *séances* with
him ; I have observed with pleasure the bewilder-
ment and rage of the medium when the word was
taken out of his mouth and spirits quite unknown
to him began to convey strange messages in
mysterious tongues ; he has shown me simple ways
in which the most startling spirit effects may be
produced ; he has drawn in my presence most extraordinary spirit portraits, and has shown me how to
produce these phenomena at will ; he has disclosed
the whole machinery, and has invented new and

ingenious contrivances and combinations for cheating the senses of those who wish to be cheated. But he has never given me the least hint that there ever was a time when he believed in the reality of the pretended spirits. Therefore, when one hears of tables lifted, pictures turned, the actual possession of Palmer himself by a spirit who made him talk Latin or whatever he pleased, one may receive the statement as perfectly consistent with the facts, but with certain reservations due to the remembrance that Palmer was a very clever man.

While he was still an undergraduate another strange and weird illness fell upon him. I have often heard him talk of it ; other friends of his have reminded me of it. But I owe to his friend the Rev. Joseph Pulliblank the following accurate account of this strange story :—

'I went to his rooms one night in the year 1865, or perhaps 1866 ; I spoke to him, and found him low-spirited, though he returned my greeting cheerfully. Suddenly he fell back on the sofa, and bent himself backwards till he lay resting on the back of his head and his heels. I got him some sal volatile, and ran to the Dean for leave to pass the gates and find a doctor. The case was one which closely resembled tetanus. Stimulants were applied, and Palmer gradually came round. For months afterwards, however, he was compelled to drink every day enormous quantities of brandy, which produced

upon him no more effect than so much water. One
night, however, some months afterwards, we were
together in the rooms of a man, who produced a
bottle of whisky. Palmer drank a glass of hot
whisky and water, and then leaned over and whispered to me, "Take me away at once, or I shall
begin to talk about rich uncles." When we got to
the bottom of the stairs, and into the open air, he
became so drunk that he could neither walk nor
stand. Fortunately I got him to the college gates,
and into his rooms without meeting a proctor and
having to explain. "You never before," he said next
day, "saw a man who did right in thanking God that
he was drunk. I was drunk last night, and now I
know that I am quite well again." In fact, the evil,
whatever it was, had worn itself out, and there was
no more drinking of brandy.'

He was at last, five years later in point of age
than most men, admitted to his bachelor's degree with
third-class classical honours. His place probably
indicated his classical attainments; in after life he
professed not to know Latin and Greek at all. In
his own sense of knowing a language this was
perfectly true; but he knew a good deal of both
languages. And now it became necessary to look
about for work and the means of support. He made,
as has been stated, an ineffectual attempt in the
direction of diplomacy. What could he do next?
For an Arabic and Persian scholar, there are a few

pupils to receive; there is the chance of getting occasional translation work in connection with the India House or the Foreign Office. Still there is not much opening in this country for an Orientalist. There is also, of course, general literature; but he wanted to follow up his special knowledge, not to write. He was already well known in the University as a remarkable man, of whom great things were expected. And, while he was still hesitating, the college again came to his help. There was, at that time, no instance on record, I believe, of a man getting a fellowship at St. John's who had not taken high honours in either classics or mathematics. Therefore the governing body must have been very much impressed indeed by the merits of their Oriental scholar when they began to consider the question of conferring a fellowship upon him. Professor Cowell writes the following account of the matter :—

I had just begun to reside in Cambridge in October 1867, after I had been elected Professor, when the late Master of St. John's, Dr. Bateson, asked me to examine Palmer in Oriental languages, in order that they might elect him to a fellowship if he were really worthy of it. I undertook to examine him in Persian and Hindustani, as I felt that my knowledge of Arabic was too slight to justify my venturing to examine him in that language. I well remember my delight and surprise in this examination. I had never had any intercourse with Palmer before, as I had been previously living in India ; and I had no idea that he was such an Oriental scholar. I remember well that I set him for translation into Persian prose a florid description (I am sorry that I forget the exact passage) from Gibbon's chapter on Mohammed. Palmer translated it in a masterly way, in the true style of Persian rhetoric, every important substantive having its rhyming doublet just as in the best models of Persian literature. In fact, his vocabulary seemed exhaustless. I also set him difficult pieces for translation from the Masnaví, Khondemir, and I think Saudá, but he could explain them all without hesitation. I sent a full report to the Master, and the college elected him at once to the vacant fellowship.

This election was everything to Palmer. He had now secured an income which, if not great, was enough for an unmarried man with such simple tastes as were his. There was, for the present, no further anxiety on the score of money; he could sit down without the necessity for doing anything which he disliked, and he was enabled to devote the whole remainder of his life, if he chose, to that work which his soul most loved. I should think that no man was ever made more completely happy than was Palmer by an election to a fellowship. There are many kinds of success more important than the winning of a fellowship; but it is a success of early manhood, when success is most valued; it is a tangible success, such as Englishmen love; not a ribbon, or an order, or a title, but a solid income, with rooms and dinners free. It is a mode of advancing scholarship which all the world can understand; in Palmer's

E

case, as it ought always to be, it was a veritable Endowment of Research. '

And so, with success and honour, closed the second period of Palmer's life.

APPENDIX I.

In 1867, Palmer printed in pamphlet form various letters and testimonials which he received. They were printed in Persian and Arabic with the English rendering. Among them is the letter from the Nawáb, already quoted. The following are also valuable, and are here reproduced in order to mark the recognition which he had already won as an Oriental student :—

From M. Garcin de Tassy, Member of the Institut de France, etc.

Paris, 25 Juin 1866.

Je soussigné, Professeur à l'Ecole impériale et spéciale des langues orientales vivantes de Paris, membre de l'Institut de France, des Sociétés asiatiques de Londres, de Calcutta, de Bombay, de Madras, d'Amérique, des Académies de St.-Pétersbourg, d'Upsal, de Munich, de Turin, de Lisbonne, etc., atteste et certifie que Mr. Edward Henry Palmer, de St. John's College, Cambridge, sait parfaitement l'hindoustani, le persan et l'arabe ; qu'il parle et écrit ces langues avec la plus grande facilité et comme pourrait le faire un natif.

GARCIN DE TASSY.

From Monsieur le Comte de Salles, Professor of Oriental Languages at the Ecole des langues orientales, Suc- cursale Impériale à Marseille.

Marseilles, 24th June, 1866.

My dear Sir,—Madame de Salles and myself thank you for your kind remembrance. We recall to memory with gratification the pleasant moments we passed in Paris and Marseilles in society with the learned, amongst whom you figured so eminently, despite of your age.

The languages of Asia, so dear to our home, and par- ticularly Arabic and Hindústání, wherein, thanks to labour and long travel in the East, I procured some honour and consideration to my life, already so long : these languages, my dear Sir, are known to you, *calamo et verbis*, in theory and practice, in a way and degree to do you much credit, and as much to your method, schools, and masters.

My illustrious colleague, Garcin de Tassy, as well as our Indian circle in Paris, and Asiatic and African in Mar- seilles, have expressed to us on the subject in question their satisfaction and wonder. I feel personally happy to join herein my evidence, as you seem kindly to appreciate what we now tender with sincerity. Please, then, to accept our best wishes for your present and further success. May they help to class you among the learned and daring *diplomats* that England may be called to launch in the affairs of Asia.

Accept, my dear Sir, our best cordial regards.

COUNT EUSÈBE DE SALLES,

Professeur de l'Ecole des langues orientales, Succursale Impériale à Marseille.

9, Rue Maguelonne, à Montpellier.

From Syed Abdoollah, Professor of Hindústání at University College, London ; and late Interpreter and Translator to the Board of Administration for the Affairs of the Punjab.

Mr. E. H. Palmer, of St. John's College, Cambridge, has been for many years my friend and pupil, and I have been continually surprised and delighted at his application to study and capacity for acquiring languages. I have now much pleasure in stating that I have found him perfectly conversant with the Hindústání, Persian, and Arabic languages, which he both writes and speaks with the utmost fluency and correctness.

SYED ABDOOLLAH,

Professor of Hindústání, University College, London ; late Translator and Interpreter to the Board of Administration for the affairs of the Punjab.

سيد عبدالله عني شنه

21, Fulham Place, Harrow Road, London, W., 29th June, 1866.

(L. S.)

From Mír Aulád 'Alí, Professor of Oriental Languages at Trinity College, Dublin.

I have much pleasure in bearing my willing testimony to the high proficiency of Edward Henry Palmer Saheb, a Scholar of St. John's College, in Arabic, Persian, and Hindústání. I have no hesitation in justly stating that in the whole course of my life I have never met one European gentleman so well versed in the Eastern languages as Mr. E. H. Palmer.

Professor MÍR AULÁD 'ALÍ,

Trinity College, Dublin.

June 27th, 1866.

Translation of a Testimonial in favour of E. H. Palmer, of St. John's College, Cambridge, drawn up in Persian and Arabic by Syed Ally Hassan, Tehsildar of Roy Bareilly, and Meer Syed Mohammed Khan Bahadoor, late Tehsildar of Jubbulpore, and countersigned by the Ulamá of Lucknow, at a public meeting held for the purpose in that town the 1st June, 1867.

After the customary solemn formulæ :

All persons of sound and steadfast minds, and blest with theoretical and practical knowledge, are aware that the rational sometimes exists and sometimes perishes, but nobility always exists and is always to be recognised. Now the existent is divided into two classes, mineral and vegetative, of which the latter is the most worthy, as all men know. The vegetative is either animate or inanimate, the former possessing the pre-eminence, inasmuch as it requires the concomitants of reason and judgment. The animate, moreover, may be either rational or irrational, and the rational is the most excellent. The rational, again, may be either learned or ignorant, but the former cannot be compared with the latter, inasmuch as it is capable of instruction and information ; and we therefore see all men of taste and genius exerting themselves for the attainment of knowledge. Amongst those who have sought and striven to reach the pastures of perfection, and to drink from the divine fount, is the accomplished and intellectual scholar, the ornament to his school and creed, who sits on the throne of reputation and honor, reclining upon the pillows of fame, who has dived into the ocean of perfection after the fairest pearls, Jenáb Mr. Edward Henry Palmer (may his rank be exalted and his length of days prolonged !), as not only I learn from the letters of my estimable nephew, Syed Abdoolah, himself of fair fame in the world and a blessing to me (God preserve his life and accomplish his desires !), who has dwelt for many years in London, and as is also attested by printed newspapers and the written and oral assertions of trustworthy narrators ; but Mr. Palmer has himself remembered me, notwithstanding the distance which separates us, and has written to me many letters in Persian, Arabic, and Hindústání,—letters fraught with original ideas, the like of which one rarely sees, as delightful as groves of trees laden with varied fruits and blossoms where the streamlets bubble by, compositions which the

Most extravagant encomiast could not describe, practised though he might be at description.

By my life he is unequalled amongst his compatriots, and unrivalled amongst his contemporaries, confirming the poet's words—

Writing is the greatest ornament of a man if he be learned too ; even as the rain is sweeter when it falls on grass, and as pearls are fairer when upon a fair one's neck.

Having made rapid progress and laid a solid foundation, after surmounting difficulties and keeping on his guard against hindrances, he has been good enough to ask me to state what I know of the extent of his knowledge and the excellence of his understanding. Nor will I disappoint his hope, and have therefore written these few lines at his request ; for, poor and insignificant as I am, I enjoy his friendship and remembrance, though circumstances keep us apart.

This accomplished and liberal-minded gentleman, as he has shown himself to be, has not studied for long, and yet, in the opinion of connoisseurs, already surpasses his contemporaries in the knowledge of Oriental languages, thanks to his exact scholarlike attainments and his constant application. His writings, which have gone the round of literary society here, are a convincing proof of his having attained the highest degree of excellence.

(Signed)   SYED ALLY HASSAN.

Son of the late Moulvie Syed Ghoolam Imam.

[An apology from Syed Ally Hassan for writing his testimonial and affixing his seal above that of his elder brother Meer Syed Mohammed Khan Bahadoor.]

It is not unknown to persons of acute intellect and scholarlike attainments that the learned in literature and the accomplished in every branch of science have from time immemorial occupied themselves with studying and promoting their special subjects of education, under the patronage of wise kings and rulers, and have thus enjoyed a foretaste of immortality, and carved out for themselves monuments of fame that will endure through all ages : 'Men die, but the learned live.' Wherefore it is that in India, and Turkey, and Persia, and Abyssinia, and China, and Tartary, and Egypt, and Europe, wise men have founded Universities and applied themselves to intellectual pursuits, that knowledge and learning may not be supplanted by careless indifference and ignorance, as is unfortunately too often the case amongst some bigoted and misguided people in our own time. Those few persons who have attained any eminence in knowledge are now too often hidden in seclusion and obscurity, and ignored by the world around them ; but 'pure musk can never be concealed, and by its scent confirms the perfumer's words.' Now, as all the wonders of the Creator's mighty power, such as establishing the firmament of heaven without supporting columns, and kindling the torches of the sun and moon, and the candles of the various stars, and mixing darkness with light, night with day, and the production of clouds and winds and dust, and of trees that grow and bear fruit and blossom, laying the foundations of the earth in

the midst of the waters, the combination of the various
elements, and the existence of the trio, youth, age, and
infancy, in the animal, mineral, and vegetable kingdoms,
especially in man, the noblest being in creation, and as it
were, 'the fountain of immortality amidst the darkness:'
as these need no argument or proof, so the fame of the
learning and scholarship, for which that honorable and
respected gentleman (the most eloquent and accomplished
philologist of his time), Jenáb Mr. Edward Henry Palmer,
Sahib Bahadoor, of the University of Cambridge, (a well-
known school of learning and science), is particularly distinguished, and with which he is specially endowed, is so
universally spread abroad in these regions, and so well
known and apparent to all men as to need no description
or comment.

I, Syed Mohammed, who have passed these seventy
years of my life in literary society, and passed a long time
in the University of Lucknow, and been for many years
employed under the English Government in the Deccan
and elsewhere, and have now, in consideration of my public
services, received a fitting pension from the Indian Government and the honorary title of Khan Bahadoor, have
carried on for some time a friendly correspondence with
the aforesaid gentleman, and received from him at various
dates letters in Arabic, Persian, and Hindústání, written in
so elegant and accurate a style that the pen cannot sufficiently indite their praise, nor the most extravagant encomiast
describe them as they should be described ; and I have
been astonished at this gentleman's unparalleled proficiency
in literature, his fluent language, and his power of expressing
himself on any subject.   He has shown himself well versed
in European literature and a perfect master of the Oriental
idioms.   Nor is this my opinion alone, for all who can
appreciate literary acumen are unanimous in his praise ; for
instance, Moonshee Kelb Hassan, commonly called Baleeġ,

a celebrated poet of Jyess, has extemporised a poem in praise of the gentleman aforesaid, which will be found in the margin of this paper ; and a number of the principal nobles and savants of this town, who are acquainted with this gentleman's published writings, have at my request corroborated my statement by countersigning this document and formally attaching their seals thereunto. With a prayer to the great originator of all things, I subscribe myself,

(Signed)   Syed Mohammed al Jyessee.

Dated 8th Zí'l Hijj. A.H. 1283.
   ,,   18th April, A.D. 1867.

(L.S.)

The statement made by Syed Ally Hassan is fully confirmed and borne out by the writings of the gentleman referred to, which I have at different times seen and perused with much pleasure. Undoubtedly they prove conclusively his scholarship and high Oriental attainments. I willingly endorse Syed Ally Hassan's encomiums.

(Signed)   Syed Ally Hassan Ashrafí.

(L.S.)

Given under my hand and seal,

Shah Ally Hassan, Sahib,
Pirzada of Jyess.

(L.S.)

The above statements in favour of this gentleman are undoubtedly correct, his letters and writings affording a conclusive proof of his talents and proficiency.

Syed Murtazá Hussain.

(L.S.)

I have seen the letters, and communications to the newspapers, of Mr. Palmer, which show a great facility for composition in Arabic and Persian, and prove that the writer
is perfectly master of these languages.   I have, therefore, much pleasure in confirming the opinion expressed
above.

SYED ALLY.

There is no doubt in it.

SYED NUJJUF HUSSAIN.

(L. S.)

Without doubt the writings of the gentleman referred to
indicate his great proficiency.   His essays are both elegant
and interesting.

(Signed)   SYED AKBAR HOOSSEIN.

(Signed)   Moonshee TAFAZZUL HOOSSEIN,
Mir Moonshee at Artl in the Deccan.

There is no doubt in it.

SYED NUJMOODDEN HUSSAIN NAKAWEE.

(L. S.)

There is no doubt in it.

NEEAZ HUSSAIN NAKAWEE.

(L. S.)

The elegant writings of the gentleman in question conclusively prove his talents and perseverance.

IMDÁD HUSSAIN BIN SHEIKH FURKHUNDA
HUSSAIN BIN MOHAMMED.

(L. S.)

The above Arabic and Persian writings testifying to this gentleman's talents are quite correct.

BAHADOOR HUSSAIN BIN SHEIKH

MUBARAK ALLAH.

(L.S.)

There is no doubt in it.

NEEAZ HUSSAIN JYESSEE.

(L.S.)

This is a book in which there is no doubt.

RIZA HUSSAIN BIN KHOJA MOHAMMED.

(L.S.)

The evidence of the proficiency of the gentleman aforesaid in literature, and of his mastery over Persian and Arabic, is conclusive.

MOHAMMED ABDUL GHAFOUR.

(L.S.)

The writing is palpably true.

SYED MOHAMMED HUSSAIN BIN

ABDOOLLAH BIN SYED MOHAMMED

ALLIE AL NAWAKEE.

(L.S.)

I, too, bear testimony to his attainments.

SYED WAJID ALLY SHAH BIN SYED MOHAMMED

HUSSAIN BIN ABDOOLLAH.

(L.S.)

The writings of the gentleman above mentioned are a conclusive proof of his literary knowledge and ability.

(Signed)   SYED HASSAN BUKSH AL NAKAWEE.

(L. S.)

I have seen various writings of the gentleman aforesaid, which prove the soundness of his knowledge, the fluency and correctness of his language. I have seldom seen his equal amongst the most distinguished persons.

(Signed)   SYED MUSTAPHA HOOSSEIN.

(L. S.)

In truth, the statements made in the above testimonials are correct.

(Signed)   Pundit MADHO PRASÁD.

Extra Assistant Commissioner.

(Sealed)   NAJUF ALÍ.

Extra Assistant Commissioner, Roy Bareilly.

The ability and perseverance of Mr. E. H. Palmer are clearly demonstrated by the style of the compositions alluded to by Syed Mohammed Khan Bahadoor of Jyess. In my opinion the gentleman referred to deserves to be considered as an unrivalled scholar.

CÁZÍ BADUL HUSSAIN.

Formerly Cází of the Purganah of Jyess.

(L. S.)

*Certificate of the Proficiency of Edward Henry Palmer, Sahib
in the Arabic, Persian, and Urdú languages, written by
Moonshee Syed Ghoolam Hyder Khan, Sáhib, at Lucknow, the 1st June, 1867, with the consent and concurrence
of the 'Ulamá of that town.*

In order to prove more fully the elegance and correctness of the essays and letters written by Edward Henry
Palmer, Sahib Bahadoor, in Arabic, Persian, and Urdú,
published in various periodicals, I have this day laid his
compositions before a full meeting of the 'Ulamá, Professors and literary men of this place, and have, with the
assistance and concurrence of the said gentlemen, carefully
examined the correctness of the documents and the idiomatic character of their composition. I now testify that
the letters and essays aforesaid are written in extremely
correct and elegant language, and that no difference whatever is apparent between it and the language and idiom
used by the natives of this country, either in expression,
metaphor, or order of words ; and certify that the gentleman aforesaid has reached the highest proficiency attainable
in the three languages specified above.

SYED GHOOLAM HYDER

IBN MOONSHEE SYED MOHAMMED

KHÁN BAHADOOR.

(L. S.)

NOWAL KISHORE,

Proprietor and Editor of the *Oude Akhbar*.

SYED ALI IBN SYED AHMED SAHIB,

Professor at the Royal University of Lucknow.

(L. S.)

Translation of a Testimonial from Mirza Ally Ackbar, of Búshire, Iran, 14 Boulevard St. Michel, Paris.

My object in writing this is to state that I have passed some time in the society of Mr. Palmer, an esteemed English friend of mine. In our conversation and inter-course he has always made use of the Persian, Arabic, or Hindoostani languages ; and he is really perfectly proficient in and conversant with them all, and never in any way at a loss.

MIRZA ALLY ACKBAR.

Paris, June, 1866.

The same pamphlet contains a list of his publications up to that date :—

الجنّة و الجنّية *El Jinnah w eljinniyah.* A translation into Arabic verse of Moore's 'Paradise and the Peri,' published in the Birgís Barís, No. 146, Paris, June 21st, 1865.

Histoire de Donna Juliana, traduite d'un Manuscrit de la Bibliothèque de King's College, Cambridge. Nouvelle Annales de Voyage Mai 1865.

Oriental Mysticism : a Treatise on the Sufiistic and Unitarian Theosophy of the Persians.   Cambridge, 1867.

Catalogue of the Oriental Manuscripts in the Library of King's College, Cambridge.   Published by the Royal Asiatic Society.

A Descriptive Catalogue of the Arabic, Persian, and Turkish MSS. in the Library of Trinity College, Cambridge.

Catalogue of the Oriental MSS. in the University Library, Cambridge. See Testimonial from H. Bradshaw, Esq., p. 23.

Javídán i Hirad, The Wisdom of Ages. Translated for the Royal Society from a Persian MS. in their possession. (Will be published shortly).

Numerous Essays, Poems, and Letters in Urdu and Persian, published at various times in the *Oude Akhbár*, Lucknow ; the *Akhbár i "Alam*, Meerutt ; the *Mufarrih ul Qulúb*, Kurrachee ; the *Naiyar i Rajistán*, and other Indian native papers.

APPENDIX II.

The following is from a letter from the Rev. Joseph Pulliblank :—

'In our long intimacy I got to know more, I think, of Palmer's inner life than most of his companions. His association with Mahommedans from India was, I believe, a great power in moulding his opinions. He hated above all things the rough and ready, but too popular way of classing Mahommedans with heathens. Their strict monotheism had a great attraction for him. But he was much more powerfully affected by the much earlier Zoroastrianism. We read together the "Dabistan," and were necessarily attracted by its teaching. The mysticism seemed to Palmer to be true to human life. A little treatise which he discovered in Trinity College Library, and translated into English, marked an epoch in his life. It introduced him to two very dissimilar books, Bunyan's " Pilgrim's Progress " and Tennyson's "In Memoriam." Of the latter he admired and used to repeat oftenest

The great intelligences fail, &c.

'The monotheism of the "Dabistan" he believed to be a genuine survival of a primitive Aryan faith.   Palmer had a project in his mind, of an examination of the whole history of Melchizedek, whom he believed (rightly or wrongly) to be an Aryan prince.   He wanted to work out the Aryan influence upon Abraham.

'He was an adept at mesmerism.   Before he entered at Cambridge he used frequently to mesmerise people, but entirely abandoned the practice when he found himself gaining a command over a young girl which might prove dangerous to her.   I believe that Professor Humphrey could give an account of a curious trial of Palmer's power made at the Addenbrooke Hospital.   I heard it only at second-hand : but it was to this effect   The young girl referred to above had a diseased bone in one of her fingers : it was examined by surgeons, who declared an amputation to be necessary.   Palmer asked them if they would try the anæsthetic power of mesmerism.   On their consenting, he mesmerised the girl at his aunt's house, making some special passes over the hand affected.   He then commanded her to go to the Hospital, wait till she had been attended to, and come back to him.   She went (about three-quarters of a mile), had the operation performed, and came back to him.   He unmesmerised her, and she declared she had felt no pain.   I knew of this only years after, under these circumstances.   I had an attack of hiccough, very bad indeed.   After about twelve hours I sent for a doctor, who prescribed, but did no good.   Nearly 48 hours after the attack began, Palmer came into my rooms—the third or fourth visit.   "What a fool I am not to have tried mesmerism !"   I could not resist saying, exhausted as I was, "You would have been nearly as great a fool if you had."

"Never mind," he said, "let me try." I did, of course, but with an utter disbelief in the whole thing. I was astonished beyond measure to find that as he made the passes across my diaphragm I could begin to breathe, and in less than two minutes the attack was over. Palmer helped me to bed, sat on my bed and made some passes over my eyes and my chest. I fell asleep and woke the next day not only without hiccough but completely free from pain. After that he explained to me the whole *modus operandi,* and frequently had me mesmerise him when he was suffering, as he did at that time, from neuralgia and sleeplessness. He has often come to my rooms, across three courts, merely in answer to a wish of mine—which he explained by the theory of *rapport.*'

The following incident is also related by Mr. Pulliblank. It is an example of the way in which stories rolled up about him :—

' Palmer was once walking with a cousin near Chesterton. There are remains of a Roman encampment there. They talked about the old Roman soldiers, and the cousin wondered whether there was any survival of the manes of the soldiers there. They arranged some kind of alphabet— how I don't know—and got a Roman name with the addition of the words " Centurion in — legion," and something about the place of his burial. Palmer said he would not believe anything of it ; then the spelling went on in these words—" Tabula reversa." " That is greater nonsense still "—and then the matter dropped. They went back to Cambridge, and Palmer went to his rooms to wash his hands before dinner. In 'his bedroom, which no one had entered since he left it, over his washstand, a picture, which he had noticed before he went out, and knew to have been then in proper position, hung *with its face to the wall.*'

F

CHAPTER III.

THE SURVEY OF SINAI.

ONE thing was now wanting. Palmer had acquired as complete a mastery over Oriental tongues as is possible without going among Oriental people in their own country. He had taught himself to read, write, and speak perfectly Arabic, Persian, and Hindustani, without counting European languages ; but he had not obtained as yet any opportunity of Oriental travel. This chance now came to him, and in a form which most powerfully commended itself to his imagination, although, for purposes of personal advancement, he would rather have had the chance of going to India. The connection between sacred history and sacred geography had in the year 1868 been recently and strongly insisted upon by Dean Stanley ; it was beginning to be understood, by those who turned their attention to the subject, that unless the geography of the Holy Land can be clearly ascertained, and the natural features exactly laid down, the history of the events which have taken place upon that

soil can never be clearly comprehended.   Already
some steps had been taken in this direction ; Captain
Wilson, R.E., had surveyed Jerusalem, partly at the
expense of Lady Burdett-Coutts, partly at his own
expense ; and the Palestine Exploration Fund had
been established for three years, though as yet it was
a small thing, and had done little indeed compared
with the great work which it has since accomplished.
But Wilson and Anderson had already made their
preliminary journey through the country, and prepared
the valuable report which formed so trustworthy a
basis for subsequent work, and Captain Warren had
been already a year at work in Jerusalem.   The value
of exact geographical knowledge, even now most
partially and imperfectly understood, was then only
beginning to be seen by a few ; in fact, in connection
with the study of the Bible there are not many,
even of those who write commentaries, who have
yet learned the value of an accurate map, who can
understand the bearings of water-parting lines, or can
follow the course of armies by the exigencies of the
formation of the country, or can bring the windings
of a valley to help in the adjustment of a boundary.
It is not very long ago, for instance, that the House of
Commons heard without surprise that if we would
take a big map we should be relieved of all further ap-
prehension about Russia's advance in Asia, as if, the
larger the map, the greater would be the distance between the frontiers of England and Russia.   Ignorance

profound still reigns absolute as regards political
geography, but as regards sacred geography a great
deal has of late been done to raise the veil. The
Survey of Jerusalem was followed by that of Sinai ;
that has since been followed by the Survey of Western
Palestine, and all by private enterprise and voluntary
contribution, and without help from the Government
of any kind, except the services of trained officers
and men. The East Country, the South Country, the
North Country, yet remain awaiting the surveyor.
When all has been planned and mapped the way of
the student will be made plain for him, and many
things yet dark will become light. Moreover, it will
be seen that what has been so useful in religious
matters may also prove useful in things political.

The Survey of Sinai, to which especial curiosity had
been attracted since the journey of Laborde, was due
to the Rev. Pierce Butler. He had long desired to
accomplish this undertaking, by which he hoped to
clear up the difficulties connected with the march of
the Israelites. His plans were drawn up, and he was
about to start upon a preliminary journey, when he
was struck down by a fatal illness. It was another
illustration of the way in which the sower of the seed
does not always live to reap the harvest. The cause,
however, was taken up by the Rev. Frederick Holland,
then the curate of Quebec Chapel, who has now also
passed over to the silent land. He brought to bear
upon Pierce Butler's proposals not only an enthusiasm

equal to that of the projector himself but also a practical acquaintance with the country, to which he had
already paid three visits, and had spent many months
in examining its general characteristics and in endeavouring to trace on the spot the route of the Israelites.

It is well known to everybody that this route
has been fiercely contested. Some place the crossing
of the Israelites and the destruction of the hosts
at Suez, at Ayûn Mûsa, and even at the mouth
of the Delta; the 'stations' have been identified in various ways. Mount Sinai itself has been
localised at Jebel Musa, at Jebel Serbal, at the head
of the Gulf of Akabah, and at Mount Hor.[1] Mostly,
however, the battle has been fought over Jebel Musa
and Jebel Serbal. When funds had been collected
and preliminary plans drawn up, the expedition was
placed under the general direction of Sir Henry James,
chief of the Ordnance Survey. The officer appointed
to command the party was Captain (now Sir Charles)
Wilson, R.E., who had already surveyed Jerusalem;
with him were Captain Palmer, R.E., and a staff of
non-commissioned officers of the Royal Engineers.
Mr. Wyatt went with the expedition as naturalist.
Mr. Holland gave his personal experience of the
country and the people; and when they cast about

---

[1] At the head of the Gulf of Akabah by the late Dr. Beke, who
made a journey to the spot in order to prove his theory, found a
mountain called the Mount of Light, and identified it at once without
further evidence with Sinai; at Mount Hor by Mr. Baker Green in
his book called *The Hebrew Migrations* (Trübner and Co.)

for a competent scholar to collect the traditions, names, and legends, to copy and decipher inscriptions, and to observe dialectic differences, there appeared, as generally happens on such occasions, to be only one man in the whole of England who was at once competent for this task and could be asked to go.   There are not many Arabic scholars in the country, to begin with.   Most of them are scholars of books, who can read the language but speak it with difficulty ; of those who can speak it, one would be occupied in other ways ; one would be too old ; one would not be disposed to encounter the risks and fatigues of such a work, and so on.   Palmer, however, was not only competent as regards scholarship, but he was also without other engagements.

Holland himself always maintained that this expedition was the one thing needed to restore Palmer to strength and health.   The hard work of the last six years, the pitiless way in which he had tasked his strength, the want of exercise and fresh air, perhaps also some lingering effects of his old disease, combined with his general tendency to consumption, had made him by this time very weak.   'We found him,' said Holland, 'a fragile creature, who looked as if he would not last a month ; we brought him home, after a few months in the strong pure air of the desert, another man, strong and upright.'

So weak was he, in fact, that during the first few days of the work he was unable to endure the fatigue

of walking a couple of miles, though long before
the survey was completed he was as perfectly fit to
undertake the difficult marches, to climb the precipi-
tous rocks, and to cross the deep valleys of Sinai as
any member of the party. It may be thought that
Palmer's previous life was not altogether the best
fitted to make an investigation into the topography
of the Sinaitic peninsula. Certainly students of the
type of Origen, Eusebius, Reland, or Robinson do not
generally come from the desks of merchants' offices,
nor even from the ranks of those who read Arabic
poetry. On the other hand, the same might be said
concerning officers of the Royal Engineers. Yet the
names of Wilson, Warren, and Conder are in the very
front rank of all as authorities on Biblical topography,
geography, and archæology. I know not when
Palmer's attention was first attracted to the subject.
There are so many fringes, so to speak, to the Biblical
instruction which we get at school, there are so many
things written in journals and elsewhere for popular
education in Biblical matters, the illustrations of the
Bible are of such various kinds, that he may very possibly have been led to consider the topographical
question long before there was any thought of his
going to Sinai. I believe that as a boy he taught
a class in a Sunday school. Probably he had learned
in a vague way, while a Sunday school teacher, something of the difficulties and controversies. When, for
instance, a year or two later, he began to discuss with

me certain disputed points of Jerusalem topography, I found that he already knew the main issues, and that in a way which does not come from a mere visit to the Holy City, which he had then seen twice ; he knew them, in fact, in such a way that he must either have read the subject or have talked it over with Wilson, George Williams, Willis or Fergusson.   It is indeed a subject which, although floods of words have been spent upon it, allows itself to be stated very briefly.   I do not think, therefore, that the topography of the Holy Land was a new subject to him when he was first invited to join the Survey expedition and go to Sinai.   However that may be, he was the first to bring a knowledge of Arabic to bear upon the question.[1]

Of course it was a great chance for Palmer.   He was actually going to visit the East at last ; not the far East, nor India, nor Persia, but that wild country and that wild people among whom Mohammed was born—the land of Ishmael.   He was also to go under the most favourable circumstances, with a party fully equipped for all purposes of exploration ; he was to be officially connected with a scientific expedition, and he was to have every opportunity of showing

---

[1] He did bring this knowledge to bear upon the Jerusalem question, as we shall presently see.   And he had promised at some time or other a work on early Arabic geography and history, which might have thrown great light upon many points arising out of the survey of Western Palestine.   Perhaps some other Arabic scholar may yet be induced to take up the subject.

what good work he was capable of doing. Further, he would go at no expense to himself—a very great consideration in those days. In fact, I believe there was some pay attached to his office; and he would get the opportunity, rarely offered to an Arabic student, of investigating the dialects of the Bedawin on the spot. Lastly, it was a great thing—it was, in fact, promotion and recognition by the outside world of his scholarship—to be connected with so great and important a work; it pleased him that he should have been thought of as a possible member of such an enterprise.

We need not here describe the work of the Survey. Suffice it to say that the peninsula contains an area of about 11,600 square miles—that is, twice as great as that of Yorkshire. The most important part of this area, about 3,600 square miles in the western half, was surveyed on a scale of two miles to the inch, and special surveys were made of Jebel Serbal and Jebel Musa on a scale of six inches to the mile. Photographs were taken, and the results of the whole were embodied in a great work published by the Ordnance Survey Department. I believe, however, that the deciphering of the well known and much debated inscriptions, which was to have been part of Palmer's work, was never published, because he never finished it. The reason of this was that he read and noted an immense number of them, and found them all comparatively modern and of not the slightest im-

portance.   It should be understood that the Sinaitic
inscriptions have no more to do with the Israelites
than the names on the wall of Shakespeare's house
have to do with the poet.   Palmer, therefore, very
naturally shrank from the useless trouble of writing
down things of no greater value than the name of a
visitor written on the wall of an ancient monument.

One of the objects of the Survey—in fact, its most
important object—was to decide between the rival
claims of Jebel Serbal and Jebel Musa.   The controversy between the two mountains may be briefly
stated.   Those who advocate Jebel Serbal point out
that it is the highest mountain in the western range,
and on that account, though one does not see why,
more likely to be the real Mount Sinai.   At its foot
formerly stood the episcopal city of Feiran, long since
destroyed, founded about the third century, whose
monks certainly asserted that Jebel Serbal had
always been considered Mount Sinai.   As regards
Jebel Musa, its name, it is said, is in favour of
the identification.   There is a convent at its foot,
whose monks, like the old monks of Feiran, advance
an unbroken chain of tradition.   There is also a third
argument which the Survey was able to furnish, viz.
a thorough examination of the country.   Palmer's
own contribution to the settlement of the question
was very important.   He observed that Antoninus
Martyr speaks of a certain oratory at Feiran as built
upon the spot where Moses stood at the battle of

Rephidim. He looked about for this oratory, and discovered the ruins of a small chapel on a hill immediately above the spot, exactly corresponding with the
description of the old pilgrim, the position, moreover,
being suitable for the prophet's standpoint, and every
circumstance connected with it tending to confirm
the idea that here was the veritable site of Rephidim.
Palmer therefore suggested that when the monks
founded Feiran they pitched upon the site which native
tradition at the time indicated as Rephidim ; but that
when their town grew and became a flourishing place
and the seat of a bishopric, there arose jealousy between the rival establishments of Jebel Musa and
Jebel Serbal, and the monks of the latter began to
claim for their own mountain the honour of being
Sinai. On the other hand, when Feiran had perished
the monks of Jebel Musa not only remained masters
undisputed of their own tradition, but they also began
to transfer bodily all the interesting sites to their own
neighbourhood, so that we have now, in defiance of
geography, all within an hour's walk of the convent of
St. Katherine, not only the place of the giving of the
Law, but also the spot where Korah, Dathan, and
Abiram perished, the site of Rephidim, and the ' Rock
in Horeb' which supplied the tribes with water.
Palmer also found a curious proof of the antiquity of
the Jebel Musa tradition. In the time of Josephus it
is clear that a definite tradition was attached to one
mountain : he says that the mountain was regarded

with awe, ' from the rumour that God dwelt there.'
Now there are two hills, both insignificant, in the
peninsula, which bear the name of Moneijáh, or the
Conference. Over the door of the convent is an old
Arabic tablet, which purports to be a translation of
the original tablet put up when the convent of
St. Katherine was founded. The mountain is called
on the tablet Jebel Moneijáh. This name, therefore,
would seem to have been the earliest name given to
the mountain, the title of Jebel Musa, or Moses' Mount,
having been borrowed from the common talk of the
people. One may add that the Survey, and the
models executed after it, ·of the two mountains,
showing the valleys and formation of the rocks, have
left little doubt that if the Law was given at one of
these two mountains it was at Jebel Musa and not at
Jebel Serbal.

The work of collecting names, which was entrusted
to Palmer, was extremely delicate and difficult, for
many reasons. The first of these is that a man may
know Arabic well, and yet, until his ear is accustomed
to the peculiarities of the Bedawin dialect, he will be
liable to make dreadful blunders ; next, the Arabs of
one part are ignorant of the nomenclature of their
neighbours, and cannot understand the motives of any ·
other person's curiosity on the subject. The difficulties
are thus summed up by Palmer.

My own work consisted chiefly in ascertaining from the
Bedawín the correct nomenclature of the Peninsula, and the

task was far from easy.   Even in our own country, with all
the advantage of ancient records and an intelligent population, it is often difficult to determine the correct nomenclature of a single district ; but in the desert of Arabia,
without civilisation and without records or literature of any
kind, the difficulties are greatly increased.   The language
also has always proved a fertile source of error in previous
investigations.   The traveller either relies upon the fidelity
of his dragoman's interpretation, or possesses a sufficient
knowledge of Arabic to question the Bedawín for himself.
In the first case accuracy is impossible, for the dragoman is
both unwilling and unable to prosecute the required investigations.   He is generally an illiterate and mercenary being,
between whom and the Bedawín no sympathy or friendship
can exist, and, strange as the assertion may appear, his
language even is not theirs.   If, on the other hand, the
traveller has obtained a previous knowledge of Arabic, I am
only repeating my own experience when I say that, until he
has mixed for some time with the Bedawín, and accustomed
his ear to the peculiarities of their dialect, he cannot rely
upon a single piece of information that he may have
received : and thus it is that the most startling errors have
crept into our books and maps.   As an instance of this, I
may mention the name *Serábit el Khádím*, which is set down
in Russegger's map of Sinai as *Serabut petah Khadem*,
evidently a dragoman's mistake, as *petah* represents the word
beta, which in the vulgar Egyptian dialect is used as a sign
of the genitive case.

The Arabs of one locality are totally ignorant of the
nomenclature of their neighbours, and cannot understand
the motives which induce another person to feel any interest
in the subject.   Shrewd and intelligent in their own sphere,
they are at a loss to comprehend the simplest ideas of
civilised life, and this want of a community of thought
between the enquirer and respondent is a great stumbling-
block in the way of accurate investigation.

The ingenious stupidity of the Bedawín was often very perplexing, as the following instance will show.   During the early part of my stay in Sinai I sought for every opportunity of mastering such expressions and idioms in the Towarah language as differed from those in ordinary use ; and not feeling certain as to the particular form of the interrogative particle 'when' employed by them, I enquired of an intelligent Arab with whom I chanced to be walking.   To make the question as plain as possible, I said, 'Supposing you were to meet a man with an ibex on his shoulder, how should you ask him when he shot it ?'   'I shouldn't ask him at all,' he replied, 'because I shouldn't care.'   'But if you did care,' I persisted, 'what should you say to him?'   'What should I say to him?   Why, I should say good morning !'   This was not satisfactory, so we walked on in silence for some minutes, when I suddenly observed, 'Sáleh, I saw your wife.   '*Mitien ?*' said he, startled, '*when ?*' and down went the word in my note-book.   On another occasion I asked an Arab if he knew why a certain wády was called *Khabár.*   'Of course I do,' he returned contemptuously, 'to distinguish it from other wádies, just as you're called Bundit (Pundit) to distinguish you from Hollol.'

Another difficulty that had to be guarded against is indicated by Robinson in his *Biblical Researches,* vol. I. p. 112. 'A tolerably certain method of finding any place at will is to ask an Arab if its name exists.   He is sure to answer yes, and to point out some point at hand as its location.   In this way, I have no doubt, we might have found a Rephidim, or Marah, or any place we chose.'

If more attention were paid to these distinctions and to the character of the people, many errors of travellers and explorers would be avoided.   I need not expatiate upon the value of such accuracy both to the Biblical critic and the geographer, for, as the Archbishop of Dublin has truly and pithily remarked, Arab tradition is 'fossilised' in their nomenclature, and often furnishes undying testimony to the truth of Scripture.

The method pursued by me was as follows :

I accompanied the officers during the actual process of making the survey, and taking with me the most intelligent Bedawín that I could find belonging to the particular locality, I asked the name of each place as its position was noted down upon the sketch.   I then made further enquiry in the neighbourhood from other Arabs, and never accepted a name without independent and separate testimony to corroborate the information I had at first received. Having in this manner satisfied myself of the accuracy of my information, I proceeded to enquire into the meaning and origin of the names, and set down against each one not only what I knew to be the signification of the word, but the meaning which my informant himself attached to it.   I found this method invaluable for testing the accuracy of my orthography ;   and although the reasons given were not unfrequently trivial or even ridiculous, they served the purpose of corroborative evidence.

That is to say, if you ask an Arab if a certain name exists he is sure to answer yes, and to point it out wherever he thinks you would prefer to place it. If you depend upon a dragoman you will get nothing trust-worthy, partly because he will not take any trouble, and partly because he does not understand the language. That is to say, both he and the Bedawin talk Arabic just as the Lowland Scot and the Devonshire man both talk English. And there is, finally, the inability of the people to understand the good of it all. Why should anyone seek to obtain proof of things which need no proof? Everybody knows about the Lord

Moses and the Beni Israel.   Why all this going about
with instruments, books, and paper?   Why all these
questions, save to hide the real purpose of the Survey,
which was, of course, undertaken as a preliminary to
taking the land?   The difficulties encountered by
previous travellers in getting names and the meaning
of names was constantly illustrated by Palmer.   Thus,
for instance, to take only one example, the Ain
Hawwárah which it is sought to identify with the
Marah of Scripture—a spring of water sometimes
bitter, sometimes palatable—is said by Robinson to
mean the Fount of Destruction, whereas it really
means nothing but the 'Little Pool.'

Another result of the Survey was a study made by
Palmer of the Sinai Bedawin.   It will be found in his
book, the 'Desert of the Exodus,' and is certainly the
best account as yet written of this curious people.
They are, he thinks, in dress, speech, and modes of
life, exactly the same now as they were in the time
of the Patriarchs.   They are not, as is generally believed, wandering continually from place to place :
they have their winter and their summer camping
grounds, and do not wander except from one to the
other ; they are not robbers or murderers, though they
resent the intrusion of an unauthorised person upon
their territory ; they have no history, they boast no
nationality, they possess no organisation.   They are
not even the aboriginal people, but came with the
Mohammedan conquest and turned out the tribes

who before them held the peninsula. Perhaps, however, the descendants of the latter may still be found
among the ' Jibaliyeh,' or mountaineers. It has been
the custom.to consider the Arab of the desert as a man
practically without religion ; yet Palmer often over-
heard them at sunset repeating a very remarkable
and simple prayer. And they have other prayers for
sunrise and on lying down to sleep. They preface
every prayer with the words, ' I desire to pray, and I
seek guidance from God ; for good and pure prayers
come from God alone. Peace be upon our lord
Abraham and our lord Mohammed.'

Palmer thus summed up the results obtained by
this most important Survey :—-

We are thus able not only to trace out a route by which
the Children of Israel could have journeyed, but also to
show its identity with that so concisely but graphically laid
down in the Pentateuch. We have seen, moreover, that it
leads to a mountain answering in every respect to the
description of the Mountain of the Law ; the chain of topographical evidence is complete, and the maps and sections
may henceforth be confidently left to tell their own tale.

The arguments against objections founded on the supposed incapability of the peninsula to have supported so
large a host, I need not recapitulate here ; in the evidence
adduced of the greater fertility which once existed in Sinai,
and in the actual measurements of its areas, the reader
has all the data for himself to decide upon these points.

We cannot perhaps assign much importance to Arab
traditions relating to the Exodus as an argument for or
against the truth of the story, but it is at least interesting to
know that such traditions are found, and it is satisfactory to

G

have them in a collected and accessible form.   Such legends, as we might expect, are chiefly attached to particular
localities ; they do not follow the Children of Israel by any
single or consistent route through the peninsula, but any
spot possessing peculiar features, wherever it may be situated,
is connected by the simple Arab with the grand, mysterious
figure of the Hebrew prophet, whose memory still lingers in
the wild traditions of Sinai.

Such spots are, (1) Moses' wells at 'Ayún Músa near
Suez, and Ain Músa on Jebel Músa.   (2) Moses' seats :
At Abu Zenímeh, on the sea-shore near Hammám Far'ún, is
shown the place where Moses watched the drowning of the
Egyptians, and in the pass of El Watíyeh the chair-shaped
rock, now called Magád en Nebí, is supposed to have received
its peculiar shape from the impress of the prophet's form.
Similar rocks are found in the valley (Wády ed Deir) in which
the convent of St. Katherine is situated, and upon the summit of Jebel Músa itself.   (3) Rocks struck by Moses ; that
in Wády Berráh supposed to have been cleft in twain by
Moses' sword : the Hajjar el Magarín in the path along
Wády Lejá and Hesy el Khatátín in Wády Feirán.   The
Hajjar Músa in the vicinity of the convent, which is pointed
out to pilgrims as the true rock in Horeb, is a palpable
fiction of the monks, and is virtually disregarded by the
Arabs.   (4) Moses' Baths ; as the Hammám Syedná Músa
at Tor.   The Bedawí version of the passage of the Red
Sea, and the legend of the building of stone huts (*nawámís*)
by the Children of Israel to keep off the plague of mosqui-
toes, I have already given.   Enough has been said to prove
that the inhabitants of the country are themselves thoroughly
imbued with the idea that their own desolate and rocky land
was once the scene of a great and wonderful manifestation
of God to man.

The Mohammedan tradition, as elsewhere current also,
evidently points to Jebel Músa as the true Mount Sinai.

The description given by the commentators on the Corăn of the ' Holy wády of Towa,' where Moses halted amidst the snow and mist, could scarcely apply to any other spot, while the distance, according to the same authority, of Midian from Egypt, exactly tallies with the position of Feirán. Whether, therefore, we look at the results obtained in physical geography alone, or take into consideration the mass of facts which the traditions and nomenclature disclose, we are bound to admit that the investigations of the Sinai Expedition do materially confirm and elucidate the history of the Exodus.

He found in this rough life in the desert the keenest enjoyment. He liked the camping in tents, the fine air of the desert, the simple fare, the fatigues of the day, and the rest of the evening. Above all, he delighted in talking with the natives. He was always in after years coming back to some story of the desert. Many of them may be found in the ' Desert of the Exodus '—a delightful book, albeit on a subject which to some may seem uninteresting. The following, for instance, is a translation which he made of a poem composed by a camel-driver, Salameh Abu Taimeh, after the great flood of 1867, when a whole Arab encampment was washed away, and forty souls, together with many camels, sheep. and other cattle, were drowned :—

> I dreamed a dream which filled my soul with fear
>   Fresh grief came on me, but the wise have said,
> When sorrow cometh, joy is hovering near,
>   Methought I looked along a forest glade,
> And marvelled greatly how the trees did rear
>   Their heads to heaven ; when lo ! a whirlwind laid

Their trunks all prostrate.   Then I looked again,
   And what but now like fallen trees had seemed
Were forms of warriors untimely slain.
   Again my fancy mocked me, and I dreamed
Of storms and floods, of fierce resistless rain,
   Of vivid lightnings that above me gleamed ;—
And yet again, dead men around me lay,
   Dead men in myriads around me slept,
Like the Great Gathering of the Judgment Day.
   I woke—a torrent through the wády leapt,
Nile had its ancient barriers burst away
   And over Feirán's peaceful desert swept ;
Nor spared he any in his angry mood
   Save one—to be the river-monsters' food !

I have spoken of the Sinaitic inscriptions, of which
Palmer did not write the translation.   There has
been so much talk about these inscriptions that one
may be permitted to give Palmer's own account of
them and their true value.

In a philological point of view they do possess a certain
interest, but otherwise the 'Sinaitic inscriptions' are as
worthless and unimportant as the Arab, Greek, and European *graffiti* with which they are interspersed.   The language
employed is Aramæan, the Semitic dialect which in the
earlier centuries of our era held throughout the East the place
now occupied by the modern Arabic, and the character
differs little from the Nabathæan alphabet used in the inscriptions of Idumæa and Central Syria.   Thus far they accord
with the account given of them by Cosmas Indicopleustes
in the sixth century ; I see no reason why, without for a
moment admitting a too remote origin, we should not believe
that his Jewish fellow-travellers read, as he asserts that they
did, inscriptions in a language and character so cognate to

their own. It is not true that they are found in inaccessible places high up on the rock, nor do we ever meet with them unless there is some pleasant shade or a convenient camping ground close by. In such places they exist in a confused jumble, reminding one forcibly of those spots which tourist Cockneyism has marked for its own. The instrument used appears to have been a sharp stone, by which they were dotted in ; a single glance is sufficient to convince the inquirer that neither care nor uniformity has been aimed at in their execution. They have been attributed entirely to Christian pilgrims, but, although some of them are undoubtedly their work, the other localities in which they are found renders it extremely improbable that they can be assigned exclusively to this class. Wády Mukatteb, being on the main road through the country, has, as might be expected, a large, even the largest, share, but there are many other remote spots in Sinai where they are scarcely less numerous. In the more flourishing times of the peninsula, and especially during the monkish occupation, there must have been *súks*, or public marts, and even permanent colonies of traders, to supply the wants of the inhabitants ; and those who frequented the fairs, speaking and writing the then prevalent dialect of the East, would be as likely to leave *graffiti* behind them as do their successors in other parts of the desert in the present day. Thus we find Sinaitic as well as Greek inscriptions not only on all the principal roads, but wherever shade, water, or pasture would attract a concourse of men ; and they occur as far as the camel-roads extend, especially in the vicinity of the ruined monasteries ; but, where these are perched upon the inaccessible rocks or at the places of pilgrimage themselves, they are, with few exceptions, seldom found. Serbál, which served as a beacon tower, and consequently became a secular place of gathering, has many such inscriptions, but Sinai's hallowed chapels and confessional archways are without a trace of them. I

imagine, then, that the greater part of the inscriptions are
due to a commercial people, traders, carriers, and settlers
in the land.   No less than twelve of those which we copied
were bilingual, being written in Greek and Sinaitic by one
and the same hand.   The existence of one of these was
previously known : it differs from the rest in being carefully
cut with a chisel and enclosed by a border line.   That many
of the writers were Christian is proved by the number of
Christian signs which they used, but it is equally clear from
internal evidence that a large proportion of them were
Pagans.   They must have extended far down into the later
Monkish times, possibly until the spread of el Islám brought
the ancestors of the present inhabitants, Bedawín hordes
from Arabia proper, to the mountains of Sinai, and dispersed
or absorbed that Saracen population of which the Monks
stood in such mortal fear.

The latter part of the Survey was marked by the
discovery of a place called Erweis el Ebeirig, remarkable as being the only place discovered in the peninsula which could be supposed to show a still existing
trace of an Israelite encampment.   On Palmer's
second visit with Drake they examined the place
more carefully, and found clear proof that it was an
ancient encampment, and that it was not a short
halting place, but a place occupied for some time ;
that it was the camp of a very large number of
people ; that Arab traditions exist to the effect that
here, a long time ago, a Haj or pilgrim caravan
pitched their tents on their way to Ain Hudherah,
and were afterwards lost in the desert of the Tíh and
never heard of again ; that the place is exactly a day's

journey from Ain Hudherah—probably Hazeroth.
Putting all these facts together, with others based on
philological points, Palmer concluded that he had
found the Kibroth Hattaavah of Numbers xi. 33–35.

I have attempted to give a short account of
Palmer's special work on the Survey of Sinai, but I
have not attempted to show the enormous importance of the Survey to that portion of the world which
is interested in the history of the Israelites. This has
been already done by many others. It is sufficient to
establish the fact that Palmer was no drone in that
hive of workers who surveyed the peninsula. He
became its historian in the book to which I have
already referred. This book is now, I believe, out of
print. It is very much to be wished that a new and
cheaper edition might be issued.

CHAPTER IV.

THE DESERT OF THE WANDERINGS.

THE Sinai Survey party returned to England in the summer of the year 1869, but Palmer's work in the Desert had only just begun.

The committee of the Palestine Exploration Fund had just accomplished, so far as it was then possible to go, the first part of their programme. Captain Warren had completed his excavations in Jerusalem and returned to England, bringing with him the splendid spoils of three years' research. They were such discoveries as, in the opinion of some, enabled us to restore the city of Solomon, and to lay down beyond any reasonable doubt the line of the ancient walls and the site of the ancient buildings ; by the confession of all he narrowed the bounds and changed the area of the whole controversy. I shall have, however, something to say about the question of Jerusalem topography when I come to speak of Palmer's share in it.

The Jerusalem work accomplished, the next point

in the programme marked out by the committee was
nothing less than the Survey of the whole country—a
great undertaking which they naturally hesitated to
embark upon before receiving promises of support.[1] At
this juncture Captain Wilson and Mr. Holland—the
former a member of the committee and the latter an
honorary secretary—brought before them the possibility of making a separate examination of the
country north of Sinai and south of Palestine. It
was then a country very little known. A few travellers
had crossed it on their way from Sinai to Palestine ;
among them were Wilton, Russegger, Robinson,
Rowlands, Williams, and I believe Tristram. But
they had for the most part ridden straight across the
country, turning neither to the right nor to the left,
and finding little. Robinson, however, made some
valuable observations, and Rowlands discovered the
fountain of Kadesh, of which he wrote for Williams's
'Holy City' so glowing a description that doubts
have been thrown upon the account, no following
traveller having been able to find anything answering
to it. Fortunately, however, an American traveller,
Mr. Clay Trumbull, has since re-discovered the place,
and found that Rowlands was fully justified in speak-

[1] So great an undertaking has it proved that the Survey of Western
Palestine alone occupied the officers of the Society, working continuously, from December 1871 until May 1875, and again for the
whole of 1877, while the results of the work are not even yet completely published. And there remain the whole of Eastern Palestine
with the Negeb and the North still to be done.

ing of its beauty and the copiousness of the spring
which emerges a full-grown stream, like the Sorgue
at Vaucluse, from the bare face of the cliff. As for
the country itself, it consists of two parts—the Negeb,
or south country, and the Tih, or desert of the wanderings.

The Tih is a large limestone plateau of irregular
surface, advancing by steep escarpments into the
peninsula ; on one side the edge of the plateau runs
nearly parallel with the Gulf of Suez ; on the other
side the edge of the plateau faces the Gulf of Akabah
and skirts the valley of Arabah. On the north it is
bounded by hills which rise like a wall from the
plain, with Jebel Araif on the west and El Mukrah
on the east. The following account is extracted from
an able *résumé* of the existing knowledge of the
country written for the committee of the Society by
Mr. Trelawny Saunders before Palmer was sent out :—

This hilly region, as far as Beersheba, includes the Negeb,
or 'south land' of the Bible, with the upland pastures of
Gerar, where Abraham, Isaac, and Jacob fed their flocks,
and held personal intercourse with the Almighty. It was
afterwards inhabited by the Amalekites, in later times by
the Idumeans, and now by the Azázimeh, the Saidiyeh, and
the Dhullâm Arabs. The Azázimeh country is the most
southerly, and quite unknown. Near the cliff Mukrah an
ancient road is supposed to have passed between Gaza and
the Gulf of 'Akabah, with a branch to Hebron. Here, too,
at its base, on the verge of Paran or the Tih, and of Zin or
the 'Arabah, some critics place Kadesh, one of the most
hotly contested sites in Biblical investigation, and the settle-

ment of which is much to be desired. The other positions of most importance in the controversy are Dr. Robinson's Ain el Weibeh, in the 'Arabah, and Mr. Rowland's Ain el Kudeirah, or Kudes, among the valleys on the west.

Just as Sinai projects into the Red Sea, and as the Tih projects into Sinai, so does the Negeb advance into the Tih. For on the west the desert skirts the hill country north-wards from Jebel 'Aráif up to Beersheba and Gaza, where the Wády Suny serves for a boundary, dividing the barren waste from the Shefelah, or fertile plain of Philistia. On the east the plateau of the Tih runs up beyond the cliff of El Mukrah, towards the Dead Sea, in the form of a narrow terrace, between the eastern base of the hill country and the great Wády el 'Arabah.

In proceeding northwards from the Gulf of 'Akabah, the traveller ascends a succession of terraces, the first of which is the Tih itself, and the next is the hill country of the Azázimeh. This is succeeded by a third, which rises pre-cipitously from the second terrace up a vast inclined plane of a thousand feet in height, and very steep. It is traversed by the Nukb, or pass of Es Sufâ, and also nearer the Dead Sea by the pass of Ez Zuweirah, both well described by Dr. Robinson. On this third terrace are the ruins of Thamara (Kurnub), Aroer (Arara), and Arad. It is inhabited by Dhullâm and Saidiyeh Arabs. Its western side is formed by Jebel Rakmah, behind which Dr. Stewart saw from Beersheba the top of another range, called Ras Tareibeh, but neither of these ranges has been explored. A valley of considerable extent, called Wády Marreh, is said to cross the high land at the foot of the third terrace, connecting Wády el Ain on the west with Wády Fikreh on the east. It is at the western end of these valleys that Mr. Rowland places Kadesh. In the same neighbourhood are said to be the ruins of Eboda; and Jebel Madherah, which rises in a conical form out of Wády Marreh, is regarded by some as Mount Hor.

The uninviting region of the Tih is nearly water-
less, with the exception of a few springs situated in
the larger wadies ; and even here water can only be
obtained by scraping small holes in the ground and
baling it out with the hand as it slowly accumulates.
You then get a yellowish solution, half of which settles
to the bottom in a cake of mud. The ground (I am
here taking Palmer's own description) is covered with
a carpet of small flints, so worn and polished by the
detritus that is being constantly blown over them as
to resemble pieces of black glass. Although, however,
the soil appears so arid, a quantity of brown, parched
herbage is scattered over the surface, which bursts
into sudden life in the time of the spring rains. In
the larger wadies there is more moisture, and therefore
more vegetation. Over the whole desert there are
no rivers, no sign of former inhabitants or of any
period of fertility ; but in the north-east the mountain
plateau called Jebel el Magráh offers many points
of interest ; on its edge is Ain Gadis, the ancient
Kadesh ; it contains the *hazeroth*, or fenced enclosures,
of an ancient pastoral people, probably the Amalekites.
In the plateau north of the desert the ruins of many
towns have been discovered, and doubtless there
are many more which still await discovery. Here,
for instance, was the town of Zephath, identified
by Palmer with Sebaita ; here the frequently re-
curring names "Amir, "Amerí, "Amerín remind one
of the Amorites ; and here were the wells of Rehoboth,

Sitnah, and Beersheba, whose names, in this land which changeth not, survive in Ruheibeh, Shutneh, and Bir Seba.

There is a great deal to be done in the country which nothing but a scientific survey can accomplish, but the field in the year 1870 was sufficiently unknown to make it a promising one for a small party or a single traveller. Probably the committee might have hesitated to take the responsibility of sending one man alone, even Palmer, among the wild Arabs of the Tîh, but fortunately an opportunity offered by which a certain amount of the danger might be avoided. They learned that although Palmer would willingly have undertaken, alone, a journey of exploration in the desert, there was a chance of finding a companion for him in the person of Mr. Charles Tyrwhitt Drake, and of obtaining a grant in aid of the enterprise from the Travelling Bachelors' Fund of Cambridge.

Mr. Tyrwhitt Drake, whose name was henceforth to be, for the short remainder of his valuable life, associated with the exploration of the Holy Land, was then about twenty-four years of age. A weakness of the chest and tendency to asthma cut short his University career, and he had already travelled in Algiers and Morocco, and visited the peninsula of Sinai in the year of the survey. He had some acquaintance with Arabic, which he afterwards greatly improved, and became fairly able to talk Arabic

though he was never an Oriental scholar. He was
an excellent ornithologist, and, indeed, a good 'all
round' naturalist. He could also sketch, and would
probably, had his life been spared, have become
a good archæologist.[1] Other qualifications useful
for a traveller he possessed. For example, he was a
man whose courage could always be depended on,
and steady in danger ; moreover, he was of equable
temper, and always, in hunger, danger, fatigue, and
illness, the same cheery companion. His great height
and personal strength were also useful to him among
a people who regard strength and dexterity with so
great respect.

'Never once,' said Palmer four years afterwards,
lamenting the early death of his friend, ' never once,
during the whole of our journey did I know Drake out
of temper, out of heart, or discouraged.' I have heard
Captain Burton pay exactly the same tribute to his
memory. It is pleasant to think that such Englishmen
are still to be found as good as the brave men of old.

The preliminaries were easily arranged. Palmer
calculated that the expedition would cost altogether
about 400*l.*, to which was added the grant made by
the University to Drake. So far as I remember he
executed his mission for rather less than this sum. His
instructions were general rather than special. He was

---

[1] He died, in June 1874, at Jerusalem, of a complication of diseases
brought on by hard work in the Jordan valley during the Survey of
Western Palestine.

to endeavour, first of all, to investigate certain points at the north-east of the peninsula which Captain Wilson wished to clear up ; he was next to examine the passes in the south escarpment of the Tih, to settle, if possible, the question of Kadesh by examination of the rival sites ; to search in the Land of Moab for inscriptions : and for the rest he was left free, and only generally instructed to throw as much light upon the desert of the wanderings as his observations permitted.   The travellers proposed to undertake this journey without dragoman or escort of any kind, to do everything on foot, and to carry with them as little as possible in the way of personal luggage or instruments.   They also received from Captain Wilson some preliminary instruction in the art of taking observations, reconnaissances, and laying down the country in field books.

Their equipment consisted of a tent, six feet square and five feet high, two mattresses, blankets, a kettle, pot, and frying-pan, with tin plates, knives, forks, and tin washing basins, and a three-months' supply of tea, flour, bacon, onions, tobacco, sugar, Liebig's extract, and brandy.   In addition they had their instruments and a photographic apparatus. Four çamels sufficed to carry the whole, and the only escort consisted of the owners of the camels. These were changed in passing from tribe to tribe, so that they may be said to have performed this journey absolutely unattended and alone.   It is

needless to say that such an expedition, among
people so suspicious and uncertain, would be impossible except for one who was already a perfect
master of Arabic and thoroughly experienced in
native habits and customs. Six months among
them, however, had given Palmer this mastery of
desert Arabic and familiarity with the ways of one
tribe, at least.   Residence among a people is of itself
perfectly useless unless one speaks their language and
not only can, but does, converse freely with them.
All over the world, for instance, we have English
merchants, garrisons, consuls, clergymen, lawyers,
physicians, engineers, living among strange people,
yet practically ignorant of their manners and their
thoughts, because they have not learned their
language.   Again, it wants more than a mere
knowledge of the tongue to become really acquainted
with a people.   There are missionaries scattered
about all over the world—thousands of missionaries,
Protestant and Catholic—they all learn the native
tongues ; their whole business is to go about among
the people ; yet it is only now and again by some
rare chance that one will be found here and there—
a Xavier, a Huc, a Martyn—able to understand and
to interpret the mind of the people with whom the
work of his life is engaged; for to do this requires
the rarest kind of sympathetic insight.   For the most
part they deliver their message with such eloquence
and earnestness as may be in them, and they have

done. But they are strangers in a strange land, they win respect, confidence, and even affection ; but they are never regarded by the people as one of themselves. Think what might have been known of the races of mankind had missionaries been able to talk as well as to preach ! Think what a missionary such a man as Palmer would have made ! Palmer among his Arabs spoke as one of them, and thought as one of them, not as a stranger. His was that strange sympathy which enables its possessor to feel *with*, as well as *for*, his friends. His extraordinary gift of sympathy was connected with his mesmeric power ; he was a thought-reader. To know what a man is thinking about goes a long way towards acquiring an influence over that man. Another thing, again, gave him power over all sorts and conditions of men : he possessed to a wonderful degree the enthusiasm of humanity. Any broken-down vagabond, any poor drunken outcast, any ragged Arab, strolling thief, or poaching gipsy interested him and gave him material for study and reflection. He was incapable of contempt for the meanest and lowest of his kind. That a man could be so mean and low moved his surprise, but not his wrath. He regarded the thing as an eccentricity. The gentleman liked rags, dirt, tramping, and begging. A curious taste ; but some men are so.

He relied, therefore, in undertaking this expedition—just as he was going to rely in undertaking

H

another, twelve years later—entirely on his power of managing the people. The result showed that his confidence was not misplaced. This self-reliance one must point out strongly and insist upon, because it illustrates the character of the man, was complete and absolute. He never doubted himself. It was not in boastfulness, but as a mere matter of plain fact, that he regarded himself as able to manage any number of Arabs, friendly or hostile. He would state the thing just as he might say that he could translate Arabic if he were asked, and as if it were no more important.

Let us follow this journey with some attention to detail. It must be remembered that, among other things, it gave him that knowledge of all the desert tribes—the Sinai Survey only brought him into contact with the Towárah—which enabled him to undertake and carry through the great Achievement of last July.

The two travellers started from Suez on December 16, and first struck southwards, making for Jebel Musa, which they reached twelve days later. Their object in going there was to examine the MSS. and library of the convent. Palmer found there, besides the well-known *Codex Aureus*, an ancient copy of the Psalms in Georgian, written on papyrus, and another in Greek, with some curious old Syriac books and one or two palimpsests. They next proceeded to visit again the curious remains which Palmer had already

discovered near Ain Hudherah, called Erweis el
Ebeirib. The second and more exact examination
proved, as has been already stated, beyond a doubt
that it was an ancient encampment, and one of a
very considerable host ; while its distance from Jebel
Musa on the one hand and Ain Hudherah on the
other exactly corresponds with the required positions
of Kibroth Hattaavah. In the neighbourhood were
also found a great quantity of *nawamis*, the strange
prehistoric stone-houses which, I believe, were first
discovered in the course of the Survey. They are
frequently accompanied by stone circles. After exploring the wadies and passes of the Jebel el Ejmel
in connection with the way of the Israelites they
struck north-west and went to Kulàt Nakhl, a place
which has of late been frequently spoken of. It is
one of the four forts which are garrisoned by Egyptian
soldiers for the domination of the Desert and peninsula of Sinai, Akabah, El Arish, and Suez being the
other three. Here they made a bargain for camels
with the Teyáhah Arabs, who, not being able to
pronounce their names, called Palmer Abdullah and
Drake Ali. Palmer retained the name, and was
always afterwards known and remembered among
them as the Sheikh Abdullah, or Abdullah Effendi.

Their progress was slow, because they were occupied in map-making as they went. Ten miles a day,
however, done on foot over a terribly rough country,
with excursions right and left, represent a fair day's

march. For ten days they walked over a plain with occasional depressions of wadies. Many stone circles and *nawamis* were passed, and several examined. They arrived at the conclusion that the Amalekites or some other early race used to bury their dead in cists, pile great cairns on the top, surround the whole with a stone circle, and offer sacrifices to the deceased in small open enclosures situated within the ring. It would be well worth the while to get these curious monuments all planned, measured, and drawn, as has been recently done by Captain Conder in the rude stone monuments of Eastern Palestine. Palmer, however, had other things to do; moreover this was a journey of reconnaissance only. If his maps showing the route be examined it will be found that a vast area of the country has never been visited at all. There is no reason to expect that it differs in any way from the part explored. Probably *nawamis* and stone circles would be found dotted all over it; still it would be interesting to have a complete record of them. Meantime there they are; they will not be destroyed, and whenever it is found possible to organise a party for the purpose they can be sought for. About fifty miles N.E. of Kulát Nakhl they came upon a ruin which probably marks the most southern position ever occupied by the people of Palestine even in the flourishing days of order and prosperity which preceded the Persian invasion and the Moslem conquest. The place is called Contellet-Guraiyeh;

it stands on a hill, and appears to be a mound erected on the summit. But on digging the mound proved to be the débris of a former wall. They also found by another excavation a very remarkable series of *amphoræ*, contained in a framework of sun-dried bricks and beams of wood with signs of mortices and bolts. They uncovered some, but could not, of course, bring them away. The wood used was the *seyál*, the Shittim wood, of which they saw only one tree remaining in the Tîh at the present day. Probably this place was an outpost to guard the frontier of Palæstina Tertia, or the Negeb, when it was full of cities, churches, and monasteries. It was, in fact, one of the many remote and solitary desert fortresses erected in the time of the Byzantine Empire ; a garrisoned place, as Nakhl is now. This also is a place where excavations might profitably be conducted. The next place of interest was the site of Kadesh, and it is very much to be lamented that they were so satisfied, after careful examination, that the place marked on the map as Ain Gadis, the place where they were standing, could be no other than the Kadesh of the Exodus, that they did not explore the neighbourhood, and so rediscover the magnificent fountains and stream of Rowlands, already mentioned.

What they missed and was found ten years later is thus described by the American traveller who hit upon the place :—

It was an oasis unapproached by any I had seen in the desert since leaving Feirán, and not surpassed, within its limits, by *that*. It was carpeted with grass and flowers. Fig-trees laden with fruit were against its limestone hill-sides. Shrubs in richness and variety abounded. Standing out from the mountain range at the northward of the beautiful oasis-amphitheatre, was the 'large single mass or small hill of solid rock' which Rowlands looked at as the cliff (sela) smitten by Moses to cause it to 'give forth its water' when its flowing had ceased. From beneath this cliff came the abundant stream. A well, walled up with time-worn limestone blocks, was the first receptacle of the water. Not far from this was a second well similarly walled, supplied from the same source. Around both these wells were ancient watering troughs of limestone. Several pools, not walled up, were also supplied from the stream. On from the line of these pools, a gurgling stream flowed musically for several hundred yards, and then lost itself in the verdure-covered desert. The water was clear and sweet and abundant. Two of the pools were ample for bathing. Before the cliff, and around its neighbouring wells, camel and goat dung was trodden down as if by the accumulations of centuries, showing that the place was much frequented for watering purposes.

One of the most important objects of the expedition was to determine the question of ancient fertility, if a time of fertility ever existed. On this important point Palmer writes :—

From Northern Syria to Sinai southwards the country seems to have certain natural divisions, marked by the comparative fertility of the soil of each. In Syria, at the present day, we have a well-watered and productive soil ; in Palestine, after the Hermon district, the soil is much more

barren, but must certainly at some time, when better cultivated, have been more productive ; south of the mountains
of Judæa, to the point immediately below which Gadis is
situated, the country, though now little more than a barren
waste (from the failure of the water-supply, consequent upon
neglect), presents signs of a most extensive cultivation, even
at a comparatively modern period. This is undoubtedly
the Negeb, or south country of Palestine, and 'Ain Gadís
may be considered as situated nearly at the frontier of this
district. Between this and the edge of the Tíh plateau the
country is even more barren, but there are still traces of a
primeval race of inhabitants, in the cairns and nawámís, or
stone huts, to which I have before adverted. At the time
of the Exodus it must have borne a similar relation to the
then fertile region of the Negeb which that now barren
tract at the present day bears to Palestine. This would
exactly answer to the description of the Bible, the Israelites
waiting as it were on the threshold of the southern portion
of the Promised Land ; and from the analogous recession
of fertility northwards we may fairly conclude that the
surrounding country was better supplied with water than it
is now, and that it was therefore at least as suitable for the
encampment of the Israelitish hosts as any spot in Sinai.
But the spies went up from Kadesh and returned thither,
bringing the grapes from Eshkol ; it may be, therefore,
objected that if Hebron be Eshkol, the distance from that
to 'Ain el Gadís is farther than the grapes could possibly
have been brought, especially by men who would have to
pass through the country with so much caution as they must
have employed in their character of spies. Now, it is a
curious fact that among the most striking characteristics of
the Negeb are miles of hill-sides and valleys covered with
the small stone heaps in regular swathes, along which the
grapes were trained, and which still retain the name of
teleilát-el-'anab, or grape-mounds. It may be that we shall

have to modify the existing theories concerning the position of Eshkol, and indeed I have no doubt but that it is to be looked for a short distance from 'Ain Gadís ; but in any case I think that no *primâ facie* difficulty need be made of the relative positions of Eshkol and the Kadesh which I am now advocating. Dr. Robinson's theory that Kadesh must be sought for at 'Ain el Weibeh, in the neighbourhood of the passes of Sufâh and Figreh, immediately below the southern border of Palestine, does not seem a tenable one, especially from strategic considerations, for the children of Israel would have been confined, as it were, in a *cul-de-sac*, with the subjects of King Arad, the Amorites, the Edomites, and the Moabites completely hemming them in, whereas in the neighbourhood of 'Ain el Gadís they would have had nothing but the wilderness around them, and certainly no very formidable hostile peoples in their rear.

Close to Gadís is a spring called the Ain Muweileh, which has been suggested as identical with Hagar's well, though orthodox Mohammedans place it near Mecca. Near this place they found caves excavated for sleeping chambers, and one for a Christian chapel, with immense quantities of stone heaps of the character already described. These lie about on the hill-tops, the sides being covered with paths. There must, therefore, at one time have been some kind of city here, but one knows not of what people or what period. The existence of the Christian chapel means nothing ; a hermit or a few monks may have carved Christian signs upon the walls of an old cave and used it for a chapel. The Edomites, however, were cave-dwellers, and the remarkable caves of Dubban, farther

north, are attributed to them during their occupation
of South Palestine.   They were now, however, arrived
at the country where the ruins of a later time begin.

Palestine was never more densely peopled than just
before the great revolt suppressed by Vespasian and
Titus.   But the frightful massacres which it suffered
at the hands of the victors, and the deportation of so
many thousands, were never thoroughly recovered,
and after the next rebellion under Barcochebas the
greater part of the country passed out of the hands of
the Jews.   There seems, so far as one can learn, to
have been few Jews left in the south country from
the fourth to the seventh century, when, save for the
Rabbinical seats of learning, the land was entirely in
the hands of Christians.   Of what race the Christians
were who inhabited the south country it is difficult
to say.   Probably they were the same people as the
modern fellaheen, and these are generally supposed
to be nothing more or less than the ancient
Canaanites, who were never exterminated, and have
always remained attached to the soil, changing their
religion to suit that of their conquerors.   In other
words, the Christians who in the fifth century built
their churches and had their bishops in the 'south
country' were Philistines, Edomites, Amalekites, and
Amorites.   Formerly they had been, in a way, worshippers of Jehovah with a little tinge of Jewish ritual and
the survival of the high places and the graves.   After
the destruction of their towns they became Moham-

medans, with lingering traditions of the Christian period and the survival still of high places and groves.

The destruction of the south country cities is due to the invasion of Chosroes, the Persian king, who swept through the country from north to south, burning, murdering, and destroying, followed by thousands of the Jews, eager for revenge upon the Christians. It was very easy to destroy a city of the Negeb. You had only to cut down the trees, fill up the wells, and break the cisterns; then the inhabitants must starve or go. Probably the officers of the Persian took steps so thorough that the people were spared the necessity of considering the alternative.

Palmer and Drake either discovered or examined afresh five or six of these ruined towns. One cannot but feel sure that there must be many others lying off the track followed by the Arabs of to-day. The remains of a fort and a church, the ash-heaps, the ruined walls, and the hill-slopes covered with stones swept together where vineyards once stood, attest the former populousness and fertility. The most considerable ruin is that of Sebaita (Zephath), where there are the remains of three churches, besides walls, towers, and citadel. When one considers the sudden nature of the destruction, and the fact that since the event no one except the Arab has been near the ruins, it becomes almost certain that excavation might yield results of the greatest interest.

The first part of the journey ended at Jerusalem.

They had walked 600 miles, and had worked on an average fourteen to sixteen hours a day.   The second part of the journey took them from Hebron across the east side of the desert to Petra.   On the way they were able to sketch and plan the ruins of Abdeh, the ancient Eboda.   At Petra they heard of two ruined cities called Dibdibeh and Banoureh, and visited two others called El Beidha and El Bárid.   This part of the country is practically unexplored and likely to remain so, for the cupidity and jealousy of the Arabs keep off all travellers except those who are extraordinarily wealthy or those who travel in great force. The remains at Petra are not of high antiquity, but yet, with those of El Barid and the other places found by Palmer, they cry aloud for investigation.

It was, further, one of the objects of the expedition to look for inscriptions in Moab.   The Arabs were at this time, a year or two after the unlucky smash of the Moabite Stone, keenly alive to the value of inscriptions ; yet none could be found.   I am, myself, of opinion that none will ever be found above ground. For, in the first place, it is evident, from the historical part of the Bible, that the setting up of such stones was by no means common ; so that one need not expect, because King Mesha inscribed one stone, that all his successors should do the like.   Next, if they did, the chance of survival would be almost infinitesimally small.   Such inscriptions as still remain will be found, I believe, as Clermont Ganneau, the

man with the *main heureuse*, found the famous tablet
from Herod's Temple—underground. Some, however,
are perhaps built up in walls. Palmer, at this time
thought otherwise ; he believed that with judicious
backshish and careful search other inscribed stones
might be found in the country. There is this to be
said in favour of his view : Eastern Palestine has been
practically left alone, while in the west the old
synagogues and other public buildings have been
ruthlessly pulled down to be built up again as
monasteries, convents, chapels ; these, in their turn,
destroyed to be converted into mosques ; these again
to furnish materials for crusaders' castles or Latin
churches ; so that hardly anything has been left.
Eastern Palestine has seen no church-building south
of the Arnon, no crusaders except at Kerak, has
suffered nothing from war since the march of Baldwin
upon Bozrah, and has known no destroyer but the
hand of time. Yet, even with these advantages, I
cannot think that any considerable or important inscriptions still remain to be found. Palmer found
none : following travellers—Tristram, Oliphant,
Merrill, Conder—have found none.

The journey was finished : for the first time two
young Englishmen, trusting to their courage and
their knowledge of the people, had walked fearlessly
through the 'great and terrible' Desert. One of
them, for his part, made so many friends among the
sheikhs and the people that ten years afterwards he

was not afraid to go back in time of war and the rage of religious fanaticism, and to travel among them again alone and unprotected.

Palmer made some stay at Jerusalem, where he copied and translated the Cufic inscriptions round the wall of the Dome of the Rock, and made other notes which were utilised later on. From Jerusalem he rode with Drake to the Lebanon and Damascus, where Captain Burton was at that time consul. It is pleasant to record that both Palmer and Drake were counted by this great traveller among his best friends. The consul went with them to the Lebanon, and I believe to Baalbek.

Among the many stories brought home by Palmer from this adventurous journey was one of a certain sheikh, Salámeh, who was at one part of it their guide. He brought to them the day after they entrusted themselves to his leadership a paper which, he said, was a testimonial of his wonderful honesty. It was a document setting forth in English that the said Salámeh was a most rapacious scoundrel, and that everybody must be on their guard against him. Next day the cook appeared, tearing out handfuls of beard and beating his breast. Salámeh, he said, was going to desert them and leave them to perish in the wilderness. This, it presently appeared, was the actual intention of the honest Salámeh, unless———. Five-and-twenty pounds bought his fidelity, and the travellers passed on in safety. When, however, they arrived at Jerusalem Palmer informed the Turkish Governor of the circumstance. The Pasha said that he knew the man, and that his tribe were behindhand with their tribute. Steps should certainly be taken. Salámeh had been already reported more than once for such acts. English travellers should see an example of the strength and justice of the Sultan's rule. Shortly afterwards they arrived at Damascus and called upon the Waly, who, in course of conversation, asked them if they should know Salámeh again. He thereupon clapped his hands, and a soldier brought in a sack containing four human heads, one of which belonged to the unfortunate Salámeh. 'Are you satisfied?' the Waly asked.

In North Syria there exists a most remarkable people called the Nusairiyeh, whose religion has been one of the most curious problems of Syrian travellers. As for the Druses, we do know part of their creed; it is pretty well established that they worship the mad Hakeem; but no one—not even Mr. Lyde, who wrote the 'Asian Mystery,' a book all about the Nusairiyeh —has been able to say why, or how they worship him. Palmer continued his journey to the north among this remarkable folk, about whom he learned many strange things. These he embodied in a paper contributed to the 'British Quarterly,' called the 'Secret Sects of Syria,' which it is hoped may be republished with other valuable papers. From North Syria he went on to Constantinople and came home by way of

Vienna, where he met Arminius Vambéry, who became and remained one of his firmest friends.

The results of this journey were summed up in a report furnished to the committee of the Palestine Exploration Fund, and published by them in the journal of the Society first, and again in the volume called 'Special Papers' belonging to the 'Survey of Western Palestine.' He wrote a popular account of it, in his 'Desert of the Exodus'; it provided him with materials for his paper on the 'Secret Sects of Syria,' and for other papers contributed to various reviews. For purposes of exploration the results were invaluable, though in many cases only suggestive of further research. He proved the former rich fertility of the south country, and the comparative fertility of the Tíh; he discovered the site of Kibroth Hattaavah, and adduced new arguments to establish the site of Kadesh; he collected a vast quantity of traditions and legends, and disclosed a prehistoric set of monuments whose existence had been previously unsuspected. In addition to this, his quick brain-power of rapid observation and retentive memory made him henceforth an authority second to none—except, perhaps, Wilson, Warren, and Conder—on matters connected with Palestine and its people.

Nor was this all. His visit to Jerusalem turned his attention to the questions of topography which have been so hotly disputed. Now, before this time the only reference to Arab authorities—who may be

supposed to know something about their own buildings in Jerusalem and elsewhere—had been through
one or two badly executed versions. Palmer began
to look up the matter, and was presently able to
give the whole story about the Temple area and the
modern buildings in it from the history related by
different Arab writers.

Stated briefly, the position of the two different
camps of disputants is this. The late George Williams
and others of his thinking held that the present
Church of the Holy Sepulchre stands on the site of
the church built by Constantine ; that it covers the
real tomb of our Lord, and that the Dome of the Rock
is a building by Abd-el-Melek on part of the area
occupied by an ancient temple. Mr. James Fergusson maintained that the Dome of the Rock is no
other than a building erected by Constantine over
the real tomb, that the Temple stood in the south-
west corner of the Haram Area, and that the tra-
ditional Church of the Holy Sepulchre was erected
by monks for the purpose of deceiving pilgrims when
they were turned out of their real church. He based
this position mainly on architectural arguments.
There is now a third school who hold that the present
church stands on the site beside which, not over which,
Constantine erected his basilica, and that the Temple
of Herod stood in the middle of the Area, but that as
to the real site of the Holy Sepulchre Constantine
had no more certainty, but rather less, than ourselves.

Palmer's view was simple. He said, 'I know nothing at all about the architectural argument; I am not even for the present concerned with the Christian history of the Jerusalem buildings. What I do know is that the Dome of the Rock was erected by Abd-el-Melek, and that the history of the building is narrated as plainly and as clearly by the Arab historians as that of St. Paul's by Christopher Wren is told by English writers.' A year later he wrote in collaboration with me a History of Jerusalem from the siege by Titus to the present day. In this work he undertook the Mohammedan part, while I told the tale from Christian sources. It was not our object to embark in the controversy about the sites, but the building of the Dome by Abd-el-Melek was part of the history, and it is told by Palmer from the Arab historians. Professors of architecture may hold any opinion they please, but if their opinion does not agree with the plain and simple story in which, without any doubt, all the Arab accounts agree—and, so far as we could see, all the Christian accounts—so much the worse for that opinion. *The Dome of the Rock was built by Abd-el-Melek.* Where he got his architects, his design, his materials, is another question altogether, though these points are also fully answered by the historians.

It was part of Mr. Fergusson's theory that the Holy Sepulchre is the cave within the Dome, and he considers the Dome to have been built by Constan-

I

tine. Now, as regards the real site of the Holy Sepulchre, that is a great question of which much has been written. I believe I am fully warranted in saying that Palmer was of the opinion, held by many, that it was completely unknown in the fourth century; that the early Christians, on their return from Pella after the siege and destruction, had forgotten where it was, and cared only to preserve one site—that of the Ascension, to which, we know, pilgrims came as early as the second century—and that Constantine's advisers knew less even than ourselves where to look for it. Lastly, he was profoundly impressed by the remarkable discovery made by Captain Conder in the year 1881 of a certain very remarkable tomb near the 'Place of Stoning,' and was inclined to believe that it was reserved for the nineteenth century, and for a centurion of an English legion, to discover the actual Tomb—the Holy Sepulchre itself.

As regards Palestine research, Palmer continued to afford the Society every kind of assistance, to advise and contribute papers. When, a year or two ago, the publication of the 'Survey of Western Palestine' commenced, he undertook, and carried through, the great labour of transliterating and translating the name lists collected by the Society's officers, and was appointed, with myself, editor of the volumes. As a fellow worker he was incomparable—rapid,-unwearied, accurate, a keen corrector of proofs, full of resource, and always knowing exactly where to find what was wanted.

CHAPTER V.

TEN YEARS OF WORK.

DURING the undergraduate years—perhaps before them—Palmer made the acquaintance of a family living at Grantchester, near Cambridge, named Widnall. At their house he met the young lady who became his first wife. She was a niece of Mrs. Widnall, and was named Laura Davis. He became engaged to her, with her father's consent, in the same year in which he took his degree, when she was but sixteen years of age. Marriage was for the moment out of the question : reputation and an income of some kind had first to be sought. Then came the Sinai and the Tîh expeditions, out of which a good beginning was made in the direction of the former, at any rate. But the income seemed as far off as ever. The engagement, however, went on ; the young lady was still under twenty, and Palmer was not yet thirty. She was a singularly beautiful girl, fair and with a lovely complexion, taller than her *fiancé.* In the 'Song of the Reed' he has preserved an acrostic

written by him upon her, and a little poem. written
for her in which he recalls in pretty flowing verse
the moment of their engagement.

> I felt the flood-gates open fly
>   And poured my secret in her ear,
> And paused awhile for her reply
>   With hope, though somewhat mixed with fear.
> It came, a little word that sent
>   Through all my frame a joyous thrill ;
> And gently on my arm there leaned
>   Those tiny fingers, trembling still.
> The merry stream flowed on apace
>   Beneath the shady chestnut trees ;
> And lo ! another smiling face
>   Was turned to catch the balmy breeze.

Mrs. Palmer herself wrote poetry, and a 'little
volume of her verses was printed in the year 1876,
called 'Thoughts in Verse.' But it was only intended
for private circulation.

The following is an acrostic written by Palmer on
the name of his mistress some time after his engagement :—

> L' addio dire quanto è cosa dura,
> Al mondo non v' ha pena piu acerba ;
> Un sol pensier il cor me or rassicura,
> Ravviserò que' luoghi, dove l' erba
> Ancor di te vestigio dolce serba.
> Deh ! pensa un poco s' egli mai pioggia,
> A noi bagnati, su quel giorno, quando
> Venivam radunati in bella foggia :
> In solitudine di te gustando
> Siëderò di te ognor pensando !

On Palmer's return in the autumn of 1870 there was plenty of work waiting to be done. First of all there was the official Report on his journey for the committee of the Palestine Exploration Fund. This document, carefully prepared, and embodying all his discoveries and observations, was published in the journal of the Society in January 1871. Twelve years have now passed since that journey, and although a few travellers have crossed the Tîh from Sinai to Hebron no attempt has been made by any of them to follow up Palmer's work and examine the strange forlorn country whose ruins he discovered and planned. In the present disturbed state of the East it is probably unsafe to make the attempt, but it is to be hoped that further research will be conducted by this country in ' Palæstina Tertia.'

In the autumn of the same year he produced his ' Desert of the Exodus.' The book was admirably illustrated, and put forth at great expense by the publishers (Bell and Daldy). It was received with favour by the press, both in America and England, and I have always been astonished that a new and cheap edition has never been issued. Perhaps it is not yet too late ; and, after the excision of a few passages which are no longer of interest, it would become a permanent and standard work on the country and the people of Sinai and the desert. In the same year he wrote the ' History of Jerusalem,' of which I have already spoken. The idea was to take up the history of the city at that point where its sacred associations cease, to tell the story of the siege, the early Christian centuries with their pilgrims, monasteries, and hermits, the Moslem conquest, the building of the Dome, the later pilgrims, the Latin kingdom, the fall of the city, the later wars, the Children's Pilgrimage, and the Mohammedan pilgrims. It was my first experience of Palmer as a fellow-worker. Our plans admitted of separate work ; he told his story, I told mine ; if there were small discrepancies here and there, one did not care to harmonise them ; we met and talked over the work when we had our proofs in our hands. I found that he had no kind of sympathy with the Crusaders, whom he regarded as a mob of ignorant and fanatic barbarians fighting for a shadow, because what did it matter, what does it matter still, who may be master of the City of sacred memories ? Nor could he ever forgive a people who could, as was done at Tripoli, destroy and burn a splendid library full of manuscripts because they were written in 'execrable characters ; ' nor could he contrast without disgust the ferocity of the knights who disgraced the later days of the Latin kingdom with the chivalrous and courteous manners of Salah-ed-Dín, commonly called Saladin.

Syria, and every part of the history connected with Syria, is inexhaustible. He who undertakes Syria must be prepared to give to his task the work of a life. He might do much worse. To begin with, he would have to read the whole of the Byzantine historians, a great part of the early Fathers, and the Arab historians. The writing of this one book of ours opened up before us whole vistas of subjects in which the collaboration of an Arabic scholar with a student of mediæval chronicles might lead to most wonderful results. We promised ourselves the joy of pursuing our researches into all kinds of interesting subjects which we had been compelled merely to touch lightly or to pass over. There was the history of the Assassins ; the secret history of the Templars ; the strange charges brought against them, and their connection with the Sheikh of the Mountain ; the rise of the Druses ; the lingering among the northern hills of the old religions ; the condition of the Jews in Palestine during the flourishing period of their Rabbinic schools ; their condition under the crusaders : the extent and stability of the Latin kingdom ; the people over whom the Counts of Edessa and Tripoli, for instance, ruled ; the fellahin ; the destruction of the ancient monuments ; the topography of the early pilgrims : all these were points to which we were going to devote our combined attention. One sees now how impossible it was to think of following up even one of these. For money must be made ; and by archæology no money can be made ; and were it not for the providential raising up here and there of a rich man who is also a scholar and an archæologist, or of a quiet country

clergyman with tastes archæological, or of some men
good enough not to marry and therefore not to want
money, there would soon be no archæology at all.
None of these investigations, therefore, were made
by either of us, and the field still remains open. We
used to meet in those years also at a certain Masonic
Lodge, founded originally for Orientals and persons
interested in things Oriental. Persians, Hindus,
Parsees, and Mohammedans belonged to this Lodge,
though I believe that it has now lost its distinctive character and become as uninteresting as other
Lodges are wont to be. Palmer was never a great
believer in Freemasonry, and he ridiculed the present
Government and practice of the Society, but he
acknowledged that its value, granting its mediæval or
ancient existence, lies in its being a standing and
practical protest against the usurpations and pretensions of the priest. In the Brotherhood, every man
stands face to face with his God, with no priest, or
dogma, or person claiming any supernatural powers
whatever between. This being so, there is surely,
he thought, a great future for Freemasonry when it
gets out of the present vicious groove and falls into
the hands of intelligent men capable of seeing what
a tremendous weapon it may be made for independence and freedom of thought.

In the same year Palmer experienced what one
is fully justified in calling the most cruel blow ever
dealt to him, and one which he never forgot or forgave.

The vacancy of the Professorship of Arabic in 1871 seemed to give him at last the chance which he had been expecting. It was clear that the scheme of Indian work must be for the present postponed : pupils, literary work, and translation work of all kinds, were beginning to pour in upon him ; his place, for. the present, was certainly in England. He became a candidate for the vacant post ; the place in fact *belonged to him* ; it was his already by a right which it is truly wonderful could have been contested by any—the right of Conquest. The electors were the Heads of the colleges.

Consider the position : Palmer by this time was a man known all over the world of Oriental scholarship ; he was not a single, untried student and man of books ; he had proved his powers in the most practical of all ways, viz. by relying on his knowledge of the language for safety on a dangerous expedition ; he had written, and written wonderfully well, a great quantity of things in Persian, Urdú, and Arabic ; he was known to everybody who knew anything at all about the subject ; he had been greatly talked about by those who did not ; he was a graduate of the University and a Fellow of St. John's, an honour which, as was well known, he received solely for his attainments in Oriental languages ; he had a great many friends who were ready to testify, and had already testified, in the strongest terms to his extraordinary knowledge ; he was, in fact, the only Cambridge man who could,

with any show of fairness or justice at all, be elected.
He was also young, and full of strength and enthusiasm ; if Persian and Arabic lectures and Oriental
studies could be made useful or attractive at the
University, he would make them so.   What follows
seems incredible.

On the other hand, the electing body consisted, as
stated above, of the Heads of colleges.   It is in
the nature of things that the Heads, who are mostly
men advanced in years, who have spent all their lives
at the University, should retain whatever old prejudices, traditions, and ancient manner of regarding
things, may be still surviving.   There were—it seems
childish to advance this statement seriously, and yet
I have no doubt it is true and correct—two prejudices
against which Palmer had then to contend.   The first
was the more serious.   It was at that time, even more
than it is now, the custom at Cambridge to judge of
the abilities of every man entirely with regard to his
place in one of the two old Triposes ; and this
without the least respect or consideration for any
other attainments, or accomplishments, or learning.
Darwin, for instance, whose name does not occur
in the Honour List at all, never received from his
college the slightest mark of respect until his death.
Long after he had become the greatest scientific man
in Europe the question would have been asked—I
have no doubt it was often asked—what degree he
took.   Palmer's name did occur in the Classical

Tripos—but, alas! in the third class. Was it possible, was it probable, that a third-class man could be a person worthy of consideration at all? Third-class men are good enough for assistant-masters in small schools, for curacies, or for any other branch of labour which can be performed without much intellect. But a third-class man must never, under any circumstances, consider that he has a right to learn anything or to claim distinction as a scholar. I put the case strongly; but there is no Cambridge man who will deny the fact that, in whatever branch of learning distinction be subsequently attained, the memory of a second or third class is always prejudicial. Palmer, therefore, went before the grave and reverend Heads with this undeniable third class against a whole sheaf of proofs, testimonials, letters, opinions, statements and assertions of attainments extraordinary and, in some respects, unrivalled. To be sure they were only letters from Orientals and Oriental scholars. What could they avail against the opinion of the Classical Examiner of 1867 that Palmer was only worth a third class?

As I said above, it seems childish. But it is true. And this was the first prejudice.

The second prejudice was perhaps his youth; he was, it is true, past thirty, but he had only taken his degree three or four years, and therefore he only ought to have been five and twenty. He looked no more than five and twenty; he still possessed—he always

possessed—the enthusiasm of youth ; his manners
which could be, when he chose, full of dignity even
among his intimates, were those of a man still in
early manhood ; he had been talked about in connection with his adventures in the East ; and stories
were told, some true and some false, which may have
alarmed the gravity of the Heads.   There must be
no tincture of Bohemianism about a Professor of the
University.   Perhaps rumours may have been whispered about the gipsies and the tinkers, or the mesmerising, or the conjuring ; but I think the conjuring
had hardly yet begun.

In speaking of this election, I beg most emphatically to disclaim any comparison between the most
eminent and illustrious scholar who was elected and the
man who was rejected.   I say only that it is always
the bounden duty of the University to give her prizes
to her own children if they have proved themselves
worthy of them.   Not to do so is to discourage learning and to drive away students.   Now, the Professorship of Arabic was vacant ; the most brilliant
Oriental scholar whom the University has produced
in this century—perhaps in any century—became a
candidate for it ; he was the only Cambridge man
who was a candidate ; he was the only Cambridge
man who could possibly be a candidate : the Heads
of Houses passed him by and elected a scholar of
wide reputation indeed, but not a member of the
University.

There were other circumstances which made the election more disappointing. It was known, before the election, that Dr. Wright had been spoken to on the subject; it was also known that he would not stand because the stipend of the post, only 300*l.* a year, was not sufficient to induce him to give up the British Museum. It seemed, therefore, that the result of Palmer's candidature would be a walk over. But, the day before the election, the Master of Queen's, then Dr. Phillips, who was himself a Syriac scholar, went round to all the electors and informed them that Dr. Wright would be put up on the following day. He was put up; he was elected; and very shortly afterwards he was made a Fellow of Queen's, probably in consequence of an understanding with Dr. Phillips that in the event of his election to the Professorship an election to a Queen's Fellowship should follow. Of course, one has nothing to say against the Fellowship. Probably a Queen's Fellowship was never more honourably and usefully bestowed; but yet the man who ought to have obtained the Professorship, the man to whom it belonged, was kept out of it. Palmer was the kindest-hearted and most forgiving of all men, and the last to think or speak evil; but this was a deliberate and uncalled-for injustice, an insult to his reputation as a scholar which could never be forgotten. It embittered the whole of his future connection with the University; it never was forgotten or forgiven.

In the same year the Lord Almoner's Professorship of Arabic also fell in by the resignation of Mr. Theodore Preston, who had long been non-resident. It is a little thing, so far as stipend goes, worth 40*l.* a year only, with, I think, an obligation to give two lectures a year. The appointment lies, not with the Heads, fortunately, but with the Queen's Almoner, then the Rev. Gerald Wellesley, Dean of Windsor. I know not by whom Palmer was introduced or recommended to the Dean, but the result was, first, that he was appointed to the post; and, next, that the Dean conceived a great affection for him, and ever afterwards held him in the highest esteem and friendship. It was preferment, also, of a most important kind, because it allowed him to keep his fellowship whether he married or not. He lost no time; the very day after his appointment he was married. It was on November 11, 1871. The wedding would have taken place before but for an unlucky and ludicrous accident. He could not be married before the whole of the formalities connected with his appointment had been properly gone through. One of the most important of these was the reception of a seal or sealed document, for which a japanned box had to be made. The artist entrusted with that japanned box delayed the work, and, with it, the marriage.

The newly married couple took a small house at first in Cambridge. Here they lived for a short time, removing to a larger house at Newnham, where they remained until Mrs. Palmer's failing health obliged her to change Cambridge for Paris first and Bournemouth next.

And here in the first three years of married life his two daughters were born. A son born at Aberystwith in the year 1877 died in infancy.

The duties of the professorship are practically nothing at all, so that as a matter of fact Palmer was now endowed with an annuity, made up of his fellowship and his small stipend, of about 350*l.* a year, with nothing to do for it. This was something to begin upon, and work of a remunerative kind soon began to come in as he became more widely known.

At the same time, Palmer was no *fainéant* Professor ; he made of his post a means of doing real and earnest work. His first and introductory lecture was given on Monday, March 2, 1872. The subject was the National Religion of Persia, and it contained an outline sketch of Comparative Theology. In this and the following term he also lectured every day, viz., on Monday, Wednesday, and Friday in Arabic, and on the other three days in Persian, together with an additional lecture in May on an Arab poet of the thirteenth century. This was giving a tolerably fair return of work for a stipend of 40*l.* 10*s.*, the exact value of the Professorship. This stipend was, however, augmented by 250*l.* a year in the following year, as a consequence of a Report of the

Council dated February 24, 1873, concerning the newly
established Oriental Triposes.   In the discussion on
this Report, the Rev. Charles Taylor, now Master of
St. John's, took occasion to remark that Palmer's 'share
of the work for the new Triposes was a very large one,
ludicrously out of proportion to his stipend.'   The
Report was confirmed by Grace of the Senate on
March 3, 1873.   The augmentation was made retro-
spective from Michaelmas 1872, but conditions were
attached, and those pretty hard, viz., that Palmer
should reside for eighteen weeks, and that he should
give three courses of lectures—in Arabic, Persian,
and Hindustani.   It must be acknowledged that the
University got full value for their money.   These
lectures were regularly given until Palmer left
Cambridge six years later.

   The new Triposes spoken of were the result of a
report furnished by a syndicate appointed to consider the best means of promoting the study of
Oriental languages.   Palmer was a member of the
syndicate.   The report, dated March 12, 1872, recommended the establishment of a Semitic and an Indian
language Tripos.   The Senate adopted the recommendations on May 7 of the same year, and the
Triposes were established ; without, as yet, creating a
rush for those languages.

   In addition to his lectures Palmer read with any
pupils who came to him ; his teaching work in all
occupied him some three or four hours every day—a

goodly slice out of the day's work. Of literary work between the years 1871 and 1874 there does not appear to have been much, but they were years of hard and unsparing work ; he established his reputation at Cambridge, and was by this time known to all European Oriental scholars, and as well, it would appear from the following little anecdote, to some people who were not Oriental scholars.

He received one day a note, ill written and ill spelt, with the Manchester post mark, as follows : 'Dear Sir, can you read the inclosed ? Yours truly, ——.' The enclosed was a short document in Persian, presenting no difficulty. Palmer replied that it was a warrant or ticket for certain goods, setting forth, in the name of Allah, that the bale with which it came contained so many yards of stuff, of such a quality, made by such a manufacturer, and so forth, a paper of the most prosaic kind. A day or two after he sent off his translation another letter came from the same correspondent. It enclosed a ten-pound note, with the words :—

'Dear Sir, Hooray for old Cambridge ! This was what the Oxford chap said it was. Yours truly, ——.'

The 'Oxford chap' was a little wide of the mark. 'This very curious and most interesting document,' he said, 'appears to be a copy of an ancient Persian inscription, probably taken from a tomb or a triumphal column. It is, however, very incomplete. It reads as

K

follows : " In the name of God. This —— was made [or erected] by [name uncertain] in the year [un-certain]. It is one thousand four hundred and seventy-five . . . long, and seven hundred and thirty . . . broad ; and it——." Here the manuscript abruptly ends.' The name of the Oxford scholar was not given.

In the year 1873, when the Shah of Persia came to this country, Palmer was presented to him by his friend Prince Malcom Khan, and acted as one of his interpreters. He wrote in Urdu a long account of his interview, and of the Shah's visit to London, for the 'Oude Akhbar,' where it occupied thirty-five columns. At the same time and for the same paper also he wrote a long and, as I have been told, a most delightful description of the Duke of Edinburgh's marriage.

Some time in the year 1873 he entered into an engagement with Messrs. Allen and Co., of Waterloo Place, to prepare for them an Arabic grammar. This work appeared in 1874. I believe that it has become the standard grammar not only for students in Arabic here, but also in India. In the same year he wrote for the Society for the Promotion of Christian Know-ledge a ' History of the Jewish Nation.' This work adds little to the previously existing knowledge on the subject, being chiefly compiled from Ewald ; but it is careful and conscientious. I remember his talking over the book ; it was out of his line, and he was not inclined at first to do it ; but he was per-

suaded to undertake it, and devoted a very considerable amount of time to it. I do not think that he
should have consented, as neither his studies nor his
sympathies lay among the Hebrew race and its
literature.

The Arabic grammar was followed by a Persian
dictionary. This laborious work occupied him from
1874 to the year of his death. The first part, the
Persian-English, was published in 1876, and the
second part has been found, nearly completed, among
his papers after his death.

In the year 1876–77 appeared, published by the
Pitt Press, his Beha ed din Zoheir, in two volumes—
namely, the text in 1876 and the English version in
1877. Of this version we shall have to speak in
another place. Suffice it to say that it is the only
complete version of the collected works of any Arabic
poet ever published in English. In the year 1880
his ' Life of the Caliph Haroun Alraschid ' appeared
in the series of biographies called the ' New Plutarch,'
published by Messrs. Marcus Ward and Co. It seems
strange that a man so well known, the hero of the
' Arabian Nights,' should have been the subject of
so little curiosity that his life was never before written.
Probably most of us have always thought that the
Caliph was no more a real personage than the one-
eyed Calendar, or Sindbad the Sailor, or Aladdin, or
the Hunchback. This little book has restored the lost
Caliph, and clothed him with real life and individu-

ality. The history of the origin and rise of the Caliphate—a subject on which most of us may confess profound ignorance without being ashamed—may also be found there, told with great clearness. It is, in fact, a very delightful little volume, not too long for readers who have neither the time nor the inclination to make an independent study for themselves, but are willing to be instructed in the meaning of old Mohammedan institutions and the history of one renowned Mohammedan monarch. To learn that the Haroun Alraschid of story was once a real and living despot ; to learn, further, that he was a king possessed of great strength of character, with the weaknesses and impulses which belong naturally to an irresponsible autocrat, was a new thing to most people. The following is Palmer's summary of the legendary monarch's real character.

He was a man of great talents, keen intellect, and strong will. Had he been born in a humbler position, he might have done something for the good of his country and the world at large, and would certainly even then have attained to eminence.

The eloquence and impetuosity of his discourse, as shown in those speeches of his which have been preserved, were remarkable even for a time when eloquence was cultivated and regarded as the greatest accomplishment. That these speeches are genuine is proved by the fact that, though related by different persons, the style is identical in them all, and they are of so remarkable a character, that even now they linger in the memory of anyone who reads them once in the original ; and at the time they were uttered,

with the tragic circumstances that for the most part surrounded them, they must have fixed themselves indelibly
upon the hearers' minds, and could scarcely have been
repeated otherwise than faithfully.

As a man, he showed many indications of a loyal and
affectionate disposition, but the preposterous position in
which he was placed almost necessarily crushed all really
human feelings in him.   It must not be forgotten that he
inherited what was practically the empire of the civilised
world ; that he was the recognised successor and kinsman
of God's own vicegerent on earth ; that he was the head of
the Faith ; that, in a word, there was not, and could not be,
a more grand, important, or worshipful being in the world
than himself.   Nor was this merely instilled into his mind
by servile courtiers ; it was the deliberate conviction of the
whole Moslem world—that is to say, of the world at large—
for no Moslem then, and few Moslems now, would regard
an infidel as even deserving the name 'of one of God's
creatures.   That such a man should not be spoilt, that such
absolute despotism should not lead to acts of arbitrary
injustice, that such unlimited power and absence of all
feelings of responsibility could be possessed without unlimited indulgence, was not in the nature of human events.
He was spoilt, he was a bloodthirsty despot, he was a
debauchee ; but he was also an energetic ruler, he humbly
performed the duties of his religion, and he strove his utmost
to increase, or at least preserve intact, the glorious inheritance that had been handed down to him.   If, in carrying
out any of these views, a subject's life were lost or an
enemy's country devastated, he thought no more of it than
does the owner of a palace who bids his menials sweep
away a spider's web.   When he could shake off his imperial
cares, he was a genial, even an amusing companion, and all
around him liked him, although such as ventured to sport
with him did so with the sword of the executioner suspended
above their heads.

In the same year Palmer finished his new translation of the Quran for the Clarendon Press.   This
important version naturally became the subject of
criticism in all the reviews and papers.   Putting together the points in which they all agreed, against
those in which they differed, it becomes quite clear to
outsiders that, even in the eyes of those most likely
to hunt for faults—namely, contemporary Orientalists
—it is a very remarkable and valuable work.   Of the
difficulties connected with the translation Palmer thus
speaks :—

The language of the Qur'ân is universally acknowledged
to be the most perfect form of Arab speech.   The Qurâis,
as the guardians of the national temple and the owners of
the territory in which the great fairs and literary festivals of
all Arabia were held, would naturally absorb into their own
dialect many of the words and locutions of other tribes, and
we should consequently expect their language to be more
copious and elegant than that of their neighbours.   At the
same time we must not forget that the acknowledged claims
of the Qur'ân to be the direct utterance of the Divinity have
made it impossible for any Muslim to criticise the work,
and it became, on the contrary, the standard by which other
literary compositions had to be judged.   Grammarians,
lexicographers, and rhetoricians started with the presumption
that the Qur'ân could not be wrong, and other works therefore only approached excellence in proportion as they, more
or less, successfully imitated its style.   Regarding it, however,
from a perfectly impartial and unbiassed standpoint, we find
that it expresses the thoughts and ideas of a Bedawî Arab
in Bedawî language and metaphor.   The language is noble
and forcible, but it is not elegant in the sense of literary

refinement. To Mohammed's hearers it must have been startling, from the manner in which it brought great truths home to them in the language of their everyday life.

There was nothing antiquated in the style or the words, no tricks of speech, pretty conceits, or mere poetical embellishments ; the prophet spoke with rude, fierce eloquence in ordinary language. The only rhetorical ornament he allowed himself was that of making his periods more or less rhythmical, and most of his clauses rhyme—a thing that was and still is natural to an Arab orator, and the necessary outcome of the structure of the Arabic tongue.

It is often difficult to enter thoroughly into the spirit of the old Arab poets, Mohammed's contemporaries or immediate predecessors, because we cannot completely realise the feelings that actuated them or identify ourselves with the society in which they moved. For this reason they have always something remote and obsolete about them, however clear their language and meaning may be. With the Qur'ân it is not so. Mohammed speaks with a living voice ; his vivid word-painting brings at once before the mind the scene he describes or conjures up ; we can picture his very attitude when, having finished some marvellously told story of the days of yore, uttered some awful denunciation, or given some glorious promise, he pauses suddenly and says, with bitter disappointment, ' *These* are the true stories, and there is no god but God ; and *yet* ye turn aside !'

To translate this worthily is a most difficult task. To imitate the rhyme and rhythm would be to give the English an artificial ring from which the Arabic is quite free ; and the same objection lies against using the phraseology of our authorised version of the Bible : to render it by fine or stilted language would be quite as foreign to the spirit of the original : while to make it too rude or familiar would be to err equally on the other side. I have, therefore, endeavoured to take a middle course ; I have translated each sentence as literally as the difference in structure between the two languages would allow, and when possible I have rendered it word for word. Where a rugged or commonplace expression occurs in the Arabic I have not hesitated to render it by a similar English one, even where a literal rendering may perhaps shock the reader.

The following passages may be taken to illustrate the flowing English into which Palmer has rendered the Prophet's utterances :—

Righteousness is not that ye turn your faces towards the east or the west, but righteousness is one who believes in God, and the last day, and the angels, and the Book, and the prophets, and who gives wealth for His love to kindred, and orphans, and the poor, and the son of the road,[1] and beggars, and those in captivity : and who is steadfast in prayer, and gives alms ; and those who are sure of their covenant when they make a covenant ; and the patient in poverty, and distress, and in time of violence ; these are they who are true, and these are those who fear.

Has not the story come to you of those who were before you, of the people of Noah, and 'Ad, and Thamûd, and those who came after them? None knows them save God. Apostles came unto them with manifest signs ; but they thrust their hands into their mouths [2] and said, 'Verily, we disbelieve in that which ye are sent with, and we are in hesitating doubt concerning that to which ye call us !' Their apostles said, ' Is there doubt about God, the Originator of the heavens and the earth ? He calls you to pardon you for your sins, and to respite you until an appointed time.'

They said, ' Ye are but mortals like ourselves ; ye wish

[1] *I.e.* the wayfarer.
[2] Easterns, when annoyed, always bite their hands.

to turn us from what our fathers used to serve. Bring us, then, obvious authority !'

Their apostles said unto them, 'We are only mortals like yourselves ; but God is gracious unto whomsoever He will of His servants, and it is not for us to bring you an authority, save by His permission ; but upon God do the believers rely !' What ails us that we should not rely on God when He has guided us in our paths? we will be surely patient in your hurting us ; for upon God rely those who do rely.

And those who misbelieved said to their apostles, 'We will drive you forth from our land ; or else ye shall return to our faith !' And their Lord inspired them, 'We will surely destroy the unjust ; and We will make you to dwell in the land after them. That is for him who fears My place and fears My threat?'

In the year 1878, owing to the appointment of Lieutenant-Colonel Sir Charles Wilson to the consulate of Anatolia, it became necessary to appoint a new editor for the great work called the 'Survey of Western Palestine.' The committee of the Exploration Society entrusted the work to Palmer and myself as joint editors. I have already spoken something as to Palmer's work on this publication.

A very important part of the work, and a particularly heavy and tedious part, consisted in the transliteration and translation of the name lists collected during the survey by the party, and written down and arranged under Captain Conder's superintendence. There are about 10,000 of these names. Palmer undertook this immense labour, and carried it through

with astonishing rapidity. The first volume of the
memoirs also received from him a large quantity of
valuable notes and additions, while, owing to the
absence in Eastern Palestine of Captain Conder, and
in Cyprus of Lieutenant Kitchener, the compilers of
the memoirs, there were countless occasions during
the printing of the first volume on which Palmer had
to be consulted in matters connected with the right
spelling of a name or the verification of a reference.
He also revised his Report on the Journey through
the Desert for the volume of Special Papers, and was
ready, just before he was called away, to join in the
preparation of the Jerusalem volume. In this labour,
as in all others in which he was engaged, he showed
the most indefatigable power of work and rapidity of
execution. He was never tired, never out of spirits,
and always the most patient, most cheery, and most
sympathetic of workmen. We were looking forward
with anticipation to getting done with the memoirs
and taking up the Jerusalem volume, in which we
might together re-open a chapter closed for ten years.
Now, alas ! that volume will have to appear without
his help, and without the accounts which he had
proposed to collect and to translate from the earliest
Arab writers on the topography of the Holy City
and the buildings on the Temple area.

I have already mentioned Palmer's singular im-
patience for grammar, and his desire to learn and to

teach languages with as little regard to the rules of grammarians as possible. During the lectures at Cambridge he devised a plan for simplifying the necessary portions of grammar. Partly to save himself trouble he put together his notes of this method, and constructed a short grammar on a new and very simple basis. He then found that the method he had adopted for Arabic would also prove equally useful for Persian, Hindustani, and, *mutatis mutandis,* for all other languages. He therefore laid his plan before Mr. Trübner. The result has been the publication of a remarkable series of grammars on this system, of which Palmer was the first editor.

The following extract from the prospectus sufficiently explains the arrangement and idea of these grammars, and at the same time shows, more clearly than could be conveyed by any language of mine, his own views on the treatment of grammars :—

The object of this series of grammars is to provide the learner with a concise but practical introduction to the various languages, and at the same time to furnish students of comparative philology with a clear and comprehensive view of their structure. The attempt to adapt the somewhat cumbrous grammatical system of the Greek and Latin to every other tongue has introduced a great deal of unnecessary difficulty into the study of languages. Instead of analysing existing locutions and endeavouring to discover the principles which regulate them, writers of grammars have for the most part constructed a framework of rules on the old lines and tried to make the language of which they were treating fit into it. Where this proves impossible the difficulty is met by lists of exceptions and irregular forms, thus burdening the pupil's mind with a mass of details of which he can make no practical use.

In these grammars the subject is viewed from a different standpoint : the structure of each language is carefully examined, and the principles which underlie it are carefully explained, while apparent discrepancies and so-called irregularities are shown to be only natural euphonic and other changes. All technical terms are excluded unless their meaning and application is self-evident ; no arbitrary rules are admitted ; the old classification into declensions, conjugations, &c., and even the usual paradigms and tables, are omitted. Thus reduced to the simplest principles, the accidence and syntax can be thoroughly comprehended by the student on one perusal, and a few hours' diligent study will enable him to analyse any sentence in the language.

The last great piece of work—in the opinion of many, his greatest and most important work—was his revision, in company with Dr. Bruce, of Henry Martyn's Persian translation of the New Testament. It was executed for the British and Foreign Bible Society, and occupied him for six or eight months, during which he received his collaborateur nearly every day at eleven o'clock and worked with him for three hours. The labour was very great, and it came at a time when his health was already suffering from other kinds of work, but the invitation of the Society pleased him, and the honorarium was at the time particularly useful, and he thought he could manage it. As soon as he had resolved on undertaking it, he faced the work with that courage with which he faced every fresh piece of work, big or little. Not only is the translation of the New Testament into Persian a great and laborious piece of work, but it is a work which brings with it the very highest kind of responsibility. One used to hear from time to time whispers, so to speak, of those long hours spent in considering how to unravel the thought of Paul and how best to convey it in Persian, and how on such occasions Palmer would, after arriving at an opinion, defend it with floods of quotations from Persian poets, showing his extraordinary knowledge of Persian literature. I know that Dr. Bruce, the work at last happily accomplished, left his fellow-worker with the very highest respect for his powers and acquirements.   That, however, *va sans dire.*

Before he started for the East he issued a proposal for a translation of Hafiz, but hardly any of it was accomplished.

I think that I have enumerated most of the learned productions which, in the years of his actual working life, came from his pen. Among scholars his Quran, his text and translation of Beha ed din, his Arabic Grammar, and his Persian Dictionary will keep his memory green. Among the outside world he will be principally remembered by his Quran, his 'Haroun Alraschid,' and his 'Desert of the Exodus.'

There are also, besides his books, a great number of valuable papers contributed by him to various journals and reviews. One of the most remarkable of these is the article already mentioned, published in the 'British Quarterly,' in the year 1873, on the 'Secret Sects of Syria.' For the 'Encyclopædia Britannica' he wrote the papers on Hafiz and 'Legerdemain.' I find from his correspondence that he was also engaged to write the articles on Mesnavi, Mecca, Medina, Omar el Kheizan, and Nizami, but I do not think he finished these. He published a translation of Moore's 'Lalla Rookh' in the 'Bírvis Baris' in the year 1865 ; he contributed a quantity of compositions in Urdú and Persian to various papers in India. And there are also many papers of his which appeared in the 'Times' and have more than ephemeral value.

In this chapter on work I am well aware that I have not been able to assign to Palmer his proper place as an Oriental scholar. General assertions of vast attainments and proficiency cannot do this. For such a purpose one must oneself be an Orientalist of the first rank. I have therefore to thank Mr. Stanley Lane Poole and Professor Nicholl of Oxford for papers in which this deficiency is supplied. Professor Nicholl's longer paper will be found at the end of the book.

Mr. Stanley Lane-Poole writes as follows :—

Palmer was a scholar of the kind that is born, not made. No amount of mere teaching could develop that wonderful

instinct for language which he possessed. He stood in
strongly marked contrast to the other scholars of his time.
Most of them were brought up upon grammars and dictionaries ; he learned Arabic by the ear and mouth.   Others
were careful about their conjugations and syntax ; Palmer
dashed to the root of all grammatical rules, and spoke or
wrote so and so because it would not be spoken or written
any other way.   To him strange idioms that a book student
could not understand were perfectly clear ; he had used
them himself in the desert again and again.   He was a
linguist rather than a philologist, and he had the merits and
faults of a linguist.   It is the German-trained philological
school of Arabists that does most of the sober scholarly
work—edits texts, collates manuscripts, writes critical commentaries, and performs the dull but necessary labours
which must precede the wide generalisations of genius.
Palmer was not of this sort : he was not given to careful
collation and revision, but sent his work out just as it
occurred to him ; he corrected his proof sheets hurriedly,
and let many a trifling error escape his eye ; he could tell
you what the right phrase was, but he could not tell you
why it was so.   Others would refer to De Sacy's ' Grammaire
arabe,' vol. i. page so and so ; Palmer did not in the least
know what rule he went by ; the phrase was such and such,
and could be none other, and that was all he cared for.
His instinctive appreciation of the niceties of Arabic did for
him what minute grammatical study effected less thoroughly
for others ; and very often his natural genius would explain
difficulties for which the grammars had provided no rule.

His work in Arabic scholarship consisted of the new
translation of the Korân for the ' Sacred Books of the East,'
his complete edition of the poetry of Behâ ed dín Zoheir of
Egypt, with an English verse translation, and an Arabic
grammar, Arabic manual, and simplified Arabic grammar,
the last three being practically one and the same book in

different forms and reduced sizes. His Life of Harûn Er-
Rashîd for The New Plutarch series, though a singularly
charming little book, hardly comes under the designation of
pure scholarship ; and his ' Song of the Reed ' is composed
of translations from the Persian and original pieces, with
but one rendering of an Arabic poem.

The most finished of his scholarly works is certainly the
edition of Zoheir. In the first place it has the merit of
entire originality : not only was there no previous translation
of this particular poet, but no Arabic poet at all had ever
been presented in his entirety in an English dress. Palmer
was the first to translate the whole of an Arab poet's
works. Of course the poet he selected is not a Dante or
a Homer. He is not even a typical Arab poet, like the
warrior singers who used to compete for prizes at the fair of
Okâdh and sang of the wild Bedawy life and the roaming
of the desert. Zoheir lived in other times than the old
poets. The Arabs were no longer merely Arabian. They
had met and conquered and mixed with many races,
and had learnt new ways and a culture not their own.
Zoheir lived in the thirteenth century, just when the great
Saladin had left an empire for his kinsmen to fight over.
One of these, Es-Sâlih, a great nephew of Saladin, was
Zoheir's patron, and it was at the court of this prince at
Cairo that most of his poetry was written. The verse is
the echo of the writer's surroundings. It is not great poetry ;
there is nothing sublime or rugged about it ; but it is often
tender and always graceful, and as good a specimen of
Eastern *vers de société* as one is likely to find. Zoheir
takes life, as a rule, in a comfortable way, except when he
has quarrelled with a mistress or offended a patron ; and he
spends his time in writing dedications and panegyrics to
princes and love-songs to innumerable fair friends ; or if
there is no prince or maiden to write to he elaborates an
elegant conceit to some friend who has called or has not

called, or has gone a journey, or who by any means has
offered a pretext for being assailed in verse. His love
songs are especially delicate and refined, and his humorous
pieces full of rollicking fun.   Into all this Palmer entered
thoroughly.   His translation represents the original with
remarkable skill ; he does not indeed attempt to preserve
the metre and local colour of the Arabic, but he chooses a
corresponding motion and equivalent ideas from among our
ordinary English poetic repertory.   Not seldom his poetry,
as English verse, is exceedingly good ; the love-song on
p. 23, beginning—

> I waited at the tryst alone . . .

contains some exquisite lines ; nothing could be more
graceful than the thought and the expression of—

> Oh, let me look upon thine eyes again,
> For they have looked upon the maid I love ;

and the picture of 'An Egyptian Garden' (p. 9) and the
drinking song on p. 280 are in their different ways admirable.

Zoheir is Palmer's best piece of work, but his version of
the Korân is a very striking performance.   It has the grave
fault of immaturity ; it was written, or rather dictated, at
great speed, and is consequently defaced by some over-
sights which Palmer was incapable of committing if he had
taken more time over the work.   Personally, too, I differ
toto cœlo from Palmer's theory of translation as regards
the Korân : I think he went at it the wrong way.   But,
in spite of all the objections that may be urged against
it, his translation has the true desert ring in it ; we may
quarrel with certain renderings, puzzle over occasional
obscurities, regret certain signs of haste or carelessness ;
but we shall be forced to admit that the translator has
carried us among the Bedawy tents, and breathed into us the

L

strong air of the desert, till we fancy we can hear the rich voice of the Blessed Prophet himself as he spoke to the pilgrims on Akabah.

Palmer's grammatical works, like everything he did, take up new ground and are unlike anything else. I have said he was no grammarian, that he went by no rules ; and it is true for his own scholarship. But he could explain and illustrate the difficulties of Arabic grammar in a way that was luminous and simple and perfectly obvious, but which had not struck anybody before. In the science of Arabic grammar, as treated by European writers, there are two distinct schools. The one, headed by the justly renowned Silvestre de Sacy, endeavours to deal with the facts of the Arabic language by the European method—in fact, to treat Arabic much as one does Latin. The opposite school maintains that Arabic is in its essence so widely different from the Aryan languages that any attempt to deal with it by Aryan methods must entail a waste of time, if it does not actually increase the difficulties which the language must present to a beginner. The founder of this school was Lumsden, whose great but clumsy work, published at Calcutta in 1813, was left unfinished. Palmer was the first, after more than half a century had passed, to follow in his steps and, boldly neglecting the Japhetic methods which had prevailed in the interval, to throw in his lot with the native grammarians. His grammar is arranged mainly upon the Arab system ; and as a result it is the best for a student who wishes to learn Arabic as a language to be spoken and not as a philological problem to be investigated. But Palmer did not merely translate native grammar ; he added here and there a clear illustration or a broad generalisation which give one sudden glimpses into the true genius of the language.

As regards the lighter work there was never, surely, any man of learning who delighted more in poetry as a recreation. I shall have in the following chapter to consider the Professor as a writer of verse : it is sufficient to note here, as part of the chapter on his works, that he wrote verse continuously, but chiefly in translation and in imitation, and almost daily ; he wrote with great facility, and I think that, had he lived and applied seriously, he would have produced original verse of great power and value. As it is he will always be unrivalled by any who desire to understand the characteristics of Arab and Persian poetry, while his Romany songs, translations from the Swedish, Welsh, and other sources, will take their chance with the great mass of published verse, out of which here and there something emerges which posterity will not willingly suffer to be forgotten.

CHAPTER VI.

VERSES AND TRANSLATIONS.

PALMER was always, then, writing verse ; when there was nothing which pressed, he either sat down and painted or he wrote verses ; he rhymed with great facility ; in his youth he imitated the Ingoldsby Legends ; later on he amused himself with writing burlesques ; throughout the whole of his life he was turning rhymes and making couplets. In some forms of verse, as I shall presently show, he attained an excellence which has seldom been surpassed, but we may search in vain among his poems for any attempt at a lofty flight. Rarely, indeed, does he touch the chords of deeper feeling save when he is translating. The reason of this is that he did not regard himself as a poet, but looked on the making of verses as one form of delight open to cultivated humanity. His published verses consist of the 'Gipsy Songs,' written with Mr. Charles Leland and Miss Janet Tuckey ; the translation of the Swedish poet Runeberg, written with Mr. Eirikr Magnússon ; the ' Song of the Reed,'

which contains, among other things, translations
from the Persian and Arabic ; a collection of verses
published in 'Temple Bar ' on 'Arab Humour ;' and the
translation already mentioned of Beha ed din Zoheir.
To these may be added certain translations from the
Welsh and sundry unpublished verses.

The volume of ' Gipsy Songs ' is very curious and
interesting.   It consists of songs written in Romany
and English, but whether the English was written
first or the Romany no one can tell. The authors are,
besides Palmer, Miss Janet Tuckey and Mr. Charles
Leland, and each contribution is signed.   A glossary
and a few hints on pronunciation are given at the end
of the volume.   One need not quote from the book,
because the Romany would not probably be understood, and the English versions without the Romany,
have no special value.

I do not know what sort of reception was accorded
to the translation of Runeberg, the great poet of Finland, which he made with Eirikr Magnússon, but I
fear the public at large are not greatly interested in
the Finnish bard.   Had Palmer been a man of craft
and subtlety, he would have prepared the public mind
for his volume by an essay here and a biography there,
a few tentative verses in one magazine and a learned
treatise on the literature of Finland in another. Then,
and not till then, public curiosity being thoroughly
awakened, he should have brought out his volume of
translations.   As it is, no one in this country knows

anything at all about Scandinavian literature ; worse than that, no one cares to know ; the English mind is not curious. Sweden, Norway, Denmark, lie close to our own doors, so to speak ; yet, save one or two, here and there, no one cares about the magnificent past and the admirable present of their literature. More surprising still, there is Holland ; it is but eight hours from our shores ; it possesses a grand history and a splendid literature, yet English students of Dutch can be numbered almost on our fingers. It is not that we are a lazy folk, but that we run in grooves ; we do not cast about for new and original work.

Palmer and his collaborateur neglected these simple precautions, and put forth their thin volume as if it were of no more importance than a new novel by an unknown writer. Therefore, I fear that the attempt to make known a Scandinavian poet fell comparatively flat. Yet the book [1] is really full of the most beautiful, the most simple, the most natural poems, things which touch the universal heart, glowing with love for nature and sympathy with humanity. I am sure it deserves to be known, and I hope that everybody who reads this memoir will make haste to get a copy. There are love-ditties among the poems, the simple aspirations of country life, old age, death, regrets, sadness, hopes—all the old, old things with which the natural poet plays upon our hearts. Sings the lover to his

[1] Johann Ludvig Runeberg's *Lyrical Songs*, &c. Kegan Paul and Co.

sweetheart, repeating his words as if he loved them
too, because they spoke of the girl—

> If I saw thee, if I saw thee nearing,
>   Steering round the foreland's birches there,
> Saw the sail first, then descried the veering
>   Purple bunting thou for flag dost wear !
> Why put off our bliss ? the year will bring in
>   Gold and goods ; thou mayst be sure of it.
> Love is like the floweret, and in spring, in
>   Spring alone it finds a season fit.

Sings the poet to the Birds of Passage—

> Ye, fugitive guests on a far foreign stand,
> When seek ye again your own dear fatherland ?
>   When flowers coyly peep out
>   In father-dale growing,
>   And rivulets leap out
>   Past alder-trees blowing,
>   On lifted wings hither
>   The tiny ones hie,
>   None shows the way whither
>   Through wildering sky ;
>   Yet surely they fly.

They find it so safely, the long sighed-for North,
Where spring both their food and their shelter holds forth;
        The fountain's breast swelleth,
            Refreshing the weary,
        The waving branch telleth
            Of pleasures so cheery ;
        And there the heart dreameth
        . 'Neath midnight-sun's ray,
        And love scarcely deemeth,
            Mid song and mid play,
            How long was the way.

The fortunate blithe ones, they build amid rest,
'Mong moss-covered pine trees their peaceable nest ;
   Though tempest and fray, too,
    And trouble may lower,
   They find not the way to
    The warderless tower.
Joy needs to be full there,
   But May-day's bright brand,
And Night that shall lull there
   With rose-tinted hand
   The tiny wee band.

Thou, fugitive soul on a far foreign strand,
When seek'st thou again thine own dear fatherland ?
   When each palm-tree beareth,
    In father-world growing,
   Thy calm faith prepareth
    In joy to be going
On lifted wings thither,
   As little birds hie,
None shows the way whither
   Through wildering sky ;
   Yet sure dost thou fly.

Or the dying man sings—the love of spring and sun-shine, and the return of the flowers, warmer in his heart than ever, though he will see the spring but once more—

   The weary night will very soon be passed :
   Is not the heaven bright and clear at last ?
   Does not the marsh snow brighter still appear ?
   Is it the blackcock's cry that now I hear ?

When, very soon, the morning sun shall glow,
And on the roof begins to melt the snow,
And when drop after drop I shall descry
Fall past the open window by-and-by.

And when the cricket grows still and I hear
The merry sparrow outside twittering near,
Then, let me pray you, make me a fresh bed,
A wisp of straw upon the hall steps spread ;

For I would there be led, would rest me there,
To see how glad is nature and how fair,
And joyous cast o'er land and sea my eye,
And then in springtime, where I lived would die.

Here is a sweet and simple poem called 'The Flower'—

When the spring once more is showing
   Sweet and clear,
Day is laughing, sunlight glowing—
   Wak'st thou here ;
On thy soft stem givest birth to
   Bud and sprout,
Like an angel seek'st from earth to
   Struggle out.

With thy scent the breeze that blows then
   Onward cleaves,
Gold-winged butterflies repose then
   On thy leaves.
With thy cheek dares no uncleanness
   Kissing play,—
Dew, wind, butterflies, sereneness—
   Only they.

Since, like plants when summer cometh
    Mild and fair,
All that's sweet is born and bloometh
    Without care,
Why should grief and danger go here
    Hand in hand ?—
Why is not our earth below here
    Peace's land ?

Lastly, I wish to quote ' The Old Man's Return,' which seems to me a most exquisite poem. What is there which touches the heart so readily as the old and simple things, common to all—love and life, old age and regret, disappointment and resignation, faith and hope ? Palmer himself seems to speak in these lines :

Like birds of passage, after winter's days returning
    To lake-land home and rest,
I come now unto thee, my foster-valley, yearning
    For long-lost childhood's rest.

Full many a sea since then from thy dear strands has torn
    me,
    And many a chilly year ;
Full many a joy since then those far-off lands have borne
    me,
    And many a bitter tear.

Here am I back once more.—Great Heaven! there stands
    the dwelling
    Which erst my cradle bore,
The selfsame sound, bay, grove and hilly range upswelling :
    My world in days of yore.

All as before.—Trees in the selfsame verdant dresses
  With the same crowns are crowned ;
The tracts of heaven, and all the woodland's far recesses,
  With well-known songs resound.

There with the crowd of flower-nymphs still the wave is
    playing,
  As erst, so light and sweet ;
And from dim wooded aits I hear the echoes straying
  Glad youthful tones repeat.

All as before.—But my own self no more remaineth,
  Glad valley ! as of old ;
My passion quenched long since, no flame my cheek
    retaineth,
  My pulse now beateth cold.

I know not how to prize the charms that thou possessest,
  Thy lavish gifts of yore ;
What thou through whispering brooks, or through thy
    flowers expressest,
  I understand no more.

Dead is mine ear to harp-strings which thy gods are ringing
  From out thy streamlet clear,
No more the elfin hosts all frolicsome and singing
  Upon the meads appear.

I went so rich, so rich from thee, my cottage lowly,
  So full of hopes untold,
And with me feelings, nourished in thy shadows holy,
  That promised days of gold.

The memory of thy wondrous spring-times went beside me,
  And of thy peaceful ways,
And thy good spirits, borne within me, seemed to guide me,
  E'en from my earliest days.

And what have I brought back from yon world wide and
    dreary ?
A snow-encumbered head,
A heart with sorrow sickened, and with falsehood weary,
    And longing to be dead.

I crave no more of all that once was in my keeping,
    Dear mother ! but one thing :
Grant me a grave, where still thy fountain fair is weeping,
    And where thy poplars spring !

So shall I dream on, mother ! to thy calm breast owing
    A faithful shelter then,
And live in every floweret, from mine ashes growing,
    A guiltless life again.

In the ' Song of the Reed ' [1] Palmer published a
small collection of translations taken from Persian
and Arabic, together with some of his early attempts,
including the ' Hole in the Wall.' We have already
spoken sufficiently of these. The Ingoldsby style
of verse has now to be very well done indeed before
it is able to please. And, besides, there has been too
much of it. The ' Song of the Reed ' itself is taken
from the ' Masnavi,' a poem in six books, in which is
expounded the whole system of Persian mystic theology. The professors of these tenets are called Sufis,
and their system constitutes the esoteric doctrine of
Islam.

It is a strange combination of the pantheism of the
Aryan races and of the severe monotheism of their Semitic

---

[1] Trübner and Co., 187 ~

conquerors, and aims at leading men to the contemplation
of spiritual things by appealing to their emotions.   The key-
note of the system is that the human soul is an emanation
from God, and that it is always seeking and yearning to re-
join the source from whence it sprung.   Ecstasy is the
means by which a nearer intercourse is obtained, total
absorption in the divinity the ultimate object to be attained.

Of this strange and curious poem I extract a
portion.

> List to the reed, that now with gentle strains
> Of separation from its home complains.

> Down where the waving rushes grow
>   I murmured with the passing blast,
> And ever in my notes of woe
>   There live the echoes of the past.

> My breast is pierced with sorrow's dart,
>   That I my piercing wail may raise ;
> Ah me ! the lone and widowed heart
>   Must ever weep for bygone days.

> My voice is heard in every throng
>   Where mourners weep and guests rejoice,
> And men interpret still my song
>   In concert with their passions' voice.

> Though plainly cometh forth my wail,
>   'Tis never bared to mortal ken ;
> As soul from body hath no veil,
>   Yet is the soul unseen of men.

> Not simple airs my lips expire,
>   But blasts that carry death or life,
> That blow with love's tempestuous fire,
>   That rage with love's tempestuous strife.

I soothe the absent lover's pain,
  The jealous suitor's breast I move ;
At once the antidote and bane,
  I favour and I conquer love.

So sings the reed, but its mysterious song
No ear attuned to harmony devours ;
Music that doth not to the age belong
Dies out symphonious with the dying hours.
Tastes are proportioned to the natural powers ;—
None but the fishes revel in the stream,
And none take pleasure in these words of ours
Whose hearts are strangers to the heavenly beam.
Peace ! it were better we should seek another theme.

     .   .   .   .   .

How shall I hope to make my meaning plain,
Who sing thus faintly as the rushes moan ?
Ah me ! the sweetest singer sings in vain,
Unless the language of his song be known.
The garden's beauty has for ever flown,
No perfumed odours float upon the air,
But the sad nightingale, who sits alone
Upon the rose-tree, singeth still how fair
The tender blossoms and the sweet young flow'rets were.

Nature's great secret let me now rehearse—
Long have I pondered o'er the wondrous tale,
How Love immortal fills the universe,
Tarrying till mortals shall His presence hail ;
But man, alas ! hath interposed a veil,
And Love behind the lover's self doth hide.
Shall Love's great kindness prove of none avail ?
When will ye cast the veil of sense aside,
Content in finding Love to lose all else beside ?

Love's radiance shineth round about our heads
As sportive sunbeams on the waters play ;
Alas ! we revel in the light He sheds
Without reflecting back a single ray.
The human soul, as reverend preachers say,
Is as a mirror to reflect God's grace ;
Keep, then, its surface bright while yet ye may,
For on a mirror with a dusty face
The brightest object showeth not the faintest trace.

The following is called Meditations—

O cup-bearer ! fill up the goblet, and hand it around to us all ;
For to love that seemed easy at first, these unforeseen troubles befall.
In the hope that the breeze of the south will blow yon dark tresses apart,
And diffuse their sweet perfume around, oh ! what anguish is caused to the heart.

Ay ! sully your prayer-mat with wine, if the elder encourage such sin ;
For the traveller surely should know all the manners and ways of the inn.
What rest or what comfort for me can there be in the loved one's abode,
When the bell is incessantly tolling to bid us each pack up his load ?

The darkness of night and the fear of the waves and the waters that roar ;—
How should they be aware of our state who are roaming in safety ashore ?

I yielded me up to delight, and it brought me ill fame at the
    last :
Shall a secret be hidden which into a general topic has passed ?

Would'st thou dwell in His presence? then never thyself
    unto absence betake ;
Till thou meetest the one whom thou lovest, the world and
    its pleasures forsake.

One of the last things projected by Palmer was a
complete metrical translation of Hafiz, the great
lyric poet of Persia. It was intended to appear in
Trübner's Oriental Series, and a prospectus was
issued, but the work was not far advanced when the
end came. The following is one of the specimens
printed with the prospectus :—

    'Twas morning, and I took my way
    Among the gardens' scented bowers,
    Where bulbuls trilled their love-lorn lay
    To serenade the maiden flowers.

    Like him oppressed by love's sweet pain,
    I wander in that garden fair ;
    And there, to cool my throbbing brain,
    I woo the perfumed morning air.

    The damask rose in beauty gleams,
    Its face all bathed in ruddy light,
    And glows like some bright star that beams
    From out the sombre veil of night.

    The very bulbul, as the glow
    Of youth and passion filled his breast,
    Forgot in song his former woe,
    With pride that conquers love's unrest.

The lily seemed to menace me,
And showed its curved and quivering blade ;
And every frail anemone
A gossip's open mouth displayed ;

And here and there a little group
Of flowers, like men who worship wine,
Each holding up its tiny stoup
To catch the dewdrop's draught divine ;

And others still like Hebes stand,
Their dripping vases downward turned,
As though dispensing to the band
The wine for which their hearts had yearned.

This moral it is mine to sing,
' Go learn a lesson from the flowers—
Love's season is in Youth's fair spring ;
Then seize like them the fleeting hours.'

And the following is also from Hafiz :—

O minstrel ! sing thy lay divine,
    Freshly fresh and newly new !
Bring me the heart-expanding wine,
    Freshly fresh and newly new !

Seated beside a maiden fair,
    I gaze with a loving and raptured view,
And I sip her lip and caress her hair,
    Freshly fresh and newly new !

Who of the fruit of life can share,
    Yet scorn to drink of the grape's sweet dew ?
Then drain a cup to thy mistress fair,
    Freshly fresh and newly new !

M

She who has stolen my heart away
  Heightens her beauty's rosy hue,
Decketh herself in rich array,
  Freshly fresh and newly new !

Balmy breath of the western gale,
  Waft to her ears my love-song true ;
Tell her poor love-lorn Háfiz' tale,
  Freshly fresh and newly new !

One ought not to pass over the translation of Behá-ed-din Zoheir, of Egypt; of which I have given Mr. Stanley Lane Poole's criticism. The book is a most curious and interesting collection of pious verses, amatory verses, panegyrics, complimentary verses, epigrams, riddles, regrets. Of a poet so little known to English readers it is fair to let his translator speak. The following is extracted from Palmer's Introduction :—

The works of El Behá Zoheir were composed at a time when the intercourse between Eastern and Western nations had become greater than at any previous period of modern history, and are especially interesting, as exhibiting the language and thought of the Desert, applied to altered circumstances, and modified by more civilizing influences.

In poetry Alexandria seems to have been, what it certainly was in philosophy and theology, the meeting-place of East and West. The inhabitants of the East and West differ so widely in tastes and habits, that we should hardly expect to find a community of ideas existing between an Arabic and an European writer ; and yet the works of Eastern authors are filled with proverbs, sentiments, and metaphors which we are accustomed to regard as peculiarly

Western in origin and character. To cite a few examples :—
The introduction to the Sháhnáma, the great national Epic
of Persia, enunciates, in so many words, the axiom that
' Knowledge is power ;' the proverb ' L'homme propose et
Dieu dispose,' exists in Arabic, with even the same alliterative jingle, *el 'abdu yudabbir wa 'lláhu yukaddir.* The
poems of El Behá Zoheir contain numerous instances of
these curious parallels ; in one case, addressing his mistress
he says :—

> But oh ! beware lest we betray
> The secrets of our hopes and fears,
> For I have heard some people say
> That ' walls have ears '—

which is absolutely identical with the English proverb.

But it is not only in such details that the works of El
Behá Zoheir remind us of the productions of the Western
poets ; the whole tone of thought and style of expression
much more closely resemble those of an English courtier
of the seventeenth century than of a Mohammedan of the
Middle Ages.   There is an entire absence of that artificial
construction, exaggerated metaphor, and profuse ornateness of style, which render Eastern poetry so distasteful to
a Western critic ; and in place of these defects we have
natural simplicity and epigrammatic terseness, combined
with a genial wit, that remind us forcibly of the *Vers de
Société* of the English poet Herrick.

In that peculiar trifling of words and sentiments, of
which the English poets of the Restoration were so fond,
El Behá Zoheir is excessively happy.   Take, for instance,
the following :

> My heart will flutter when she's near—
> Pray does it very strange appear
> To *dance* when we rejoice ?

Even to the hackneyed hyperbole of dying for love he
contrives to give a new and original turn :

> Oh ! torture not my life in vain,
> But take it once for all away,
> Nor cause me thus with constant pain
> To die and come to life again
> A thousand times a day !

Or this :

> Thou art my soul, and all my soul is thine,
> Thou art my life, though stealing life away !
> I die of love, then let thy breath divine
> Call me to life again, that so I may
>
> Reveal to men the secrets of the tomb.
> Full well thou knowest that no joys endure ;
> Come, therefore, ere there come on us our doom,
> That union may our present joy secure—

where he has worked out the last idea more seriously, changing what was a mere prettiness into a really poetic sentiment.

Approaching old age, and the first appearance of grey hairs, furnish him with many pleasing and novel conceits—

> Now the night of youth is over, and grey-headed dawn is near
> Fare ye well ye tender meetings with the friends I held so dear :
> O'er my life these silvery locks are shedding an unwonted light,
> And disclosing many follies youth had hidden out of sight.

It is seldom that we see a metaphor so well carried out, or so pregnant with meaning as this ;—the contrast between the dark tresses of youth and the white hairs of old age, the sudden awakening from the night of folly and inexperience at the dawn of maturer judgment, and the comparison of the streaks of grey amidst the massy black locks to rays of wisdom lighting up the dark sky of ignorance.

For a delicate turn of expression I may quote his apostrophe to a messenger who had brought him news of his beloved :

> Oh ! let me look upon thine eyes again,
> For they have looked upon the maid I love !

When polygamy prevails, and women are kept in degrading ignorance, we cannot expect to find much sentiment and affection.   The Eastern poets, it is true, are often eloquent on the theme of love, but love with them is either mere sensual admiration or affected passion.   The poet either expends his ingenuity in depicting his mistress's charms, and in heightening the colouring by the employment of striking imagery, or he raves about the burning passion that consumes his bosom.   Power and imagination there nearly always is in an Eastern love-song, but feeling and true sentiment are for the most part entirely absent from such compositions.   It is precisely in this respect that El Behá Zoheir differs so widely from his co-religionists ; his utterances of love come direct from the heart, and are altogether free from conventional affectation.   What can be more full of genuine feeling than the tender apology for a blind girl with whom he was in love, beginning

> They called my love a poor blind maid—
> I love her more for that, I said.
> I love her, for she cannot see
> These grey hairs that disfigure me ?

But, if an ardent lover, El Behá Zoheir seems to have been an inconstant one, even by his own showing :

> I'm fickle, so at least they say,
>   And blame me for it most severely;
> Because I court one maid to-day,
>   To-morrow love another dearly.

And for this fickleness he accounts by a quaint conceit :

> 'Tis true that though I vow and swear,
>   They find my love is false and hollow,
> Deceiving when it seems most fair,
>   Like lightning when no rain-drops follow.
> You'd like to know, I much suspect,
>   The secret which my conduct covers :
> Well, then, I'm founder of a sect,
>   Grand Master of Peculiar Lovers.

Solomon and his miraculous power over the spirits of earth and air are favourite subjects with El Behá Zoheir, as with most Arabic poets. Thus, apostrophizing the Zephyr, and beseeching it to carry a message to his beloved, he says :

> And now I bid the very wind
>   To speed my loving message on,
> As though I might its fury bind,
>   Like Solomon.

These constant allusions to the history and traditions of the Arabs, make the Diván of El Behá Zoheir particularly valuable as a repository of Oriental learning.

When we remember the servile adulation which Eastern despots are accustomed to exact from those about them, and the unworthy behaviour to which their favourites are too often compelled to descend, it speaks volumes for El Behá Zoheir's high character and principles, that he was able to retain his position at court for so many years without the least sacrifice of his self-respect. But that such was the case his own poems show : a free and independent spirit breathes through them all ; and the rebukes which he occasionally administers to persons high in office, from whom he has received a real or fancied slight, are as frank and outspoken as they are free from ill temper and querulousness. Take, for example, the following remonstrance addressed to the Vizier Fakhr ed din, from whose door he had been rudely repulsed by the domestics :

> My wrath is kindled for the sake
>   Of Courtesy, whose lord thou art ;
>   For thee I take it so to heart,
> No umbrage for myself I take.

> But be thy treatment what it will,
>   I cannot this affront forget :
>   I am not used to insult yet,
> And blush at its remembrance still.

Although Eastern poetry abounds in glowing imagery, and in metaphors drawn from natural objects, such as trees and flowers, rocks and streams, yet it must be confessed that a real appreciation of natural beauty is rarely exhibited either by Arabic or Persian authors. Behá ed dín Zoheir, on the contrary, seems to have been a passionate lover of Nature, and to have derived the keenest enjoyment from the contemplation of her beauties. Witness his description of a garden upon the banks of his own majestic Nile :

> I took my pleasure in a garden bright
>   Ah that our happiest hours so quickly pass !
> That time should be so·rapid in its flight.
> Therein my soul accomplished its delight,
>   And life was fresher than the green young grass.
>
> There rain-drops trickle through the warm still air,
>   The cloud-born firstlings of the summer skies ;
> Full oft I stroll in early morning there
> When, like a pearl upon a bosom fair,
>   The glistening dewdrop on the sapling lies.
>
> There the young flowerets with sweet perfume blow,
>   There feathery palms their pendent clusters hold,
> Like foxes' brushes waving to and fro ;
> There every evening comes the after-glow,
>   Tipping the leaflets with its liquid gold.

Can anything be more graceful than the comparison of the dewdrops on the branches to pearl-beads on a maiden's neck? The vivid picture of the after-glow will be appreciated by anyone who is familiar with Mr. Elijah Walton's exquisite sketches of Egyptian scenery, or who has been fortunate enough to witness a sunset on the Nile.

Behá ed dín Zoheir is eminently the poet of sentiment, and shows but little sympathy with the metaphysical school of philosophy. As if, however, to display his wonderful versatility of genius, he occasionally breaks out into strains as mystic as those of Háfiz himself, the arch-priest of

metaphysical poets.   Elsewhere his Anacreontic utterances
are innocent of any allegorical interpretation.

The author of these poems was a master of satirical
verse, but in panegyric he is less happy.   Nor is this to be
wondered at, for the official congratulatory verses of a poet-
laureate are seldom to be compared with the spontaneous
efforts of his own unfettered genius.   But even here, if not
always strictly poetical, Zoheir is always original.

These compositions have, nevertheless, a special interest
of their own, inasmuch as they contain many allusions and
details which are of the greatest use in enabling us to understand the history of the period, and in making us acquainted
with the personal character of the principal actors therein.

Here is a specimen, for instance, of the ' Confessions
of a Wasted Youth : '—

Youth has fled ere I have tasted joys that should have been
    my 'lot ;
Fair were youth in seeming but for follies which its pages
    blot.
I have sent my tears behind it, haply it may come again.—
No alas ! it neither hears nor answers, and I call in vain.
Well ! the night of youth is over, and grey-headed morn is
    near ;
Fare ye well, ye tender meetings with the friends I held so
    dear !

O'er my life these silvery locks are shedding an unwonted
    light,
And revealing many follies youth had hidden out of sight.
Yet though age is stealing o'er me, still I love the festive
    throng,
Still I love a pleasant fellow and a pleasant merry song ;
Still I love the ancient tryst, altho' the trysting time is o'er,
And the tender maid that ne'er may yield to my caresses
    more ;

Still I love the sparkling wine-cup which the saucy maidens fill,

And I revel in the pearly whiteness of their bosoms still.

How long have I hid my passion ?   God alone the secret knows—

God whom now I ask for pardon, God from whom forgiveness flows.

And here is a pretty little poem:—

> They called my love a poor blind maid :
> I love her more for that, I said ;
> I love her, for she cannot see
> These grey hairs which disfigure me.
> We wonder not that wounds are made
> By an unsheathed and naked blade ;
> The marvel is that swords should slay,
> While yet within their sheaths they stay.
> She is a garden fair, where I
> Need fear no guardian's prying eye.
> Where, though in beauty blooms the rose,
> Narcissuses their eyelids close.

Enough has been quoted to show that Palmer, if not an original poet of good position, was able to translate poetry of a very high order.   But there was one *genre* in which he excelled.   In his poems to illustrate Arab humour he simply writes verses of their kind, as good as can be written.   In them, as the Americans say, he ' let himself rip,' and gave full play to the mirth and merriment which formed so large a part of his character.   These poems, or many of them, were given in the first instance to the Rabelais Club, and were printed, not published, in the first volume of the 'Recreations' of that learned Society, of which Palmer was an original member. They were next, with additions and some explanatory letterpress, published in 'Temple Bar.' I have received Mr. Bentley's permission to quote from these papers. The hero of the following story is the famous Abu Nawâs, poet and jester to the Caliph Haroun Alraschid :—

> One fine evening the Caliph
>   Had indulged in heavy wet,
> Till he didn't know an *alif* [1]
>   From the neighbouring minaret ;
>
> And awaking on the morrow,
>   With (what all must feel at times)
> Red-hot coppers, thought with sorrow
>   On his fellow-creatures' crimes.
>
> 'Shall not Allah's own vicegerent,'
>   Said he, 'break the drunkard's glass—
> Crush in man this vice inherent?
>   Here, you sot Abu Nuwâs !
>
> ' My great clemency prevailing,
>   Grants to thee the choice to make
> 'Twixt beheading and impaling,—
>   Shall it be a chop or stake ? '
>
> But the still undaunted poet
>   Takes it all for pleasant fun.
> ' How your Majesty does go it !
>   May I ask what I have done ? '

---

[1] The first letter in the alphabet. The proverb quoted, ' *Ma ya'rifsh al alif minnal mâdneh,*' is equivalent to the English, 'He doesn't know big B from a bull's foot.'

'Done !' the Caliph cried with curses :
   ' Is it not thy wont to sing
Dissipated doggrel verses,
  . Bidding men the wine cup bring?

'I suspect from your condition
   Men do bring it very oft.'
'Would you slay me on suspicion?'[1]
   Asks the bard in accents soft.

'Then religion, too, you scoff at ;
   Here, for instance, when you say,
"Come along, my noble Prophet,
   We will fight with fate to-day !"'

'Well, and *did* we ?' asked the poet.
   ' How should I know ?' said the King.
'Then, when you yourself don't know it,
   Would you kill me for a thing ?'

'Cease,' cried Haroun, 'this contention :
   Thou hast often in thy verse
Owned to things too bad to mention,
   And deserving death or worse !'

' Allah told us long ago that
   What I say I never do ;
And your Majesty must know that,
   Since you've read your Koran through,

"THE ERRING FOLLOW IN THE POETS' WAY :
SEEST THOU NOT HOW IN EACH VALE THEY STRAY?
AND HOW THEY NEVER DO THE THINGS THEY SAY."'[2]

This Koranic erudition
   Left the King no more to say ;
So the other with submission
   Took the chance to slip away.

[1] ' Verily some suspicion is a sin' (Koran, ch. xlix. v. 12).
[2] Koran, ch. xxvi. vv. 224-226.

Reader ! it should make us humbler
    When of men like this we read.
Let us take another tumbler,
    Just to drink to er Rashîd.

. Here, again, is the story of the Astrologer, supposed
to have been told by an Egyptian colonel, a descend-
ant of Abu Nawâs :—

Alack a day, for the days of old
    When heads were clever and hearts were true,
And a Caliph scattered stores of gold
    On men, my Ali, like me and you !

Haroun was moody, Haroun was sad,
    And he drank a glass of wine or two ;
But it only seemed to make him mad,
    And the cup at the Sakis' head he threw.

Came Yahya [1] in ; and he dodged the glass
    That all too near his turban flew ;
And he bowed his head, and he said, ' Alas !
    Your Majesty seems in a pretty stew ! '

' And well I may,' the monarch said ;
    ' And so, my worthy friend, would you,
If you knew that you must needs be dead
    And buried, perhaps, in a day or two.

' For the man who writes the almanacks—
    Ez Zadkiel, a learned Jew—
Has found, amongst other distressing facts,
    That the days I have left upon earth are few.'

[1] Yahya the Barmecide was Haroun al Raschid's Prime Minister.
He was the father of Jaafer, whose incognito walks through Bagdad are
a favourite theme in the *Arabian Nights.*

'Call up the villain !' the vizier cried,
   'That he may have the reward that's due,
For having, the infidel, prophesied
   A thing that is plainly quite untrue.'

The Caliph waved his hand, and soon
   A dozen dusky eunuchs flew ;
And back in a trice before Haroun
   They set the horoscopic Jew.

'Now tell me, sirrah !' says Yahya, 'since
   From astral knowledge so well you knew
The term of the life of our sovereign prince,
   How many years are left to you ?'

'May Allah lengthen the Vizier's days !
   His Highness' loss all men would rue ;
Some eighty years, my planet says,
   Is the number that I shall reach unto.'

A single stroke of Yahya's sword
   Has severed the Jew's neck quite clean through—
'Now tell me, sire, if the fellow's word
   Seems, after that, in the least bit true ?'

Haroun he smiled, and a purse of gold
   He handed over to Yahya true ;
And the headless corpse, all white and cold,
   The eunuchs in the gutter threw.

What loyalty that act displays,
   Combined with a sense of humour too—
Ah, Ali ! those were palmy days !
   And those Barmecides, what a lot they knew !

I do not, I repeat, claim for Palmer a place among the poets, but I think the quotations I have made justify one in ranking him high among the versifiers and in the very front rank of translators. His verses are easy, natural, and flowing ; his style is free ; he can rise with the subject ; he is mystic with the Masnavi, humorous with Abu Nawâs, and full of tenderness with Runeberg. I confess that as regards the version of Beha ed din I find too much of him, but then that is a fault with most poets. They should in their own lifetime be boiled down by sympathetic friends, who would allow none but the best to remain, so that a dozen pages might fitly represent the whole of Beha ed din which an English reader would care to possess. No doubt to the Oriental scholar there are in the original charms in style and expression which elude the most accomplished master of translation.

CHAPTER VII.

THE RECREATIONS OF A PUNDIT.

A MEMOIR of Palmer would be incomplete indeed
without reference to that side of his character which
rendered him the most delightful of all professors. He
was, before everything, a man who loved the sunshine
of the present. Had he been able to follow his own
desires he would never have lectured, never taught,
never written grammars and dictionaries at all. He
would have gone on accumulating knowledge and
acquiring languages, as if life were to be lengthened
for him as for Father Noah ; he would have become
more and more steeped in Oriental fashion of thought
and speech till he would have grown to resemble
Father Abraham. But the acquisition of knowledge
would have been to him, like his many minor accomplishments, only one of the delights, though the chief
delight, open to him.

He was a man who entered at all times into the
pleasures of life, and especially those pleasures which
are associated with some dexterity, skill, and craft.

He was no athlete, for instance : he could never throw a ball, or jump, or run races ; nor did he play at football ; nor did he play cricket, or tennis, or racquets, or fives ; nor did he row in a college eight : for all these things he had no inclination, nor did he take the smallest interest in them. On the other hand he was good in the gymnasium, where he could do clever things on the bar. Once he found a bar at the top of St. John's Chapel tower, which was then being built, and swung from it, toe and heel, hanging over a drop of 300 feet. He admired the dexterity and coolness of head required of a gymnast, and therefore he desired to attain something of it. The only absolutely lazy amusement which he liked was fishing ; he would go fishing in the Fens or on the Ouse, and sit patiently for hours watching the float bobbing idly, but not disappointed at not catching anything. The silence and solitude of the sport rested him. It is recorded, however, that on one of his fishing excursions he once surprised himself by catching an immense jack, and brought it home to the inn, carrying it in his arms like a baby. I think he required, more than most men, an occasional retreat. We all want sometimes to get away from each other, and from the monotony of work ; but to Palmer it was absolutely necessary that he should have intervals of silence. He always spoke of the holidays which he used to take in the Fens as the happiest he ever knew ; he came back from them refreshed and strengthened by the silence and solitude. In the same way, perhaps, the air of the desert always revived and strengthened him ; and later on we shall see how he loved to get up in the early morning, pull out to sea, and enjoy the silence and repose of the dawn upon the Welsh coast.

His principal companion in these excursions was one of his most intimate private and personal friends, a Cambridge man of his own standing, named Pretyman, a son of the late Dean of Lincoln. The two used to go about together and live for weeks in the Fens. The life is rough ; there are no well-appointed hotels, only village inns ; their costume used to become, at the close of the expedition, picturesque for rags and mud. The place which they loved most was Holywell, near St. Ives, a village which is much frequented by gipsies. As we have seen, Palmer first learned to talk Romany as a boy. He knew all the varieties of it, from the pure gipsy language, spoken in its integrity by very few English gipsies, to the tinkers' road talk and thieves' patter. He never, in fact, omitted an opportunity of talking to the gipsies. They attracted him by their strange lawlessness, their absolute lack of religion, ignorance of morality, hereditary opposition to all government and order, contempt for the sanctity of property, and the out-door life they lead, always in the road, among the fields, beside the rivers, and beneath the woods. They, for their part, held in great respect

N

the little man who came to sit at the doors of their tents, and would talk, though he was a gorgio, like a Romany of the purest blood ; in fact, they believed that he belonged to them, but that for some un- known reason he chose to go about among the swells and dressed like them.   They never concealed anything from him, but talked freely in his presence of their horse transactions, their poachings, pig- poisonings, thefts, cheateries, and palmistries, as if he was a veritable Romany.   Thus, one evening, Palmer met, sitting by the roadside, a gipsy friend of his, named Petulengro. He informed Palmer, casually, that he had walked forty miles, carrying with him a sack full of pheasants, and that they were at that moment lying in the ditch at his feet. Without ex- pressing any opinion on the character of the exploit, praise or blame being equally out of place as regards so natural a proceeding, Palmer merely advised him to wash his wrapper round his neck ; otherwise, as it was covered with blood and feathers, suspicions might be awakened. ' See now,' said Petulengro, hastening to obey, ' what it is to talk with a man who knows a thing or two !'

To some this association with gipsies, this love for the wanderers, this constant yearning to escape from the houses and the books and to be in the open, is a stumbling block. What does it mean ? What is the charm of it ? Why should we be called upon to admire it ? Well, one might write a great deal about it, but I think the best reply is to quote certain words of Leland's, from his book on the gipsies[1] recently published, because he sums up in better words than mine exactly what I would wish to say :—

It is that if one has a soul, and does not live entirely reflected from the little thoughts and little ways of a thousand other little people, it is well to have at all times in one's heart some strong hold of nature. No matter how much we may be lost in society, dinners, balls, business, we should never forget that there is an eternal sky with stars over it all, a vast, mysterious earth with terrible secrets beneath us, seas, mountains, rivers, and forests away and around ; and that it is from these and what is theirs, and not from gas-lit, stifling follies, that all strength and true beauty must come. To this life, odd as he is, the gipsy belongs, and to be sometimes at home with him by wood and wold takes us for a time from 'the world.' If I express myself vaguely and imperfectly, it is only to those who know not the charm of nature, its ineffable soothing sympathy,—its life, its love. Gipsies, like children, feel this enchantment as the older-grown do not. To them it is a song without words ; would they be happier if the world brought them to know it as words without song, without music or melody ? I never read a right old English ballad of sumere when the leaves are grene or of the not-broune maid, with its rustling as of sprays quivering to the song of the wode-wale, without thinking or feeling deeply how those who wrote them would have been bound to the Romany. It is ridiculous to say that gipsies are not 'educated' to nature and art, when, in fact, they live it. I sometimes suspect that æsthetic culture takes more true love of nature out of the soul than it inspires. One would not say anything of a wild bird or deer being deficient in a sense of

---

[1] Trübner and Co., 1882.

that beauty of which it is a part. There are infinite grades, kinds, or varieties of feeling of nature, and every man is perfectly satisfied that his is the true one. For my own part, I am not sure that a rabbit, in the dewy grass, does not feel the beauty of nature quite as much as Mr. Ruskin, and much more than I do.

As regards these experiences among the gipsies, I am also indebted to Mr. Leland for a paper of recollections, which I may as well insert here, upon his own and Palmer's experiences at a somewhat later date. He says, in a letter written to me from Philadelphia in December last :—

I think it was in 1874–5 that I first knew Palmer. He in the beginning wrote to me asking some questions as to Romany. We jumped at once into intimacy. I was planning with Miss Janet Tuckey our book of English gipsy ballads, and as Palmer had translated Tennyson's ballad, 'Home they brought her warrior dead,' very beautifully into 'the black language,' we invited him to join us.

Romany was the first language which Palmer learned— after English. I remember that he said that when he was a boy he used to save up his pocket money in order to take lessons of a tinker. For these lessons he paid a shilling or a sixpence. Once when he complained to his teacher that the gipsies whom he met refused to *rakker*—i.e. to talk Romany—the preceptor replied, 'Tell 'em you'll stand tuppence for beer if they'll talk, and nothin' if they won't. That'll set 'em off.' And Palmer found that it invariably did.

I never saw but one man in my life in whom the organ of language, phrenologically speaking, was so developed as in Palmer. This man was also a teacher of languages. His— Palmer's—eyes were those of a linguist. Though he was a grammarian and one who wrote grammars, he made no use of them in acquiring a language. It is very difficult to explain how it was that he learned languages at all with such marvellous rapidity and perfect accuracy. He always cleared his way clean of all errors from the very first step. There are occasionally Russians and Orientals who have this surprising faculty of not merely learning rapidly, but of intuitively speaking and pronouncing a foreign language with absolute correctness from their first attempt in it. I have heard of a man who was by nature so strong and always in such condition that he hardly required training for a fight. Nature had gifted Palmer so that he needed less study to learn anything than any man I ever knew.

Five years ago, at the annual celebration of St. John's festival at his college, it occurred to Palmer that he would invite three guests, and that these should be Bret Harte, the heathen Chinee, and ' Hans Breitmann '—i.e. myself, albeit I have never used that cognomen for a pseudonym or *nom de plume.* For the heathen Chinee he selected our highly accomplished and learned friend Tsao Ping Lung of the Chinese legation. Harte accepted, but was unable to come, so Mr. Tsao and I represented the invited.

After dinner, when in the Combination room at wine, Mr. Tsao remarked that *Pal-mer* or *Pal-ma* in the Mantchu language meant *hemp-land* (not long after I observed a Hempland Lane in Lowestoft); also that Le-land was a common Chinese name, meaning *plum flower.* I observed that hemp-land indicated that Palmer would be hung some day, to which Mr. Tsao, indicating with a wave of his hand the portraits of the great and wise and good men which hung on the walls, replied that he would doubtless be hung in after years on those walls as an honour. I was very much struck with the identity of this courteous remark with a passage in Ben Jonson referring to certain fortune-tellers.

> One told a man
> His son should be a man-killer and be hanged for't,
> Who after proved a great and wise physician,
> And after that in later days his portrait
> Was hung up in the University
> As a wise example.

It is forty-eight years since I read the text, so that I probably misquote.

In one respect Palmer was truly remarkable. He combined plain common sense, clear judgment, and great quickness of perception into all the relations of a question with a keen love of fun and romance. I could fill a volume with the eccentric adventures which we had in common, particularly among the gipsies. To these good folk we were always a first-class mystery, but none the less popular on that account. What with our speaking Romany 'down to the bottom crust' and Palmer's incredible proficiency at thimble-rig, 'ringing the changes,' picking pockets, cardsharping, three-monté, and every kind of legerdemain, these honest people never could quite make up their minds whether we were a kind of Brahmins, to which they were as Sudras, or what. Woe to the gipsy sharp who tried the cards with the Professor! How often have we gone into a *tan* where we were all unknown and regarded as a couple of green Gentiles! And with what a wonderful air of innocence would Palmer play the part of a lamb and ask them to give him a specimen of their language; and when they refused, or professed themselves unable to do so, how amiably he would turn to me and remark in deep Romany that we were mistaken, and that the people of the tent were only miserable mumpers of mixed blood who could not *rakker!* Once I remember he said this to a gipsy, who retaliated in a great rage, 'How the devil could I know that you were a gipsy, if you come here dressed up like a gorgio and looking like a gentleman?'

One day with Palmer in the fens near Cambridge we came upon a picturesque sight. It was a large band of gipsies on a halt. As we subsequently learned they had made the day before an immense raid in robbing hen-roosts and poaching, and were loaded with game, fowls, and eggs. None of them knew me, but several knew the Professor as a lawyer. One took him aside to confide as a client their late misdoings. 'We have been,' said he——

'You have been stealing eggs,' replied Palmer.

'How did you know that?'

'By the yolk on your waistcoat,' answered the Professor in Romany. 'The next time you had better hide the marks.'

A very remarkable incident took place here. I sang a verse of a gipsy song which by the merest chance contained certain allusions and names which literally startled and appalled the *old dye*, or mother of the tribe. I saw that I had made a wonderful hit, but did not know till a long time afterwards what it was. The party had come forty miles, travelling all night without stopping, as gipsies always do after such forays. I must explain that *inter alia*, among other things quite as strange, my song alluded by mere chance very pointedly to such raiding, and as I was a total stranger singing in Romany the *coup* was a grand success. Palmer learned all this long after from the old woman, and did not fail to greatly 'improve the occasion.'

He was wonderfully amiable, full of Cambridge softness and refinement, combining with it all great *savoir faire* and *savoir plaire*. He had too the art of doing droll things with a grave face and of leading others on and into all his freaks. I never shall forget how one rainy, gloomy afternoon we 'carried on' in the closed shop of a friend of mine, a Jew from Constantinople, who sold carpets, arms, and jewellery. When a *musnad*, or praying carpet, was produced, Palmer, to illustrate its use, went down on his face and knees, touching his forehead on the spot which is always made to indicate the place. From this he began to howl his prayers in Arabic ; and, as the sight of Salaman in his red *tarbuche* and his brother suggested business, he interlarded the prayer with bargaining, as Orientals often do. ' *Illah ul Allah !*—I'll let you have it for five hundred piastres—*O Thou the Merciful, in Thee only is my trust !*—Why, you son of a dog, it's worth a thousand—*Allah kerim, Thou alone art the Conqueror !*— *Ya hinzir*, O swine, it cost me more than you offer—*O Thou Omnipotent, I confess Thy Unity*—Take it, then, you *kefir*, for two hundred—it's a dead loss.' So familiar was this to the two Constantinopolitans that they roared with laughter and assured me that nothing could be more perfect.

I omitted to say that during the thirty hours in which Mr. Tsao was in Cambridge Palmer learned from him so much Chinese, both written and oral, that fears were seriously expressed by his friends that if the Chinese gentleman should remain a day longer the Professor would learn Chinese to perfection, and add it to his course of instruction.

Palmer contributed to Arabic and Persian newspapers or magazines. His Arabic, or Persian, or Hindu, with dialects, like all of the ten languages which he spoke, was simply perfect as that of a native. Several times I interviewed in his company, in London, a native of India who had been a *Rom*—that is to say, a gipsy. Palmer examined the man long and closely in his native language—that is to say, as a shrewd lawyer would examine a man whose assertions he wished to discredit. The result of the interview was that there is, in Palmer's opinion, one distinctive race of gipsies, who call themselves *Rom*, who speak a language which is not identical with any Indian tongue, though much like Panjābi, but which is identical with Romany. The man assured me subsequently that he should never have known from his language that Palmer was not a born Hindu. It was, by the way, very remarkable that this man, the only Hindu to whom I ever spoke in England, and whom I met casually in the street, should have been in all probability the only real Indian gipsy in Great Britain.

Palmer had wonderful presence of mind. Once during his first visit to the East he was led away by a treacherous guide and betrayed into the power of a gang of Arab robbers, who intended to rob and kill him. The day before the betrayal, when it was too late to retreat, he received an intimation from one who had quarrelled with the others as to what was to take place. Very soon his captors—for such they effectively were—began to treat him rudely. He affected to take no notice of this. Then the insults became more pointed and finally unmistakable. As if it had occurred to him for the first time, he sprang up in a rage and cursed them all. ' This to *me!*' he roared ; and drawing from his pocket a letter from an English lady, he exclaimed as he flourished it, ' Down on your knees, you dogs, and kiss the handwriting *of the Sultan!*' And down went the whole three hundred of them on their faces, utterly subdued. Truly I think that the Arabs who slew him at last must have been themselves remarkable, for no ordinary Oriental could have resisted Palmer's extraordinary personal influence.

He was extremely benevolent and generous, and very thoughtful in his gifts. Once, when I had given to another a valuable book, Palmer bestowed on my bookcase, to fill the gap, a copy of the Koran which he had bought from an Arab in the desert, who had bought it in Mecca. He was very good to all poor people, and I have known him to pay doctors' bills and buy medicine for them many a time. He was a man of a thousand as regarded nursing the sick and in bestowing those attentions which only a woman or a man endued with miraculous tact and kindness can think of.

When I recall his rooms in Cambridge, the charming old-time views, the ' Bridge of Sighs,' the company who met around him, it all seems to me here in far-away Philadelphia like a memory of a dream, or poem, or romance of earlier days. Palmer was a charming host, an inimitable story-teller, never telling too much, a perfect anecdotist, one who never wearied and who never seemed weary.

It was in his company that I discovered the man who first taught us *Shelta*. Palmer considered this as a very remarkable discovery. We had but a limited vocabulary between us ; however I have since greatly enlarged it here in America, but the more I study it the more I agree with the Professor that it is a philological puzzle. It is Celtic, but I cannot succeed in identifying it with any known Celtic dialect, nor does it appear to be a mixture of them. For a very long time Palmer was the sole depositary of the vocabulary which I wrote out from our joint queries. I had no copy and he thought it was lost. Finally, to our great joy, it was found. *Shelta*, let me add by the way, is a language spoken by the old tinkers. It is passing away very rapidly and will soon be extinct. It was from a wanderer in Aberystwith that we obtained the first specimen of it which we had ever met with.

It is bitterly painful to recall the merry sayings and genial jests of one departed ; but we seldom met without ' having fun ' of some kind. Study there was, however, of many kinds. He revised the manuscripts of all the works which I wrote after making his acquaintance, and a better friend in this respect no man could have. It was at his suggestion that I made many an alteration ; it was at mine, after hearing him *intone* a passage from the Koran, that he translated the whole of that work in such a manner that it might be chanted as the Muslim read it.

Once I wrote a letter in *Schmussen*, or German-Hebrew slang, such as is spoken among the poorer Ashkenazim. It was made purposely very slangy. This I sent to Palmer, who for a joke took it to a learned and very pious old rabbi, who succeeded in translating it, but opined that it must have emanated from a very disreputable Hebrew, and never suspected that it was the work of one of the Gorgim.

One day in Paris he entered into conversation with a Zouave, or Turco, a native Arab. After awhile the man exclaimed, 'Why do you wear these clothes?' 'Why, how *should* I dress?' exclaimed Palmer. 'Dress like what you *are*,' was the indignant reply, 'like a Muslim.'

When I lived in London it was usual on Saturday nights, after a reception in my house, for Palmer, and certain other spirits to meet in my study. Then Tsao Ping Lung would favour us with Chinese songs, each gentleman doing something according to his gifts; but the *pièce de résistance* was the singing by Palmer of an Arab song called 'Doos ya lee lee.'

> Doos ya lee lee !
> Doos ya lee lee !
> Esk'ke ma bubee fetense.

He had an inimitable and exquisitely Arab manner of giving this with a nasal twang and a drawl, while ever and anon at any convenient interval somebody yelled out, 'Ya Allah il Allah!' He accompanied himself on the *darabuka*, or tambourine, with Oriental skill, while another twanged the Egyptian mandolin. Here is a book called 'Sand and Canvas,' by a man named Bevan, in which there is a picture of Arab minstrels who really look as Palmer looked when he sang this song. I do not think he ever heard a strange word, or saw a strange face, or heard a strange thing that he did not remember it.

When we were at Aberystwith we were wont to hunt daily for stones which abound on the beach at that place. It was very strange that while I was the most skilful at finding topazes he chiefly discovered amethysts. Now an

amethyst in the rough is a very difficult stone to detect,
while a topaz is easy in that respect.

Palmer's industry was something appalling. Work had
no terms for him. He would write an Arab lexicon as
earnestly and with as much interest as other men write
romances. I never could understand how he could do so
much work and yet find time to be about town—at the
Savile Club, and in society,—as he did. One might
suppose, from the character of the anecdotes which I have
given and this continual mobility, that Palmer was a
frivolous man. He was so far from this that I do not think
I ever knew anyone in my life who was more serious or
earnest as regarded great duties. He had in this respect a
great likeness to Abraham Lincoln. He could pursue a great
purpose unweariedly for years. There was also in him something of Hamlet and of Omar Khayam, to whom life was
at once a terrible enigma and yet a passing show, as of
shadows on the wall. It was very remarkable that he
thought nothing of wonderful things, while he, however,
perfectly understood them.

He was altogether a *very* remarkable man. He was
very quiet and very brave, and had often been in great peril
and extricated himself by sheer coolness and pluck. He
surpassed any man I ever met in bearing great sorrows and
terrible trials with more that Spartan coolness. He could
be cheerful, and make others happy and cheerful, as not
one man in a million could have done when undergoing
incredible suffering, mental and physical. He was pluck
itself. I have been with him daily for months, and never
suspected that he had any secret sorrows, and found out
afterwards that his heart must have been torn all the time
with trouble which would have maddened many a strong-
minded man.

I regret, my dear Besant, that I cannot write more, since
it is almost time for the mail to close, and I know that if I

miss this you will be obliged to omit my memories of Palmer from your memoir. I could have easily given you many more. I was never more intimate with anyone than with him. Now that he is gone it seems as if in returning to England I shall suffer continually because he is not there.

Palmer, while he lived, never missed an opportunity to do a kind act. He by his genius and industry greatly aided learning and literature. He was one of the great scholars of his time. As a teacher he was literally a marvel. Finally, after a life during which he did far more good to others than to himself, he died, in the service of his country, a death so heroic that it is a poem in itself. Had he left none to mourn him his death could not have been regretted ; it was such a fitting ending to his strange yet noble life. If Palmer had been a soldier he would have been simply incurring the risk which a soldier is bound to undergo. But that an eminent man of letters, a professor of the University of Cambridge, a man whose life had other aims than war, should have been employed on a mission in which there were a hundred chances for death to one of survival is truly terrible. He deserved for this a great reward, and he still lives in his wife and children to claim it. It is not a question of *que diable allait-il faire dans cette galère ?* but 'why was such a man employed in such business ? '

Among other amusements may be added that of yachting. His friend Pretyman had a boat in which they used to sail about among the Norfolk Broads and go a-fishing together off the Norfolk coast. At one time Pretyman bought a fishing smack, and then they all went a-herring fishing off Yarmouth. Palmer for his part, brought back from the voyage a confused mass of nautical terms, which he used up in the production of a ballad without the least reference to their meanings. The first lines are as follows :—

> Upon the poop the captain stands,
>   As starboard as may be,
> And pipes on deck the topsail hands
> To reef the topsail gallant strands
>   Anon the briny sea.

In the year 1877 or 1878 Palmer sustained an irreparable loss in the death of his friend Pretyman. It was the loss of a friend of early manhood, one of those who can never be replaced.

He was always sketching, painting, and drawing. He had a true eye for colour, and could generally produce an effective sketch, though his drawing wanted firmness of handling. But he succeeded best in caricature, and there exists a whole portfolio full of drawings in which nearly all his friends, and many who were not his friends, college dons, members of the Savile, and others, are caricatured, good-naturedly, cleverly, and in a very original fashion. But I do not suppose that he would ever have arrived at so much power with brush and pencil as one may meet on the walls of almost every picture gallery from the work of amateurs like himself.

I have already mentioned his fondness for burlesque writing. Of course there are many to whom it will seem impossible that a man should be at once a profound scholar and yet be able to find amusement in the making of extravaganzas. It is a waste of

breath to remind men who never laugh, that it really
is better to laugh than to cry ; that life may be made
much happier by cheerfulness ; that most things have
a comic side, and that to be able to see that comic side
is not in the least degree inconsistent with wisdom of
the highest kind.   Beneath the wisdom and melancholy of Koheleth may sometimes be discerned the
mirth of Rabelais.   Nor will it, I fear, convert such
people to remind them that this Rabelais, a most
learned anatomist, physician, linguist, and scholar,
not only wrote a book brimful of laughter, but also
once wrote and acted a farce ; that Shakespeare,
generally allowed to be a man of some wisdom,
wrote many scenes at which even a fool may laugh ;
that Luther, More, Erasmus, who were grave men,
loved laughter, jokes, songs, and mirth : *enfin*, that it
is much better to be cheerful than to be gloomy ; and
that one of the surest outward signs of inward dulness
is the solemn face.   Now, as most English scholars are
pure grammarians, and as an intimate knowledge of
grammar is quite possible for perfectly dull creatures,
and, as dull creatures frequently get front places and
then try to make people believe that dulness is
wisdom, we may readily understand how this prejudice in favour of persons unable to laugh may
have arisen.   Another reason is of course the very
recent and still partial emancipation of scholarship
from the Church, which once laid her universal and
comprehensive hands on everything, and from which

we have not even yet quite succeeded in wresting all
away. Palmer, for his part, was so entirely free from
this old-fashioned prejudice that he was seen playing
in his own burlesque after he became a fellow of his
college. He played no more, it is true, and perhaps
remonstrances were made in high quarters. The
burlesque in question was the work of four men who
formed themselves into a society called the O.B.C., or
Original Burlesque Club. They had a 'larder' into
which jokes, puns, and ideas were thrown as they
occurred. Three of them did the literary work, and
the fourth arranged the music. They produced two
burlesques, if not more, one of them called 'Peleus
and Thetis,' and the other, which was the one acted
at the Cambridge Theatre, called 'The Bandit of
Bohemia, or the Knave of Hartz.' This, however,
was a piece with an original plot, and not therefore,
strictly speaking, burlesque. The piece was printed
in the 'Eagle,' the college magazine, of which Palmer
was for a time one of the editors. A copy of the
work is before me. It is written after the approved
style of burlesque in fashion about fifteen years ago,
and is remarkable for the extravagance and abundance of the puns. The songs are set to simpler
music than obtains in such pieces at present, and
the whole thing is just the work that might be
expected of young men full of life and fun, one of
whom had some experience in stage business. Later
on he became a supporter and joint editor of 'Momus,'

an occasional periodical. The other editors were Mr. Walter Pollock and Mr. Edwin Forrest.

This paper appeared once every term, and ran, like most University productions, for a year or so, when the contributors went down, or grew tired of it. I have before me the second number, which is adorned by an admirable drawing made for the paper by Matthew Morgan. The contents of the number are almost entirely of local interest with a few political verses. It is full of life, spirit, and ' go.'

He became, about the year 1868, very strongly attracted by conjuring. While still an undergraduate he used to study this curious art, of which the highest form of success is that where the spectator is forced to state as an absolute fact, evidenced by the infallible test of his own eyes, the thing which is exactly opposite to the truth. It is an art which requires more than a mere knowledge of the way in which tricks are performed ; anybody can read, or can be taught, how things are done ; but dexterous fingers, quick eyes, a plausible face and speech, and long practice, are necessary before one can become a conjurer. After Palmer had acquired some knowledge of the simpler things, and perhaps some skill in manipulation, it delighted him to attend the entertainments of conjurers, and to find out how they did their tricks. Generally he was successful. 'For instance,' writes a friend of his undergraduate days, 'one evening after

O

Maskelyne and Cooke had given a performance[1] we talked over the box trick.   Before we separated Palmer discovered how it might be done, and only needed a little of my help in planning the mechanism to be quite certain.   We swore a carpenter to secrecy, and had a box made into which he could be placed, locked up, corded in, and carried to the gyp room, where he would emerge almost immediately.'   This same box unfortunately nearly killed another carpenter, who had to execute some repairs in the vacation and stood upon it.   The box broke, and the unlucky man got mixed up with the machinery and had to be carried to Addenbrooke's Hospital, whence he was presently discharged, but goeth lame and halt to this day.

The conjuring was afterwards developed into a really scientific study of the art.   Palmer was joined in this pursuit about the year 1869 by Mr. Gordon Wigan.   They began by the investigation of spiritualism, and made an electric rapping table, by means of which surprising communications were effected from great men departed.   They then proceeded to higher flights—Palmer always maintaining that medium tricks were among the lowest forms of the art.   In course of time they arrived at a proficiency more than respectable.   Among other things they

---

[1] This was before these ingenious gentlemen came to London, and I beg that I may not be understood to mean that Palmer found out their later and more famous deceptions.

invented a trick which was performed at the Poly-
technic for eight or nine months with great success.
The directors called it 'Arabian Magic;' the post
bills called it, in Arabic character, Darb el Mendel,
which means, I believe, 'coup de magic.' Now everybody knows that the writing of the Arabic character
is an art in itself: the letters must be carefully proportioned, and every line must follow its true curve.
Palmer was so pleased with his own writing of the
bill that in the pride of his heart he wrote his own
name on the corner, 'Abdullah Effendi.' Great, then,
was his disgust to find that the printer had reduced the
size of his words and thereby had altered and spoiled
the beautiful proportions of the letters. Worse than
all, his name remained of the same size for all stray
Persians or Indians to read. As for his own attainments, he was great in the 'pistol' business, and excelled in the manipulation of cards and what is known
in the profession as the 'dingers'—that is, the various
effective and surprising tricks done with balls, cups,
and handkerchiefs. The two friends gave several
public performances, one in a village near Cambridge,
one at Slough for the benefit of some school, one at
Halstead for a church organ, and the last at the Eyre
Arms, two years ago, for the benefit of an hospital.

In the year 1870 or 1871 he entered the Middle
Temple, still with the thought of India: perhaps he
might be called and practise at the Bar at Calcutta
or Bombay. He was, in fact, called in the year 1874,

but by this time he had given up all idea of an Indian
career. Probably he read little law,—how could he
find time to read law?—but he made himself acquainted with the procedure of the courts, and was
sufficiently familiar with criminal law to take such cases
as were offered him. He went on the Eastern Circuit,
and was regularly seen for two or three years at the
assizes of Cambridge, Bedford, Huntingdon, Norwich,
and Ipswich. He also attended quarter sessions at
Huntingdon, Bedford, Cambridge, and Peterborough.
In fact, his circuit business was just an excuse to
get away from Cambridge, and from work, if it was
nothing else. He got a fair amount of business, but it
was interrupted and quite destroyed by the long illness of his first wife. He is said to have made a very
good advocate; but that he should do well any work he
put his hand to is a matter of course. One need not
greatly regret that he was forced to give up this kind
of work. It was never more than an amusement to
him; he liked to study judge, jury, counsel, prisoner,
and witnesses; if he was not engaged he would look
on, and this was more amusing; the contemplation
of the prisoner especially was always a curious study
for him; and he was constantly admiring the irony
of fate by which one man gets set in the dock and
another, no whit the better, in the witness-box.

I have spoken of his experiments in spiritualism.
They led, latterly at least, to an unfeigned contempt
for all pretenders to supernatural powers, whether they

call themselves mediums or anything else. Yet he
had a fondness for weird and strange stories, and I
am quite ready to believe—in fact, I do firmly believe—
that there was a time in his life when he would have
been rejoiced could he have proved the pretensions
of spiritualism.   It is, indeed, so tremendous a thing,
so stupendous a thing, this communication between
the present world and the silent world, the world
beyond the veil, that we could not choose but welcome, with a joy above the power of words to express it, the actual proof of that existence beyond the
grave which has hitherto belonged, and will always
belong, to the province of faith.   But to find out, as
Palmer did, how the thing might be done, how he
could himself do the thing as well as any professional
spiritualist, and to consider, next, as he was always insisting, that not one single message worth considering,
not one communication worth having, not one scrap
of real information about the next world, has ever been
received from all the countless dead to those who
still upon this earth cherish and love their memory,
is fatal to belief.   Most of us, however, are ready to
own that the messages are worthless, and yet—and
yet—how to account for the appearance and the phenomena?   Palmer accounted for all, and could do all.
Thus, a well-known trick is the 'levitation' dodge.
The room is almost darkened ; a body is seen floating
in the dim twilight ; it is not so dark but that the feet
or the boots are discernible ; and after the light is

restored a spirit message is found written on the
ceiling.   If, now, a conjurer be found to produce
exactly the same effects, if the ' message ' be found uni-
formly worthless, what becomes of the belief in spiritualism ?   This is the way in which it is done by men
like Palmer ; how Sludge does it may differ in detail,
but is probably the same in principle.   The heavy
body which is seen floating is nothing else than the
sofa cushion, the sofa having previously been placed
in position near the window curtains ; the boots are
indeed, real boots, the actual boots of the operator
himself ; they are taken off and brandished by his own
hands ; the ' message ' on the ceiling is also produced
oy his own hands, and by means of a lump of
charcoal placed in a telescopic pencil.   Again, a
very beautiful ' spiritualistic ' effect has been produced
by ' spirit portraits,' which have thrilled and convinced
many ; I do not mean spirit photographs, which, considered as a fraud, are quite too ' thin,' but spirit
drawings.   The way to do them is extremely simple,
but to do them well wants practice ; otherwise your
eyes will not be straight, nor your nose in the centre,
nor your mouth sensibly and justly placed.   Palmer,
while talking on other subjects, and looking you
straight in the face, would produce most delightful
spirit portraits, some of them quite startling.   And
while they grew upon the page his eyes never looked
upon the page, so that you could swear that they grew
without his knowledge, which was absurd.   Of one of

these he used to tell a queer story. I have already observed that he was fond of weird stories, and perhaps he dreamed this one. There was a certain murder committed some years ago, the victim being a girl; a man was arrested on suspicion, but eventually discharged for want of evidence. One day about this time Palmer was drawing these 'portraits,' when he began thinking over the mysterious murder, and drew a 'spirit' group representing the murdered girl and the face and hand of the murderer. The portrait of the latter, when he came to look at it, presented a rather remarkable face of the low type, of which he thought no more. Six months later he went one day to the Grantchester meadows to skate, when a man brought the usual gimlet and bit of carpet and offered to put on the skates. Palmer looked at him, and instantly recognised his own portrait. 'You?' he cried; 'why, you ought to have been hanged six months ago for murdering——.' The man started and fled without a word. If this is not true it ought to be. Let me tell another odd story of this kind, which was connected with his friend Tyrwhitt Drake. They were in Venice together. An importunate beggar followed them; they tried to drive him off with every form of abuse known to them; but still the man hung upon their heels and still demanded alms. At last Tyrwhitt Drake bade him begone, adding a word which Palmer had never heard before. The effect on the beggar was remarkable ; he glared, turned pale, spat, made the sign of the cross, and ran off as hard as he could, with every indication of terror. Then Palmer asked Drake what was that strange word. Drake did not know what it meant, or to what language it belonged ; but repeated the word for him. Presently they arrived at St. Mark's, where, after going the round with a verger, Palmer asked that functionary if he would kindly explain the strange word. The verger behaved in the same surprising manner as the beggar, and entreated them that they would leave the place immediately. They came away, therefore, and took a gondola. To the gondolier the same question was put, with similar results of terror and uneasiness ; nor would the man speak one other word to them until he had landed his passengers. They then called their hotel-keeper. He laughed uneasily, said that an English gentleman, to be sure, could not know, but— here he too went through the same performance of terror and fled hastily. Subsequent enquiries only resulted in the assurance from everybody that there was no such word, and that there could not possibly be such a word. It is, in fact, a word the mere utterance of which is supposed to bring disaster upon him who speaks it or upon those who hear it. Under these circumstances I shall not write that word.

When thought-reading began to be talked about, now two years ago, it was natural that Palmer should

endeavour to find out how it was done, if it really
was done, and was not a trick and cheat. With a little
trouble, and the application of the knowledge and
skill derived from his mesmeric practice and his legerdemain he arrived at results quite as extraordinary
as those recorded of Mr. Bishop. At the same time
he was always ready to point out how he did them—
unless, as sometimes happened, they were really
tricks of cunning and sleight of hand. The thing was
much prettier to look at than legerdemain, because it
was so much fresher and apparently so inexplicable.

One ought to add, though it has been said before,
that he was always ready to go to a show, to an ex-
hibition, to a performance of any kind ; that next to
a show, he liked to go to some out-of-the-way place
—say far Poplar or picturesque Wapping—where
strange humans may be seen and conversed with,
and odd things witnessed ; and that to the last, going
to the play was the greatest recreation and rest to
him that the world afforded.

Among the recreations must also be enumerated
the rapid acquisition of European languages. It is
not too much to say that he had completely mastered
the whole groups of the Latin, Scandinavian and Teu-
tonic languages, with their dialects ; besides these he
knew modern Greek ; he knew Welsh ; he had begun
the Slavonic languages, and knew some Russian
and a little Polish. I think he never attempted
Basque, and the only language which he is said to

have tried and abandoned—I know not whether on account of its difficulty or its want of interest to him—was the language of Cochin China. His memory must have been, of course, prodigious, but it must never be supposed that he acquired any language without a very considerable amount of labour and painstaking. The history of his learning Italian is an illustrative example of the way in which he learned all. Not even for Palmer was there any royal road to a language.

There is a certain book written by one Fonseca, a Portuguese, which pretends to be an introduction to English for Portuguese students. The compiler of the work meant well, but unfortunately he knew no English. He therefore made it up by means of a dictionary of French and English. The result is the most astonishing thing possible. Señor Fonseca has produced a language of his own. This language greatly pleased Palmer, who loved to talk it among those who had, like himself, read the work, and on one occasion he gave a friend the following lines. The book itself may still be procured. I saw a copy in Quaritch's list a short time ago ; and an account of it, with some of Palmer's verses, is given in Dobson's ' Poetical Ingenuities : '—

> I don't had any greatest treat
> As sit him in a gay parterre,
> And sniff ones up the perfume sweet
> Of much red roses buttoning there.

But who it want my friendly miss
   Which make to blush the self red rose ;
Oh ! than I was the flower what kiss
   The end's tip of her splendid nose.

Who I have envy of to be
   Which herb neath her pantoffle push,
Ah ! too much happy seemeth me
   The margaret which her vestige crush.

The sing bird gurgles on the bough :
   Them put out a superior note :
But she is a agreablest row
   What bubble from my miss's throat.

The heaven space it seemed me blue
   (I anciently approved the skies !)
It want to be the robbed her hue
   At charmant miss's cobalt eyes.

But I will meet her nose at nose,
   And take occasion for the hairs,
And make a statement all my woes
   That she in fine agree my prayers.

Wilt thou, she quothed, love me alone
   And cease of ever more to roame
But yes ! I tell her for the stone
   What roll not heap up any foam.

THE ENVOY.

I don't know any greatest treat
   As set him in one gay parterre,
With Madame which is too more sweet
   As every roses buttoning there.

Palmer was a man about whom countless stories have been told, some of them true, some untrue ; some foolish, some witty, some serious. Some of them are of felicitous repartee, as, for instance, when the late Master of St. John's met him returning from one of his excursions in the Fens with Pretyman ; he was clad in oilskin, water boots, and flannels of the coarsest, stained with weather and mud. ' I suppose, Professor,' said Dr. Bateson, ' that this is Eastern costume.' ' Eastern Counties costume,' he replied. The dress of the pair on these occasions used to become so disreputable that one day a railway guard asked them if they were aware that they were in a second-class carriage, and once a compassionate old lady gave Pretyman a shilling and a glass of beer. On another occasion Dr. Bateson found him sitting at the door of a gipsy tent, talking with one of the old witches of the encampment. Palmer, then an undergraduate, saluted the Master and explained that he was about ' to take a cup of tea with the lady.'

The story which follows, however, as Palmer used to say, is ' really true.' There was a certain burglary committed in Cambridge, and the burglars got off safely ; nor was there any trace or clue to their detection except a little piece of paper with curious marks upon it. The police brought the paper to the man who was supposed to know all languages and all alphabets. At all events he knew this character ; it was a notification in ' Yiddish,' or ' Schmussen,' to the effect that there was another crib about to be cracked. Palmer read it, and the burglars were actually caught while engaged in cracking that crib. Yiddish is the language of the German and Polish Jews ; it consists of Hebrew mixed with German, and is not only a very curious and remarkable dialect, but is very widely spread over the whole of central Europe.

Here is another story which is also true. Palmer was once required by the Greek lecturer of his college to write an account of the Persian war. He did so at length, but he took as his authority the Persian ' Shahzama,' or ' Chronicles of the Kings of Persia,' an account which differs in many important points from the Greek accounts. This independent version was calculated to please his lecturer very greatly.

He was an excellent *raconteur*, and had the art of seeming to possess an inexhaustible store of anecdote, only his most intimate friends even being able to convict him of repetition. Many of the stories he told were based upon his own adventures. To this class belong one or two already narrated ; another was the adventure of Salameh's head, already told.

There is, however, no end to the stories which might be told about him, and one must come to an end.

In most of these recreations may be observed the remarkable intellectual activity which Palmer brought to bear upon everything. He wanted to do for himself, and to understand, everything. While others wondered how things were done he wanted to find out the way. As it was with conjuring, spiritualism, mesmerism, so it was with thought-reading, acting, gymnastics, painting, and modelling : he wanted to get behind the scenes. Always the most unconventional of men, the ordinary standpoints of observation were not enough for him. He regarded humanity from a Moslem as well as a Christian point of view—nay, from the different point of view which belongs to every different nation. It was as if, whatever he did, wherever he went, whatever new language he learned, he was always studying humanity, from the criminal in the dock, from the gipsy by the wayside, from the Arab of the desert, from the Turkish pacha, from the Indian prince, from a congress of clergy, or from a learned syndicate of Cambridge professors. I do not say that he is to be especially described as one who ' loved his fellow-men,' because philanthropy and sentimentalism were not by any means cultivated by Palmer. On the whole I do not think he loved, so much as he wondered at, his fellow man. He loved his friends, it is true ; but he studied his fellow-men ; he was pleased to find, under thick or thin varnish, disguised with one code of morals or another, following one faith or another, speaking one language or another, whether you stick a crown on him, or a mitre, or a turban, or a biretta cap, or a cowl, or a chimney-pot hat, or a college cap, always one and the same Man. It is indeed a curious creature to study, and Palmer, for one, was never tired of finding out new things about him, new customs, new manners, new thoughts, all lying round the same central nature.

CHAPTER VIII.

THE END OF ONE CHAPTER.

LIFE for four or five years went on in great tranquillity and happiness. Palmer, as has been seen, was full of work ; at Cambridge and in London he had a great many friends ; he came up to town constantly on business for the Civil Service Commission, where he examined in Oriental languages ; he had become a member of the Savile Club, whose quarters were then in Savile Row ; and he had begun to write for some of the literary journals. Everything promised a long and tranquil academical career. His connection with Cambridge, indeed, was not severed until the year 1881, but his household was destined to be broken up.

Two daughters were born to him in the house at Newnham, but after the birth of the second his wife's health began to decline, and it soon became evident that the lungs were affected. It was, in fact, the old, melancholy story of consumption : one of those too common cases in which the patient is always hoping, her friends always seeing improvements and prophesying recovery. But the damp, cold air of Cambridge is not good for consumptive people, and it was necessary to take her away to a milder climate and softer air.

It was in 1876 that Mrs. Palmer was taken to Aberystwith for the spring and summer. I do not think that either she or her husband had any idea of the gravity of the case ; it was not until a year later that he first realised the fact that his wife must die. Indeed, there was at the beginning great improvement in her symptoms, and it was decided that Paris should be tried for the winter. Thither, therefore, they went, Palmer going backwards and forwards between Cambridge and Paris as often as possible, spending all the time he could spare from his work with his wife and children. It is needless to say that the heavy expenses of this arrangement taxed his resources to the uttermost ; with an income which was then a long way short of a thousand, he could ill afford to maintain a double establishment, and the charge of continual travel to and from Paris. However, in the spring of 1877 it became too certain that the end was only a question of time. A boy was born early in the year, but it was a frail and sickly child, who died of consumption when a few weeks old ; and after the birth of this infant the mother herself began again to show the most alarming symptoms.

Palmer, but for this continual anxiety and the dread of the future, found residence in Paris very pleasant. There are plenty of Oriental scholars there

—more, perhaps, than in London ; he attended the meetings of the Institute ; he found Turcos and Zouaves to talk with, and it was always a happiness to him to walk about the sunny streets and watch the people.   He admired very greatly some of the characteristics of the French, the clearness and swiftness of their intellect, their cheerfulness, their wonderful manual dexterity, their cordiality and readiness to please, and their dramatic instincts.

They left Paris in the autumn of 1877 to try, first, Wales ; and then the last chance of the consumptive —Bournemouth.

There is certainly no more beautiful place in England than Bournemouth ; the fragrant pine-woods, in which the villas are planted like log-houses in a Canadian forest, the low cliff, the tranquil sea which washes the shore softly, as if anxious not to break the last slumbers of the dying, the silent and peaceful streets, the garden, pleasant all the year round, the beautiful churchyard on the sloping hillside, make it the sweetest of all English watering-places.   But the air of the town is full of sadness ; the crosses in the churchyard are all in memory of dead boys and young girls cut off in the early bloom and spring of life, young wives, young mothers, young breadwinners ; the presence of death is always felt ; and the streets are crowded with chairs carrying up and down those who are about to die.   To those who are vigorous, residence at Bournemouth must be a continual sadness; to those who are stricken it must be as a sentence of death, to be deferred awhile until one's mind should be soothed, rather than terrified, with the contemplation of death.

It was in the early summer of 1878 that Palmer lost his wife. The long illness and the heavy expenses attending her removal from place to place had by this time quite crippled his means, and he found himself seriously embarrassed. His friend Pretyman, however, came to his assistance and lent him a sum of money sufficient to clear him of his more pressing liabilities, with the generous assurance that he need not feel anxiety about speedy repayment. Unfortunately Pretyman himself died soon afterwards, and the liabilities were therefore only transferred. I shall have to speak of his pecuniary affairs in the next chapter.

Another thing occurred about this time to disgust him with Cambridge. Among other recommendations and reforms it was proposed to augment the stipend of the Arabic professorship to 500*l.* a year. No recommendation at all was made as to the Lord Almoner's Professorship: this was to continue at 40*l.* a year with, as before, a grant of 250*l.* a year, made by the University, subject to the conditions of teaching two other languages. What was, what could have been the reason why the University thus went out of the way to insult and neglect Palmer? And can one wonder if after all these years of work, he should feel that the limit of patience was reached?

The death of his wife terminated this period of Palmer's life. I have shown how full of work were these years. It will have been partly understood how full of misery were the last three of them. His work had to be done in the midst of anxieties, in journeys backwards and forwards, in the face of expenditure which was devouring his future as well as his present. It seems impossible that a man so harassed and worn should have been able to meet his friends with a smiling face, or put any heart into his work. But he did; his work was bravely faced and conscientiously executed; his lectures, examinations, teachings, translations, went on without any abatement of zeal, though every moment was full of torture. The troubles were manifold—troubles besides those caused by money and illness—they need be no more than hinted at. They were borne with such fortitude as is rare ; he never let his friends know more than was necessary. Let them go. This chapter was closed, and a brighter, happier time—too short, alas ! alas !—was to begin for him.

CHAPTER IX

THE LAST THREE YEARS.

WE have come to the last chapter of his life at home, the final three years, in which so much happiness, good work, love, and friendship were suddenly brought to such a tragical end as has been the fate of few men in the history of the world.

In the summer of 1879 he married again. The following lines speak for themselves, and proclaim their own authorship. They are written by a hand accustomed to think and write in German, therefore a few words in them have been made English :—

We stayed in London for the first few weeks, and I taught him German.

'Der Erlkönig' was our beginning. He made such rapid progress that in three weeks he talked better than some natives of Germany would do. He astonished me by singing the little songs in Swabian, such as ' Muss i denn, muss i denn zum Städle hinaus.' I had not taught him that ; he bought a song-book at Kolckman's, and took his 'Singstunde,' as he called it, on the top of an omnibus. He always sang the right tune, although he did not know

music at all, but he repeated the words until the rhymes
and the metre fitted themselves to an air, and it was generally the right one.   Mr. L. used to play the guitar while
Edward sang, and sometimes it was a dreadful concert.

We spent the first few weeks in little studies.   We
painted a good deal, but he could paint much better than I.
One day I drew a flower so badly that I felt ashamed of it and
got angry ; then he took a brush and made it into the face
of an old gentleman.

Then in August Eddie and I, the two little girls, and
Lieschen, went off to Wales, to Aberystwith, where there are
lovely rocks and a beautiful sea.   The sea always had some
kind of power over me which I cannot explain.   It saddened
me.   Edward saw this ; he knew all my thoughts, and
talked until the threatening voices which I used to fancy
were coming up with the waves became sweet and musical.
After that our favourite place was among the rocks on the
sea-shore ; we went there every day, painting, reading, and
sometimes writing poetry.   I have still some verses which
he wrote then.   And we went shooting, fishing, and sailing ; for he made me great friends with the sea.   We got
up at three and four o'clock in the morning, and used
to find the boat waiting for us.   Oh ! it was very, very
beautiful.   So early as this there lay a veil over the sea,
and only Eddie and I were upon it.   Ashore, the towns-
people were all asleep, thinking themselves so happy because they did not feel nor know anything about themselves.
But we did !

Thus we sailed on and on.   The sun arose and looked
over the rocks to bid us good morning ; the veil became
thinner ; one rock after the other came to the front.   They
were no longer rocks of stone ; they were great temples
where Nature would have her glory preached.   The murmur
of the rocks was like little silver bells.   We sang—

Wie schön bist du, Natur !

Then the sun rose high. How little did we think how soon it would go under, never to shine again.

Once we were sailing in a frightful storm. He was glorious. The waves came over our heads ; our boat danced about ; the water came in, and we could not get to the land. At last Edward sprang out to the beach. I wanted to follow, but a wave knocked me back again until the next wave brought me to him. Then he made a large fire as the gipsies had taught him, and we dried our clothes and made some breakfast of the things we had in the boat. The people in the hotel were surprised to see us return, because they had made up their minds that we should never get back again.

Another day we went for a long walk, visiting some little villages. We took our way back along the beach, and as we were walking along the sea grew higher and higher, and the waves rougher. We could neither go back nor get forwards ; we were caught by the tide. It was impossible to climb the rocks, and we saw nothing before us but death. . . . Presently a boat came in sight and saved us. Ah ! It would have been better had our lives ended then—together.

But the summer came to an end and term began.

They took a house in the Belsize Road, near Swiss Cottage ; and Palmer, who still kept his college rooms, used to go down from Monday to Friday to give his lectures. This divided life, coupled with his change of mind towards the University, became irksome to him, and he was now chiefly anxious to leave Cambridge and find his work in London. 'The very worst use a man can make of himself,' he said, bitterly, 'is to stay up at Cambridge and work for the University.' In fact, his heart was gone out of his work.

Let me take another extract from a journal already quoted. It refers to a visit made to Lübeck the year after his marriage.

In the spring of 1880 we went to Germany. As yet Edward had seen very little of Germany and German life. A little party of a dozen people went to the station to receive him. I remember that my aunt, who only speaks German and Italian, was afraid that she would not be able to talk with him, but presently she whispered, 'Surely he has known German all his life long ; he speaks it as well as my old grandmother, who would now be a hundred and twenty years old.'

Two or three days after he arrived he visited Ludwigsburg, where you go from Lübeck to get to Norway, and talked to the sailors in their own language (Platt-Deutsch).

One old woman who brought her son's dinner on board kindly added a spoon for her friend—namely, Edward. He politely thanked her in the purest Platt-Deutsch.

With my father, who is now old, he had the opportunity of learning the Slavonic languages, of which he already knew something. One day he heard my father talking to some Slavonic people and listened. The next day he hunted them up and began to talk with them. Another time my father and he met some Italian gipsies, and Edward asked one of them to read his lines. She looked at his hand and said, ' You are a *Schwarzkünstler* yourself.' Then he showed the gipsy folk some tricks, until they begged him to go away or keep quiet, for fear he should bring discredit on their own performances.

One day he was talking in Platt-Deutsch with some peasants ; the next Sunday they sent him a great wooden cart (*Leiterwagen*) to take him for a drive.

At the Zoological Gardens at Cologne as well as in London he made the camels obey him and kneel down by talking Arabic to them.

He was called a *Wunderkind* by the people, because he
could do so many things.   In the morning he went sailing
and fishing in the river ; then he painted, then he did some
work in Arabic or Persian, then he put down everything
he saw which pleased him or turned it into verses, and in
the evening he was ready to talk all languages with anyone
who came.

He was more sad to leave Lübeck than even I was.
About fifty people came to the station to say farewell and
to bring flowers and refreshments for the journey.   One of
my nephews, a child of four, got into the railway carriage
and hid himself under the seat, where he was found by the
guard.   He wanted to go away with his uncle Edward.

He only grew cheerful when we arrived at Brussels,
where he found a great number of Persians, Arabs, and
Orientals, with whom he talked.

Allusion has been made to pecuniary embarrassments.   It is not the concern of anyone to know how
these were caused ; but it is the duty of the biogra-
pher to state, emphatically, that they were due to
no personal extravagances or follies on Palmer's part.
We have seen that the illness of his wife was one, and
indeed the main cause ; but soon after his second marriage things which he believed settled and done with,
assumed unexpectedly a threatening aspect and had
to be confronted.   Palmer in all money matters was
the easiest and most careless of men ; therefore he
fell a ready victim to those weaker brethren who
can never resist the temptation to borrow, beg, and
appropriate, as well as to the sharks, hawks, and
crocodiles, who plunder, rob, and steal.   It is, indeed,

a grave blot upon his character that he was so careless. For instance, he would never take the trouble to ascertain even so simple a thing as the amount standing to his credit at the bank, and would show you with a smile of surprise, as if it was a curious and amusing thing, a cheque of his own which had just been returned with 'no effects' stamped upon it. He would never go into his own affairs and ascertain exactly what his liabilities were and how they could be met. Yet they were not enormous; and at the rate of income which he had begun in the last year to make they would certainly, with reasonable, careful management, such as he was then under, have been cleared off in a couple of years. One cannot too strongly insist on the fact that he was a man of the most simple and inexpensive habits. He had no extravagant tastes at all, he never bought things, not even books, because he could borrow all the Oriental manuscripts he wanted; but he was somehow careless of money: it slipped through his fingers; people came and took it away from him, and then he laughed and undertook another dictionary, or some such light and easy task, in order to make more.

Also he was singularly unfortunate in his money affairs. His aunt, the lady who brought him up, was possessed of a comparatively large sum of money which she intended to bequeath to her nephew. This intention was perfectly well known. Palmer, in fact, finding himself on one occasion actually in the possession of a few hundreds, gave them to his aunt to keep for him, and add to her own. She did so, using the money in her own name, and investing it with her own. Then she married, somewhat late in life, but by marriage settlements preserved the disposal of her own fortune. Some time later it was arranged between her husband and herself, for some reason or other, that the marriage settlements should be set aside, but that the husband should leave Edward Palmer an equivalent sum by will. The settlements were accordingly set aside, but that will was never made, because both husband and wife were taken ill together and died within a quarter of an hour of each other ; so that all the money, including poor Palmer's hundreds, went to the heirs at law, and the unlucky Professor lost not only his inheritance but his savings. The man being, then, what he was, embarrassments could not fail to fall upon him, and it became necessary to face them. In order to do something towards clearing off the liabilities he first sequestrated his fellowship and professorship—that is to say, he set aside 350*l.* a year, a not inconsiderable portion of his whole income—and then, burning his boats, threw up his readership in Hindustani and Persian, gave up the college rooms, and was seen no more in Cambridge. Then he had nothing left at all. This was early in 1881. He had now a household in Belsize Road with a wife and little boy. The two little girls had been sent to Germany, where they were comfortably and happily bestowed and well taught. His only chance of making an income was by writing, taking pupils, or examining. He was already an occasional writer for the 'Saturday Review,' the 'Athenæum,' and the 'Academy;' he wrote reviews and papers on Oriental subjects when they were wanted for the 'Times;' he examined for the Civil Service Commission. But all these things together were only a precarious means of keeping the pot on the fire. He turned his attention to journalism. An introduction to the editor of the 'Daily News' procured him some work; but he was really successful with the editor of the 'Standard.'

It is well known that it is an extremely difficult thing for a man to force his way into the upper ranks of journalism. There are, to begin with, so many men before him—perhaps men as good; certainly men who have been trained in a sharp, practical school, who know the lobbies, who are behind the scenes, and can write articles which are full of hidden meanings, suppressions, and hints to those who know. Journalism has become a close profession, into which a man must enter early and make of it the business of a life.

At the age of forty-one, then, Palmer became a journalist. He became a journalist just as he became an Arabic scholar, by dint of pluck and perseverance. He was always to be found at the office of the paper at the right time. He was discovered to be one of those useful men who can write pleasantly on almost any subject. As a speciality there was Turkey and the East: there was also Italy; he had travelled, he had read, he had observed. He preserved in his writing, as well as in his talk, the elasticity of youth; he was one of those men who would never have become old. He did not care how late he sat up writing; he picked up the points of the subject with astonishing swiftness; in fact, he seemed born to be a journalist, just as he was born to be an Oriental.

From August 1881 till his departure from Egypt he was employed upon the 'Standard,' going to the office of the paper every afternoon and evening when he was wanted. Sometimes he was able to get away early; oftener it was two o'clock in the morning before his work was finished. It is fatiguing work: one has to be always ready to produce an intelligent and pleasant article, taking the right view, on any subject which may occur. Sometimes there are no subjects; then one must be invented. Sometimes, when the work has been already half completed, a telegram comes in which alters the aspect of the case or presents a new subject of paramount importance. Then all has to be begun again, with the boy standing at your elbow to snatch the slips as they are completed and carry them off with the ink still wet to the compositors. Palmer liked the work, and did not at all mind the late hours. Of course he made new friendships.

Palmer's work as a journalist is thus described in

a letter to me from his friend, Mr. Robert Wilson, at that time assistant editor of the ' Standard : '—

I am only too glad to be able to send you any information I can give regarding the newspaper work of the friend and comrade we have loved and lost.

To the best of my recollection it was during midsummer of 1881 that Palmer first became connected with the 'Standard.' He once told me he had long wanted some kind of literary work that would be a diversion to his mind, then absorbed, and as he thought too deeply absorbed, by Oriental study. He had a horror of becoming a mere bookworm, and of passing all his days mewed up in a library. I don't think he knew much of Carlyle's teaching, except perhaps what he collected from the talk of his friends. But in so far as it is embodied in the maxim—the end of life is action and not thought, it seemed to have had much influence on him at this time. He often lamented the unpractical nature of University life. It was a favourite crotchet of his that he never really began to live till he was partially emancipated from academic trammels. The great world of London, with all its strife of personal ambitions and clashing of public interests, fascinated him. The great game of life is always being played there, and he had some notion that, with his acquirements and experiences, he was fit to take some hand in it. Through the portals of the press he fancied he saw a short way of plunging into the thick of this vortex. The experience he might get in a newspaper office, he thought, would compensate for that want of knowledge of public affairs which he felt was lacking in him, and which the nature of his youthful pursuits had prevented him from gaining. Very many conversations he had with me on these subjects, but what I have said now represents the gist and pith of them.

When a man like Palmer wants to form a connection with the London Press, he has only one difficulty; that of getting known to the conductors of some newspaper. The possession of solid information about a few special subjects, combined with even a very moderate ability to give it readable expression, will do the rest for him. In Palmer's case the difficulty of introduction was got over in rather an odd way. He became, like many eminent journalists—notably another Oriental scholar, Edwin Arnold, of the 'Daily Telegraph'—a newspaper writer by simply answering an advertisement. The conductors of the 'Standard' wanted a good ready all-round writer. They advertised for one, and selected Palmer from a shoal of candidates, as being worth a trial. At first he did not 'promise well.' He had little knowledge of, and no interest in, politics—but, luckily, at the time he began his newspaper work a good many questions relating to the East were at the front, and upon these Palmer had always something to say that was not only worth saying, but worth reading. If he had nothing to say, he invariably knew where to go for information ; and as he himself never spared either time or trouble in helping other people, everybody seemed to enter into a kind of conspiracy to help him.

At first he had no very regular connection with the 'Standard.' His capacity for writing on certain phases of the Eastern Question, on matters connected with political geography, and on a great variety of social topics, however, determined the conductors of the paper 'not to lose sight of him.' So he was every now and then invited to contribute an article, and it was noticed that he always did it with great care and promptitude. He was so scrupulous about his newspaper work that he made a point of coming in at night and delivering his 'copy' with his own hand, and this led to his becoming very friendly with the men on night duty in the editorial department. He would sit chatting with them in his cheery prattling way for half an hour or so, until his visits began to be looked for with pleasure.   One night 'something happened'—I forget what, a murder, a railway or mining accident—some sudden disaster which demanded editorial comment.   There was nobody at hand to write about it, and accordingly when one of the assistant editors suggested that they should 'try Palmer,' who happened to be in the way, he was tried and not found wanting.   There and then he sat down, and by aid of a hasty scamper through some books of reference hurriedly collected for him, he scribbled off a very neatly written and interesting article in something like an hour and a half.   This habit he had of 'dropping in' at nights for a little chat, caused him to be appealed to in similar emergencies, and gradually it came to pass that he was regarded as an institution in the office.   Nobody knew exactly —he used to say he did not know himself—how he dropped almost insensibly into a position on the staff, just as if he had been formally engaged as a regular contributor.   But the secret of his success, as one thinks of it now, was very simple.   He was eminently loveable.   He was indefatigably obliging—ever ready to do anything in the way of work put before him in the cheerfulest spirit and to the best of his ability.   He was always helpful, bright and gay-hearted ; in fact, his very entry into the dingy premises in Shoe Lane was like that of a glint of sunlight.

It was his custom to call at the office every day about 3 P.M.   He would then make his way to the little room where several of the members of the staff used to sit waiting for 'instructions,' and at his appearance every face used to brighten.   At these meetings, where there was so much good talking, his talk was ever of the best—I need hardly say that, where so many jokes were cracked, Palmer was not backward in cracking the merriest of them all.   He used to relish these gatherings very keenly.   He liked those he met, and they liked him ; for, though he was not one who 'gives the bastinado with his tongue,' a delicate thread of playful satire ran through his conversation, and he was one of the most delightful of *raconteurs*. To get among his colleagues was a sort of tonic to him—for they were all men living in the present, busy about the affairs of the present—with no strong professional interest in the past save in its bearing on the present. He who had by the bent of his life been fated to live so much in dim antiquity found their society peculiarly fascinating, and he told me more than once their talk was positively refreshing to a mind like his, overstrained with the grinding toil of the grammarian and philologist. He used to declare he could never degenerate into a pedant whilst he kept his footing on the 'Standard.' I need hardly say how much his friendship and society were prized by his comrades. He was not only admired, but loved by them. When he left England it seemed as if something very bright and precious had gone out of their lives. When it became certain he would return no more there was not one who did not feel as if stricken by a grief too deep either for words or tears.

To the excellence of his journalistic work his colleagues all bear frank and hearty testimony. He was not, perhaps, a strong writer, but he wrote rapidly and readily, and his style was smooth and elegant. He never was very successful as a political critic—in fact, about what may be called party politics he never wrote at all. The only exception to this has been already given, namely—where reference was made to the points of Oriental policy concerning which he had special information. He had a marvellous faculty for swiftly grasping the pith of any instructions given him, and his quickness in 'getting up' a subject was very remarkable. Men used to say of the late Sir William Hamilton—whose metaphysical writings prove the extent of his omnivorous reading—that he never read a book. He simply 'tore the heart out of it' in less time than an ordinary man would require to make his way through the opening chapters. Palmer at his newspaper work somewhat resembled the great Edinburgh metaphysician. He would now and then sit down in a state of almost blank ignorance to write on a subject, and blue-books and books of reference were soon piled up beside him. After some plunging about among them he would emerge in less than an hour with a most extraordinary collection of facts, all useful and to the point. These seemed to arrange themselves in his mind without any apparent effort on his part. In a few minutes his busy pen would scamper over the paper. In an hour and a half a little heap of beautifully clear manuscript was to be found lying by his side, which, when ' touched up ' here and there by the writer, represented what he proudly called 'my leader.'

I have been often asked what sort of subjects Palmer liked to write about. The answer is, he wrote with delight about anything that was suggested to him, provided it had human interest in it. Hence he discoursed best upon certain themes such as gipsies, vagrants and vagabonds, Oriental life and manners, folk-lore and popular antiquities. He was very fond also of writing about crimes and disasters, and strange law cases or famous trials, and his light and playful wit stood him in good stead when he dealt with what are called social questions. He had an idea that he was an authority on questions of Free Trade and Commercial Tariffs, but I never discovered that he had any profound knowledge of economic science ; and from his talk I came to the conclusion that what he knew of the subject, accurate as it was, went little beyond the speeches in Parliament, and the ephemeral criticism of the day. Perhaps there is no better illustration of his power of rapidly mastering a subject than the suddenness with which he came to take a great interest in Elementary Education, especially in connection with the politics of the London School Board. I really think he was one of the few men in London who could write well and safely on this topic. Yet nearly all his knowledge of it he acquired, in the first instance, by having a few conversations with an intelligent member of the Board, from whom he obtained a vast pile of formidable-looking documents, the contents of which his friends used to regard with awe, as containing—so he used with serio-comic solemnity to aver—the key to one of the most inscrutable of mysteries. Palmer considered his career as a journalist in London, short as it was, one of the pleasantest episodes of his life. Those who were associated with him in that career professionally can say that they reckoned his companionship one of the brightest and happiest of their experiences. He was—

> The dearest friend to me, the kindest man,
> The best-conditioned and unwearied spirit
> In doing courtesies ;

and what he was to me he was to all who worked with him.

The exposure to the night air and the fatigue of getting from Fleet Street to Belsize Road in the middle of the night made Palmer resolve upon living nearer town. 'It has always,' he used to say, 'been the dream of my life to live in London, and not only in London but in Bloomsbury.'

The old *quartier*, now unfashionable, has a strange attraction for many, with its well-built solid houses, whose rooms are spacious and staircases broad, its great squares and gardens. For my own part, I look to a return of fashion when people are tired of gimcrack villas in the monotonous roads of dingy suburbs : there will be a re-migration ; Bloomsbury

will become what Campden Hill and South Ken-
sington are now ; even Soho and Drury Lane shall
put on again their old splendours.   To Bloomsbury,
therefore, Palmer came, and took a house in Mecklenburgh Square in the spring of last year.

At this time Palmer was certainly happier than
he had ever been before.   He was released from the
University, which had treated him with such un-
merited, strange, and cruel neglect ; he was fully
occupied ; his attainments were now known and
widely recognised ; lucrative work came in from all
quarters ; he was surrounded by friends ; he was living
in London.   There was the Savile Club for an afternoon talk ; there were all kinds of interesting places
to visit, and people to talk with, of all classes, from
his friend the Persian Ambassador to the meanest
Lascar in the Foreign Sailors' Home or the poorest
gipsy on the road.   The articles—not only for the
' Standard,' but also for the ' Times ' and the ' Saturday Review '—which he wrote during the last few
months of his life show an astonishing variety of
knowledge and experience.   They were mostly written in the office of the newspaper, with no access to
his library or note-books.   In style, as Mr. Wilson has
pointed out, they are pleasant and simple, and free
from the pedantry of lugging in big names and far-
fetched allusions and learned quotation.   Palmer never
wrote fine English, but he could make what he wrote
agreeable to the reader, whatever was the subject.

During the first six months of the year 1882 he was absolutely laden with work. He wrote reviews for the 'Saturday Review,' the 'Athenæum,' and the 'Academy'; he was editing the 'Memoirs on the Survey of Western Palestine;' he was writing for the 'Encyclopædia Britannica'; he examined for the Civil Service Commission; and at odd times he was compiling his Persian-English dictionary and his series of simple grammars. All this, with three hours out of the morning for the New Testament and four hours out of the night for his newspaper, make up a tolerable share of work for one man. He did not complain, but he certainly expressed his delight when the last chapter of the New Testament was finally revised, and that laborious and responsible piece of work completed. And he found time for an hour or two in the afternoon, which he generally spent at the Savile, for an occasional visit to the theatre, for a dinner at the Rabelais Club, for an expedition to some unknown region of London for a little painting, for making a translation or for writing verses. Lastly, if a man was in trouble or anxiety, if a man wanted advice, if a man wanted instruction, if a man wanted anything, except money, Palmer was always ready to give that man what he could.

These labours were more than one man could stand. In the cold spring he was again attacked by his old enemy, asthma. He was always more or less subject to the complaint, but on this occasion it was accompanied by a most violent and distressing cough.   Then he disappeared from his usual haunts, and we learned that he could not go out of doors, but must remain within and be nursed.   There was formed an accumulation of veins in the throat, and these burst and caused a hemorrhage of a very alarming character.   However, two or three weeks of care and rest restored him, and he presently resumed work, with his usual elasticity and vigour, only looking, perhaps, more fragile than before, and with a deeper lustre in his eyes.   Yet, though we knew it not, his life's work, except for one great thing which remained still to be done, was ended.

I have endeavoured to draw the portrait of this man so that it may not only be recognised by his friends as the true *effigies*, with the true expression, but may also, if that may be attained, show to those who did not know him something of what manner of man he was.   But only something.   It is not possible, indeed, in any words to convey the singular charm which belonged to him.   It was a charm of manner utterly unlike any that I have seen in other men ; it is difficult to explain in what it lay ; yet it was there, and it subdued all men, except those whom he did not like : and these were few.   It was caused chiefly by his extraordinary sympathy ; it seemed as if, whoever approached him, Palmer involuntarily put himself into that man's place and assumed that man's attitude.   It was not effort, or affectation, or pretence, or hypocrisy, or acting. It was a natural, gracious, and extraordinary sympathy. Women, who possess this strange faculty generally to a much greater degree than men, are liable to be led away by it into extravagances, hysterical passions, blind obedience, absolute submission of the will. They are carried into slavery by means of it. Palmer, on the other hand, by means of his strangely sympathetic nature, influenced or commanded those whom he knew. I am sure there is not one of his friends who will not own, without any shame, that Palmer could, and very often did, influence him more than any other man. We all, though we do not, perhaps, like to think so, lean greatly upon each other, and are guided and influenced by the opinions of our friends far more than we believe ; to use the expression of the artisan when he wishes to describe a man who is easily influenced by others, we are all, more or less, ‘cakes’: that is, we may be moulded like dough. Palmer was the man to whom everybody confided his affairs, even the most secret and private affairs, and asked his counsel and advice.

Another cause of this strange charm was certainly his gentle manner, his soft voice, his large and luminous eyes. Small as he was in stature, he was never insignificant ; whenever he entered a room one felt there was another man, of larger growth than most, in it. And this although he never in the least degree asserted himself, anywhere or in any way, but always retained the same quiet, unpretending manner, as if a back place, somewhere in the pit, at the Play of the World would perfectly content him, and others might occupy the stalls.   And then, again, there was the curious contrast, which the prejudices of some unhappy persons may present to them as more or less of an incongruity, between the won- derful learning of the man, his unrivalled linguistic power, and the boyish playfulness which he always retained, so that, without ever being a jack-pudding, or a tom-fool, or a buffoon, or a practical joker, or a comic man, or in any way losing his self-respect, he was always surrounded with a pleasant atmosphere of cheerfulness, which he carried about with him.   Why should not a great scholar be also a man of joyous nature?   Partly because, as I have said already, great scholars were formerly all Churchmen, and we have not succeeded as yet in separating learning from its associations with the Church, and so we connect learning with theological gravity.   It will be indeed a bad look-out for the Church if she ever cease to number scholars among her ministers and clergy : but scholarship is not necessarily a part of theology.

Again, one could never forget with him the intensely earnest and serious side of his character. There never was any man with a greater ardour for knowledge, a greater enthusiasm for learning, a stronger resolution to achieve learning.   I have endeavoured to show this in the story of his early years, where it has been seen how he taught himself Romany, Italian, and French, with no other assistance than his own dogged perseverance and determination; and in the story of his early manhood, when, with a kind of ferocity, he threw himself upon his three Oriental languages and 'tore the heart out of them;' and in his ill-paid work for an ungrateful University; and in his journalistic work; and even in those things in which he made his amusement. And, as there has never been any greater master of Persian, Arabic, and Urdu—though there may have been, and perhaps still are, greater *scholars*, as we commonly reckon scholarship—that is, by grammar—so there never has been, since the time when the first alphabet was created by Providence for the use of the first man who loved letters, any more determined, resolute, and enthusiastic student.

There were two reasons why he was able to do so much—two, I mean, without counting his determination. First of all, he read very little; he did not, as most of us do, waste his time in ascertaining what everybody thinks and says about every conceivable subject: that was an immense gain. Think of all the time that might be saved if people would only cease to trouble their heads about what they cannot understand and cannot mend! Palmer left all—that is, as much as a man can leave—which did not concern him. The mess and muddle which one Government makes after another disturbed him little ; the endless controversies over fashions and passing phases of thought did not interest him in the least. No one ever saw on his table any of the 'thoughtful' magazines ; no one saw him reading them at the club. He took very little interest in the new books of the day ; he neither read them nor talked about them. Yet he knew what was going on, and generally had an opinion which was worth hearing. And another reason was that he did not waste his time, but worked in odd moments, using up the half-hours before dinner, and taking freely, if necessary, from the night. A third reason I might put forward with regret. He took very little exercise ; in fact, not nearly enough for his general health. On the other hand, a great deal of the time which others spend in walking or in exercise of some other kind Palmer gave to those small arts and little dexterities which amused and pleased him so much.

Let us remember with real gratitude that the last three years, in spite of the grievous money troubles which harassed him, were by far the happiest in his life. They were cheered and hallowed by the deepest affection and devotion ; they were spent in the place he loved best of all places in the world, among the friends he most valued, in work which he found entirely congenial. Palmer had the most extraordinary capacity for happiness : his heart was always ready to bask in the sunshine of love, sweet thoughts, and 'doux parler;' no one could be more contented than he, in the simplest and best of all ways, with wife and children, and friends; with sympathy, tenderness, and love. Yet from this pure and simple happiness he was to be suddenly and cruelly torn away.

<hr />

APPENDIX TO CHAPTER IX.

PALMER had an excellent plan of preserving and pasting in books all the articles, reviews, and communications which he contributed to papers and journals. I have read through one of these books in order to learn how many and various were the subjects which he treated : some of them carefully and quietly written in his own study, but many written at a moment's notice and without reference to any books—some, even, with the boy standing over him waiting for 'copy.' Among them are, for instance, papers on Afghanistan, the Ceremony of the Doseh, Gipsy Children at Board Schools, the Greek Question, Jewish Marriages, the Night Side of Nature, Phœnician Inscriptions, the Rising of the Sonthal, Rogues and Vagabonds, Trained Elephants, Thought-reading, Brigands, Modern Indian Magic, the Wandering Jew, French Slang, Whittington and his Cat, Newgate, the Modern Rough, George Borrow, the Cannibal Islands, Arabian Pilgrimage, An Occult World, the Jehad, Arabs and Arab Stories, the Survey of Western Palestine, the Sufis, and many others. I have already mentioned the 'Secret Sects of Syria,' contributed to the 'British Quarterly.' For the same journal he wrote two other valuable papers, one on ' Monotheism,' and one called 'Among the Prophets.'

CHAPTER X.

THE GREAT RIDE OF THE SHEIKH ABDULLAH.

IN the midst, then, of his greatest happiness, with
health once more restored, full of work for the present,
and with the certain assurance of as much work in
the future as he could possibly accomplish—came the
end.

As nothing ever happened to Palmer as to other
men—as his life was strange, so was his death. He
was not to die peacefully, after the pain and endu-
rance of disease, amid the tears and tender farewells
of wife and children, but suddenly, and by violence,
and unexpectedly, after he had braved successfully
the greatest danger and prepared for himself and his
companions a way of safety.

When it became evident that the rebellion of
Arabi must be put down by force, and that he
intended to measure his strength with that of the
British Empire, two great causes of anxiety arose.
The first was concerning the safety of the Canal, the
second was as to the support which Arabi might
receive and the allies on whom he could depend. A

religious war of unknown magnitude might arise out
of it; no one ever knows what control Turkey can
exercise over her subjects in Asia, even if she may
be desirous of exercising any control ; no one knew
at this time how far Turkey was intriguing to back up
Arabi ; and, in reluctantly entering upon the war, it
was felt that we might be opening the gates for a
gigantic conflict very little imagined at the outset.
The question of fanaticism—how it may be awakened,
how strong it may be, to what lengths it may carry
a people—is one which presents very many difficulties
and very few points of certainty. Egypt is nearly
the geographical centre of Islam ; when the great
conflict between Christians and Moslems is fought
out for the last time, it may be in Egypt or it may be
in Syria, but most probably in Egypt, for the latest
and most zealous converts to the cause of the Prophet are those of Africa.

As regards Arabi, it is tolerably certain that he
reckoned on other support than that of the so-called
Egyptian National party.   For this support he would
perhaps look to Upper Egypt, to those parts of Africa
where the Faith has of late been so widely extended, perhaps to Tripoli and Tunis, certainly to the
Arabs of the Desert on both sides of the Canal, and
through them to the hordes of Mohammedans in
Arabia and the great Syrian Desert.

If one looks at a good map, it will be seen that
a road runs across the north of the Sinai Peninsula

from Suez to Kulat Nakhl and from Nakhl to
Akabah. This is the Haj road by which the pilgrims
pass every year on their way to Mecca. It joins the
other Haj road from Damascus about fifty miles
N.E. of Akabah. Another caravan road runs from
Suez to El Arish on the coast of the Mediterranean,
fifteen miles east of the Lake Serbonis. These roads,
or tracks, are still, and always have been, military
roads. They serve, now, for the passage of troops to
and from the three castles of El Arish, Akabah, and
Nakhl. In the hands of a good Government they
would be strongholds for the repression of the
Desert tribes : in the hands of Egypt they have fallen
into ruin, and serve for little more than as an outward sign that Egypt claims this territory as her own.
Also, in such circumstances as those we have recently
experienced, they are important as centres to which
the Sheikhs may be summoned and treated with.
These places have all been recently visited and described. Of El Arish, Mr. Greville Chester writes in
his ' Notes on a Journey from Sân to El Arish ' :—[1]

'The town, or rather village of clay-houses, stands
between the desert and the sea, at the distance of
about one mile and a quarter from the latter. It is
dominated by a dilapidated fortress erected by Sultan
Selim. To the west of the entrance of the Wady,
close to the sea-shore, and near a Wely called Nebi

[1] *Quarterly Statement of the Palestine Exploration Fund,* 1880,
p. 158.

Jasar, are the remains of some ancient houses, one of which shows a ground plan of no fewer than seventeen rooms. Occasionally in winter, when heavy rains have fallen amongst the mountains inland, the Wady of El Arish (the 'River of Egypt') is temporarily a turbulent, rushing torrent, but as, during the rest of the year, it is a wide, dry Fiumara, it is to be hoped that the company of revisers of the Old Testament will exscind the word " River," which to an English ear conveys an entirely different idea. El Arish, or rather the Wady at that place, is the natural boundary of Egypt, and appears as such in many maps. It is not, however, the political boundary between the Turkish Empire and the Vice-realm of Egypt. That is a day's journey farther on towards Gaza, at a place called Râfeh, the ancient Raphia, where two ancient pillars have been re-erected as a landmark to the left of the track out of Egypt into Syria.'

Kulat Nakhl was visited by Palmer himself in the year 1869. He thus speaks of it briefly :—

' Nakhl is a wretched square fort in the midst of a glaring desert plain, the picture being backed up with some rather pretty limestone mountains. Here a few miserable soldiers are maintained by the Egyptian Government, for the protection of the caravan of pilgrims which annually passes by that road on the way to Mecca. We were received by the captain of the guard, a dark noseless Arab, and presently the Effendi himself, the Názir, or governor of the station, joined us, and we drank coffee with him and smoked pipes on the great divan at the end of the hall. None of the soldiers were in uniform, and they were as scoundrelly a set as one could well conceive.'

As regards the fortress of Akabah it has been described by Laborde (1829)

'The fortress of Akabah is built on a regular plan, and exhibits the same arrangement and system as all those which have been constructed for the protection of the caravan from Mecca. It is at present, externally at least, in a sufficiently good state to resist the inroads of the neighbouring tribes, who, though not deficient in courage, have no means for enabling them to assail it with success. Within the fortress several good habitations have been suffered to fall into decay, while others have been constructed of mud in a most slovenly manner. The governor has taken to himself the south-western bastion, and enlarged it considerably. The gunner, who is the military chief, inhabits the bastion to the south-east, and, like a veteran artillery man, sleeps by the side of a cannon. This gun, a twelve-pounder, and another which is planted in the north-eastern tower, are the only pieces capable of being discharged in case of an attack,—an event, however, of which happily there is little danger. The gunner adds to his warlike occupations the more peaceable pursuits of a merchant: he has converted a ruined mosque into a warehouse. A well lately excavated, and a palm tree, are the only objects which attract attention in a court indifferently levelled, and surrounded by ruinous buildings blackened with smoke.

'A few mud huts belonging to Arabs, who live on the small profits they derive from selling butter and other provisions to the soldiers of the garrison ; some tombs of former inhabitants of the fortress, and of pilgrims arrested on their pious expeditions by that malady which a sight of the Prophet's sepulchre would have cured, occupy the northern borders of the fortress ; on the east, hills of sand, forming part of the ranges of Djebel el Akabah descend even to its walls.'

These places, with Suez and the little Christian village of Tor, are the only Egyptian settlements, so to speak, among the Arab tribes. They are in fact very much like the old Roman outposts, which were dotted about along and beyond the frontier of the Empire, whether in Britain in the north or in the Hauran in the east : and like them they are places practically of banishment, whose officers are in disgrace, and whose soldiers are men whose characters make it desirable that they should be kept out of the way of their fellow-men.

The governors of all these places were, at the beginning of the Rebellion, fanatic partisans of Arabi. So much was known for certain. He had therefore an easy means of access to the Bedouin sheikhs.

Of the tribes among whom the forts are placed, the northern part of the Desert, which is part of the old Negeb or south country, is held by several. Our information is incomplete on the subject, even after the accounts given by Palmer and by Burton, but the following is tendered as an approach to the truth. First, there are the Azazimeh, described by Palmer as one of the poorest and most degraded of Arab tribes : 'they are superstitious, violent, and jealous of intrusion upon their domain, suspecting all strangers of sinister designs upon their lives and property.' The Saidiyeh and the Dhullam occupy the mountains to the north-west, and the Jehalin the country on the north-east.[1] The central plateau of the Tîh is occupied by the Teyahah, a great and powerful tribe. This country produces no grain, and they have therefore to purchase the necessaries of life at Gaza, or some other of the outlying villages of Palestine. They live by furnishing camels for the pilgrims between Suez and Akabah, and when there are any travellers across the desert they have the right to conduct them. They sell also the milk of their sheep and camels, and sometimes have nothing else to live upon. Once a year they organise a plundering expedition, and set off on camels for the country of the Anazeh, which is the

---

[1] It is an illustration of the general carelessness about political geography that even in Johnstone's *Royal Atlas*—a most excellent and careful work—no mention is made of the tribes. This is much as if we were to give a map of Europe with the rivers, mountains, coast and English consular stations, without the names of the nations.

district round Palmyra, a twenty days' journey. Their object, in which they frequently succeed, is to surround and drive off some large herd of camels, grazing at some distance from the camp. One remembers how the Chaldæans made these bands and fell upon the camels and carried them away: yea, and slew Job's servants with the edge of the sword. They have been doing this ever since, and will no doubt continue to do this until the end of time. The neighbours of the Teyahah are the Terebin, also a large and powerful tribe, whose territory extends from forty miles south-east of Suez as far north as Gaza: and the Haweitat who occupy the mountains west of Akabah. The Arabs who possess the peninsula itself are called, collectively, the Towárah, that is, the people of Tor, which is the ancient name of the peninsula.

The principal tribes of the country East including Petra and the Akabah are the Jehalin, whom Palmer found tractable and good tempered, the Hejayah, the Hamaideh, the Ammarin, and the Liyáthench. The last named are an interesting people, who, though they call themselves Mohammedans, are of Jewish descent and belonged originally to the Khaibari Jews of Mecca. These are the people in whom Dr. Wolff and others have discovered the descendants of the Rechabites. The Liyáthench still retain the distinctive physiognomy and many of the customs of the Jews, such as wearing the Pharisaic love-locks.

It is impossible to arrive with any accuracy at the

number of fighting men who can be got together among these tribes. The Towárah, not the most numerous, say that they number 4,000 men. The sheikh of another tribe, called in the Blue-Book the 'Deymat Sowaki,' was ordered by the Governor of El Arish to send up a force of four to five thousand men. Of course every man, unless he is disabled by age or disease, is a fighting man. As we shall presently see, the whole number of Sinai Arabs capable of military service, taking the Desert as far east as Petra and the Peninsula itself, was estimated by Palmer at about 50,000. But, in the case of a war for religion, these are not the only people to consider. Behind them are the whole people of Arabia and the great Desert, whose rising would be like the moving of sand. Insurrection is a highly contagious disease ; fighting for the faith is the most stimulating form of war ; the religious sense, as we understand it, may be at its lowest among these people, but there is always in abeyance a possible force, namely, the same fanaticism which animated the troops of Omar and of Saladin. True, there has been of late years little display of the old spirit ; yet even between Omar and Saladin there was an interval of five hundred years, during which the first strength of the new faith might have been supposed to have settled down. Yet it had not. It seems more likely that it will revive again, if only for a great final effort, than that it should wholly expire and vanish away. Fanaticism is a factor which will have to be considered in any doings with Moslems so long as the Haj caravans go yearly 'to Mecca, and the worshippers are daily called to prayer, and the Koran is taught to the children. As regards such an invasion as our own, we must also consider the natural suspicion with which a wild man regards a stranger, and the hereditary suspicion with which a Moslem looks on a Christian. And as a proof that the Bedawins have power to unite, the fact may be mentioned that only two or three years ago they mustered forty thousand strong, and marched north across the Desert, one knows not on what pro-vocation, with intent to destroy and pillage Damascus. As for the power of any number of Arabs in a pitched battle against regular troops, that need not be greatly considered. But they can harass ; they can hover round an army ; they can cut off stragglers ; they can plunder—in short, they can give trouble ; and they might make a march, such as that of Lord Wolseley's, impossible, except with twice as many troops.

One thing, in fact, was certain. There is an immense recruiting ground in the Desert east of the Canal, provided the recruits can be persuaded to enlist. They are recruits who do not enlist volun-tarily or singly, but by whole tribes or not at all. They rise or they remain quiet at the command of their sheikhs. The sheikhs are supposed to know best what is to the interest of the tribe. Now, to get at these sheikhs, Arabi had, as we have seen, four

centres, at El Arish, Nakhl, Akabah, and Suez. At
each of these places he had a governor belonging to
his own party ; he expected with confidence—there
are plenty of indications that he had already begun
to treat with some of them—that he could as easily
attach these sheikhs to his cause as those of the Nile
Bedouin ; a very few arguments would suffice ; it was
the cause of the Arab against the Christian ; it was
the cause of religion ; the Feringhee wanted to take
the land for themselves—that is, Egypt ; then they
would have the command of the Desert ; then they
would make the tribes dwell in huts and grow crops
like the Fellaheen ; they would even take away their
camels and guns ; Egypt was the only friend of the
Arab ; and, lastly, there would be plunder, great
quantities of plunder.

And behind these tribes more, and still more ;
a countless multitude ; so that a simple rising of a
single tribe in favour of Egyptian Home Rule might
be followed by a rush of all the others, and so might
lead to a conflict between the Crescent and the Cross
with Arabi himself—who knows ?—playing the much-
coveted part of the long expected Prophet and Saviour
of Islam.

It was early in June last that the Government
appears to have begun the serious consideration of
the question from this point of view. No doubt the
negotiations with Turkey were carried on with the
view of averting the danger of a holy war ; and there

can also be little doubt that they failed because Turkey saw that such a war might plunge England into the most serious difficulties, and therefore that it was an enterprise, on the whole, to be desired. It became, therefore, evident that the work would have to be carried out by England single-handed, and that all the dangers of the situation would have to be faced. At first the thing most to be dreaded appeared to be the destruction of the Canal, and questions began to be asked about the people on the other side. The other dangers which might arise were considered afterwards, as they became more apparent. Apparently, no one had ever heard of Palmer, or his travels, or his book on this very subject, and some time elapsed before he was discovered.

It was on the evening of Saturday, June 24, that Captain Gill first called on Palmer at his house in Mecklenburgh Square. He came from the Admiralty, and he was instructed to ask for whatever information Palmer could give him as to the character, the power, the possible movements of the Sinai Arabs. The interview was short, because there was an engagement for the evening, but it was long enough for Palmer to point out in general terms the character of the people, the nature of the dangers, and the best way of meeting those dangers. The most direct and most trustworthy method, he said, without thinking of himself, was for some one whom they could trust to visit the sheikhs, and to arrange matters personally with them.   On Gill's departure Palmer realised the full force of his own advice, and said to his wife: ' They must have a man to go to the Desert for them: and they will ask me, because there is nobody else who can go.'   On Monday Gill came again, and remained with Palmer discussing the question from various points of view the whole morning.

Let us at this point remember that Gill, whose unhappy fate it was to perish with Palmer on the expedition which they planned together, was not a man without experience of Orientals.   Moreover, he was the last man in the world to be scared by a bug-bear or to magnify danger.   At this interview it was agreed that no time ought to be lost in detaching the tribes, if possible, from Arabi, in preventing any injury to the Canal, and in quieting fanaticism which might assume such proportions as to set the whole East aflame.   It now became perfectly evident to Gill that Palmer was the only man who knew the Sheikhs, and could be asked to go, and could do the work; it was also perfectly evident to Palmer that he would be urged to undertake this difficult and delicate mission; he had, in fact, already laid him-self open by speaking of the ease with which these people may be managed by one who can talk with them. When Gill left him on that Monday morning he was already more than half-persuaded to accept the mission.

He thought about it all day; in the afternoon an invitation came from the First Lord of the Admiralty

to breakfast with him the next morning. He went
to the breakfast. There were present, besides Lord
Northbrook, Colonel Bradford, Captain Gill, and I
think, but am not sure, the First Lord's Naval Secretary. Palmer found that all the notes and reports
which Gill had made during the interviews on the
subject were already set up in type and laid on the
table. The whole conversation at breakfast was concerning the tribes, and how they might be prevented
from giving trouble. Palmer stated, again his belief
that the sheikhs might, if some one could be got to
go, be persuaded to sit down and do nothing, if not
to take an active part against the rebels.

It has been asked again and again, why Palmer,
a man of peace, a scholar, should wish to make or
meddle in a soldier's business. He did not wish.
But even a scholar may feel his heart glow within
him, if the chance arise to do even a small service for
his country. And this was no small service : it was
a great and splendid thing which he was asked to do.
Consider the position. We were entering upon an
enterprise which might be quite easy and short, but
might develop into a vast flame of religious fanaticism. Palmer seemed the only Englishman available
who could even attempt to avert the danger : the service he would render his country by merely making
the attempt was certainly very great, and might prove
beyond all power of reward if he should succeed.

The only Englishman who could do this thing !

Is there any other man, in any other conceivable affair, of whom the same thing can be said?

Yet Palmer ought not to have been allowed to go. On this point there seems no doubt or dispute whatever. So long as there was a single soldier in Her Majesty's dominions who could be entrusted with the work, this scholar should have been spared. That Captain Burton would have undertaken the work had he been asked, no one who knows him can doubt for a moment; but he was not asked, he was not referred to. Palmer, therefore, was allowed to go. With such powers of persuasion as he possessed, with such confidence in those powers, with such knowledge of the services he might render to his country, with the love of adventure which always possessed him, I see no reason for wonder that he should have gone. It has been stated that Palmer volunteered. In a sense it is true. But not in the sense in which the word is generally used. It must not be imagined that he sent in his name and offered his services as an officer who desires to join a campaign. To volunteer is generally understood to mean a free and unasked-for offer of personal service. In this sense Palmer certainly did not volunteer. Nor, on the other hand, was he officially asked to go. For five days, he had the matter in his mind and talked it over with Gill and with his friends, before he finally decided to give his services.

We are, however, as yet, only at the Tuesday. I

know for certain, and from his own lips, that he had on that very day made up his mind that if he did not go himself the chance would be lost. It was either on that day or on Thursday that he saw Lord Granville and gave him the same information as he had given the First Lord of the Admiralty. On Wednesday he received another invitation to call on Lord Northbrook on the Thursday. He went to the Admiralty at ten in the morning and remained there till noon, when his wife called for him and he came out, accompanied by Colonel Bradford, saying that it was now decided that he should go. In fact, when Lord Northbrook put the question to him, ' Do you know anyone who would go ? ' he replied, ' I will go myself.'

He had been considering since the Saturday whether he should go or should not go. It was not until he had carefully thought over the whole situation, and laid down a plan of action, and weighed well his chances of success, that he accepted the mission. There are other Englishmen who are Arabic scholars ; there are one or two Englishmen, such as Captain Richard Burton, who have lived with natives as a native, and are accustomed to go about in momentary peril of death.[1] But Palmer was the only man who personally knew the Sheikhs of the Teyáhah and Terebin Arabs and would travel among them as an old friend. Therefore he consented to go.

[1] Captain Burton knew the Hawaytat tribe, having transacted business with them on his journey to the land of Midian.

Great precautions were adopted to secure secrecy. It was given out that he was going to the East for his health ; for a geographical mission : it was believed that he was going for the 'Times' or the 'Standard.'

Let us note very carefully, because it is characteristic of the man, that he made no bargain beforehand and asked for no reward. A self-seeking man would have stipulated for a sum of money : a merely prudent man would at least have secured ample provision for wife and children in case of his death. Palmer did neither : he accepted the mission without even a verbal promise—except in the most general terms—of reward for himself or provision for his wife : he simply said he would go, and he went.

It was necessary that he should go at once, and he proceeded with all speed to make the necessary arrangements. I spent Thursday evening with him, and heard his plans. He had already laid down the route he was to take, and the order in which he would see the sheikhs. He did not at all disguise from himself that he was going to encounter great dangers : but not, he said, from his friends the Arabs : with them he thought that he would be perfectly safe, even if they should be excited by fanaticism : the danger was from Turk and Egyptian, at the beginning and the end of his journey. He received the sum of 500*l.* for the expenses of his journey, and another sum was advanced for the expenses of his household : as regards remuneration for himself in case he succeeded, or provision for his wife in case he failed, nothing at all, as said above, had been arranged.

On Friday he drove round to shake hands with some of his friends. Alas! he bade us farewell with a light in his eye and a laugh on his lips : he should soon be back again, in two months, most likely : certainly in four months : he should take the greatest care of himself; he was only going among his friends. Afterwards, one remembered that gaiety of heart which among the Scotch is thought to precede disaster. Byron used to say that whenever he felt more than usually happy, he knew something horrible was going to happen to him. The approach of Azrael is attended to some men, as to Falkland, with gloomy forebodings : with others, as to Palmer, it is attended with lightness of heart and gaiety. Perhaps, however, this gaiety was partly assumed to soothe the anxieties of his wife, whose presentiments were of evil from the outset. Certainly, on Thursday evening he did not disguise in conversation his full appreciation of the danger.

So he went from us, and we were to see his face no more.

.   .   .   .   .   .

The Government have caused two or three statements to be made in Parliament as to the nature of the mission with which he was entrusted. In an early semi-official statement it was said vaguely that he was sent off to report upon the disposition of the

tribes.   In the House of Commons, the expedition
was spoken of, once by Mr. Gladstone, and Palmer's
conduct was characterised as 'patriotic and gallant.'
This is very well, as far as it goes : but that is
very little way.   Then Mr. Campbell-Bannerman
spoke at length (on Thursday, March 1) of the mission
and its objects.   But he did not tell the whole.

His mission, in fact, as he understood it, was as
follows.   He was to proceed to the Desert and Peninsula of Sinai : he was to get there the best way he could,
at his own peril : he was to travel about among the
people, to pass from tribe to tribe, and—this was the
first thing—to ascertain the extent of the excitement
aroused among the people, and how far they were
inclined to join Arabi.   Next, he undertook to attempt the detachment of the whole of the tribes, if
he could, from the Egyptian cause, and in order to
effect this he was to make arrangements with the
sheikhs : he was to find out on what terms each
would consent to make his people sit down in peace,
or, if necessary, join and fight with the British forces,
or act in any other way for our interests which might
seem best.   He was, if possible, to agree to those
terms, and his promise would be regarded as bind-
ing.   Thirdly, as to the Canal : it was the time when
the anxiety about the safety of the Canal was very
great : he was to take whatever steps he thought
best for an effective guard of the banks of the Canal
on the Eastern side, or for the repair of the Canal, in

case Arabi should attempt its destruction. Indeed, before he left England he had submitted to the Government careful estimates in detail of the probable cost of preventing the destruction of the Canal, or repairing it if damaged in any place. The safety of the Canal seemed at that time the most important point of all. I think there was another point in his instructions which he probably received at Alexandria, namely, to ascertain if camels in sufficient numbers could be purchased, and at what price.

These instructions were not written down. I believe that he had no written instructions at all: they were conveyed to him in conversation only, and were never further formulated. But these were his instructions: his actual mission was exactly what I have stated. There are two ways of writing the history of war: the one is from the despatches of the general in command and from the results visible to all: the other is from the history of the secret service, when that can be obtained. Now as regards Palmer's mission, it seems to me that the only reason why it was a secret was that he would be murdered at the very outset were it known. The territory of Egypt includes the country he was going to travel in: therefore it belonged to the Khedive for whom we were nominally fighting: Arabi was a rebel: therefore an emissary exhorting the Khedive's subjects to remain loyal to him and giving full and persuasive reasons why they should be loyal—which was exactly Palmer's position—need seek to preserve this secrecy of his mission just so long as was necessary for his own safety and no longer. The thing once done— why not let all the world know it ?

However, for the sake of secrecy, it was arranged that his reports and telegrams should be sent to his wife, who was to transmit them to the Admiralty. And as soon as he arrived at Alexandria a telegram was sent to him, with orders to receive instructions from the Admiral.

Most fortunately Palmer kept, during his first expedition, a short journal, which arrived home safely : this, together with a few private letters also written in the Desert and posted at Alexandria, forms the only record, except one or two other documents to which I shall presently refer, of this adventurous journey. It is greatly to be wished that the journal was longer, and that it contained a day by day log telling of the sheikhs he saw and the places where he met them. Also, it was not written for general reading, but for the eyes of one person only, and it cannot, therefore, be printed entire, even though it shows, in every page, the affectionate nature of the man and his passionate love for wife and children.

I am permitted to transcribe such portions as relate to the work he had to do and the way he did it :—

'S.S. Tanjore : Tuesday, July 4.

'I am writing this on deck in the middle of the Mediterranean. It is such lovely weather. . . . I got to Brindisi at three o'clock on Monday morning, very tired and dusty after three days in a railway carriage, and as we never stopped more than twenty minutes at a time after leaving Paris I could not get any regular meals and felt rather queer.   But a bath and the quiet on board soon made me all right again. . . . I have some very pleasant passengers, two Indian officers, an old college friend from St. John's, and the new Consul at Alexandria, a very pleasant young fellow, who came up and introduced himself to me, saying that he had been told about me at the Foreign Office. As three of us have young wives who saw us off, we are great friends and get on very well.   The Consul had no longer notice to get ready than I had.   It is very hot indeed, but there is a little breath of wind, and we sit under the canvas awning, which is like a tent, and do nothing.   The complete rest has already made me feel much better, and my throat, which the dust and fatigue of the railway had made rather bad, is getting all right again.   We expect to get to Alexandria late to-morrow night or Thursday morning. I may have to stay there a few days on my way to Jaffa, but I will telegraph to you as soon as I get there, so you will get it before you do this.   I am longing for a letter. . . . I am sure this trip will do me an immense deal of good, for I wanted a change of air and complete rest from writing, and now I have got both.   Of course, the position is not without its anxieties, but I have no fear. . . . It is such a chance!   The special artist of the " Illustrated London News " is on board, and has drawn a picture of me talking to an Arab pilot.   It is not much like me, but you will recognise it when it is published.   I shall keep this open, to add a line when we arrive. . . . Just got into harbour, and boat come for mails.   Adieu !'

The two important facts brought out by this letter are, first, that his plan of action was prepared in England,[1] and secondly, that the magnitude of the enterprise was understood at head-quarters.

As regards getting into the Desert there were two ways open to him.   First, he might go through the Canal and be landed at Tor in the Peninsula, whence he could make his way to the convent of St. Catherine and watch for a favourable chance for going north.   The chief objection to this method was the length of time required, because he would have to retrace his steps, for there would be no possibility of getting out by way of Syria.   On the other hand, if he could get into the Desert from Gaza he could go straight through and be taken up at Tor.   In this case his worst danger would be at the beginning. Going into the Desert by any other way—by way of Moab for instance, or by way of Akabah : or from Suez, which was still in the occupation of the Egyptians—was absolutely impossible.

Perhaps a better and safer way would have been for the English simply to have taken and occupied

---

[1] So detailed was his plan that he had prepared estimates showing (1) what it would cost to preserve the Canal by native patrols, and (2) what it would cost to repair the Canal if it were damaged.

the forts of Akabah and El Arish, an operation which could probably in either case have been conducted with a company of marines. This would have given Palmer a safe starting-point and place of retreat ; on the other hand, it might have excited the hostility of the tribes. At all events, it was decided, before he went out, that he should attempt the journey from the North.

The next letter begins on July 5, and ends on the 11th :—

'Directly I got your telegram [1] I went on board the Admiral's yacht, and was told to go at once to the Desert and begin work. Sir Beauchamp Seymour has given me a revolver and a rifle, with plenty of cartridges, so that I am all right in that way. I am going to breakfast with him to-morrow morning at 8 A.M., and at 11 A.M. I start by Austrian Lloyd's steamer to Jaffa—three days' journey. The heat is tremendous and I am already as brown as a berry, but am in very good health. I am staying on board this ship until I leave. There are a lot of people here from the town—all the English people in fact— because they expect that there will be war at once, and perhaps it may begin to-morrow. The town is quite deserted, and the poor people are all thrown out of work. I am glad there is going to be fighting. Though I shall be a long way off, I shall be able to do something towards winning for our side.

[1] This was the telegram instructing him to take orders from the Admiral.

'The harbour here is a grand sight : there are thirty-seven huge men-of-war, and the batteries in shore have got three guns mounted, so all is ready for an outbreak.   I have been about the harbour all day long—once in an Arab felucca, once the captain's gig, rowed by sailors, and once in a boat rowed by six Egyptian harbour police.   I have to talk now French, then Italian, then Arabic, till I don't know what my own language is. . . . The Admiral said to me that he congratulated the country on finding so able a man to undertake such a difficult task.

'The next morning, after writing the above, I breakfasted with the Admiral, and after waiting to see the political agent, came on board the Austrian steamer.   It was a change.   The first class was crowded with Greeks, Armenians, Italians, Germans and all sorts of people, among whom a certain Signor B. was very civil to me.   I gave him a note to H., in case he should come to London.   But what shall I say of the rest of the ship ?   Jews and Syrians packed like herrings, fighting, being sick, howling, poor babes and little children screaming.   I never saw or smelt anything like it before.   The sea was very rough, and the first day I felt quite ill and miserable.   Then we went to Port Said, the beginning of the Canal, and I went on shore for a few hours.   There were English men-of-war there too, and the people in a dreadful fright.   The heat was terrible.

'On board the ships were some Turkish ladies, the wives and mother of a great Pasha, and with them two eunuchs in fashionable Paris costumes. With the next morning I got to Jaffa, where I am writing this. The town is built on a rock facing the sea, and this was crowded with noisy picturesque people when we arrived. The custom-house people were very uncivil and searched all our things, but I managed to get my guns and powder on shore, although there was a strict order that all weapons were to be taken away ; —— was very kind to me, and sent down to Gaza a letter from me to an Arab sheikh, and I am waiting here till one of the Bedouins can be found, when I start for the Desert.

'To-day I bought a lot of things for my journey : Arab costumes, coffee, flour, onions, rice, candles, lanterns and other things, which took me from seven till twelve, when I came back to lunch and afterwards went to sleep. This letter I am writing just after waking up again. I have not as yet had a single hour's rest since I left home, and feel rather knocked up, but I think my Arabs will be some three or four days before they come to Gaza, so I shall take it easy and rest a bit. The heat here is just like a Turkish bath, and the perspiration runs down my face. In the Desert it will be hotter still, but better to bear because dry, and this is so damp. I am already as brown as a gipsy. I have had to cut my hair quite close, and I already begin to look a savage.

'There is going to be an English occupation of Egypt. That seems pretty clear, and this journey I make to see how the Arabs are, but afterwards I shall have all the troops and war ships at hand to back me up, and be in constant communication with head-quarters. . . . We are very anxious to know how things have gone at Alexandria since I left, for the Turks have stopped all telegrams about political things. . . . I have been talking all about myself, because I thought you would like to hear about my doings. . . . It is bad enough here where I find plenty of people to talk to and be civil to me, but how will it be when I am in the Desert with no one but wild Arabs to talk to ? Not that I am a bit afraid of them, for they were always good friends to me ; but it will be lonely, and you may be sure that when I sit on my camel in the burning sun, or lie down in my little tent at night, my thoughts will always be with you and our dear happy home. I am quite sure of succeeding in my mission, and don't feel anything to fear except the being away for a few months. I have nearly engaged a servant, a great Syrian, but he can't quite make up his mind because of the Desert. I am staying at the Jerusalem Hotel, which is kept by a German. The two or three other people in the house are also German. The English Consul is an Italian, and does not speak English, while in the bazaar of course they only speak Arabic. There is a beautiful view from my window of gardens, with apricots and palm trees, and beautiful flowers for miles around, and the town and sea behind.

'*July* 11.—I have just got a telegram from Gaza that Sheikh Suleiman whom I want is five days from Gaza, so I have telegraghed to —— to hire me four camels from the Teyáhah Arabs who are there, and I leave to-morrow morning for Gaza, and shall be in the desert the next day. I telegraphed to you at once *viâ* Constantinople. I hope you got the one I sent on reaching Jaffa, but I have just heard that the Egyptians have cut the telegraph wires that way. I have hired a strong hardy servant, a native Jew named Bokhor, for 5*l.* a month.

'So the most important part of my trip begins to-morrow. . . . I feel very homesick, but quite con-fident. . . . I have still got a lot of things to buy, and all my packing to do.

'Adieu. . . . Remember me kindly to all friends. . . . I shall add a few words in the morning before I start. . . . I hope to be able to send a letter from Suez in about a fortnight, so in from three weeks to a month you will hear from me again. . . . I shall write to you every day. . . . but I can't send the letters, though there may be a chance of an Arab coming in. Just a line to say that I am off. I will write a letter the first opportunity I have, and ask the P. and O. agent to telegraph to you from Suez.'

This was the last letter received until after the

first expedition was finished. It will be understood that very little is omitted, except the fond messages of love to wife and little ones which make these letters and the journals which follow inexpressibly sad. It was not vanity which prompted him to repeat the Admiral's words ; any man to whom such words can be honestly said ought to be proud of them. Few indeed are there among us for whom the good old country can be congratulated. When these letters reached England he had been gone into the Desert for ten days. He was doing something to help the winning of the cause for which we fought. You shall see, directly, how he did it.

It should be added that Palmer was armed, or protected, or imperilled, as the case might be, with a pass from the Khedive of which the following is his own translation :—

'To all the *employés* of the Viceregal Government on the sea-coasts, Port Said, and the Canal generally.

'The bearer of this order is a person in whom we place especial confidence, and wherever he may go he is to be received with respect, and any questions he may ask are to be strictly answered without reserve or hesitation, since he is sent especially from us, and you are to rely upon him and turn to him for instruction. I hope your loyalty will send him back grateful for your assistance in this his commission.

(Signed)   'MOHAMMED TEWFIK.'

Then followed a month of great suspense. The two or three who knew the secret had to sit mute while men speculated on what took Palmer to the East at such a time ; some suggested political business ; most thought that he was gone to Syria for a newspaper ; a few knew exactly for which newspaper and why he was sent to Syria. For by this time it was very well known in some mysterious way that he had gone on to Jaffa. At length came the news that he had arrived safely at Suez, and some days later came home the little journal written for his wife, and two or three letters to those who were in the secret. One of these I will presently quote. Let us return to the letters. On leaving Jaffa Palmer disappeared ; he was no longer Palmer ; in his place there is the Sheikh Abdullah, the old friend of the Teyáhahs, and going back after ten years and more to see them again ; he is much richer than when he was here last ; he was then shabby and went afoot ; now he is splendidly dressed and rides a camel ; he has beautiful guns and pistols with him ; he gives presents because he is so glad to see his old friends again ; he can give many more presents because he is so rich. As for his former companion, who was with him before, the tall and strong Ali Effendi, he is dead ; he had no time to grow wealthy like the Sheikh Abdullah ; why did the great Abdullah ride across from Gaza by night ? why should he fear the Egyptians ? He will make all rich ; courage, brothers ! the good time long dreamed of by the Beni Ishmael has come at last.

And then the journal tells its tale.

'*Gaza, July* 15.—I have stayed here two days, getting information from the Arab tribes who are crowded here. I am writing this with a room full of Arabs, two of my old men among them ; my boxes are loaded on the camels, and I am just off. I heard secretly of the bombardment, which is not known here, and I am going through to Suez. I have written to head-quarters for a boat to take me off at a safe place. Things are very bad here, but it is quiet in the Desert. I will write to you a long letter to send off at Suez, and tell you all. Good-bye !

'*July* 15, 1881.—I spent my first evening in my little tent here on the border of the Desert writing to you. . . . I started after a great deal of difficulty in the afternoon, and we camped at sunset. My tent is very comfortable, and my servant a capital fellow. He had the tent up, and a nice dinner—soup, and roast fowl—ready in no time, and I took it in the twilight sitting on a carpet outside. I have also got capital Arabs ; the sheikh is a cousin of the one to whose place I am going, and I am quite safe with them. The journey to Gaza was dreadful, eighteen hours sitting upright in a jolting carriage. We stopped for three hours at midnight, and slept on the ground just as we were. The road was bad in every way, and they killed a man a few hours before I passed by a certain olive grove. In the town they are expecting that the Mohammedans will rise and murder the Christians. I expect they will as soon as the news of the bombardment becomes known. I heard of it secretly by telegraph. The people are so afraid, that I could not at first get anyone to go with me. I offered one man fifteen shillings a day and his food to come with me because he knows some Arabs I want to see, and he would not take it, though he is only a poor blacksmith and quite used to the Desert. . . . I know my way here better than you would think, and am most cautious. I am going to Suez straight. I shall get there after staying with Sheikh Suleiman in about ten days. I shall not go in myself because of the Egyptian outposts, but send a Bedouin rider in to tell them where to find me on the sea-shore.

'My man Bokhor has got a little square tent I bought him, and I have got some camels and a man for each. We have a camp fire and all sleep with loaded guns at our side, it is quite picturesque and romantic. My sheikh has just come, and I have had a long and very satisfactory talk with him. I think the authorities will be very pleased with the report I shall have for them. I am so looking forward to getting to Suez to hear from you. . . . I haven't had time or opportunity to paint, but shall try to take a sketch or two when we get to Suleiman's camp. We get up before sunrise, to start as soon as it is light.

The air is beautiful at night and in the morning, but from eleven to four it is like a burning furnace. I never felt such heat. Good-night. . . . I shall go to sleep thinking of you. . . . We are camped in an open space where we can see for miles, and two of my men are always on the watch, so there is no fear of our being surprised.

'*July* 16*th. In the Desert.*—I can only write you a few lines to-night because I am so tired. I was up at five and travelled for twelve hours, riding on my camel through the most scorching heat, wind, and dust that I ever felt. We stopped for two hours at noon and slept, but the heat was so great it did not refresh me at all.

'However, when the sun went down and we had camped it was better, but it is still very trying.

'We saw a great many Arabs to-day of the Turbani (Terebin) tribe. They were very curious to know who I was and what I wanted—my man said I was a Syrian officer on the way to Egypt—of course I am dressed in full costume like a Mohammedan Arab of the towns. I found out more about them though, than they did about me. I now know where to find and how to get at every sheikh in the desert, and I have already got the Teyáhah, the most warlike and strongest of them all, ready to do anything for me. When I come back I shall be able to raise 40,000 men! It was very lucky that I knew such an influential tribe. I wonder whether our troops have landed yet on the Canal banks. Good-night. . . . It is about ten o'clock with you. . . .

'*17th.*—I found the journey to-day terribly fatiguing, as it was over nothing but white glaring sand. I had a little headache before I started, and then rode for eleven hours in the burning heat—but I am all right again after a rest. We saw nothing of importance to-day except two Turkish soldiers belonging to a troop who are in this part of the desert. Fortunately they did not come up to us, for which I was very glad, for if they had made a row, my men would probably have killed them, which would have been inconvenient. I get on capitally with my mission, and am longing to get instructions from Suez and know if our troops have landed. I did not expect to find out as much as I have done this first trip. . . . I am going to bed though it is only half-past eight, because I was up at four and must be up before sunrise to-morrow. . . . Good-night.

'*18th.*—I have been quite well to-day, but as usual came in very fatigued. I had an exciting time, having met the great sheikh of the Arabs hereabouts. I, however, quite got him to accept my views, and, what is more, have sent in for letters. I dare not trust this to the men who are going, but hope to be at Suez myself and post it in about ten days. . . . It was really a most picturesque sight to see the sheikh ride into my camp at full gallop with a host of retainers all riding splendid camels as hard as they could run ; when they pulled up all the camels dropped on their knees and the men jumped off and came up to me. I had heard of their coming, so was prepared, and not at all startled, as they meant me to be. I merely rose quietly and asked the sheikh into my tent.

' 19*th*.—I had a better day to-day, though the heat was more terrible than ever as we got further south. I slept well for eight hours last night and had a nap when we rested for noon, so that I am not so tired. Then again we saw no one, 'and the sheikh who came on with me had the headache, and I had not to be always talking to him, which was a comfort. The Bedawi I sent on to Suez is going at a quick pace all the way, and will I hope be at Magharah, where I stop, by Tuesday next as I am looking forward. . . . to getting letters from you. . . . It seems an age since I heard anything of you all. . . . I hope to be able to make a sketch or two at Magharah, but in this dreadful heat it is impossible while travelling, and when I get into camp I am too tired after riding for nine hours and sitting for three in a little tent at noon with the thermometer at about 130 in the shade. The country is nothing but sand with a few stunted bushes on it, and the glare of the sun on it is something terrible. I think I am the only European who ever made such a journey in midsummer. Even the Arabs are knocked up, but I keep quite well. The nights are getting hot too, which is a nuisance. If I find they do not want me to return to Suez at once (as

I hope they do) I shall go to the Convent at Sinai and wait there in the cool mountains and send for the sheikhs of the Towarah—they are not such an independent set as these Bedawin. It is wonderful though, how I get on with them—I have got hold of some of the very men whom Arabi Pasha has been trying to get over to his side, and when they are wanted I can have every Bedawin at my call from Suez to Gaza. I have also found out the right men to go to in every tribe, and where they are camped, and what men they have got with them, so you see I have not been idle during my journey. Of course I know nothing of what has been done in Egypt since I left except that Alexandria was bombarded, as the Admiral told me it would be soon. But I hear from the Arabs that the Egyptian military party are still in arms, so I suppose our troops must have landed by now. My man is a capital fellow, and as he speaks Italian I have a little relief now and then from shouting in gutturals all day. I so look forward, when all the trouble and fatigue is over, to spending a quiet two or three weeks with you in Italy.

'*20th.*—To-day our journey lay again over a level plain, but to-night we camped at the foot of the mountain where Suleiman, my old sheikh, has his tents. The only incident on our journey was that the sheikh flew into a rage with one of the men, rode up to him, drew his sword and tried to cut him down, which he certainly would have done if the other had not slipped nimbly out of his saddle. The sheikh, who is the brother of Suleiman, is one who engages all the Arabs not to attack the caravan of pilgrims which goes to Mecca every year from Egypt, so that he is the *very man* I wanted. He has sworn by the most solemn Arab oath that if I want him to, he will guarantee the safety of the Canal even against Arabi Pasha, and he says that if I can get three sheikhs out of prison, which I hope to do through Constantinople and our Ambassador, all the Arabs will rise and join me like one man. In fact I have already done the most difficult part of my task, and as soon as I get *precise instructions or see Colonel Bradford the thing is done, and a thing which Arabi Pasha failed to do, and on which the safety of the road to India depends.* It has cost me some anxious moments to break the subject, and I do not mind saying, now that I am in comparative safety, that I have had a most dangerous task. I am now in the Teyáhah country, and no one can hurt me here. Was I not lucky just to get hold of the right people? . . . I have seen a great many other sheikhs, and know that they will follow my man Sheikh Muslih. I would give anything to be able to telegraph to Admiral Sir B. Seymour, but I must wait. Good-night.

'*21st.*—At last I have arrived at the Arabs' camp, which is some way up in the mountains and therefore a little cooler. Suleiman has gone to Cairo, but they expect him back on Thursday, the day when I hope

the man will bring me letters from you. . . . I am only
three days' journey from Suez, and if all is safe and
the way open I may be there in another week—if not
I shall have to return to Jaffa and go by steamer to
Port Said. I hope I shan't have to do that, for the
journey is so fatiguing and one has to be so cautious.
The Arabs are very nice to me, and have just
brought me a lamb as a present : Bokhor is going to
kill and cook it to-morrow. I already feel much better
for getting up into the cooler air—down in the plains
the heat was so oppressive that I had no appetite, but
to-night I ate a good dinner—some bacon, a ham
and tongue sausage (one of a stock of tinned meats
the Admiral gave me), an onion and some Arab
bread—so I did not fare so badly. To-morrow
morning I shall try and make a sketch, as I mean to
stay in camp and rest. I shot a partridge to-day, but
it fell over a precipice and we could not get it. It
seems quite sociable to hear the dogs bark in the
Arab tents close by, after the tiresome stillness of
the desert plains. I am anxious to get to Suez,
because I have done all I wanted by way of preliminaries, and as soon as I get precise instructions I can
settle with the Arabs in a fortnight or three weeks
and get the whole thing over. As it is the Bedouins
keep quite quiet and will not join Arabi, but will wait
for me to give them the word what to do. They
look upon Abdullah Effendi—which is what they call
me,—as a very grand personage indeed ! I have

made my tent quite cosy. . . . with a little carpet I bought at Jaffa and the black rug spread on the ground and my bed and two trunks. My guns are tied up to the tent-pole in the middle, and I have a lantern with one of the candles you gave me in it, and am just going to bed with the comfortable feeling that I need not get up and pack everything up at half-past three to-morrow morning, but sleep on till the sun gets up at five, when my man will bring me a cup of tea—Good-night. . . . I go to sleep and my thoughts are always on you. . . .

' 22*nd.*—I have rested in camp all day, but though not travelling have had plenty to do. I hear from a Bedouin who has just come on from Egypt that Arabi Pasha has got 2,000 horsemen from the Nile Bedouins and brought them to the Canal—but when I get to Suez they will soon go back, for my men know them, and if fair means won't do I shall send ten thousand of the Teyahah and Terebin fighting men and drive them back. I have got the man who supplies the pilgrims with camels on my side too, and as I have promised my big Sheikh 500*l.* for himself he will do anything for me. To-morrow I expect my letters. . . . You may imagine my anxiety about them—first I want to hear from you, . . . and then I want to know how they propose to get me into Suez, because I shall have to cross the Egyptian guards—or rather to slip through them—and I do not want to have to fight my way, though of course I

T

can get as big an escort of Bedouin warriors as I
want, but it would make a disturbance which I want
to avoid. However, I sent a letter to the Admiral
before I left Gaza, and I have no doubt it will be all
right. It may seem a vain thing to say, but I did not
know that I could be so cool and calm in the midst
of danger as I am, and I must be strong as I have en-
dured *tremendous fatigue* and am in first-rate health.
I am very glad that the war has actually come to a
crisis, because now I shall really have to do my big
task and *I am certain of success.'*

The whole distance from the starting point at Gaza
to Suez as a crow flies is about a hundred miles. But
with all this riding backwards and forwards a great deal
more than a hundred miles must have been traversed.
The ' Magharah,' of which the Journal speaks is the
' Jebel Makrah' of the map, of which mention has
already been made as a mountain range in which the
' South country ' terminates and where the Tîh begins.
It is a central position, and I think that the whole of
the last letter must have been written from his camp
there.

The evidence of the Sheikh Meter abu Sofieh,
taken by Colonel Warren and published in the Blue-
book, gives information not found in the Journal,
which allows us partly to lay down Palmer's actual
route across the desert. He was conducted by
Hamdân, a head man of the Teyahah, from Gaza to a
place called Bowâteh. This is marked on Murray's

map as El Bawâty, lat. 37° 10′ and long. 34° 12′, and is in Egyptian territory.

It was at Bowâteh that the Sheikh Misleh met Palmer accidentally. With Misleh was Meter abu Sofieh, who was introduced to Palmer as the Sheikh of the Lehewats, occupying all the country east of Suez. This was not true. Warren states in his narrative that the Lehewats do not live in that part of the country at all, but south of Palestine, and that their Sheikh is Alayan, and that Meter was simply the head of a family who had separated from their tribe and taken up their abode with two or three other families near Suez. 'They called themselves,' Warren goes on, 'the Sofieh tribe, but they had no power or influence whatever. In fact, as Meter abu Sofieh had broken off the connection with his own tribe, and had not succeeded in establishing another tribe with any influence, he was a most undesirable person to act as escort to travellers at such a critical time.' It is indeed, Colonel Warren thinks, to this unfortunate deception, against which it was impossible to guard, that the unfortunate termination of the second expedition was principally attributable. In person, Meter abu Sofieh is described as a man of commanding stature, and haughty and peremptory manner. He was about seventy years of age.

Palmer sent Meter to Suez for letters, and remained at the camp of Suleiman, Sheikh of the Teyahah, from the 21st to the 26th of July, when

Meter came back with papers. Suleiman was at Cairo during this time. On the 27th Palmer left Misleh and, under the escort of Meter, started for the coast. Their first stage was to a place called by Meter Airif, doubtless the Jebel Arif of Murray's map. The next two places, the Wady Hadîreh and Jidi mentioned by Meter, are not on the map at all, and the Wady El Haj must be in the range of hills which run parallel with the coast. Its name sufficiently determines its locality ; it must be near the Haj road.

As regards the last words quoted from the Journal, 'certain of success,' they seem to require explanation. Palmer had already succeeded in what seems now the most important part of his task : he had got the men over to his side : he could depend on getting as many men and as many camels as he wanted. But we must remember that when he left England there were two dangers equally important : one that the tribes of Sinai, followed by the tribes of Arabia, would join Arabi, and the other that the Canal would be destroyed. To Palmer the latter danger still seemed as great as ever : he knew nothing of what had happened : he was most anxious therefore to get the Admiral's instructions in order to place his men and guarantee the safety of the Canal. Then the Journal goes on :—

'23*rd.*—Thank goodness to-morrow ought to bring me letters from you. . . . To-day we had a little excitement. Some Arabs made a raid on the camp a little

lower down the valley, and our men went off after
them, but finding themselves outnumbered were
obliged to come back after firing a few shots.   I lent
the sheikh my rifle, and it so astonished the enemy
when the bullets came in the middle of them from
such a distance that they ran away, taking the stolen
camels and sheep with them however.   No one was
killed after all, so it does not matter, but it shows
what sort of a country it is just now. . . .

'I shall listen to every footstep to-morrow, hoping
that it may be my Bedouin with letters.   If I get
good news I may be at Suez in five days' time, and
then I will telegraph to you at once.   Good-
night. . . .

'24*th.*—I have been in a state of excitement ever
since sunset, expecting the return of my man with
letters, but he has not come.   Every time the dogs bark
I think it is he and jump up.   I do hope he will come
soon.   The day was fearfully hot, a scorching wind
blowing that seemed to dry up one's blood.   But it
is better now it is dark. . . . I can't write any more.
I feel so excited with expecting the Arab.   Fancy,
I had to give 6*l.* to get a man to go—postage
in the desert in war-time is expensive, and I don't
wonder at it, for the man runs great risk going alone.
I hope nothing has happened to him.   Good-night.

'25*th.*—Another day has passed without my man
coming with letters.   I am getting so anxious about
them.   To-day the heat was so terrible that, although

I did not go out of the tent till just before sunset, I had a splitting headache, and my man Bokhor was just as bad. Even the Arabs complained of the same thing. I never felt anything at all like it, and the flies nearly drive me mad. At sunset I went out into the mountains a little way to shoot a partridge, but I was obliged to come back because my head ached so. Fortunately it is a nice cool moonlight night, and as I have been lying on my rug outside I feel much better. . . . As soon as I know when I can come home I will write you full particulars. . . . I hope my letters will come to-morrow. Good-night. . . .

‘ *26th.*—My man came in, but fancy my dreadful disappointment when he only brought me some newspapers sent me by the P. and O. Company's agent ! They had been on board ship for fifteen days and could not send for letters. However, I find it is possible to get to the ships near Suez, and I start to-morrow, and hope to be on board in five or six days.

‘ I have had a great ceremony to-day, eating bread and salt with the Sheikhs in token of protecting each other to the death.

‘ *27th.* (7 o'clock p.m.)—We got off to-day at ten, and after travelling till .three o'clock, stopped and pitched the tents. It was frightfully hot, and all loose sand over which we had to go. I have just had some dinner, and as there is a moon and I want to get on I am going to travel all night. You may fancy me in Arab dress on the back of a camel riding along in the moonlight over a broad sandy plain with a lot of ragged cutthroat-looking ruffians—yet I am quite safe with them. I have made them respect me by always insisting on having my own way, and never letting them see that I had the least fear of anything or anybody. I do not really think there are many men who would have made the journey I have done. I hope in five days' time to telegraph to you. . . . that I am safe. Good-night.

'*28th.*—We travelled last night by moonlight as long as we could, then I had my bed made up in the open air without the tent, and slept till four, when the sun rose and we were once again on the road. After resting at midday we went on again till five o'clock, and camped in a hot fierce sand-storm—it was so miserable, the heat intense and the sand filling our eyes and mouths, and the wind blowing the tent about. But thank goodness it got better after sunset, but I am very tired. I have got the great Sheikh of the Haiwátt Arabs with me now, and get on capitally with him. In fact I have been most wonderfully successful throughout. I have been sitting out in the moonlight, repeating Arabic poetry to the old man till I have quite won his heart. Now I must go to bed. In three days I hope to be in Suez and get my letters. . . .

'*July 28th* (14*th Ramazan.*)—My letters get tiresome, for they are all about one thing—the heat and sand—but I know you like to read them. I

could not sleep if I did not write a few lines to you
—it seems like being able to talk. . . .

'The day after to-morrow . . . well . . . I have
not had a line from you since I left, a month to-
morrow. . . . All I fear is that the mail which arrived when all the Europeans had left Alexandria
was brought on to Suez, and as there was no one
but Egyptians at the post-office, the letters may
have been lost or destroyed. But I live in hope,
and it is a great thing for me on this tedious part
of the journey to be able to look forward to a letter
in a day or two. . . . Good-night.

'30*th.*—It is just a month to-day since I saw
you. . . . to-morrow evening I hope to be in Suez
and the next morning to get your letters. . . .

'To-day we travelled through a narrow valley
with high banks of glaring sand, and the heat was
so intense that at seven in the morning the Arabs
wanted to stop and not go on till night, but I was so
anxious to get on that we went on all day. I had a
frightful headache when I camped, but some dinner
and a rest outside in the cool moonlight made me all
right, only I mean to go to bed so as to be able to
start before sunrise in the morning. I shall be glad
of a rest in Suez and some good food, for living on
soup and maccaroni and onions is not nice, and the
water we get is half sand and the colour of tea, and
tastes horribly. Good-night.

'*Aug.* 1.—I am safe on board the P. and O. boat,

and have got your letter. I did not write yesterday because I did not get here till between three and four this morning, having been travelling by camel and felucca (i.e. native sailing boat) for twenty-four hours. I have had only two hours' sleep, and nothing but a piece of bread and a cup of tea, since ten yesterday morning, but I am just going to have a good meat breakfast, and then I go on board to report myself to the Admiral on the station. I got here by going to a part of the coast above Suez and got on board at midnight.[1] It cost me a lot of money, nearly 10*l.*, but I escaped the Egyptian sentries. The troops are coming on Thursday, and this is Tuesday.

---

[1] They arrived at Moses' Wells on the night of July 31. The party consisted of his cook, Bakhar (a Jew from Jaffa), Meter abu Sofieh, and six Teyahahs. They stopped at Mr. Zahr's gardens at the Wells, the Teyahah having refused to take the baggage down to the beach.

The wells of Moses are brackish springs of water, which rise in the sand of the desert about a mile from the seashore to the south-east of Suez. Here gardens have been planted belonging to the native Christians, viz. : Messrs. Costa, Medowar, Zahr, and Georgio. The families of Messrs. Costa and Zahr were staying at the gardens when Professor Palmer arrived. The gardens had been threatened by Hawetat Bedouins of Moweileh on July 29, and the Christians had obtained the services of several Bedouins of the Aligât tribe as guards to their property ; among others were Ode Ismaileh, Sheikh of the Aligât, and Umduckhl, a minor Sheikh.

Umduckhl supplied Professor Palmer with three camels, which, with the camels of Meter abu Sofieh, were able to take the luggage down to the beach, while the party walked.

The six Teyahah returned to their tribe, Meter abu Sofieh went up to his camp at Tusset Sudur, while Professor Palmer embarked in a dhow, and after beating about all night arrived on board the P. and O. barge at 4 A.M. on August 1, and was received by Mr. Hammond there. — *Warren's Narrative*, p. 10.

The last thing I saw in the Desert was the bones of a camel and the head of its rider ! I am quite well, a little thinner and dried up perhaps, but quite strong. Fancy being up for twenty-four hours hard at work and for fifteen hours without food, and yet I only feel a little tired. After I have seen the Admiral I shall go to sleep. I will just add a line when I have seen him and then send this off, for the mail goes out to-day. . . . I have just seen the Admiral, he is delighted with the results of my work, and has telegraphed to Lord Northbrook. He had three boats' crews watching the coast for me, but I got here by myself. I am going to dine with him to-night. . . . Kind regards to all friends who may enquire. . . . .'

The rest of the Journal belongs to the second expedition, but it may be as well to follow it on to the end in this chapter. He goes on :

' *Suez, Aug* 2.—Yesterday I had a most interesting day. I called on the captains of all the men-of-war, and met with a most pleasant reception. They all insisted on my drinking iced champagne with them, and in the evening the Admiral gave a dinner party on board the flag-ship in my honour. It was a beautiful dinner, and I did not get back to my ship till one o'clock this morning.

' I am off again to the Desert for a short trip in about two days. I have been asked to go to the coast and cut the telegraph wires and burn the poles on the Desert line, so as to cut off Arabi's communication with Turkey. Captain Gill arrived at Port Said yesterday, and will be here this morning. I can only write a few lines, as a ship which is just going into the Canal will take this for me. I am wonderfully well, and getting on capitally. . . . Good-bye.

' *Suez, Aug.* 4.—I have got a few minutes at last, and write to you. Ever since we came here I have been worked dreadfully, but thank goodness we are getting settled and it will be easier. I have only been to bed once for three nights. On Monday I was ordered to accompany the commanding officer who went to take Suez. We landed with three guns and 500 men. The Egyptian soldiers ran away, so we had no fighting to do. I was in the first boat which landed. We then made the Governor give us up the town and 50,000*l.*, which he had in his possession.

' The day before yesterday Lord Northbrook telegraphed to the Admiral to congratulate me on my safe arrival, and informing me that I was appointed " Interpreter in Chief " to H.M.'s Forces in Egypt and placed on the Admiral's staff. I am living here in great state at the Hotel at Government expense, and have all my meals with the Admiral. I am going up to Ismailiyeh the day after to-morrow in a gunboat, and the Admiral here said, "Don't let the other Admiral keep you—you are on the books of the ' Euryalus,' " his flag-ship. I have got a staff of about forty men working under me. . . . They won't let me go to the Desert for the present at least,

as they want me here ; it is certainly much pleasanter
if it were not for getting occasionally too hard worked.
The other night the enemy were reported in the
neighbourhood, and we had to go off on foot and find
out ; it was a false alarm, and I went back to the
same place with the Admiral, making twelve miles'
walk after dinner, still I keep in excellent health and
my work will soon be easier.

' I am one of the chief officers of the expedition,
and an awful swell. The 72nd regiment are coming
to-morrow, and I have got to see about camels for
them. Good-bye. . . .

' The pay is to be what I suggest, but I haven't
settled it yet. . . . Address E.H.P., Chief Interpreter,
Admiral's Staff, Suez, Egypt. Capt. Gill has just
come, and placed 20,000*l.* at my disposal for the
Arabs. . . .

' *Suez, Aug.* 6, 1882.—I find I have just a chance
of sending you another line with the Government
despatches. I start to-morrow for a few days in the
desert to buy camels. Capt. Gill and the Admiral's
Flag Lieutenant go with me, and we shall be all
jolly. My position seems like a dream—the Admiral
said, as I preferred leaving the Government to settle
my pay, that in the meantime I might draw to
any amount for private expenses. To-day 20,000*l.*
in gold were brought by ship and paid in to my
account here. I have *carte blanche* to do everything.
To-night I have been interpreting while the Governor

dined with the Admiral. I have servants, clerks, and interpreters at my beck and call, and in short I could not be in a better position. We are very securely entrenched here, and the enemy is eighty miles off, and to-morrow the Indian troops are coming. Of course it is war time, but as I am on the staff of the Commander-in-Chief I am not likely to get into risky places. I have seen active service though, having been one of the first to land when Suez was taken. The Admiral, I am told, never forgets his officers, but pushes them on to promotion. Good-bye. . . .'

Well, the journey was done. It has been ex plained what he went out to do: it has been seen what was done, and how it was done. We have seen, moreover, what the man himself thought of his exploit. He knew that it was a great thing ; and *in a journal intended for his wife's eyes alone,* he confesses that he is proud of himself for having done it : he exults in the reception accorded him by the Admiral. As for what he did it amounts to this. *Alone and single-handed, he induced the tribes to trust his promises, to rise at his bidding; to guard the Canal ; to line it with guards, if necessary ; and, if called upon, to fight Arabi's Nile Bedawin with fifty thousand men.*

As regards the Canal, Arabi did not destroy it when he had the chance, perhaps because he wished to stand well with the French : by the 1st of August, as it seems to those who only have the telegrams of the newspapers to go by, his chance was practically gone, because our gunboats were going up and down.

The story told by the journal is quite clear and distinct : no doubts can be thrown upon its absolute truth. It is supplemented by two or three private letters addressed to those who knew the secret of his mission. They all tell exactly the same story. From one of them I extract the following passage. The letter is written from the Wady Mughárah Desert of the Tih, and is dated July 22, 1882.

'This is not nice—thermometer at about 110 in shade here, in the mountains and in the plains, over which I rode for eight hours a day for seven days running, it is, I should think, about twice that, judging from my sensation. Then, again Arabs are such a nuisance ; for instance, this morning some of the Aiyaidi made a little gentle raid on us and appropriated some camels. They considerately avoided waking me from my forenoon siesta, as they did not come so far up the valley, but the Sheikh and most of the men have gone off on the war track thirsting for blood, and I and my man Bokhor and two or three ageds and youngs will have to do any fighting that may be necessary till they come back. This country is not exactly what you would call in a truthful spirit safe just now. I have had to dodge troops and Arabs and Lord knows what, and am thankful but somewhat surprised at the possession of a whole skin.   The pleasing part of my present journey has yet to come, I have somehow to dodge the Egyptian sentries.   I may know when I get letters to-morrow, by a Bedawi whom I have sent on, how it is to be done, but at present I don't unless I rush them with a couple of hundred men.   You see if the Egyptians get hold of me there will be but short shrift for me, as I shall undoubtedly be shot.

'This business has its anxieties, but I feel quite calm about it, only it is necessary to keep one's head clear, as you may imagine.   Many thanks for the revolver; it is a charming little weapon, but as the Admiral gave me one of the new pattern navy revolvers, which puts a bullet in a six-inch board at 200 yards and is self-extracting, I have armed my man with yours, but it is a most useful addition to my small arsenal.   I could get no one to come with me at first, people said it was dangerous, but at last I managed to engage a Jew, none of your old clothes-man lot, but a sturdy native who cheerfully eats my bacon.

'He speaks a little Italian too, so that I can express my opinion without my Arab friends understanding.

'I have thus far succeeded in my preliminary run through the desert beyond my wildest hopes, but it was often risky opening the game.   For instance, when I made certain propositions to the big boss of

these parts, he replied sententiously, "Ahmed Pasha
Arabi is with the Muslims—you belong to our
enemies," and would not for some time vouchsafe
another word. They tried to bustle me one day—
about forty Arabs rode up to me while I was halting
at midday, brought their camels to a standstill on their
knees with one simultaneous motion, and then jumped
off and ran to me. But I spotted my friend the Sheikh
whom I had seen before, and simply addressed him
by name and asked him to sit down and smoke a
cigarette, which he did. It was a pretty "blow of eye,"
but I don't think I even let them see that it interested
me. What a game it all is. How I long for the cool
smoking-room at the Savile, and the cooler drinks.
I dread the three or four days' march to Suez, as it
gets hotter the further south we go. Hoorah! my
Sheikh's party is twice as strong as the Aiyaides;
if they catch them, as they expect this evening, there
will be some murder done.

14*th Ramadhan (somewhere about the end of
July).*—I regret to say my marauders got clear off,
and the Tiyahah and Terebin are raging in a manner
that does one good to see. I wish to remark that about
the fifth consecutive hour (noon) of the fifth consecutive day's camel ride with a strong hot wind blowing
the sand in your face, camel-riding loses, as an amusement, the freshness of one's childhood's experience at
the Zoo. The necessity of allowing one's tea to settle
and sipping the comparatively clear residue of theine

and ammonia is the only excitement of a day when one meets no suspicious characters. I am now two days from Suez, and before the third sun sets shall be either within reach of beer and baths or be able to dispense altogether with those luxuries for the future. The very equally balanced probabilities lend a certain zest to the journey. However, I shall make my documents into a parcel, and give them to a Bedawi to take care of.

'My man stole some melons from a patch near some water (if I may use the expression), and I feel better for the crime. Still I am dried up and burnt and thirsty and bored.

'*August* 1.—Just got into Suez safe, twenty-four hours' consecutive travelling and have had only a piece of bread for fifteen hours, no sleep. Mail just going out. Au revoir.

'Ever yours,
'E. H. P.'

In addition to this letter I myself received one written at the same time, and conveying exactly the same information in almost the same words. I put the letter aside in a safe place, where I should be sure to find it again when I wanted it. And I have not been able to find it since, though I have searched everywhere. The journal, the knowledge which we had of his instructions before he went, this and two or three other private letters constitute the proofs, if any are wanting, of the expedition itself, its audacity, and its success.

There is also one other document. Palmer drew up an official report of the journey for the Admiral. That report has not yet been published. When it is, if it be published without omission or alteration, it will be found exactly to substantiate the foregoing narrative. I have also received an extract from Gill's journal[1] which entirely bears out, so far as it goes, the statements made on the authority of Palmer's.

It seems incredible that a frame so slight and fragile could bear the fatigues of such a journey. But the same indomitable spirit which had made him the foremost of Arabic scholars sustained him and carried him through. I know not what honours, if any, would have been bestowed upon him had he survived. What he got after death was a hesitating and vaguely-worded recognition of services in the House of Commons, and a statement by Mr. Gladstone that his conduct had been 'gallant and patriotic.' But the Prime Minister did not think the time had yet come for an explanation of this conduct, and a statement of the immense services rendered by this simple scholar and man of peace.

We have looked in vain among all the despatches

---

[1] I wrote this before seeing the report. I have since been allowed to see it (see p. 297), and am happy to say that it entirely bears out the statements I have advanced on the authority of the letter and the journals.

and accounts of the war for any allusion to this exploit : it has not been thought fit to tell the country how, at the bidding of one man, many thousand wild Arabs laid down their arms : there has not been any formal acknowledgment and official account of that ride across the great and terrible Desert in the burning heat of a Syrian summer, among a people wild with excitement and ready for a fanatical outburst. Is it, then, so common a thing for a peaceful scholar to leave his books and papers, his wife and his children, and, at a moment's notice, to go forth on such an errand ? Is it so common a thing even for a soldier to volunteer on such a mission, with certain death, unless avoided by extraordinary precaution, at either end ; and in the midst death only too probable unless avoided by the most wonderful dexterity, courage, coolness, and discretion ?

It has thus been left to Palmer's private and personal friends to tell this tale : they have, providentially, been enabled to tell it in the very words of the man who performed the feat. The story stands in the simple and familiar language of the letters written to a young wife loved with a tenderness and passion which break out irrepressibly in every other line. To publish these letters, even with the messages of love and the words of endearment left out, seems a desecration. Yet these letters are the only record, and they must be published.

It is idle to ask what would have happened if

Palmer had not taken that journey.   It is, however, pretty clear that we should have had to deal with a vast horde of fanatics.   What they would have accomplished one does not know.   Perhaps the destruction of the Canal : perhaps only the lining of its banks with hostile natives firing into every ship : perhaps the addition of an immense army, formidable by their numbers though badly equipped, to the ranks of Arabi : perhaps only a crowd hovering about and harassing the English troops.   We found, *after Palmer made the tribes quiet* and there was no enemy on the banks of the Canal, that we could guard it by a patrol service of gunboats : we found, *after Palmer had removed all chance of an attack in the rear*, that the operations which led to Tel-el-Kebir were possible.   What if he had not gone through the Desert first ?

However this may be, the audacity of the exploit remains.   And I think and believe that the ride of Abdullah Effendi will never be forgotten—never— even when future generations of Englishmen shall have fought greater wars and rejoiced for greater victories than their triumph over a rebel Fellah.

APPENDIX TO CHAPTER X.

AMONG the papers found by Colonel Warren lying about the Wady Sudr and sent home, were some torn scraps and shreds with writing on them, belonging to Palmer. The Rev. Dr. William Wright, of the Bible Society, has made a careful examination of these, and has furnished me with a description and translation. They are as follows :—

1. An account of money expended in stores, written in English.
2. The same in Arabic.
3. A list of names.
4. An envelope addressed to Abdullah Effendi.
5. Four envelopes addressed to the Governor of Ismailia, and to several Sheikhs of tribes, viz., the Tahawi, the Nassiat, and the Kabile Henain tribes.
6. A sheet of note paper from the ' Euryalus,' with these names in Arabic and English, viz., 'The way of Wady Remliah,' the 'Way Atrabîn,' and the 'Way of the Hajj.'
7. A very important note-book, full of little scraps of writing made in the first journey :—

> Pages 1 and 2.—Telegram, and the names, in Arabic, of El Haj Zaid, El Bkhairi in Ismailia, and Shakir Effendi el Bhari.
> On page 5.—In Arabic, ' daughter of a dog.'
> Page 6.—Name in Arabic, Ali Bash Sherif.
> Page 8.—Arabic names for some of the articles bought at Jaffa.

Up to p. 8 the notes contain merely rough entries day by day, thus :—10th. Buying goods in Jaffa. 11th. Telegram from Jussuf Amzalek—getting ready to start to-morrow. Engaged Bokhor for servant at 5*l.* a month. 12th. Getting ready for start.

On page 11.—There is the Arabic name *Makhshit*,
with a rude scrap of a map, and the words in
English characters 'Yel of Feli.' This tells us
nothing, except that he evidently wished to note
some spot observed on his journey. On a loose
page there is a note of expenses after leaving
Magharah, and a note in English, written evidently
at Suez, about borrowing a donkey.

On page 12.—There is written in Arabic, but erased
with pencil, 'Fendi, I have only with me little,
but with the Government there is much, and
what I say now it is from myself, and I only am
a man commanded, and not rich.'

On page 13.—In Arabic—'What do you think of
returning with me, O Sheikh Foul?' Also in
Arabic—'Ten pounds, but do not tell to any
besides me, and what comes after me has no
point (edge) from the Government.'

On page 14.—The following also in Arabic :—'Greed
of the Arabs for money.' 'It is necessary that
one be with you. It is my desire to go, and
weighing a little while return quickly. Please
God I will not part from you now.'

On page 15.—Also in Arabic, but fragmentary :—'It
is known to you how many piastres wheat we
weighed for our boys.' 'Do not fear me nor . . . .
- the grace of God.'

On page 16.—He hopes that someone will come
with him, and on the way he will make known to
him the affair, and he is to tell it to Muslih.

On page 17.—In English: 'To Gaza 110 francs.' In
Arabic: 'Thalib, son of Atâyat,' and in English:
'A great and rich Sheikh of Tyaha, but friend of
Blunti.'

On page 18.—In Arabic: 'Please God the thing

sought by you shall only be with Musleh.' 'If I spoke to Musleh no doubt he will speak to his brother also what is in him of unpleasant words.'

On the next page are the words in English : 'Found them very grasping and covetous as before, but as I could not leave any in bad humour, or play one off against another, as I did when merely exploring, I had to give so many presents in token of the right of my proposals, and pay so extravagantly for escorts, that it has nearly exhausted the funds placed at my disposal.' The funds he had at his disposal consisted only of the 400*l.* or so with which he started. He brought more than 200*l.* of this amount out of the Desert, so that the backsheesh, &c., was for the most part in promises.

Lastly, there are a few notes about backsheesh promised or paid, and the names ' Suliman Ablajy,' ' Bani Aby,' and ' El Khalis.'

8. The names of certain Sheikhs imprisoned in Jerusalem.

9. Three telegrams, and two Egyptian proclamations stating that the bearer goes to their place and must be received with honour.

10. A letter from some man (apparently an interpreter of some kind), giving an account of the massacre of the 11th, and stating that there were more Arabs killed than Europeans. This letter, and another with it, do not seem to be connected with Palmer in any way.

CHAPTER XI.

THE DEATH OF THE SHEIKH ABDULLAH.

WE have seen from the Journal how the last days
were spent. After his safe arrival at Suez Palmer
reported himself to the Admiral, and prepared a
Report on the results of the journey. In this document he states that he has obtained from the most
influential men in the country promises of adhesion.
The Report, as might be expected, contains a great
deal more information than that contained in the
journal already quoted. The Bedouin, whom he
found in a very unsettled and turbulent condition,
had already been disturbed by agents from Arabi
endeavouring to stir up a war of religion. The
Sheikhs had also been summoned to Cairo. As
yet, however, the only tribes who had obeyed the
summons were those under the protection of the
Shedides of Cairo. He enumerates the various tribes
of the Desert, and gives an estimate of their number;
he states that he can engage, if necessary, 50,000
men to protect the Canal, furnish camels, &c., and

proposes a plan of action. The Report is a confidential State document, and must not be quoted at length. One may, however, state that it is a perfectly clear and calm account of the results of the journey. The writer has certainly not been carried away by his imagination or by any enthusiasms. He speaks gravely, pointing out the dangers of the situation and suggesting the best means of averting them. He states his opinion, as given in the private journal already quoted, that an expenditure of 20,000*l.* to 25,000*l.* would secure the services of 50,000 men, and he gives his reasons for that opinion. This sum, it must be again insisted, was not to be spent in bribing, but in fair payment for services rendered in patrol of the Canal, camel-driving, and so forth. There is not one word about bribing, unless we call the few hundreds given or promised to the sheikhs for backshish, bribing. Without backshish, of course, nothing whatever can be done in the East. One part of the plan proposed was that afterwards resolved upon, viz. to call a meeting of sheikhs to be attended by himself armed with authority to engage the tribes. Palmer also suggested that a company of 300 or 400 Bedawin should go with him 'for the sake of effect.' It is deeply to be deplored that this suggestion was not acted upon for the sake of caution. He concludes by saying that the Arabs will keep quiet till they hear from him, and that he is ready to go back to the Desert at a day's notice.

Meantime he was appointed Interpreter-in-Chief to Her Majesty's forces in Egypt, and placed on the Admiral's staff. No arrangement as to pay was made, but it was proposed that he should himself suggest the rate of pay. With characteristic carelessness about money matters he neglected to suggest anything ; and when the Admiral kindly told him to draw on account if he wished, Palmer thanked him and put it off—a putting off which led to a good deal of trouble afterwards. During the few days which he spent in the capacity of Interpreter-in-Chief he was terribly hard worked, as one supposes were most of the staff; one day he had to walk twelve miles after dinner ; during three days he only went to bed once ; he accompanied the expedition which took Suez with five hundred men and three guns, and he had a staff of forty interpreters under his orders. An important part of his duty as interpreter was to re-assure the people and to make them bring in camels. His doings from August the 2nd to the 8th —that is to say, between his arrival at Suez and his departure on the second expedition—are thus told by Colonel Warren :—

On 2nd of August Suez was occupied by the British forces, and Professor Palmer was occupied in assisting to reassure the inhabitants. He received instructions to buy camels, and gave a camel-contractor of Suez, named Sheihk Salameh, the sum of £40, and sent him to look for camels. This man left Suez on the 2nd or 3rd of August, was taken prisoner by Raschid Pasha of the rebel forces at Chalouf next day, and was only liberated from prison after the occupation of Cairo ; he is known to have given information to the rebels concerning the English at the time of the occupation of Suez, and it is probable that he went to Chalouf for the purpose of giving information concerning Professor Palmer's enterprise, and was imprisoned merely on account of the money in his possession, which was taken from him.

In an official report of 25th September this man is confounded with both Meter abu Sofieh and Sheikh Suleiman of the Teyahah, and this mistake led to the supposition at first that Meter abu Sofieh had not betrayed the party.

On 3rd August, Professor Palmer appears to have visited Moses Wells for the purpose of obtaining the assistance of Ode Ismaileh in buying camels, but found him not disposed to assist ; and on the 4th August he sent a letter to Meter abu Sofieh, requesting him to come to meet him at Moses' Wells with twenty armed men, to escort him to Nakhl. This letter was taken to Tusset Sudr, where Meter was encamped, by Sualem N'Mair, a Lehewat. This man states that he was not given any verbal message, and, as Meter was unable to read, it is not clear why a letter should have been sent to him instead of a message. Meter received the letter on the 6th August, and started for Suez the same evening.

On 4th August, Professor Palmer went to Moses' Wells, and requested Mr. Zahr to buy camels for him ; he also sent another message to Ode Ismaileh, who again refused to assist. He states that he was afraid to go, not on account of the Bedouins on the eastern side, but for fear that some Egyptian Bedouins might cross the Canal and attack the party. He also states that he sent a message to Professor Palmer, intimating that it was not the proper time for entering the Desert, and that he advised Umduckhl not to go. It seems very doubtful whether he acted in any way for the interests of Professor Palmer, and there is a general impression among the Bedouins that he is in some measure responsible for the disaster.

On 5th August some Jebeliyeh Bedouins brought down eleven camels to Mr. Zahr, who sent his son into Suez to Professor Palmer for the money. Mr. Zahr's son brought out the money, and paid £181 10s. for ten camels ; another camel was bought, but Professor Palmer made Mr. Zahr take it back, on account of the high price. There appears to be some reticence about the eleventh camel, the reason for which has not yet been found out.

A reference to the Blue-book supplements this information on August 1. Sir William Hewett telegraphs to the Admiralty :—

Mr. Palmer has arrived from Gaza. All well. Reports Jehad being preached at Gaza. Saw Turkish soldiers there. Bedouins loyal. Camels procurable in quantities, but no place to bring them to until Suez is occupied.

On August 4, Sir William Hewett telegraphs :—

Professor Palmer confident that in four days he will have 500 camels, and within ten or fifteen days 5,000 more.

He waits return of messenger sent for 500, so he cannot start for Desert before Monday.

On August 5, a telegram is sent to Jerusalem with a special message for the Sheikh Misleh to meet Abdullah at Nakhl.

On August 6, Sir Beauchamp Seymour telegraphs as follows to the Admiralty :—

Palmer, in letter of August 1 at Suez, writes that if precisely instructed as to services required of Bedouin, and furnished with funds, he believes he could buy the allegiance of 50,000 at a cost of from 20,000*l.* to 30,000*l.*

Palmer with Hewett still. Gill there also. Will Admiralty communicate with Palmer direct ?

On the same day he telegraphs that Gill has gone to Suez to make arrangements with Palmer, and that 'authority has been given to Hoskins to expend for this service.'

The orders of the Admiralty are also sent on to Sir William Hewett on the same day.

Admiral reports Palmer's proposal of August 1. Instruct Palmer to keep Bedouins available for patrol or transport on Canal. A reasonable amount may be spent, but larger engagements are not to be entered into until General arrives and has been consulted.

On the morning of August 6 Gill arrived. He brought with him—as is stated in his own, as well as Palmer's journals and letters—a general authority from the Admiral for Palmer to carry out his plans at the cost, if necessary, of 20,000*l.* ; this, as is clear from the Blue-book, was only an approval on the part of the Admiral, subject to confirmation by the First Lord, whose reply I have quoted above. The sum of 20,000*l.* was also brought down by a naval officer on the gunboat by which Gill went through the Canal, and was paid to Sir William Hewett. It is certain that Gill considered this sum as an advance to Palmer. We may assume that if the Admiralty had sanctioned the expenditure, the money would

have been used for that purpose; and it is evident
that Palmer considered the money as paid 'to his
account'—that is, placed by Sir William Hewett in
the hands of his paymaster for him to draw.   The
telegram from the Admiralty would, however, set
that matter right.   It was arranged on the same day
—viz. August 6—that Palmer should take a naval
officer with him on his next journey to meet Misleh
and the sheikhs.   Seven officers volunteered for this
service.   Palmer asked that Flag-Lieutenant Charrington should go with him.   It was further decided that
Captain Gill, with a dragoman, should accompany
them for part of the way, and that he should then
strike northward in order to cut the telegraph wire.

In accordance, then, with Lord Northbrook's
telegram, Palmer was instructed to expend no more
at first than 3,000*l.*   From two letters which are
among his papers, it is proved that he was going to
negotiate for the purchase of 750 camels for the
Indian Contingent, and that the price of a camel was
about 12*l.*, though he paid more for some, according
to Warren's narrative.

Let us again point out, because so much has been
said on this point, that it is absurd to suppose that
he was going to bribe the sheikhs with the money.
He had shown the sheikhs already that it would be
for the interest of the tribes to work for the English;
and he had paved the way, after the Oriental fashion,
with backshish of comparatively insignificant amount:

that is to say, the largest sum promised to one man was 500*l.* Certainly this is a very large sum to an Arab sheikh ; but most likely sums of ten or twenty pounds each had been promised to most of the sheikhs. The purpose of the second expedition, then, was to engage them to patrol the Canal, and to bring in plenty of camels ; Palmer was going to pay his promised backshish, to give swords to the sheikhs— he had got a dozen regulation naval swords from the 'Euryalus' for the purpose—he was going to pay something on account for camels and pay of men ; and he intended, in the presence of an English naval officer, who carried his uniform with him for the occa- sion—*but did not wear it* on the journey as was at first stated—to address the sheikhs on the greatness and power of England.

A great deal of fuss has been quite unnecessarily made about the 20,000*l.* mentioned in the two jour- nals. It really seems to require no other explanation than that offered above. Gill recommended that Palmer's report should be acted on : he went down to Suez to tell him that the Admiral had approved of it : he thought the 20,000*l.* brought on board the boat intended for him : but the First Lord, though he approved in general terms, limited the preliminary expenditure : Sir William Hewett gave Palmer the sum of 3,000*l.* out of the 20,000*l.* to begin with. These are facts which can be proved, and which perfectly explain the whole matter.

There is, however, a note book or account book of Palmer's in which there is an entry of certain other sums of money. The Rev. Dr. William Wright has kindly translated these entries. There are only three pages on which entries are made at all, and we have to do with one page only, on which there are the following. The handwriting is not Palmer's.

(1.) Received from the part of the Government to use by the hand of Mr. Abdullah . . . 20,000 francs.

(2.) By the hand of His Excellency the General from the hand of Mr. Abdullah . . . 18,000 francs.

(3.) By the hand of Sheikh Fahîr El Yadoub, francs ten.

(4.) By the hand of El Farey, francs sixty.

On the opposite page the first entry is 'for buying camels.'

It has been questioned whether the payment of this money is consistent with the statement that all the money received by Palmer was the 3,000*l.* for the second journey. There need be no difficulty in the matter at all. Palmer was buying camels in large numbers. The 800*l.* and the 720*l.* of the account book would together buy at the lowest estimate of 12*l.* per each camel only 128 camels. If the money was not expended in this way, it may possibly refer to the transfer of the money found in possession of the Governor of Suez, of which he speaks in his Journal.

I am allowed to insert in this place the following passage from Gill's Journal :—

August the 6th.—Saw Palmer. He has travelled much in the Sinaitic Peninsula, and knows all the Arab sheikhs. He has just come from among them, and is hopeful of bringing about 50,000 Arabs over to us for 25,000*l.* Had a long talk with him, and determined to go and cut the wire myself. . . . Palmer has arranged for a great meeting of sheikhs in a few days, and if he were to go north to cut the wire he would miss this meeting, which might do incalculable injury. There is no one here to send except military and naval officers who have never travelled among this sort of people, and for every reason it is best for me to go. . . . I brought Palmer authority to spend 20,000*l.* among the Bedawin. . . . Of course, I had to set to work to buy an outfit—Arab clothes, pillows, cooking pots, detonators, axes, &c., and am now ready to destroy one of the greatest works of civilisation—a telegraph line.

It has been asked why a naval officer went with them at all. In the first place, one may be pretty certain that unless some useful end was in view Palmer would not have encumbered the party with companions who could not speak Arabic. Nor was Gill at all the man to add unnecessary danger to the expedition.[1] The presence of an officer, I take it, was to be a guarantee that Palmer now returned to the Desert in an official position, and with authority to make

---

[1] I have felt that to speak concerning the high character and reputation of this officer, or of his unfortunate companion Lieutenant Charrington, would be an impertinence on the part of one who did not know either personally. It may be permitted, however, to say that Gill's loss was as great to the army as Palmer's was to Oriental scholarship. A short memoir of his life and work, written by his friend Colonel Yule, will be published before long, with a condensed account of his travels.

arrangements. There was no reason why he should not have been accompanied by a dozen officers ; the special danger arising from the presence of the Egyptian garrison of Suez was gone ; the sheikhs of the interior had met and sworn solemn brotherhood and friendship. No one can doubt that, but for one or two tribes, reported by himself to be still hostile—the Haiwatat, for instance, under the control of the Shedides of Cairo—the Desert was nearly as safe for him and his party as it is for any ordinary travellers going across under the conduct of a sheikh : that is to say, not exactly so safe as Hyde Park in the afternoon. Let us remember, however, that travellers, two or three together—English, Americans, Germans, French, Russians—cross the desert backwards and forwards every year, relying not on the revolvers they carry, but on the safe-conduct of the sheikhs. That confidence is not often misplaced. It may be urged that this was a time of war. It was ; but there was no war in the Desert, as is proved by the fact already quoted (Blue-book, p. 23), that the tribes refused obedience to orders that they should send men to assist Arabi. It may also be pointed out that Palmer himself in his Report bears witness to the turbulence and the hostile attitude of the tribes ; but he had quieted those of the interior, and his only or his chief danger lay among those of the western edge. It must not be said that Palmer showed want of caution in going : it should rather be said that he went—and the officers with him went—knowing the danger and hoping to escape, as he had escaped before, by the aid of Meter abu Sofieh, whom he trusted, and who betrayed him.

We will consider presently the probable motive, cause, and instigation of the crime which followed. Let us first tell the dreadful story itself, from Colonel Warren's 'narrative,' dated February 21, and compiled by him from the evidence of the men whom he caught and examined. Colonel Warren says :—

It is stated in evidence (Hassan Ateyeh) that on this day the Hawetats sent a message to Cairo to inform Sualem Hassan Farag that there were plenty of Christians at Moses' Wells to plunder, and a party of English with money just going to start into the Desert.

Some say that Sualem Hassan Farag came down himself to Marbook ; others that he sent Mosellam Suleiman, a Hawetat. This man Mosellam is the spy that visited Professor Palmer subsequently on the 9th August.

On the 6th August the Admiral sent from Suez a special message to the Consul at Jerusalem : 'Send trusty horseman at once to Gaza, and let him deliver the following message to Misleh, who is in the neighbourhood expecting the communication—"Kawadja Abdullah wishes Sheikh Misleh Ameer of Teyahah to ride a swift camel and meet him on the 12th at Nakhl."' As will be subsequently related, it was Sheikh Suleiman who went to Nakhl in lieu of Misleh.

On the afternoon of the 7th August, Meter abu Sofieh, with his nephew Salameh ibn Ayed and the messenger Sualem N'Mair, arrived at Moses' Wells and asked Mr. Zahr to read to him the letter he had received from Professor Palmer. Mr. Zahr states that it contained a request from Professor Palmer that Meter should bring down one

hundred camels and twenty armed men ; it was signed
' Abdullah.'   Mr. Zahr sent his son with Meter into Suez by
water ; they called on Professor Palmer, and in the evening
Meter was presented to Admiral Sir William Hewett and
Mr. Consul West in the drawing-room of the Suez Hotel,
and received a naval officer's sword as a souvenir of his visit.
Mr. Zahr's son (Farag) states that Meter gave him the sword
that night to keep for him, and has since produced the
sword and handed it over to the Consul.   Meter, on the
other hand, when under examination asserted positively that
he never gave up the sword, that he kept it with him all
night when at Mr. Zahr's house, and took it into the desert;
that it was put up with the other swords, and was stolen by
the Bedouins when the baggage was plundered in Wady Sudr.
Considerable stress has been laid on this transaction, as it
appears to indicate Meter's foreknowledge of the possibility
of an attack upon the party ; and if the evidence of Mr.
Zahr's son is correct, it seems certain that Meter was, to say
the least, fully aware that there was great danger to the
party in their expedition.   He states that Meter came to
him at night and asked him to keep the sword, saying he
was afraid, because he had with him some English gentlemen, and the Bedouins were not quiet at that time, and
might kill him if they saw him with a sword.

Meter states that Professor Palmer informed him that
he had sent a message to Sheikh Suleiman ibn Amar,
brother of Misleh of the Teyahah, asking him to meet him
at Nakhl, and requesting him to escort him as far as Nakhl.
Meter replied that he had brought no camels with him for
the purpose.   Professor Palmer replied that he had ten
camels, and could get camels and camel-drivers for 5 fr. a
day, and requested Meter to take him by Wady Sudr to
Meter's camp, so as to get Meter's camels, and send back
those he had bought or hired for use of the troops.   Meter
further states that he said the country was quite quiet, and

that he had camels at his camp. He also frequently reiterated his assertion that the country became disturbed after he came to Suez, and that he was not aware of what was going on.

It appears from the evidence of Salem es Sheikh and Hassan Ateiyah el Kadaf (the thief) that on this or the following day a Hawetat named Nâfil took a message from the Shedides at Chalouf to the Bedouin at Marbook, ordering them to stop the Christians going into the country at the risk of their throats. This message did not arrive at Dukilallah's camp until the 10th August.

On the 8th August all necessary preparations were made for Professor Palmer's expedition, but no formal agreement was made with Meter abu Sofieh before the Consul as to escorting the party into the Desert.

Professor Palmer received from the 'Euryalus' during the afternoon a bag about eighteen inches long, containing three bags of 1,000l. each in English sovereigns. This sum appears to have been taken into the desert intact, all Professor Palmer's expenses in Suez, amounting to 467l., having been paid for by the Admiralty separately. The party embarked in a boat from Suez, and arrived on the beach near Moses Wells after sunset ; here they put up in one of the tents of Mr. Zahr. The party consisted of Professor E. H. Palmer, Captain W. Gill, R.E., and his dragoman Khalil Atek (Syrian Christian), Lieutenant Harold Charrington, R.N., and a Jew called Bokhor, who had been engaged at Jaffa by Professor Palmer as cook, Meter abu Sofieh, and Salameh ibn Ayed, his nephew. The Lehewat, Sualem N'Mair, also joined them here. During the evening messengers were sent up to Moses' Wells (about two miles distant), and four camels and seven camel-drivers were engaged at 5 fr. a day, to go as far as Meter's tents, for six days—three days there and three days back. Six of these cameleers were of the Aligât tribe, and one of the M'Saineh tribe, branches of the Towarah. If Ode Ismaileh had wished to warn the party of impending danger he ought at this time to have come forward ; but he did nothing. It is not certain who hired the camels and drivers, but 'it is probable that both Mr. Zahr and Meter made the engagement. Several of the men engaged were employed in Mr. Zahr's garden as guards at the time. The party rose before the sun on the 9th August, and the camels were brought down to them from Mr. Zahr's garden. The names of the cameleers were as follows.

Aligât.— Umduckhl Umduckhl, Sheikh of half the tribe, possessed one camel ; Silmeh abu Niefeh possessed one camel ; Hamdam Jemar Chowishe possessed one camel.

M'Saineh.—Salameh ibn Omar abu Farag possessed one camel.

Aligât.—Saad Mosellam, Owad Salameh, Salam Salameh, had charge of Professor Palmer's ten camels.

While the party were loading their camels it is related by Umduckhl that an important conversation took place between Salim ibn Subheh and Meter abu Sofieh ; but other witnesses state that this conversation took place on the evening of the same day at Wady Cahalin. Salim ibn Subheh asked Meter why he was taking Christians into the Desert at so disturbed a time, and hinted that they might be attacked. Meter only made light of the matter, but Umduckhl got frightened, and told Meter that he would not go with the party ; he was then brought before Professor Palmer, who stated that he had come down from Syria with Meter, who was better able to judge of such a matter than Umduckhl, and then added that Umduckhl need only go as far as Meter's tents, and persuaded him to go on.

It appears that Ibn Subheh merely made these remarks for the purpose of ascertaining from Meter an account of where the party was going to.

The party started soon after sunrise, and consisted of

three Englishmen, dragoman, and cook, three Lehewats, and seven camel-drivers—six of the Aligât and one of the M'Saineh tribe; there were sixteen camels—two of Meter abu Sofieh and his nephew, ten of Professor Palmer, and four of the cameleers. They went direct over the Desert towards Wady Cahalin; but Meter left them, and rode round to Moses' Wells to engage another camel-driver. Here he met Ode Ismaileh, and an altercation is said to have ensued between them; but little information on this point could be obtained. Ode Ismaileh states: 'I saw Meter abu Sofieh come to Costa's garden after the party had started; I saw him hiring a man, and did not like it, but did not wish to interfere. I heard Gobran Costa ask him, "What are you doing here?" and he answered, "I come to take Professor Palmer to Nakhl."' It seems that Ode Ismaileh was angry at this time, because Meter was acting as guide in his country; but it is doubtful whether he took any active steps to injure the party. Meter engaged as cameleer an Aligât named Salim Hamad. The whole party halted for lunch at noon at Wady Lahasie, about ten miles from Moses' Wells, but some of them did not eat, it being Ramadan. While they were resting here two Hawetat Bedouins, mounted on camels, came up and joined them, named Salim ibn Subheh and Mosellam abu Aiyeneh abu Nar. They had some private conversation with Meter, and the Abu Nar received from him some gold pieces. Meter states that he gave him two sovereigns to make purchases in Syria. It is probable that Mosellam was one of the spies sent out to see which way the party was going, in order that notice might be given at Dukilallah's camp. He left after lunch in the direction of Marbook. Salim ibn Subheh joined the party, and went on with them to their camp in Wady Cahalin, where they pitched their camp at sunset, at a distance of about eighteen miles from Moses' Wells.

Later on in the evening three Bedouins arrived at the

camp on foot, named Musleh Oweideh, a Hawetat; Salim Silman, an Aligât; and Said M'Said Genouneh.   These men had started that morning from Moses' Wells, and had been passed on the road by Ibn Subheh on his camel.   Musleh ran after him, and conversed with him for some time, and then joined the others and stated that Salim ibn Subheh had told him that he was going to catch up Meter to get some money from him.   It is surmised that at this point Salim ibn Subheh suggested to Musleh that he and his . companions should join Professor Palmer's camp, in order that they might be ready in case they were required to assist him in arranging for the attack upon the party.

At the time that the party started from the seashore there was at Moses' Wells a low-class Terebin called Ali Showeiyer.   This man was also acting as spy upon the party, and states that Salim ibn Subheh came in the morning after the party had left and said that he had had a quarrel with Meter abu Sofieh about money, and that they must stop him coming into the country.   It appears that Ali Showeiyer first went to the tents of Dukilallah and called for men to attack the party, but the old sheikh threw sand on his people and forbade them to go, saying that the affair would come to no good.

Ali Showeiyer met the camel of Suleiman Amar Abouse, a blind man, and rode on it to Ain abu Jerad, at the mouth of Wady Sudr, and stopped there that night (9th August) in company with Salem es Sheikh and another Bedouin.

It has not yet been ascertained how Salem es Sheikh discovered where the party was going to, but it is probable that he had made his arrangements with Ibn Subheh early in the morning.

During the evening of August 9 there appears to have been a good deal of conversation between Salem ibn Subheh and Musleh Oweideh at a distance from the others, and it is probable that at this time he persuaded Musleh to delay the party by stealing two of the camels during the night. It is also apparent from the evidence that Meter and Ibn Subheh had much conversation together of a nature similar (according to Salim Silman) to what Umduckhl states took place on the seashore. Salim Silman would make it appear that Musleh was the chief culprit in stealing the camels. He states that he was woke up in the night by Musleh to continue their journey, and that about thirty yards from the camp they saw two of Professor Palmer's camels standing, which Musleh proposed they should steal; to this Salim Silman agreed, and accordingly in company with Said M'Said they went off with the camels at a quick pace to the south towards Gharundel. It is to be remarked that the stealing of these two camels was a most necessary arrangement for the execution of Salem ibn Subheh's project, as otherwise the Bedawin of Wady Sudr could not have come down in time to attack the party.

On the morning of August 10 it was discovered that the three guests had disappeared and two camels were missing. Professor Palmer surmised at once that they had been stolen, and sent some men in search. They are said to have consisted of Salameh ibn Ayed, Umduckhl, and Owad Salameh, but there has been some reticence on this subject. At first the witnesses one and all declared that the camels had strayed, and had been found browsing by themselves. Possibly they said so to screen Salim Silman, one of their tribe, or else, perhaps, to cover their own negligence. It has been frequently suggested by Moslems that these Aligât cameleers were in the conspiracy, but there cannot be a doubt that there is some prejudice against the Aligât for going in with the Christians at such a time, and it is more probable that these cameleers were merely very careless, there being nothing to gain for them by the transaction.

They found the camel-tracks to go along the road to the south, and followed them full speed about twenty miles

until they caught the fugitives up in a wady beyond Ain
Elifeh. Salameh ibn Ayed appears to have been first, and
caught Salim Silman and conversed with him; both these
men state that there were four cameleers in pursuit, and that
they sat down and drank water with Salim Suliman; but
the cameleers declare that they never saw him, and that
Salameh ibn Ayed alone met him. In any case the man
was allowed to escape and the camels were driven back to
the camp. On the way they found Said M'Said by the
water of Elifeh, and Umduckhl took his gun away from him
and beat him, although he declared that he had not assisted to
steal the camels. Musleh was not seen by those in pursuit.

On return to camp Professor Palmer noted the names
of the three men in his note-book, and remarked that he
would teach them to steal camels.

This occurrence delayed the party till about 3 P.M.,
and the camels which had been in the pursuit were too
tired to travel fast. Meter Abu Sofieh is said to have now
appeared to have become alarmed at the incident, and
proposed that the Englishmen should go with him at once
while the baggage followed more slowly. Umduckhl asked
to be allowed to go with the party, but this was objected to,
and it was decided that he should go with the baggage.

Meter abu Sofieh's line of action on this occasion is
not intelligible, except on the supposition that he was in
some manner in league with the hostile Bedouin. If he
had really hurried the party on they might have reached his
camp by midnight, and thus have escaped attack. Or if
they had stopped behind and travelled with the baggage
the Bedouin would have hesitated to attack them. Or,
again, they might have left the two camels which had been
stolen and gone on with the rest in the morning, as there
were no heavy loads. On the other hand it does not seem
that Meter contemplated the murder of the party. It seems
rather that he favoured the idea of an attack in order that

he might get away with the money while the Bedouin got the baggage, possibly thinking that Professor Palmer and his companions would be allowed to go into Suez, or not caring what became of them. On the morning of August 10 Ibn Subheh left the camp at Wady Cahalin and joined Salim es Sheikh and Ali Showeiyer at Ain abu Jerad in Wady Sudr. Here he related about the party having been delayed in consequence of the camels having been stolen, and he and Salim es Sheikh sent Ali Showeiyer by a mountain path to the camps of Hassan ibn Murched, a Terebin, and Salim abu Talhiadeh, a Debour (Hawetat). Ali Showeiyer travelled all day on foot by a mountain path until he reached the site of the Bedouin camps at Jebel Rahah, situated on a mazaireh or piece of cultivated ground. Here he arrived in the evening after sunset. It was Thursday evening, the feast of the dead, during Ramadan, and there were several guests feasting at the camp. They had finished eating and were drinking coffee when he arrived. Ali Showeiyer informed Hassan ibn Murched and Salim abu Telhiadeh of his errand, and these two called out to their comrades that the Christians were coming up the Wady with much money, and invited them to attack them. They at once collected together and, some on camels and some on foot, ran helter-skelter down the mountain side, by the pass of Madullah, until they reached a point on the Sudr road near the water of Abu Regim in Wady Sudr. Here they lighted torches, and commenced looking for camel-tracks to see if the party might have slipped by them, it being after midnight. While they were so employed, some men on the look-out distinguished the party approaching ; they hastily concealed their lights and placed themselves so as to form an ambuscade. They had been seen, however, by Meter, who was in front, and had he acted honestly he might yet have saved the party by entering into conversation with the attacking party while they got off. There appear to have been about twenty-five Bedouin engaged in the attack, and they placed themselves on either side of a path, on a spur of a small hill, so that in firing they would not shoot into each other.

It is now necessary to turn to Professor Palmer's party on the afternoon of Thursday August 10. They were all dressed in Arab costume outwardly, but their underclothing was of the usual European make. They arranged to carry with them simply what things they considered valuable and essential. These were Professor Palmer's despatch-box, with about 234*l.* 10*s.* in cash and notes, a black leather bag containing 3,000*l.*, two boxes with the stores of Captain Gill, a small kitchen tent, and two bags of clothing.

The following is the order in which they started :—

Meter abu Sofieh on one of Professor Palmer's camels with two deal boxes of Captain Gill's and the kitchen tent.

Professor Palmer and Salameh ibn Ayed on Meter abu Sofieh's dromedary with despatch-box and black bag containing 3,000*l.*

Captain Gill on Salameh ibn Ayed's dromedary with two bags of clothing.

Lieutenant Charrington on camel of Umduckhl with some clothes and food.

Khalil Atek on one of Professor Palmer's camels.

They left Wady Cahalin about 3 P.M., reached Wady Sudr about 5 P.M., and appear to have gone very leisurely, as they did not reach the place of attack (called Mahârib) till after midnight.

The baggage left Wady Cahalin about 4 P.M., and after going for two hours stopped for the night near the 'Ain abu Jerad. There were seven Aligâts (including Umduckhl), one M'Saineh, and one Lehewat, and Bokhor the cook. There were eleven camels, eight belonging to Professor Palmer and three to the camel-drivers.

No evidence has been produced to show that they spoke

to any Bedouin on the way of Wady Sudr, but there was a rumour that they were met by about a dozen men, who asked for tobacco and behaved rudely. This account, however, seems improbable. On their road during the darkness, Salameh ibn Ayed states that they passed two men sleeping (Salem es Sheikh and Salim ibn Subheh), and that when he pointed them out to Professor Palmer he proposed to shoot at them, but he was dissuaded. It seems most improbable that Professor Palmer should have wished to disturb them. No clear account has been obtained of the method of attack. It was very dark, and each Bedouin probably only thought of what he could get for himself. The Bedouin appear to have opened fire upon the party, and it was returned, but little damage was done on either side. The camel of Salameh ibu Ayed, on which Captain Gill rode, was shot in the head and disabled ; and there is a rumour that Aiyedeh, a Terebin, was shot in the foot, but this all the Bedouin deny. Meter abu Sofieh stated in his evidence that he took Professor Palmer's revolver from him and fired it, and attempted to show that he had done much to assist the party before he left them ; but all the Bedouin state that he ran away as soon as they commenced to fire. He escaped up the Wady to his camp beyond Tusset Sudr, where he arrived about sunrise.

The others are said to have knelt down behind their camels, so as to get cover while they defended themselves ; and there is a bazaar rumour that Salameh ibn Ayed, who was riding behind Professor Palmer, struck him off the camel and rode off with the money. He himself states that both Professor Palmer and Meter told him to take the camel with all the money, and ride away quickly. He states he was not told to take the money into Suez or to give any notice, but other evidence shows that he was sent into Suez.

He states that he rode quickly down the Wady and passed Salem ibn Subheh and Salem es Sheikh still asleep on the road, and that he saw nothing of the cameleers or baggage, although his tracks, which were subsequently examined, show that he passed within a few feet of them. He knew where they were going to stop, and if he had taken the trouble to warn them the life of the cook would probably have been saved, and in that case it is very possible that the lives of the others would not have been sacrificed.

Salameh ibn Ayed passed down to the mouth of the Wady and then turned off towards Marbook. He might either have gone into Suez or to Moses' Wells, to warn the Christians there that their turn would probably follow, but instead of this he went up the Hadj route on to the desert of the Tih, and on the following day hid the despatch-box and money in the ground and arrived at the camp of Meter abu Sofieh in an exhausted state. There is no certain information as to how the party were captured, but it is probable that the Bedouin, finding they were so few in number, rushed in upon them and disarmed them. They stripped them at once of all their Bedouin clothes, leaving them only their drawers and probably their under jerseys. The men who appear to have taken their clothés, &c., are Hassan ibn Murched, Salem M'Haisn, and Ayed, his son, and the Abu Telhiadehs. Professor Palmer's watch fell into the hands of Salameh Owadeh, but it is not certain how he obtained it. The method of taking any loot by the Bedouin is to hold the hand over it, as a signal that it is taken, but as it was dark it appears that articles were taken and retaken several times.

After the attack the four prisoners were taken down into a hollow among some rocks, about 200 yards from the place of attack, and then left in charge of Salameh abu Telhiadeh and Aiyedeh. The former, however, who had taken the camel of Umduckhl, soon left his charge and rode down the Wady after the rest of the Bedouin, who were in hot pursuit of Salameh ibn Ayed with the money. On their way it appears that they were joined by Salem es Sheikh and Salem Subheh, though Ali Showeiyer asserts that these two were in the attack.

On arrival near 'Ain abu Jerad they saw the cameleers loading up and rushed in among them, firing their guns and threatening them with their swords. On seeing them come up the cook gave his revolver and fowling-piece to Owad Salameh, who concealed them under his abba and succeeded in going off with them. They first asked after Meter abu Sofieh, who they supposed had run off with the money, but their attention was soon diverted to the baggage, and they gave up the pursuit of Salameh ibn Ayed. The cook attempted to get away, but Murched ibn Sard threatened him with his gun, and Ayed M'Hiasn fired at him, and he was captured by Modan, who stole 21*l.* from his girdle. The Bedouins quickly cut the cords of the baggage, broke up the various boxes, and distributed the spoil, and the revolvers and swords.

When they found there was no money with the luggage they got angry and repeatedly asked where Meter Abu Sofieh had got to ; but Umduckhl replied that, if they had seen the man escaping with the money, they also would have gone away with the baggage.

They not only took Professor Palmer's camels, but also those of the cameleers ; however, these were returned to them on the cameleers swearing to them. Three of the cameleers without camels, noticing this, came down and swore that four of Professor Palmer's camels were their property, and went off with them.

These men now state that they only took these camels to keep for Professor Palmer, but it is probable that they were not averse to keeping them for themselves, should circumstances admit of it ; however, they brought them into Suez at the end of the war, and they have been given the benefit of the doubt after trial before the Tantah Commis-

sion.   Umduckhl, whose camel had gone on with Professor
Palmer, now asked to be allowed to proceed up the Wady,
and accompanied the Bedouin for about three miles to a
spot where Ibn Murched wished to divide the spoil.

Here a carpet was spread, and some of the Bedouin
came up and handed in what they had looted ; others, however would not agree to this, and eventually it was arranged
that each should keep what he had taken.   At this spot the
despatch-box of Captain Gill was broken open and the contents strewn about, but whether it was taken from him or
found in the baggage does not seem certain.   Umduckhl
now saw Salameh abu Telhiadeh coming down the Wady
riding his camel, and, having claimed it, was told to go away ;
he gives a long story of how he tried to go up and assist the
party, but this is probably apocryphal ; it is probable that,
having obtained his camel he was satisfied to go away without further trouble.

It is to be noticed that the cameleers all assert that the
Bedouin talked of having an order to kill Christians, and
Abu Telhiadeh and Ibn Murched appear to have frequently
made remarks to that effect ; but during the enquiry they
would not acknowledge that they had received such an order,
although they were aware it might mitigate their offence.

We may remark, at this point, that it is perfectly
clear that most of the party were simply gathered together with the hope of plunder ; on the other hand,
the story which follows seems to show almost conclusively that more than money was wanted.   The
evidence as to Meter's conduct is very confused ; it
does not seem at all certain how much money he
offered ; it is not certain what the robbers knew
about the money in the bags ; it is by no means
intelligible why they should want to kill their prisoners,

on the theory that the attack was made for the purpose of robbery only, when one of them, as we shall
see directly, was continually offering them ransom,
and large ransom. On the other hand, when we
consider the indications of information about the
expedition having been sent to Cairo ; the order sent
from Cairo to arrest all Christians travelling in the
desert ;[1] the intrigues of the Governor of El Arish
among the tribes—he is reported (Blue-book, p. 28)
to have issued orders for Abdullah to be brought in
dead or alive ; the exasperation produced by the
refusal of the sheikh of the Deymat Sowaki tribe to
send any men to assist Arabi (Blue-book, p. 23) ; the
attempt to shift the blame to the innocent Towarah
Arabs ; the persistent obstruction with which the
Shedides subsequently met Warren's attempts to elicit
the truth,[2] and the fact that they let prisoners escape ;
the refusal of the Porte to allow Hussein Effendi, a
Turkish subject, to assist in getting information, with
many other indications, all seem indications that
murder, and not simple robbery, was planned and

[1] Warren says in his narrative that, 'it is nearly certain that the
order given by Nakhl to Dukilallah at Marbook, about stopping Christians
coming into the country, arrived some hours after the attack and murder
of Professor Palmer : but the Governor of Nakhl was on the spot, which
seems to prove that the attack was planned by superior authority.'

[2] 'In consequence of the constant opposition of the Shedides
throughout our work, I brought their conduct to the notice of the
Acting-Governor of Suez, and pointed out that on two occasions Hadj
Mohammed had allowed the important prisoners to escape, and that
the only inference I could form was that they were so implicated that
they were afraid to bring the prisoners in.'—Blue-book, p. 70.

ordered. As for the complicity of the Governor of
Nakhl, who happened to be on the spot at the time—
of course, by the merest accident—that, so far as the
stopping of the party was concerned, seems pretty
clear—was he acting by orders? Whether he compassed their murder is not clear. He says, himself,
that he should have taken them to Nakhl and kept
them there. Again, when Meter refused to give up
the money, why did they—knowing that his nephew
had ridden off with the whole of it—let him go and
murder the prisoners who had none? Why not
murder Meter? Why not take the money from him?
Why not go to his tents and take his camels till he
gave up the money? Meter was very rich; he could
be forced to pay. And the murder was not resolved
upon in a fit of rage or on an impulse of the moment :
it was solemnly considered, as will be presently seen,
and deliberately arranged. The theory that the party
were murdered because Meter had refused to give up
the money, may be true. Some of the men in their
evidence state as much. Meter, who may have been a
great villain, but may yet have told some of the truth,
said that he went away at last because he saw they
were resolved to kill the party. In other words, their
murder was no question of money. But that it was a
question of money is the theory held by Colonel Warren,
who has the strongest right to be heard with attention,
and who is, indeed, the only man who has got the
unwritten evidence of place, appearance of witnesses,

manner of confession, prevarications or lies afterwards
corrected, and so forth. Moreover, he had abundant
opportunities of observing the Bedouin manner of
thinking and acting. But to one who simply reads
the evidence in the Blue-book—there is more which
I have not seen—it certainly seems that the causes
of the murder may be looked for outside the Wady
Sudr. However this may be, we may acquit Meter of
conspiring to murder, while admitting his treachery
and complicity in the attack, since Colonel Warren
assures us that the evidence proves it—indeed, his
narrative seems to prove it clearly. It is pretty
certain that it will never now be clearly known whether
the murder was caused by a kind of chance and the
blind rage of these wild robbers disappointed of the
gold—which I, for one, cannot understand, looking
at the matter with English eyes and inexperienced in
Arab ways ; or, which seems to me the only way of
explaining it, by order of somebody. In any case there
can be little doubt that Meter deliberately led the
party out of their way, for the Wady Sudr is a long
way south of the direct road to Nakhl, in order that
by previous arrangement they might fall in the
Haiwatat. Palmer trusted this man, and was deceived.
Let us return to Colonel Warren's narrative.

The cameleers appear to have all gone off south except
Sard Mosellam, Hamdam Chowische, and Umduckhl, who
went towards Moses' Wells. The former travelled on foot,
and arrived near the wells early on the following morning,

when he met Umduckhl returning from the Wells, and was told by him to hurry on and give warning of the attack. Umduckhl on getting his camel went down the Wady and followed the track of Salameh ibn Ayed, who is supposed to have been Meter abu Sofieh. He saw that it turned round to the north, and followed it, thinking it might be a short cut to Moses' Wells ; but on finding, after some time, that it went towards Marbook, he crossed down into the usual road, and thus passed Sard Mosellam without seeing him. He arrived at Moses' Wells at dusk on the evening of the attack on baggage (August 11), and at once gave notice to Ode Ismaileh that the wells were likely to be attacked, having heard some words to that effect passing among the Bedouin.

To return to Meter abu Sofieh. Having escaped up the Wady he hastened to his camp, and collected his four sons and several other Bedouin, and came down again to the place of attack, ostensibly for the rescue of the party.

They came to the place where the camel had been wounded, and finding nobody there they shouted out, and were answered from the four prisoners in the hollow. Meter abu Sofieh and Haneyek went down and found the four sitting in their underclothing, free, Ayedeh having run away at the approach of Meter's party. Some valuable time appears to have been lost in useless expressions of pity, &c., on Meter's part, and in Bedouin interchanges of ceremony, so that when the four were brought up to Meter's camels the hostile party were just in sight, having arrived from the plunder of the baggage.

This was the last fatal accident which led to the murder. The party of Englishmen were at this point absolutely unguarded. There was nothing to prevent their escaping. More than this, Meter seems now to have done his very best to assist them to escape.

Perhaps his own mind was at rest about the money, which his own nephew had carried off and would perhaps keep in safety—for themselves. When, at the first attack, Palmer orders the nephew to escape with the money, Meter hurries away for help ; brings back camels and men : finds the party uninjured and un-guarded, and proceeds to bring them up to his camels. What more could the man be expected to do even if he was quite innocent ? And why should we not 'believe that he spoke the truth when he said that he offered 30*l.* for each of the party? They knew or suspected that there was a great deal more which had been carried off. And would they listen to an offer of 30*l.* for each when Palmer was offering the whole of the money—*all they had*? When Meter went away at last there seems reason to believe that he went sorrowfully because he saw that no ransom at all would be accepted, but that the murder was resolved upon ; and that he, who thought only to plunder the man who had trusted him, had compassed his death. He went away ; first he hid himself; then he gave himself up: but he was torn by remorse ; he wandered in his mind ; and presently he lay down and died.

M'Saifeh, who has given his evidence very straightfor-wardly, states that the men with him said, ' Let us protect the Englishmen,' and threatened the hostile Bedouin with their guns ; but Meter said, ' No, we must negotiate the matter,' and he allowed his men to be surrounded by a superior force. He then went through a pantomime by putting his abba on Professor Palmer, and his kefieh on one of the others, and kissing them ; but he appears to have shown by his half-hearted manner that he was not entirely anxious that his charges should be released.   Meter's evidence on the subject was most confused and unsatisfactory, he was ever oppressed with the concealment of something, and contradicted himself, and prevaricated continuously.   He asserted positively that Professor Palmer never spoke to him, except to say, ' Oh Meter, Meter ! ' and that he received no orders about a ransom.   There is, on the other hand, unanimous testimony, both from the attacking party and also from those who accompanied Meter from his camp, that Professor Palmer constantly offered all they possessed if their lives should be spared, and stated that Meter had got all the money.   It seems probable that Meter, having got the money, was not sorry that the party should be made away with.   He states that he offered 30*l.* for each of the party, but it is only certain that he offered 30 camels for the whole party, which is tantamount to no offer, as the camels were his own, and he could have recovered them after at a ' Talaba,' according to Bedouin custom.

It does not appear that Meter remained very long endeavouring to release the party, probably half an hour, and then they were left to their fate, it being understood by Meter and those who accompanied him, that the party were to be killed.

The cook had been placed with the other four on his arrival.

There is a report that at one time Hassan ibn Murched went after Meter to offer the party for some money, but was stopped by Salem es Sheikh ; and there is another account that when Hassan ibn Murched found that they could get no money, they offered the party unconditionally to Meter, but that he refused to take them.

The chief men all through the affair were Salim es

Sheikh, Salem ibn Subheh, Hassan ibn Murched, Salem abu Telheidah, and Zaiyed il Surdeh, and these men agreed together that the five must be killed, and then put it to the vote of the Bedouin, who also agreed.

Then arrangements were made how the murder was to take place, and two of the prisoners were told off to the Debour and three to the Terebin. Of the Debour the family of Abu Telheideh was to kill one, and the family of M'Hiasn another. Salem abu Telheideh told off his brother Salameh ; Salem M'Hiasn, being an old man, did not feel equal to the task of killing, and as his sons had left soon after the plunder of the baggage, he hired Merseh el Rashdeh to do it for the present of a sword.

Of the Terebin, Said el Ourdeh and Harash were told off, and subsequently Ali Showeiyer was told to kill Bokhor the cook. At first it was doubtful whether they would kill Bokhor, as he was supposed to be a Moslem. The preliminary arrangements having been made, the five prisoners were driven in front of the Bedouin over some rough ground for about a mile to the ravine of Wady Sudr. This appears to have occurred during the heat of an August day, and as none of the prisoners had on their hats, it seems likely that by the time they arrived at the place selected for the murder they were almost unconscious. The Bedouin have been unwilling to state whether they used violence in driving the prisoners down, but the probabilities are that they were subjected to very rough treatment.

Professor Palmer is reported to have repeatedly said that he would give all the money if their lives were spared, and referred to Meter, but as the latter had refused to give up anything the Bedouin would not listen.

On arrival at the Wady they were obliged to climb down some steep cliff in order to arrive at the plateau overlooking the gulley into which they were to be cast ; this being accomplished they were placed in a row facing the gully, with five Bedouin, one behind each, told off to shoot them at a given signal. They were then driven towards the edge of the gully, but, before the signal was given, Merseh el Rashdeh fired at Professor Palmer and killed him. Salem abu Telhiadeh, who was standing near, was also supposed to have fired at the same time. The fall of Professor Palmer appears to have caused the others to realise their danger, and they made a dash forward, some for the bottom of the Wady, down a cliff about sixty feet deep, and one (Khalil Atek) ran down along the edge of the gully, and was overtaken and slain by Salameh abu Telhiadeh and Salem Sheikh. The others were shot in endeavouring to get down the cliff by Teyeid el Ourdeh, Harash, and Ali Showeiyer. Several now descended to the bottom, and not only despatched those who still breathed, but appear to have thrust their swords through each of the party. Captain Gill only is said to have been alive when they got down to the bottom of the Wady.

It was reported very soon after the murder, and among the first rumours which reached Cairo—another indication that the murder was ordered—that the Sheikh Abdullah before being killed solemnly cursed his murderers. Some of his friends have been pained to think that his last moments should have been spent in cursing his enemies. It must, however, be understood that cursing in the hands of an Oriental who understands how to curse is a most powerful weapon of defence. Palmer knew every form of Arab cursing. He was driven to this, as his last resource. If he could not deter them by cursing, he could do no more. And again, to understand an Oriental curse, one must go to the Old Testament, and not to a gathering of English or American roughs. Such a curse is a solemn and an awful thing. It falls upon a man, and weighs him down and crushes him ; it brings with it a fearful foreboding of judgment ; it lies like lead upon a guilty heart ; it helps to bring the crime to light and the criminals to justice.

I make no doubt—no doubt whatever—that the denunciations of woe, ruin, desolation, and death— Palmer's last words—which fell upon the ears of those wild desert men, and were echoed back from the rocks around them, became to them a prophecy, sure and certain, as is the vengeance of the Lord.

'O my God!'—it is the voice of Asaph the singer, 'make them like a wheel, as the stubble before the wind ; fill their faces with shame ; let them be confounded and troubled for ever ; yea, let them be put to shame and perish.'

The curse has fallen upon the murderers already ; they are confounded ; they are put to shame ; they have perished.

Thus died the Sheikh Abdullah.

.   .   .   .   .   .

Eight months later we stood in the crypt where England buries her heroes, to pay the last honours to the three who fell in the Wady Sudr. While the words of our magnificent service for the dead resounded among the shadows of that ghostly place, while the voices of the choristers echoed among the tombs, there were some present who wept, and some who thanked Heaven for English hearts as true and loyal now as in the brave days of old, and some who thought of Palmer's strange destiny, and how a brave boy should win his way from obscurity to honour by indomitable courage and persistence, and how the mortal remains of a quiet scholar and man of books should find a place beside the bones of Wellington and Nelson.

APPENDIX I.

PALMER'S WORK AS AN ORIENTAL SCHOLAR.

By G. F. NICHOLL, M.A.

Lord Almoner's Professor and Reader of Arabic in the University of Oxford ; Oriental Lecturer of Balliol College, Oxford ; Professor of Sanskrit and Persian in King's College, London.

PALMER'S WORK AS AN ORIENTAL SCHOLAR. ✦

PROFESSOR PALMER commenced his Oriental studies with the Saiyid 'Abdu'lláh (or, as he called himself, Syed Abdoollah). For two or three years he read vigorously—I may say voraciously—Urdú, Persian, and *some* Arabic with Syed alone.[1] I have searched among the mass of papers Syed entrusted to me on his departure from England for scraps of Palmer's early compositions, and have found but one scrap—a sketch of the story of Llewelyn and his dog in charming Persian—apparently in Palmer's handwriting (or rather in one of Palmer's handwritings). And yet, as Syed told me, Palmer was " constantly writing prose and verse exercises for him "—an employment, we all know, he delighted in. No exercises, however, were left in Syed's hands, it is clear. Now the secret of Palmer's success was that, whatever he read and digested, he could reproduce, redistribute, and reconstruct; and

---

[1] Palmer, when asked by the Sháh from whom he had learnt his Persian and Arabic, replied—" I learnt my Persian from Syed Abdoollah, and my Arabic from Arabs here and in Arabia." (*See his account of the Shâh's Visit further on.*)

all his friends know well that he did reproduce, redistribute, and reconstruct in the most marvellous manner.   At the very outset we find him sending *original* Arabic couplets to Professor Theodore Preston and turning 'Lalla Rookh' into what he called his "favourite language."   For purposes of comparison these compositions, if they could be found, would be invaluable; though* I doubt not that, in respect of his later writings, it is as well that—

> Omnes illacrimabiles
> Urgentur ignotaeque longâ
> Nocte, carent quia *vate sacro* (alias ' *the printer* ').

Palmer's *best* work in Arabic was, no doubt, begun and consolidated under the Nawáb.   Almost co-ordinately he was constantly associating with, and studying Persian and Urdú with, a number of Indian Mussulmans, no less able than educated.   And with these we must not fail to mention (though he comes on the scene a little later and from a different part of the East) Rizḳu'lláh Ḥassún Ḥalabí—"my very dear friend," as Palmer termed him—a man whose influence on Palmer's writings, aye and on his character too, can be distinctly traced.   We all remember, of course, the article on this extraordinary man which appeared in the 'Saturday Review' of June 27, 1868.   Ḥassún's was a "life of romance and poetry," albeit he was clearly a shrewd man of business; and Palmer, who was his ' affinity ' was quick to appreciate and copy one whom, in a letter addressed to me over four years ago, he called "the best Arabic scholar and poet of the age." *Ex Ḥassún disce Palmer !*

The interval between 1864–1866 was no doubt the season of Palmer's blossoming, so to speak. Of the work of that interval, however, I have but a few meagre examples, most unfortunately. No doubt, from the native papers he wrote in and for, might be culled flowers of poetry and prose which sprang full-blossomed from his restless brain, but I have no time to search for them. I have several Persian *ruḳ'as* of the dates mentioned, which show that *then*, at all events, Palmer had learnt his *inshápardází* very well indeed, but no poetry; and we may be sure that where he wrote an inch of prose he wrote a nail of poetry or its equivalent. But the loss, at all events, is not very serious ; for it was at this period (1866) that he must have been busy with his Catalogues, which seem to me to be his most arduous and wonderful works ; and of them we have records.

Of his work for the University Library, I know nothing : I never had occasion to seek its aid. I have by me, however, a copy of his ' Trinity College Catalogue,' which seems to me an all-sufficient exemplar of his catalogue work. Now any one who glances at the title-index of this Catalogue will see that, whereas there are a great many subjects—Jurisprudence, Mathematics, Medicine, &c—which Palmer could not have understood (for instance, he once wrote me of his "ignorance of mathematics"), there are very many subjects—Kur'ánic Science, Muḥammadan Tradition, Philosophy, Grammar, Lexicography, &c—which he knew a great deal about. We may safely affirm that any man, be he small or great, would require a good deal of assistance in cataloguing books on subjects he did not understand, especially when treated of in languages like Arabic and Persian. But, the question is—*how much* assistance had this man, who (be it remembered) was within half-a-dozen years of his *alif-be*, in subjects he already, as far as I can judge, fairly understood. Palmer, we all know, had access to able assistance all round ; Hassún even must have been well known to him at this time. Did he toil through the MSS. himself, or get his friends to read them and simply register their reports ? *I* think he read them, or did his best to read them, himself ; *for he could and did quote from them on occasions.*[1] Now, there is a volume in the Trinity Collection (R. 13. 32), which Adam Bowen gave to the library. Palmer describes it as " a collection of short works and treatises on Religious, Philosophical, and Historical subjects, principally in Persian [, a little in Turkish]," and, to judge by the detailed account he gives of its thirteen component

---

[1] Here is a trifling incident which throws a little light on Palmer's mode of going through the MSS. In a Persian letter to be subsequently given, Palmer speaks of an ' *old note book* ' (*baiyáz̤-i kuhna*), from which he quotes two couplets to be found in the *Kitáb-i badá'i'*, a rare portion of Sa'dí's works, scarcely procurable except in a *Kullíyát*. Among the Trinity MSS. there is such a *Kullíyát* (R. 13. 101). *I* can conceive Palmer wading through it, and *noting* everything that struck his fancy.

parts, it must be a work requiring much and varied knowledge to catalogue. That Palmer had gone through it, is as clear as can be from a small work of his entitled ' Oriental Mysticism,' which he published in 1867, and prefaced with a Persian letter to the late Emperor of the French. It is but a small book, a mere tract ; but, it throws a clear light on Palmer's mode of dealing with the College MSS., as any candid person who peruses it will admit. There were, of course, many *common* volumes in the Collection—Sa'dís, Jámís, Mu'allakáts, Ḳur'áns, &c—which only required to be identified, to be known ; but, there were also numbers of other MSS., requiring learning and research of a high order.

After carefully weighing a good deal of direct and indirect evidence, I have come to the conclusion that, though we may deduct a good percentage of credit for the extraneous aid Palmer must have received in compiling this Catalogue, we must leave him enough to make a fair reputation, especially when we consider that he could almost count on the fingers of one hand the years he had been an Oriental student. But, there is another point which seems to me to suggest caution in deducting credit, and that is—I never knew Palmer take credit for anything he did not do himself. And, in the Chronogram he has written at the end of the Trinity Catalogue, so far from acknowledging aid, he *virtually* declares he

did the cataloguing himself. As this Chronogram is
a fair specimen of the kind of Arabic poetry Palmer
wrote at this time, I give it. It is in *Ramal*; and,
though fairly open to attack in two or three places,
is a striking example of Palmer's early powers of
composition :—

من كلام الاقدمين الخبرا   فتشوا الكتب لكى تستكشفوا

من علوم وفنون اثرا   درجوا لكنهم ابقوا لنا

دام في أحوالهم معتبرا   خلدوها في القراطيس لمن

يجتني في الدرس منها الثمرا   ليس يخلو المرء من فائدة

هذه الدنيا علي ماض جرا   وقيس الآتي من الأحوال في

شبهه قد مر فيما غبرا   لاترى شيئا جديدا إلا ما

نغنم الفهم و ندري السيرا   ولهذا نحفظ الكتب لكى

في بيوت صونها مدخرا   ومن الواجب اتقانا لذا

كنت في تدوينها مستبصرا   إنني أورد يأمر الذي

بين لترنتي الدفترا   قال لي الطالب لما تم أرخت

I subjoin a close bald translation that even a tyro
may follow :—

'Search the scriptures,' that you may try to discover,
   In the discourses of the ancients, information :
They passed away ; but they left us,
   In sciences and arts, remains :
They perpetuated them (i.e. scriptures) in papers for those who
   Continue ever, by their experiences, to be warned.
There is not a person who is without profit,
   As he gathers, in reading, from them fruit.
And estimate thou the future of events in
   This life by the past that is fled :
Thou seest not aught new but that the
   Like of it has already been in that which is gone.
And, therefore, we preserve 'the scriptures' that
   We may easily acquire wisdom and get to know of exploits.
And of that which is needful in effecting this end
   (Is) in edifices keeping them (i.e. scriptures), treasured up.
It is I Edward Palmer who was,
   Of the cataloguing of them, making a study :
Said to me a student—"when [1] was it (i.e. the cataloguing)
   finished ? " I gave (him) as
Date—"study the Trinity Catalogue." [2]

It is as well to observe the self-sufficiency of the couplet in italics. Palmer was honest, as I have said, and the amount of credit we allow him should depend on the dimensions of the word *mustabṣir*, so far as they can be fairly ascertained in the case. For my part, I do not hesitate to declare that, if we are to judge of Palmer's catalogue work by this one Catalogue, it is simply wonderful. We may be sure that the man who took

---

[1] As I view the hemistich, Palmer's *lammá* shouldn't stand.
[2] The sum of the numerical values (by *abjad*) of the letters of the three Arabic words will, of course, give the date of publication—1868.

such great pains to ascertain the character of the paper and handwriting of a MS. would take still greater pains to get at its contents. That he had rare intelligence, no one will deny ; that he had in-domitable perseverance, every undertaking attests. What wonder, then, that he was enabled, in grappling with the manifold difficulties of cataloguing, to eke out his comparatively small Oriental experience by qualities which are essential to success in everything ?

Palmer must have been very busy in 1867–1870, not only with serious writings, but with those little *études* or fetches of mimicry he was so fond of. With him αἰσχρόν ἐστι τὸ μὴ μιμεῖσθαι was a strong motive. He was inspired by examples, great and small ; let us take two instances of this.

At the end of 1867 his dear friend Ḥassún issued a little work entitled *Nafaṭhát* or ' *whiffs*,' in imitation of Kriloff, a Russian Æsop, so to speak. This work has a preface in rhyming prose, followed by fables, &c, in very graphic verse. At the beginning of 1868 there appeared in the ' Times ' a notice of the death of Syed's father, Muḥammad Khán, formerly Collector of Jubbulpore. There was nothing at all to inspire a poet in this notice ; nor can I believe that, under ordi-nary circumstances, Palmer would have accentuated it as he did ; but he had the recent exemplar of Ḥassún before his eyes ; and *he*, too, would have a *brochure* with a rhyming prose introduction and a *quantum* of verse—prosaic verse, if you will, as he had but a

prosaic story to tell ; but, a prosaic story, if it be only
apropos, is better than no story at all! I extract
from this tract, by way of sample, a few sentences at
the end of the prose introduction, half-a-dozen couplets
at the beginning of the verse (*Basît*[1]) translation of
the notice, and the epitaph in *Ramal*[1] :—

ممن نصح لدولتنا المنتصرة بالله

وتبوَّأ من ذنايتها ما تمنّاه

وارتقى الى رُتب المجد السامية

وتشرف بالمناصب العالِيَة

ولم يزل يتسامى اشتهاراً بين الخاص والعام

حتى تغمده الله برحمته فى هذا العام

وكنى بالثناء علي محامده المأثورة

ما كتبه تيمس فى مراثيناه المشهورة

وقد نظمتُ هذه الترجمة في لغة العرب شعراً

تخليداً لذكر هذا الرجل الشريف مجداً وفخراً

لانه كان من الناصحين لدولتنا المنتصرة بالله سراً وجهراً

---

[1] Palmer's English representatives of these metres will be subsequently given.

[2] A marginal correction of Palmer's, apparently.

بِئْسَ ٱلزَّمانُ دهانا بِٱلفجِيعةِ فى

فقدِ ٱلأميرِ ٱلخطيرِ ٱلمَجِدِ ذِي ٱلشَّمَمِ

مُحمَّدٍ عينِ أعيانِ ٱلزَّمانِ و مَن

في ٱلهِندِ كَٱلبدرِ يجلو حالِكَ ٱلظُّلَمِ

شمسُ ٱلدرَايةِ في ٱلأحكامِ فطنتُهُ

وقَادةٌ بِٱلذَّكا و ٱلرَّأيِ و ٱلحِلَمِ

قَدْ ذَاعَ صِيتاً ¹ وهذى فِرصةٌ عرضتْ

لِذكرِ أخلاقِ هَذَا ٱلباهرِ ٱلشِّيَمِ

نِيطَتْ بِهِ ٱلرُّتَبُ ٱلعُليَا فقامَ بِها

عِندَ ٱلبَلاءِ قِياماً ثابتَ ٱلقدمِ

مُذْ عَامِ خمسةَ عَشَرَ ٱلأنكليزُ عَلَى

أعمالِها ٱسْتوزرتْهُ و في ٱلتخدُّمِ

ٱلأميرُ ٱبنُ نجاةٍ ذُو ٱلتُّقَى

و ٱلحسبِ و ٱلفخرِ و ٱلمَجِدِ ٱلخَطِيرِ

¹ So Palmer printed.

كَانَ فِي ٱلثَّالِثِ مِن شَعبَانَ عَن

هٰذِهِ ٱلدُّنيَا لَهُ خَيرُ ٱلمَسِيرِ

قَد قَضَى ٱلعُمرَ ٱصطِلَاحًا نَابِلًا

نَجُودَ سَعدٍ ذٰلِكَ ٱلفَوزُ ٱلكَبِيرُ

I subjoin a very literal translation, to help my inexperienced readers to follow the original, which, though extremely able, is not wholly immaculate. I have tried to give an idea (poor and faint, indeed) of the rhyming prose.

'He [i.e. Syed's father] (was) of those true to our Power,
  dominant thro' the *Adored* ;
And had command of its support (in) all that he *implored* :
And rose to grades of honour *eminent* ;
  Was, also, honoured with appointments *excellent*.
Nor ceased to stand out notably 'mong commoner and *peer*,
  Until 'God veiled him with his mercy' in this *year*.
And ample for commending of his virtues racially *traceable*
  Is what the 'Times' records in its obituaries *notable*.
And I have set this version in the Arabic to *poetry*,
  Perpetuating the remembrance of this man distinguished
    for renown of race and pride of *ancestry* ;
In that he was of those true to our Power, dominant thro'
  God, (both) *covertly* and *overtly*.'

' Bad is the Time that smote us with affliction in
  the loss of the *amír*, the great in renown, the straight-
    nosed,[1]
Muhammad, chief of chiefs of the Âge : and who
  in India (is) like a full-moon, clearing the darkest of the
    zulam[2] :
Sun of knowledge in precepts ; his intelligence (is)
  aglow with acuteness, judgment, and soberness.
Is bruited (his) fame : and this (is) an occasion that is
    opportune
  for describing the character of this (man), superior in parts.
There were attached to him dignities very high ; and he
    held them
  'mid trials, as (one) holds firm of foot.
Since the year '15 the English, over (a portion of)
  their territories, made him *vazír*—(him) true to duties.'

The *amír*, son of Salvation, man of piety
  and sagacity, and of great (ancestral) pride and renown—
His, on the third of *Sha'bán*, from
  this life was the best departure.
He has discharged (his) life [as debt] to a text[3] conveying
  abundance of bliss[4]—*zálika 'lfauzu 'lkabír.*

---

[1] Indicative of 'self-pride,' 'generosity,' &c.
[2] *hálikun* is an intensive of *aswadu*, and seems here to be used and
constructed like an ordinary *af'alu*. (See Lane *sub vocibus*.) Of course
zulam suggests *zulm*, which is the point.
[3] *Istildhau* is somewhat awkwardly used here; it should hardly
stand as it is, if I understand the couplet.
[4] That is *assa'ádatu'l'ukhráviyat*, implied by the quotation that
follows from Ķur. lxxxv. 11, the letters of which, added to those of
jílda sa'd, (by *abjad*) give ' *the tomb-stone date*' (*ta'ríkhu hajari'zzarïh*),
1284 A.H.   This is an extremely clever stroke, as any one may see.

The other instance I would mention of Palmer's mimicry is as striking as it is interesting. In 1868 Syed issued an edition of the *Akhlák-i Hindí*, and wound up his *Khátima* with an *Urdú* poem he had seemingly communicated to Palmer before publication. As might have been expected, Palmer matched it at once by a poem of his own in the same metre, which, to quote Syed's words, "judged even by a native standard of excellence, is remarkable for its correct expression and chaste imagery." "I insert it without correction or alteration," continues Syed, "and I believe it may safely defy competition from any living European scholar." Here then is an *Urdú* poem which Syed declares he has not 'touched up,' the production of a man who had not studied that difficult language much more than half-a-dozen years! In the *Khátima* Palmer's poem stands side by side with Syed's. Anyone can see that they are distinct mental properties—a contrast in matter, manner, and diction. Syed's poem may be roughly described as prose in verse—*mansúr*, though *manzúm* in a sense ; Palmer's, as poetry in prose—*manzúm*, though *mansúr* in a sense : the former deals mainly with *facts*, easy to construe ; the latter, mainly with *imagery*, hard to connect. But, the literary merit of the work, as it stands, is but one feature of it ; how many hours of tentation and toil must have been spent on it by the author, who, eight years later, on my congratulating him on his wonderful *Urdú* review of the Sháh's

Visit, replied—"the writing of such things is *a laborious
and artificial task* to me, as I am not as familiar with
the Urdú of everyday life as I am with the Persian"!
I give my readers, with a literal translation, the first
portion of this poem (in *Ramal*)—a monument of
ability and perseverance alike :—

جونکہ ہے حمدِ خُدا تاجِ سرِ نُطق و بیان

چتر نعمتِ عیسیٰ گردوں نشین ہو سائبان

کیا عجب برسے اخترکے جواہر آسمان

کہکشاں کے جوہری بازار سے ہو شادماں

مورچل طاؤس لاۓ اور کلغی خود ہُما

دے رزِ گل کی بنی پوشاک پُرزر بوستان

بوتلیں غُنچے بنیں گلہاے گلشن ہوں گِلاس

اور گلابی ہوے بس رنگِ بہارِ گلستان

شاہدِ نازِ چمن رقاص ہوکر آئیں پھر

دے انہیں زہدِ ثُریّا کا وہ جھومپا آسمان

سب جوانانِ چمن گائیں بجائیں پیش گُل

نغمۂ بُلبُل کو سُن چکر میں آۓ باغبان

یوں صدا نِکلے ہم مِلکر بجائیں ساز جب

دھوم در پر دھوم در پر در یہ تیرے شادیاں

کہکَشاں تو ہو سڑک ذرّاتِ تاباں، ہوں نجوم

روشني میں اُس پہ سیّارون کی دَوڑیں بگّیاں

آسماں بن جا ے پُل خورشید و مہہ ہوں لَال تیم

اور بجلے سِلسِلہ تارِ شُعاعي ہوں عَیاں

چرخ بن جاۓ عماري برق، تاباں جُھول ہو

فیل ہو ابر سیہ اور رعد دوے فیلباں

دَنمیں مستی کي ھوَا پر جب چلے وہ جُھوم جُھوم

مَوج دریا اُسکي بیٹي ہو قدم کوہ کلاں

ہمرکابِ آبلۂ دَوراں ہو یہ سارا جُلوس

اور سَواریمیں ہرے ممدوح کي ہوے رواں

کون ہي وہ صاحبِ اقبال و عِزّت نارتھ کوٹ

رایت آنربل سِر اِستافورڈ ممدوح زماں

' As praise of God is *the diadem* of the head of utterance and
eloquence,

Let *the umbrella* of eulogy [1] of Jesus on high shade
(it).

What wonder (if) Heaven rains *star-gems*,

In the Gem-Mart of the Milky Way [2] rejoicing !

Let the peacock bring *a chámar* ; and the phœnix its *plume* ;

Let the garden supply *a brocaded robe*, wrought of rose-
gold.[3]

Let buds turn *bottles* ; flowers of the flower-garden be
glasses ;

And let the *gulábí* be but the vernal freshness of the
gulistán :

Let the fresh *beauties* [4] of the parterre set a-dancing once
again ;

Let Heaven give them the *heap of coin* [5] of the Pleiades :

Let every *gallant* of the parterre sing (and) play to *the
Rose* [6] :

Listening to the song of the bulbul, let *the gardener* set
a-whirling.

[1] Observe the neat and adroit substitution of the *na'tu 'ísą* for the
na'tu'nnably.

[2] As indicating Palmer's subtle fancy, it may be observed that ' *the
Milky Way* ' is called *aṭṭaríḳu'lmaḥsúsa*, i.e. ' the way sensibly perceived ; ' and *jauhar*, as coming from *jahr*, would also imply ' being
sensibly perceived.' Observe, also, the play on *khud* and *khild* (implied)
in next line.

[3] Having spoken of royal *insignia* &c, Palmer seems next to
suggest a *jashn*, ' the flowers ' *(sháhidán-i čaman)* being dancers, ' the
nightingales ' *(jawánán-i čaman)* being singers, &c.

[4] *Sháhid* is defined in the *Kashfu'llughát* to be *amrade khúbṣúrat*,
applicable to tree and flower. Of course, *naukhez* and *naurasta* are
common meanings of *náz.*

[5] As a sort of *mujrá*, apparently. A not uncommon suggestion of
extravagant reward, as in *Akhláḳ-i Jalíli* (p. 13) &c.

[6] As *gaddí-nishín*, perhaps. No doubt, in Palmer's mind, *bághbán*,
also, had its billet.

Thus let acclaim go forth, as all in concord play (their)
    instruments—

Clamouring (and) clamouring at Thy door, whereat (are
    offered) *mubárakbáds.*

Now let the Milky Way be *the road*; let *the glittering
    specks* (i.e. *lamps*) be the stars ; [1]

'Mid the glitter along it let the Planets' *cars* speed :

Let Heaven become *the bridge* ; the Sun and Moon be *the
    red lights* ;

And for *the rails* let radiant streaks [2] be visible :

Let the Firmament become *the howdah* ; let flashing light-
    ning be *the housings* ;

Let *the elephant* be the black cloud ; [3] and thunder be *the
    mahout* :

In pride of passion on the air as it (i.e. the cloud-elephant)
    moves, swaying to and fro, [4]

Let the sea-wave be its *fetter*, (its) *foot* the big mountain.

Accompanying *the Dun-steed of the Age* [5] let all this caval-
    cade be,

And in the train of my Patron let it proceed.

Who is that favoured and honoured one ? Northcote,

    The Right Honourable Sir Stafford, Mæcenas of the
    Time !

---

[1] The *majarra* or '*Milky Way*' is the track of 'the planets.' A
good deal of this it is not easy to point as Palmer's mind must have
pointed it. He is evidently parodying some well-known scene—a railway, perhaps.

[2] As of an *Aurora Borealis.* My turn of *silsila* depends on the con-
text, of course.

[3] One is reminded much by this of Kálidása's description of
Airávat.

[4] *Jhúmjhúm* is very cleverly pointed both at the elephant's swaying
and the clouds' gathering.

[5] Alluding rather to *the eulogist's pen* than to *the eulogised*, as might
be shown.

So much of Palmer's *mimicry*; now for his *sarcasm*, in which he was particularly strong. A stinging *Urdú* satire, of nearly a hundred lines, which Palmer launched against the Nawáb's Maulaví Wiláyet Husain, suggests an interesting episode which shows the marvellous progress he had made in correct thought and expression, almost within a decade of his novitiate. It appears that Wiláyet Husain had accused Palmer of plagiarism from the *díwán* of Khusrú. The charge was indignantly denied by Palmer. The *díwán* was, accordingly, procured from the India Office Library and closely examined, when it was found that Palmer had only to answer for the *wazn* of his *ghazal*, the subject-matter thereof being wholly different from that of Khusrú's. Briefly, then, a very learned Maulaví judged one of Palmer's undoubted productions to be *too good for him*, and fathered it on Khusrú!

I give my readers four couplets of this satire as they were given to me by Syed, who quoted wholly from memory and probably erred in several particulars (metrical even) ; for instance, he gave me *jur'at* for *jur'a* or *jur'at*, clearly. As will be seen, the *language*, like the *thought*, is unmitigated Persian— affording a short but good specimen of Palmer's ordinary " un–Hindí style," as he called it :—

هان غازئ مطلع تو لگا تیغِ دودستي

ششِ پارہ کراِس مَولوي کا پیکرِ دستي

هان ساقُ دوران هي دمِ رندي و مستي

هُشيار که دم مين نه بلندي هي نه پستي

نے خم هي نه شيشه هي نه ساغر هي نه باده

هربار فكرِ نشهُ جُرعت هي زياده

آ ساسهنے يه گو هي يه چوگان هي يه ميدان

مَين علم هون تو جهل مَين آدم هون تو شيطان

The two latter couplets of this specimen are, I
think, clear enough. In respect of the first couplet
of the two former ones, my readers will not fail to
observe the extremely clever play on the word *taktí*
'*cutting up*' or '*scansion,*' suggested by *matlaʻ* as
opposed to *maktaʻ*. I suppose *ghází-e matlaʻ* to imply
the '*critic*' or '*critic's pen.*' Of the second couplet, the
sting is not quite clear to me. Perhaps in *sáki-e
daurán* the Maulaví is satirically apostrophised—'*is
there a whiff of inspiration? (be) sober enough (to
mind) that it neither elevates (by intensity) nor de-
presses (by crop-sickness)*'—scathing enough for the
poor Maulaví! I think Palmer, under the common
masti ú rindí of Ḥáfiẓ, &c (—*gar man az sarzanish-i
mudda'iyán andesham + shíva-ı masti o rindí naravad
az pesham*—), veils '*literary inspiration.*' There is

also a neat contrast in the *masti* and *hushyár*, as
in the line—*áh azán mast ki bá mardum-i hushyár
chi kard?*   Confer, also, *sákí bahosh básh ki gham dar
kamín-i má ast, &c.*

The following satirical lines in Persian are interesting, as having been addressed by Palmer to myself.
I had sent him, in the form of a letter, a *farrago*
of *Jámí, Háfiz,* &c—a somewhat jagged production
of the *Ghálib* type—which was certainly not to his
liking.   He replied promptly by a *foolscap* (!) of
bright "*shírází* badinage," as he called it, in which the
following *hazaj* lines, evidently *impromptu*, were em-
bedded :—

$$\text{تو ميداني زِ قِطميرو نقيرم}$$

$$\text{كه از تحرير خود من در نفيرم} ^{1}$$

$$\text{نمي آيد مرا رسم كتابت}$$

$$\text{چه ميپُرسي زِ اِنشاءِ ضميرم} ^{2}\text{؟}$$

---

¹ Translate—'thou knowest, by my peddling, that I am protest-
ing against my own writing !'   *Kitmír* is, properly, '*the thin pellicle
of a date stone ;*' *nakír,* '*a small groove in it* '; the two words together
imply *minuteness* or *minutiæ.* (Vide Ḳur. iv. 56, xxxv. 14.) A distich
of *Jámí's Tuhfatu'l'ahrár* runs (unmetrically, of course)—*ánki tú
kh'ániyash ṣarír-i ḳalam + az ḳalamat hast nafír-i ḳalam* = ' as to what
thou callest the scratch of the pen, it is the cry of the pen against
thy pen.'   Both the Burhán and Haft Ḳulzum explain *nafír* by
faryád.

² *Inshá-e ẓamír* implies ' literary creations or conceptions.'

دوات انگُشتِ حیرت در دهان است ۱

پیِ تحریر اگر من خامه گیرم

همین قِرطاس میپیچد زِ غصّه

گرش بهرِ نوشتِ نامه گیرم

قلمدان مینمایدِ سینه را چاک

که من در جیبِ نادان جلے گیرم ۲

زنم گر دست در آغوشِ مضمون

جوانی کے نمایدِ عقلِ پیرم؟

فقیرانِ سؤالِ فقر دارم

که پیشِ فقر کمتر از فقیرم ۳

---

[1] Conf. *Jámí's bait*, as above—*tú basih angusht shuda kháma-zan + khalk dih angusht zi tú dar dahán*, which Palmer may have imitated. Conf. also *Rukʿát—chu níst hadd-i zabán sharh-i hál-i dil dádan + zabán chirá niham az kháma dar dahán-i dawát.* Similarly, in the 'Arabian Nights,' we read—*afwáhu 'lmahdbiri tashtakí + 'alama 'lfirdki bi'alsuni 'l'aklámi.*

[2] Seemingly the *oratio recta* of the *Kalamdán.*

[3] The word *fikr*, which Palmer apparently makes the plural of *fikra*, denotes ' *the best points* ' of a composition—' *the vertebræ,*' in fact. The word *fakír* is, apparently, used by him in the sense of ' *broken-backed* ' (*shikasta-pusht*) or ' *invertebrate.*' And the distich seems to mean—' I pray for *points* (or *vertebræ*) as a suppliant + I who am, in regard to *points* (or *vertebræ*), worse than invertebrate !' I call to mind a similar idea—*zibaski fikra na dárad fakír ast.*

چه میکاوی جگر بیهوده پامر؟

همین باشد نداهے صریرم

پیِ تحریر حالاتِ ضروری

مگر وقتِ ضرورت ناگُزیرم [1]

من و اِنشاء و اِملانُم همه بوجّ [2]

پذیر این قولِ من ای دلپذیرم

بنه بر دوشِ من بارِ دبیری

حقیر ام من حقیر ام من حقیرم

These lines are not very difficult to follow by the aid of the notes I have added. They cannot fail to be appreciated by my readers.

The work by which Palmer is best and widest known is, of course, the *magnum opus* of 1871. 'To hold the mirror up' to this work is quite outside my purpose; I merely mention it here to draw attention to one or two very interesting letters, which appeared in an *Akhbár* of December 1871. Palmer, as is well known, was at this time " labouring day and night " at

[1] Somewhat obscure, but apparently means—'About things that I should, I cannot help writing except when I should.' Surely *pay-e* here should have been *az*?

[2] 'My diction and spelling are bad.'

his book, and was all but crushed under the pressure of the editorial work. Contemplate, then, the mental yearning of a man who, working as he was working, found time to "look into an old note-book" and mimic a *ghazal* of *Sa'dí* by one he enclosed Syed in a long Persian letter of the usual charming and bantering type. It is much to be regretted that more of such letters are not to be found ; for they show the man in colours he himself laid on. Palmer, in his letter-writing, was often prolix—he had mostly a good deal to say and he was restless enough to say it, but he was not like Lucilius '*lutulentus.*' His very handwriting suggested and bespoke a remarkable clearness of diction, whether he wrote you in English, Arabic, Persian, or Urdú. Had we but a score or so of Palmer's *foolscaps*, we might be content to let them tell the story of his life, unannotated. The letter I am about to quote from the *Akhbár*, where it was lithographed, with the usual complement of blots and errors, will have great interest for my readers :—

برادرِ عالي‌جناب فيضمآب والاخطاب ذي المجد و

الجاهِ سيّدِ عبد اللهِ صاحب دَامَ عنَايَتُه—الله الله ! اين‌چه

تحرير حَيرت‌افزا است كه از كلكِ مرواريد-سلكِ آن

والا-همم سر زده—سببِ عدمِ تحرير . محبّت ناب‌رجات

ذ غفلت ذ تساهُل—بلكه حقيقتِ حال اين است كه سر

تصنيفِ كتابِ سيروسِياحيِ عَرَب و ترتيبِ نقشجاتِ
هر دِيار و امصار و جبالِ بحروبرّ كه گذرم بر آنها افتاده
وحالاتِ تواريخِ باستان و وقائع و كيفياتِ اوقاتِ سَفَر و
حَضَرِ خود و دِيگر سوانحِ از حُكمِ حاكِمانِ مدرس براے ياد
داشت بر صفحاتِ لَيل و نَهار همه تن مشغول ام —
و شرطِ اينست كه در همين سال از خُلفِ طبع مُكمَّل
شود — زياده از دو هزار اوراقِ تقطيعِ كار تمام شدند — علاوه
تصنيف تصحيحِ اوراقِ مُسوَّداتِ مطبع — در آن شب را . بـ
روز و روزرا بِ شبِ بسرے برم — كمالِ احتياط ضرور است كه
گفته اند مَنْ صَنَّفَ قَدِ اسْتَهْدَفَ — آهوگيرانِ بيكار دل آزار
كه نكته چينيِ خواهند كرد — از اوّلِ اصلاحِ كار بايد كرد —
پس چگونه از طرفِ آن بِرادر كه اوستاد و مُحسِن و مُربِّيِ
اين هيچميرزانِد بر دلِ صُحبت منزلم غُبارِ كدورت و ملال
جاگيرد — بِجز لُطف و عنايت چه كرده ايد كه من خُدا نه
خواسته ناخوش شوم — بهر كيف لانِيِ عفو و اَجْر ام نه
قابلِ زَجْر چراكه دلم از محبّتِ شما مُدام معمور است —
راه اگر نزديك و گو دُورست بـے

دل جُدا دیده جُدا سوے تو پرواز کند

گرچہ مَن در قفَسم بال و پرم بسیار است

در بنولا در بَیاضے کهنہ این دو بیت بنظرم آمد و از غزلِ
سعدیٔ شیرازي طَابَ ثَرَاهُ

گر کسے سرو شنید است برفتار این است

یا صنوبر کہ بناگوش و برش سیمین است

نہ بلندي است بہ قامت کہ تو معلوم کني

کہ بلند از نظرِ مردمِ کوتہبین است

حالا این ثابت نیست کہ مالِ حضرت سعدي است یا
دیگرے—من هم برین غزلے گفتہ نزدِ آن برادر براے اصلاح
میفرستم کہ جاے اوستاد خالي است—ازروے اخبار معلوم
شد کہ کسے شقّی ازلیّ متعصّب جمع نارمن صاحب را
خنجرزده هلاک کرد اَسْتَغْفِرُ اللّٰہَ رَبّي—کسے را بیگناہ
و خصوصًا در غفلت کُشتن نهایت درجۂ شقاوت است—
این معلون کسے مجنون و خونریز جبلي بودہ باشد—
و کسانیکہ طعن بر مُسلمانانِ هند میزنند وهمہ را بدنام میکنند

اوشان هم کوتاه-اندیش و مزاجِ پُرظنون دارند چه در

همین ولایتِ مُهذّب چند بار بر تاجداران و حُکّام

حَرامیان حمله آورده اند پس تمام یوروپ را چرا خونخوار

و متعصّب نمیگویند؟ درین حرف اینست که ناخوانده

جاهل اُمّی و عَمّی ظاهر و باطن مُسلمانانِ هند متعصّب

میباشند نه اینکه خونِ معصوم و بیگناه کنند—بتاریخ هشتم

ماهِ حال قریبِ لندن قسّیسی که عالمِ متجرد مُعتکفِ

جیّد و دیرینه که عبارت اورا مردمان مثلِ حِرزِ جان

میداشتند پادری جان سِلبی واتسُن نام عمررسیده زوجهٔ

خودرا یکایک از نهایت بیرحمی کُشت و انداخت که از

خواندنِ آن جگرحَجَر چاک چاک میشود و امطارِ اشک

از هر دیدهٔ نمناک—پس تمام پادریانِ عیسوی را خونی و

ظالمِ سفّاک گفتن نشاید—آن برادر هم خوب تحریر و تردید

نمایند نَعُوذُ بِاللّٰهِ مِنْ شَرِّ الشَّیْطَانِ—عند الفرصت اگر معلوم

باشد از حالِ این طایفهٔ وهّابیّه مشروحًا مطّلع فرمایند از

قلّتِ فُرصت نمیتوانم که تلاش در کُتُب نمایم—از استماع

بهم رسانیدنِ انگلهای نغز و فرستادنِ چند دانه برای آن برادر

بطور تحفه از طرفِ حافظ احمد حُسین صاحب بهادر
من نیز حظِ روحانیّ و لذّتِ صوریّ برداشتم—حافظ
صاحب را از همین تردّداتِ خط زنگاشتم—وقتِ ملاقات
از طرفِ آئم بسیار بسیار آداب و تسلیمات بخدمتِ
عالیدرجتِشان خواهند رسانید—زیاده بندگی و نیاز—
بخدمت بی‌بی صاحب کورنشات—رقیمهٔ نیاز اڈوڑڈ پالمر—

۲۷ اکتوبر سنـــــع ۱۸۷۱ منمقام کیمبرج

غزل

ساقیا فصل بهار وگهِ فر نزدیک است
گر غنیمت شمُری وقتِ غنیمت این است
بعد ازین از من و تو خَلقی حکایت گوید
آنچه افسانه که از کوُءکَن و شیرین است
دام دلها نبوَد گر سرِ زلُفت ز چه رو
حَلقه‌در‌حلقه و خَم‌در‌خَم و چین‌در‌چین است

در خیالِ سرِ زُلفت نرَود دیده بخواب

سرِ عقرب زده کو در هوسِ بالین است

صاحبِ حُسن اگر بنده بُوَد سُلطان است

بندهٔ عشق اگر شاه بُوَد مِسکین است

با خیالِ لبِ آن خسروِ شیرین دهنان

گر خورم زهر بکامم چو شکر شیرین است

زاهدم از مَي و معشوق کند منع چه باک

يی بِ معنی نبرَد دیده که صورت بین است

با صفِ طُرّهٔ جانان چه کند جان چه کند

یک کبوتر که گرفتارِ دوصد شاهین است

در جوابِ غزلِ حضرتِ سعدي غزلی

پالمر گفته که شایستهٔ صد تحسین است

I will now give a literal translation of the letter
and *ghazal*. The letter opens in the usual flowery
style and is addressed to Syed, as I have said :—

*My dear Saiyid 'Abdu'lláh—(whose) resort (is) exalted,
(whose) retreat (is) bounty's, (whose) address (is) lofty, &c[1]—
may your support never fail!*

Good Heavens ! what an astounding letter it is that has
sprung from the eloquent[2] pen of him (whose) aspirations
(are) lofty[1] ! It is not from carelessness or remissness that
(I) have ceased writing friendly letters (to you). But, the
fact of the matter is—I am exclusively and continuously
engaged in editing (my) book of travels in Arabia, and in
arranging the engravings of the districts, towns, and mountains I visited *en route* by sea and land ; and (in setting
forth)[3] the old historical particulars (relating thereto), the
circumstantial details of my own occasions at home and
abroad, and other incidents—to serve as a *Memoir*—at the
instance of the University authorities. And it is stipulated
that the Syndics of the Press shall finish (the book) this
year, more than 2,000 sheets of which are already complete.
Besides editing, (there is) the correction of proof-sheets, at
which I work from night till morn and morn till night.
(One) must be very careful ; for, (as the Arabs) say, ' *he who
edits, makes a target of himself.*'[4] There are good-for-nothing
fault-finders to harass one, sure to pick holes. Best put
things right from the first. So, how can a feeling of dis-

---

[1] A thoroughly accurate and philosophical estimate or description of the facts of construction of Aryan compounds of this sort, which
Palmer perfectly appreciated, has yet to be written. To avoid the
common *paraphrases*, I have, by way of example, turned these compounds rigidly and baldly, as (I know) Palmer viewed them, following
principles of Sanskritic *vigraha*. The common expression, *jandb-i
'álí*, by the way, rigidly = ' exalted (object of) resort.'

[2] A brief paraphrase, of course : the pretty conceit *marwárid-silk*,
literally = ' (whose) string (is like one of) pearls,' and has a very interesting history.

[3] Of course *tartíb-i* runs through the sentence.

[4] But Palmer might have added, justly, with Káshifí—*man ṣannafa
ḳadi 'staṭrafa.*

pleasure and annoyance [1] due to my dear friend—who are my poor self's master, benefactor, and patron—take hold of a heart so attached [2] as mine ? You have shown (me) naught but kindness and favour; that I should be dissatisfied—*God forbid it !* Anyhow, I ought to be excused and rewarded, and not rebuked ; for my heart is ever full of affection for you. ' Be the route near or be it far,

> Now heart, now eye—each wings (its way) to thee :
> Although I'm caged, I've wing and feather much.'

By the way, in an old note-book I met with the two (following) couplets, as (belonging) to a *ghazal* of Sa'dí of Shíráz—' *may the earth lie light on him* ' [3] :—

> ' If one has heard of a cypress in motion, it is he ;
> Or a pine with cheek and bosom of silvery white :
> Nor is (his) highness of the stature you wot of ;
> In that it is beyond the ken of those who see not far.' [4]

Now one's not sure whether they are Sa'dí's or another's. I have, however, written a *ghazal* on them and send it to you for correction, as it needs correction. [5]

---

[1] *Ghubár* is somewhat extravagant here, no doubt.

[2] ' *ṣuḥbat-manzil* ' literally = ' (whose) goal (is) companionship.'

[3] Said of a deceased shaikh, &c ; Palmer's own rendering.

[4] These couplets are from Sa'dí's *Kitábu'lbadá'i'*, where, instead of Palmer's *baraftár*, I read *ki raftast*. As everybody knows, of the *sarv* and *ṣanaubar* terms denoting parts of the body are often fancifully used ; thus, Ḥáfiẓ speaks extravagantly of the *dil-i ṣanaubar*, a mere ' *knur* ' (*girih*), likened to a ' *heart.*' So in the couplet—*chu sarve ki paidá kunad dar chaman + zi gísú bunafsha zi 'áriẓ saman.* The sentiment here may be compared with that in the Ḥáfiẓ couplets—

> *ḥadís-i sarv ki goyad bapesh-i ḳámat-i dost ?*
> *ki sarbulandi-e sarv sahl zi ḳámat-i o'st.*
>
> et seqq.

[5] A common saying of this purport.

(I) see by the papers that a miscreant, fatalist [1] (and) fanatic, has murdered Mr. Justice Norman with a dagger— *God forgive him !* To kill an innocent man, and particularly off guard, is the very acme of crime. This wretch may have been a born lunatic and murderer ! so, people who taunt the Moslems of India and give them all a bad name (through this act), themselves reflect but little and have minds full of prejudices. Thus, in Europe itself, which is civilised, kings and judges have been attacked by assassins on several occasions ; yet, no one would call all Europe murderers and fanatics. The point in this case is that the unread (and) ignorant Moslems of India, illiterate and blind *temporally and spiritually*, are fanatics, not shedders of innocent and guiltless blood. On the 8th instant, near London, a parson who (was) thoroughly learned, an excellent and experienced author, whose writing people valued as an *elixir vitæ*,[2] Rev. J. Selby Watson, advanced in years, murdered his wife outright with extreme heartlessness, and got rid (of her). To read of it breaks in pieces a heart of stone, and (brings) showers of tears from every tearful eye. Yet, it would not be right to call every clergyman a murderer and bloodthirsty villain. My dear friend, too, should write and repel (the accusation) firmly. *God protect (us) from the malevolence of Satan !*

When you've time, if it's not out of the way, give (me) an explicit account of the doings of the *Wahhábí* sect. I cannot search (for them) in books, as (I) have no time.

I, too, derived mental pleasure and sensual delight from hearing of Ḥáfiẕ Aḥmad Ḥusain's [3] having secured some fine mangoes and of (his) having sent a few to my dear friend, as a present. I've not written Ḥáfiẕ because of (my)

---

[1] This, following another use of the word by him, is Palmer's meaning.

[2] Conf. Jámí's *náma-ash ta'wíz-i ján*.

[3] This man was one of the referees in the Maulaví Wiláyet case aforementioned.

present labours. When (you) see him, please convey to His Eminence from the delinquent (my) very best respects and salutations, &c. Regards to your wife. *Humble epistle of*

Edward Palmer.

Cambridge: October 27, 1871.

Ghazal.

CUPBEARER ! the season of spring and time of loveliness is
  at hand :
  if you deem it a godsend, now is the time for the godsend !
Hereafter, of me and thee let story-tellers repeat
  the romance of Farhád and Shírín.
To snare hearts if thy ringlets are not, for what reason
  (are they) ring-in-ring and coil-in-coil and fold-in-fold ?
In dreaming of thy ringlets goes not (my) eye to sleep :
  the head of one scorpion-stung, does it ever long for
  the pillow ?
A Beauty, though he be a slave, is Sultán :
  a Slave of Love, though he be a sultán, is (but) a
  Misérable !
While dreaming of the lip of that monarch of sweet-mouthed
  (ones),
  if I take poison, to my palate like sugar it is sweet.
I'm a zealot ; what qualm bars Wine and Beloved ?
  the eye that sees (but) 'matter' guides not the foot to
  'mind.'
With the file of the ringlets of Beloved what can Soul do ?
  what can it do ?
  'tis (but) one dove held in captive by two hundred
  falcons !
In reply to the *ghazal* of Shaikh Sa'dí, a *ghazal*
  Palmer composed, which is worthy of a hundred
  bravos !

The *Persian* letter and *ghazal* of Palmer just given were enclosed in a letter Syed sent to the *Nawáb Niżámu'ddaula Bahádur*, who, apparently, sent both to the editor of the *Akhbár* with the following very interesting and complimentary remarks in *Urdú* :—

صاحبِ من محبّي مشفقي همدانِ فخرِ هند عزيزِ
دلهاے اهلِ انگلئڈ سيّد عبد الله صاحب بهادر پروفيسر نے
مقامِ دلكش لندن سے اپنے خط ميں يہ قندِ مكرّر خط
مع غزل فاضل اجلّ حكيم و جهان‌ديده جهان‌آشنا خُلقِ
مُجسّم فخرِ انگلستان مِستر اَڈورڈ پالمر صاحب بهادر كا
ميرے پاس اِس غرضسے بهيجا هى كہ اونكي فارسي غزل سے
مَين بهى لُطف اوٹهاؤن اور اون كے هاتھ كا لِكها ديكهكر
سوَيدلے سوادِ خط سے چِشمِ جان كو منوّر كرون اور بعدَہ
واسطے اُولُو الآبصار اهلِ هند كے برِلے درج اخبار بهيجون——
تاكہ اهلِ هند جانين كہ نازپرورده ولايتِ دوردست
انگلئڈ كے باَلطبع ايسے لائق فائقِ طباع محنتي اميرِ شائق
هوتے هين كہ گهِر بيٹهے علومِ شرقي مين جِسمين اكثر

اہلِ مشرق تو عاری و عاطل ہیں وہ کمالِ خداداد حاصل

کرتے ہیں—سیّد صاحب نے اپنے خط میں لکھا ہے کہ

صاحبِ جوانسال جوانبخت علوم دانِ نہایتِ یورپ کے

سوا جیسے علومِ مشرق میں دستگاہ رکھتے ہیں ویسے ہی

اوسکی خط کتابت اور تحریر و تقریر میں یدِ طولیٰ—اور طُرفہ

یہ کہ مرزوقی طبع سے شعر بھی فرماتے ہیں چنانچہ غزلِ

سعدی پر ایک غزل جو بھیجی ہے کیسی لُطف انگیز بلکہ

حیرت خیز ہے—اس قابلیّت کے صلے میں صاحبِ

موصوف کو پندرہ سو ماہانہ کا ایک اعلیٰ عہدہ بمبیٔ میں

ملتا ہی مگر ابھی تامّل ہے—زہے بختِ ہند! جہان

ایسے لائق اورعالِم کارفرما ہوں—صاحبِ ممدوح سے میرا بھی

غائبانہ اتّحاد بہت برسوں سے ہے مگر اون کا شَوقِ علم

و زبان وافی روزافزوں ہے سُنتا ہوں—چنانچہ اب عربی علم

اور زبان میں بھی کمال حاصل کر لیا اور خود عرب جاکر

نام کر آۓ اور اب اوسکی تأریخ لکھ چُکے ہیں جسکا ذکرِ

خیر بھی اون کے خط سے واضح ہے—خدا اون کے علم

اور عمر میں خیر برکت بے—زیاده زیاده و السلام—
مقام دارالمنصور جودپور—محمد مروانعلیخان غفرّہ—

۱۸۷۱
دسمبر سـنـہ ع

My dear and learned friend &c, Saiyid 'Abdu'lláh, has
sent me from charming London, in his letter, the (enclosed)
very nice [1] letter and *ghazal* of the accomplished, very eminent, *savant*, and the travelled, well-informed, *gentleman*,[2]
pride of England—Mr. Edward Palmer—to the end that I,
too, might enjoy the charm of his Persian *ghazal*; and,
beholding his handwriting, refresh my soul's eye with the
collyrium of (his) letter's inkiness ;[3] and, then, send it for
insertion in the *Akhbár* for the (benefit of the) intelligent
people of India. So that my countrymen may know that,
delicately nurtured in the distant country of England, there is
by nature so apt, so very able, (and) so painstaking a personage that, without leaving his country, he is acquiring a preter-
natural proficiency in Eastern learning of which most of the
people of the East, themselves, are destitute and devoid.

Syed tells me in his letter that this young and promising
gentleman, besides (being) extremely proficient in European
learning, is as strong in Eastern learning as he is clever[4]

[1] *Kand-i mukarrar*, defined in the *Burhán* and *Haft Kulzum* to
be *kindyah az labhá-e ma'shik báshad*, can only be paraphrased here.

[2] *Khulk* is often used in the sense of *muríi'at* or *futúwat*, qualities
'embodied' in our word '*gentleman*' in its strictest sense.

[3] *Suwaidá* in this phrase suggests, at least, 'a collyrium '—may be
the ' *black*' (*suwaidá'u*) berry of the *Kuhlu'ssúdán*, for instance, which is
good for the eyes. And as to *sawád* here, *apropos* of the *sawád-i
nuskha* &c, Káshifí says—*sawádash ki kuhlu'ljawáhir-i ma'dni-e 'ibárat
azánast*.

[4] My readers will, of course, call to mind the point of the Arabic

in epistolary correspondence, and in writing and speaking[1] (in general). The wonderful thing, however, is that he writes poetry, too, with a natural giftedness. Thus, a *ghazal* he has sent on one of Sa'dí's is a very charming—indeed, a very marvellous—(production).

As *a* reward for such ability, Mr. Palmer has been offered a very important post in Bombay worth 1,500 a month, and (he) is now considering (the offer).[2] Lucky India in having such apt and learned officials !

I, too, have had, for many years, friendly, though not personal, relations with Mr. Palmer (, and know a deal of him) ; further, I am informed, his love of learning and language is thorough (and) growing every day. Accordingly, (he) has just mastered the Arabic learning and language, too; has himself been to Arabia and gained a reputation ; and has just finished writing his account of it (i.e. Arabia), of which he makes fit mention, also, in his letter, as is clear. May God grant him exceedingly abundant learning and prolonged life, &c.

Dáru'lmanṣúr Jaudpúr :
Muḥammad Marwán 'Alíkhán.

December, 1871.

---

expression—*lahu yaduu ṭúlq fi'l'ilm* = 'he is an eminent scholar,' which has been transferred to Persian ; thus, Abu'lfaẓl says—*dar ḳal'-i aḥjár yad-i ṭúlq namúda* &c.

[1] According to the *Kashfu'llughát, taḥrír = nek navishtan* and *taḳrír = sukhun guftan.* Jámí often emphasizes this distinction— *ba-taḳrír-i zabán wa taḥrír-i banán; ḳalam-i taḥrír wa zabán-i taḳrír.* That consummate Urdú stylist, *Ghálib,* also writes in one of his *ruḳ'as—tumne taḥrír ko taḳrír ká pardáz de diyá thá.*

[2] Palmer must have seen his way to living by his Oriental attainments long before this, the date of his appointment to the Cambridge Chair. So early as the beginning of 1869, Syed wrote me—*tájdárán-i Hindústán baẓarl'a-e ín hechmaddán iẓhár-i muláḳát wa ham naukarí tá duwázda ṣad líra sáliyána wa ráh-i ḳharch navishta and ammá Mistar Pálmar bar koh-i Túr ast. Agar darínjá múlbúd Nawáb Náẓim-i Bangála bar tanḳh'áh-i hazár rúpíya máhwárí naukar bará-e dars-i farzandán-i ḳhud múlláshtand ammá majbúr mándaṇd.*

The letters I have quoted and translated testify, both on his part and on that of others, to Palmer's intellectual activity and transcendent abilities. They tell their own tale and need no comment.

There can be no doubt that to Palmer's confirmed habit of versifying the translations he made from other tongues must be attributed many seeming, and some palpable, instances of his unsound scholarship. During the printing of his *Bahá'u'ddín* he sent me, among others, a specimen-proof of p. 71 (*Káfíyatu'-rrái*) wherein he rendered the grammatical conceits of the remarkable couplet— ·

جَعَلتُكم خبري في ٱلْحُبِّ مُبتَدِئاً

وَ كلُّ معرفةٍ لي في ٱلْهَوَى نكرهْ

by 'thou art to me a lover's fallacy: alas! my love is all indefinite.' (I would observe that the latter half is a correction by him in ink of his printed rendering— 'and undefined, that was so definite'). I was so much struck with the utter inadequacy—I might justly say, inaccuracy—of the turn that I wrote to him calling his attention to the juxtaposed 'enunciative' (*khabar*) and 'inchoative' (*mubtadá*), to 'the determinate' (*ma'rifat*) and 'the indeterminate' (*nakira*), and suggesting a rendering more in accordance with the principles laid down in his preface. I feared he must have missed—partly, at least—the grammatical allusions, and even the grammar itself; and had I not been in constant correspondence with him, I should have put this case down to loose or unsound scholarship. I was, however, quickly reassured; he replied by return of post with a neat little essay, saturated with apt quotations, which dissipated all my doubts respecting his not fully understanding the passage : indeed, the essay is of itself a proof of his being a consummate grammarian of an advanced (native) type. "Perhaps," said he, "my rendering is not as precise as it might be"—a suggestive admission he often made to me.

I could point out very many passages in his writings (common and uncommon), where, under the influence of poetic phrensy or of downright heedlessness, he has laid himself open to charges of bad scholarship ; but I can prove that in most cases he *knew* better. In 1872 he sent me a copy of two *ḳaṣídas* of the Persian poet Anwarí, which he, in conjunction with that unrivalled English Sanskritist, Professor Cowell, had published. It cannot be denied that Palmer's metrical version of these *ḳaṣídas* reveals a great number of blunders more or less serious, aggravated or generated by poetic fancy or exigence. I pointed out to him a number of such passages, in which I thought I had the better of him ; but I was surprised to find that in the majority of cases he had a perfectly clear and scholarlike view of his author, and that he had *deliberately* sacrificed that view to a pretty rhyme or a telling antithesis. In the minority of cases I found him generous and quick enough to acknowledge his mistakes ; and, what is more, ready to support his critic's views by actual *quotations against himself !* I take one glaring instance of what metrical and incautious translation can do for a fine idea. On p. 34 of the pamphlet, ll. 15, 16, is found the very fine punning couplet—

$$\text{آنك گر آلَے اورا گنج بودی در عدد}$$

$$\text{نیستی جذرِ اصمّ را عیبِ گُنگی و کَری}$$

which Palmer turned—'till the dumb man shall make an oration, till the stocks and the stones shall find voice, till the whole of the silent creation in language rejoice.' I need hardly remind a careful reader that *jaẕr-i aṣamm* (opposed to *jaẕr-i munṭiḳ*) is 'a surd square-root'—a fit metaphor for the *never-ending* 'blessings' (*álá*) of Him.

While pursuing the shadow, Palmer often lost the substance, though nobody was more likely than he to have grasped it. He would exclaim—"but to put that into my verse was beyond me," "my expression being hampered by verse may be a little vague," &c. To all of which should be given the answer—as your object in translating an author is to present him *as nearly as possible* in your own language, why adopt a mode of expression in that language which 'puts beyond you' the attainment of your end? Very many indeed are the pieces of a *general* character which Palmer has clothed in an English dress with pointed elegance and befitting grace ; but, on the other hand, not a few pieces of his, in the originals of which lurked peculiar conceits of language, which even an apt translator's prose could not have reached, seem to have served but one purpose, to imperil his reputation for sound scholarship. Conceits of language, which experts of long standing can hardly fathom, Palmer believed he could 'popularise' by paraphrasing in English poetry! He deliberately left, with lamp of knowledge in hand, a road he should have carefully followed, to pursue an *ignis fatuus.*

I may mention here, by the way, another grand poem of Palmer's—an *Urdú Masnaví*—on the marriage of the Duke of Edinburgh. I don't know whether he ever printed it : at all events, I never met with it. The following couplets were sent me as a specimen, and as such I give them :—

کِس کی یہ شادي هى کِسکي هي يہ فوج

جوش مارے هي يہ کِس دريا کى موج

تب کها ايک شخص نے تو اِس قدر

حال سے هيگا جهان کے بےخبر؟

ڈیوک آف ڈنیرہ ہی جِس کا نام

دھاک سے لرزے ھی جِس کے رُوم و شام

. . . . .

. . . . .

سُنکے یوں بولا دُعاکر پالمر

نِت رہے اِس شمع سے پُرنور گھر

Elegant and spirited enough, it will be admitted, to make one yearn for more, particularly as Palmer at this time wrote his best.

Before I proceed to notice Palmer's celebrated account of the Sháh's visit in the *Akhbár*, I should like to draw attention to his 'Concise Dictionary of the Persian Language' published in 1876—a small work of a common kind, but with some singular and suggestive points. In using the book, anyone will not fail to note the brevity and pointedness of most of the English equivalents, and the sprinkling of idiomatic and colloquial phrases which run through it and show that Palmer was no mere 'dictionary-man.' Take the following phrases—*úrá tarjumán kardand, tír kun, ham khurmá wa ham sawábast, gosh-i tú dú dádand wa zabán-i tú yake, man ḥáfiẓa-e khargoshe dáram, danda-ash narm shavad, man jastam az rúe dú ṣafḥa, ín pashmast, wa'ssalám,* &c—evidences of

the *practical* bent of the man who noted them.
But Palmer could have filled his book with striking
and philosophical information, had he purposed doing
so.   Take his curt, but suggestive, note on *khún-i
jigar* (or *dil*) *khurdan*—an expression usually, because
easily, paraphrased—how many are there who grasp
the precise and philosophical ideas covered by this
expression and its congeners in Firdausí, Sa'dí, Ḥáfiẓ,
Jámí, &c ?   Palmer, I know well, had grasped them ;
for I owe to him a number of profound strictures and
observations on my own protracted and laboured
attempts to define and settle this most interesting point.
It is a pity he did not give his readers many notes of the
khún-i jigar kind.   He fitly paraphrases *núshíján*, for
instance, but does not elucidate it.   And yet I know
well how heavily he bore on the intelligent Indian
probationer who knew no more of *nosh-i ján farmánd*
than Forbes gives, and how deftly he transfixed the
expression with an arrow of exegesis, to the surprise
and delight of the examinee !   Two or three trifling
instances, also, of Palmer's fine sense of humour in
matching a proverb or a nickname are to be found
in this little volume—*barát bar shákh-i áhú, ḳazalbásh,
káfúr*, &c.   Palmer was exceedingly great at this sort
of thing ; and the wonder is that almost every page
of the book has not a *mot*.   In short, it is not so much
to the book as a mere dictionary I would draw attention as to the singular and suggestive points it contains, which, though but straws, for the most part, are

unmistakable indicators of the veering of the author's mind and scholarship. In explaining his words, Palmer has, in many instances, explained himself.

A year or two previous to the publication of his Persian Dictionary, Palmer had published an Arabic Grammar, in the construction of which he " followed [for the most part] the system adopted by the native grammarians, believing it to be more suitable than the Greek or Latin methods." He forgot, no doubt, that he was writing for those who, for the most part, have been trained in ' Greek and Latin methods,' to say nothing of the Aryan modes of thought which form part of their mental state. It cannot be said of the Etymology and Syntax of this work that they are superior to, or even equal to, those of its great predecessors ; at all events, they are far from superseding them. But, though it is difficult to find adequate grounds for the publication of this Grammar in its Etymology and Syntax, the case is very different when we turn to its Prosody and Glossary. The Prosody, despite its many deficiencies and even errors, is a solid *raison d'être* for the book. Palmer knew, as every first-rate Arabic scholar knows, that without a thorough knowledge of the rules of versification, one cannot properly *construe* an unpointed poem. " Prosody," says he, " is a most valuable aid to the critical study of the language and literature ; " " it enables one to correct the errors of copyists and printers, and, in this way, to understand

passages which would be otherwise obscure." In all
this he is emphatically right. If the book needs an
excuse, it has it alone in the contribution to Arabic
Prosody it contains. It was Palmer's intention, I
know, to have corrected the errors and supplied the
deficiencies of his essay in the second edition of
the work. He thought of giving short rules for
ascertaining the metres, and English counterparts
for rhythm and rhyme. He sent me a *rough*
sketch of these rules and counterparts in 1875 ; and
as the *formulæ* of so consummate a versifier may be
of interest to others, I will transcribe from his MS.
six of his counterparts. The *principal* accent he
marked = (subscribed), the *secondary* one — (subscribed), and the *cæsura* ‖ (erect). Counterpart of

I. Basiṭ :—

> Let us have a | little sport ‖ if 'tis but an | hour or two :
> Oh that I could | only say ‖ what is best for | us to do !

II. Hazaj :—

> We sing all day ‖ we dance all night ‖ we quaff till morn
> The pure red wine ‖ so clear and bright ‖ the brimming horn.

III. Kámil :—

> In a merry dance ‖ in a shady spot ‖ on a summer day,
> We love to sing ‖ and we love to sport ‖ and we love to play.

IV. Khafíf :—

> This is all that | men have ever ‖ yet attained to :
> Just to find them | selves delighted ‖ aye and pained too.

V. Madíd (our *blank* verse) :—

Long we wandered | while the way ‖ seemed a dreadful | wilderness : [1]
Like a host of | people led ‖ by a prophet | on we press.

VI. Ṭawíl :—

May God par|don thee this sin ‖ Oh ! where is | the love I pray ?
And where is | the kindly heart ‖ thou didst here|tofore display ?

Such information as this is as useful as it is interesting : it breathes a little life into dry bones, as anyone may see by comparing Palmer's English counterpart of the metre (*ṭawíl*) of the first *Mu'allaḳa* with the Latin counterpart of Sir William Jones—

amator| puellarum |miser sæ| pe fallitur |
Ocellis| nigris, labris| odoris, |nigris comis|

Neither *rhythm* nor *rhyme* are represented in this mere detail of 'longs and shorts.' Why not write at once *fa'ílun mafá'ílun &c*?

It is to be hoped that some other hand will, in due time, simplify and vivify Palmer's Prosodial facts, and enlarge and elucidate his '.Glossary of Technical Terms,' and so give his Arabic grammar that individuality which, I am sure, he meant it to have.

The next piece of Palmer's work I wish to consider is his celebrated account in Urdú of the Sháh's Visit, to which I have more than once alluded, and which appeared in the *Akhbár* of December 2, 1873. This article, so '*charming and wonderful*' (*dilchasp*

---

[1] Proper form, without last foot.

aur 'ajá'ib ghará'ib, in the editor's words), fills thirty-six columns of the paper, or, taking the superficial measurement, contains as much matter as twenty columns of the ' Times '! I cannot do more than select and present a number of salient points, so as to enable my readers to guess the massive proportions of this monument of Palmer's skill and perseverance—skill, for it is full of " idiomatic phraseology and poetical genius ; " perseverance, because " the writing of such things was a laborious and artificial task " to him. One is sure in selecting portions of such a production to do injustice to the rest ; for, where an entire article is evenly worthy of attention, it is really paying it but a poor compliment to single out particular parts : *al'intikháb al'intiháb*, as the Arabs might say in such a case.

I have quoted the *Akhbár* verbatim, as much as possible, not without frequent misgivings as to the accuracy of the lithographer, who is more likely to have abused Palmer's copy than Palmer is to have written badly. I have added here and there notes, which, though mainly designed to explain or defend Palmer, may be of use to my younger readers.

Palmer prefaced his article with a Persian *ruḳ'a* in which he craves indulgence for inevitable errors, explaining that "he had learnt his *Urdú* in England, and had never even set foot in India." [1]

---

[1] *Aḳḳar taḥṣíl-i zabán-i Urdú dar hamín wiláyat karda, wa gáhe dar Hind ḳadam ham na niháda.*

After mentioning the position and character of the
port of Dover, the *posse* of noblemen and officials
awaiting the Sháh's arrival there, the costly preparations of the Corporation for his reception, the '*gallant
troops*' (*sipáh-i jarrár*) and '*huge guns*' (*atwáp-i
azhdar-dahán*) drawn up for '*the salute*' (*salámí*), the
concourse of sightseers from London and elsewhere
in their '*best clothes*' (*libás-i ma'kúl*), &c—he proceeds :—

اوسوقت ایک عجب بہار تھي کہ—کسُي کوس سے
جو سلامیان بادشاہ کے واسطے ہوتي تِھیں اونکے دہوُون کي بہار
جیسے معشوقرن کي پیچدار زُلفین نمودار کنارۂ بحر پر ایک
چہہکچہہ ہو رہاتھا—اور ہرایک متنفس بادشاہزادون سے
لیکر فقیر تک اِسطرح منتظر تھا جیسے روزہدار¹ ہلالِ عید
کے ہون —

از بسکہ چشم دارم کآن مہ زِ در درآید
از جا چہم جو ناگہہ آواز در درآید

---

¹ In allusion to the '*Festival of fast-breaking*' ('*Idu'lfitr*), at the
end of *Ramazán*. The couplet that follows is clear enough, *mah*
being used for '*a beauty*' or '*mistress.*'

The Sháh in due course arrives at Dover—

تو ہزاروں آدمیوں نے صدائے دُرّا سے کان کَروبیوں کے کر

کرڈالے—اوّلا میر ڈوور کے مع اپنے عملوں کے خلعتِ

فاخرہ زمانۂ قدیم کي درباری اور جواہرِ زواہر سے مغرق

آدابِ پیشوائي بجالائے—بعد اسکے وزیرِ دولتِ خارجہ² لارڈ

گرینول مشرف بملازمت ہوے—ابتو ہر لمحہ بڑي گرماگرمي

ہونے لگی—اورباجہ سلامتيُ ملکہ اور بادشاہ³ ہرطرف سے

بجنے لگے — پھر حاکم ڈوور نے ایک تہنیّت نامہ

بحضورِ بادشاہ بزبانِ انگریزي بڑي فصاحت اور بلاغت سے

پڑھا—اور ایک رومال ابریشم کا جسپر موتیوں کي جھالر

اور الماس ٹکے ہوے تھے اور اوسپر اوسکا ترجمۂ فارسي⁴

نذر گذرانا—

Palmer's description of the scene at Charing Cross Station is exceedingly graphic and poetical :—

[1] ' *With his robes &c on,*' as we say.
[2] ' *The Foreign Secretary.*'
[3] ' *God save the Queen and Sháh.*'
[4] This translation was Syed's, and was much admired by the Sháh. As Palmer adds—*bádsháh ne pákízagi-e tahrír aur khúbi-e inshá par áfrín kí.*

ایک کوس تک تمام دیوارین سُرخ چادروں

سے مڑھي—کیلوں کے کھنب اوپر سنہرے کلَس¹ اور

جھنڈے بادشاهي آویزان—پھولوں کي خوشبو سے مغز معطّر هو

رهے تھے—تمام چھت مقامِ راهِ آهني پر علَم شاهي اور

آئینے حَلبي لٹک رهے تھے اور اِنمیں نقش جو زمین پر

تھے پرتے تھے—هزارون گاڑیاں دواسپ اور چاراسپ اور

چھهاسپ اوںپر جو کوچوان اور خواص² تھے لباس طلائي

اور هار زمرّد اور الماس کے گلوں میں—اور چوبدار بڑے بڑے

عصے طلائي³ جنکے سر پري سرچهرہ⁴ اور الماس سے مرصّع

—اوس شام کو شدتِ گرمي آولا تو⁵ زیرِ سقف بلّوريِ

ریلوي اِستیشن—اور کثرت بھیڑ لیڈیاں عرق سے عرق—

عرق کے قطرے گُلرخوں پر موتیوں کي لڑي سے چمکتے تھے

اور اون پریوں کے گورے گورے مُکھڑوں پر زُلفیں اِس طرح

سے بِکھر رهي تھیں گویا آبِ حیات کي طمع سے افعال اوڑکر

---

¹ This looks like a fetch of *Prem Ságar—kele ke khambh au subaran kalas* &c.

² ' *Coachmen and footmen.*'

³ Something like *háthon men* is wanted hereabout.

⁴ ' *Like a fairy's forehead*,' as I read it.   ⁵ Virtually = *khuṣúṣaṇ.*

چاند کو جا لگے دھوں—پنکھے جو بعضوں کے ہاتھوں سے
جھلتے تھے تو ایسا معلوم ہوتا تھاکہ ابرِ سیاہ رُخِ آفتاب پر
چھا رہا ہي—

The Sháh's train being expected to arrive every
moment—

اب ہر لمحہ امیدواريُ دیدارِ فرحت آثارِ¹ شہریارِ
کامگار تھي—کبھي خبر اوڑتي تھي کہ اب ریل گاڑي شاہي
قریب آن پہونچي—

بسکہ در جانِ فِگارم چشمِ بیدارم توُئ
ہرکہ پیدا میشود از دورِ پندارم توُئ²

باوجود گرمي اور انتظاري کے ایک طرح کي چُھل اور
زندہدلي سبھوں کے دِلوںپر چھا رہي تھي کہ یکایک شلکِ

¹ Palmer was great at compounds of this kind, as I have said
before. He did not use them glibly, as many do; but knew well their
true origin and exact meaning.
² '*In that of my weary* (i.e. from long watching) *soul the constant
expect art thou,*
Whoever appears on the horizon, I fancy thou art (he).'
Here, apparently, *dar iṣṭiláḥ-i 'áshiḳán chashm-i bedár kindya az
maḥbúb-i fitna-angez báshad.*

سلامي قلعہ لنڈن سے بمجرد چھونے نافِ لنڈن کے دنادن [1]
دغنے لگین—اب کوئي دقیقہ کي بات باقي نہي [2]—لیڈیان
معزز مسوش حُوررِشک یکبارگي جیسے کوئي کل کہ کھینچتا
ہو اوٹھ اوٹھ کھڑي ہوئین کہ ترینِ شاہي بھي جیسے کہ مہر
از مطلعِ انوار برآید طالع ہوئے—روزِ انتظار آخر اور شام
اضطرار کو سحَر [3]

دوبارہ لب نہ کُشاید صدف بہ ابرِ بہار

کریم سائلِ خودرا غنی کند یکبار [4]

ایک ہلچل سي ہوئي حتّیکہ گاریون کے گھوڑے بھي ٹاپین
مارنے لگے اور سببون کي انکھین نرگسوار ایک طرف پرہ
تیروارہ [5] جم گئین—

Palmer next describes the meeting of the Sháh and
Prince of Wales, and the subsequent royal procession

---

[1] This word (clearly lithographed) for *damádam*, no doubt.
[2] ' *Now all trifles are dropped.*'
[3] A little abrupt, perhaps, but plain.
[4] Every one knows of the conceit of the 'pearl-oyster.'
[5] A good deal might be said and quoted on this *simile*; but Palmer seems to me to be playing on *nargis*, of which *tlr* is a sort of synonym.

to Buckingham Palace, introducing eleven couplets of excellent poetry. Among other ' *salutes* ' is that of *thunder*—

جب سواري قريب محلِ شاهي كے پهونچي تو

آسمان نے بهي سلامي رعد سے ادا كي

فرو بگرفتہ گيتي‌را بباغ و راغ و كوہ و در

نم ابر و دم باد و تفِ برق و غوِ تُندر

شخ از نسرين هوا از مہ چمن ازگل تل از سبزہ

حواصل‌بال و شاهين‌چشم و هدهدتاج وطوطي‌پر

زِ ابرو اُقحوان ولالہ و شاہ‌اسپرم گوے

هوا اسود زمين ابيض دمن احمر چمن اخضر [1]

[1] These three couplets (in *hazaj*) are exceedingly clever and difficult. Through each runs a clear compound antithesis. In the *first* couplet, the *ba*-words being descriptive or restrictive of *gítí*, we must arrange and construe—*farú bigirifta gítírá babágh nam-i abr, wa barágh dam-i bád, wa bakh taf-i bark, wa badar ghav-i tundar*—*dar* being ' *a mountain-pass* ' here. In the *second* couplet, which may have been suggested by the expression *túti-e ṣaḥrá* (= *sabza* in the *Kashf* and *kind-ya az sabza-e ṣaḥrá* in the *Haft*, &c), we must arrange—*shakh az nisrín ḥawáṣil-bál, wa hawá az mah sháhín-chashm, wa chaman az gul hudhud-táj, wa tal az sabza túti-par* ; and, minding the compound epithets, construe—' *the peak in* (*its*) *eglantine* (*looks*) *like the wing of a pelican ; the sky in* (*its*) *moon, the eye of a falcon ; the parterre in* (*its*) *rose, the crest of a hoopoo ; and the upland in* (*its*) *verdure, the plumage of a parrot.*' In the *third* couplet, arrange and construe—

تو ایک عجب گڑبڑ پڑی—پریوں کے اکھاڑے آدمیوں کے

غت کے غت بھیگتے بھاگتے ہانپتے جدھر جسکے سینگ

سمائے ۱ دکھلائی دیتے تھے—راقم بھی ایک مکانِ بلند پر سے

دوربین لگاکر سیرکر رہا تھا—

I pass over Palmer's sharp description of Buckingham Palace, of the banquet where the wines were
' *four hundred years* ' (*chár sau baras kí !*) old, and
(partly in verse) of the *suite* of the Sháh on his first
visit to the Queen at Windsor. The Eton boys and
school children cheer and cheer again and make the
welkin ring, when

یہ ایک عجب ماجرا گذرا کہ لاکھوں کوے خودبخود جو

باغات اور جہازی میں تھے آسمان پر کاؤکاؤ کرتے تھے اور اونکی

آواز کی ایسی سمان بندھی تھی جیسے شا شا نکلتی ہو—

He next describes (partly in verse) the costly
preparations of the Corporation of London—the
artistic ' *cards of invitation* ' (*wasliyán da'wat kí*),

C C

&c—and the state visit to the Guildhall, where the Sháh receives addresses and, among other promises,

وعدهٔ موقوفِ رسمِ قبیحهٔ بَردهفروشي یک قلم اپنے
قلمرو سے کیا—

Whereupon, Palmer pats the Sháh on the back, and says—

في آلحقیقت اعلٰی حضرت بادشاهِ ایران کوہِ دانش و
دوراندیشي عادل و باذل بري از تعصّب ہیں

Next comes Mír Aulád 'Alí's Persian address on behalf of the authorities of Trinity College, Dublin, which Palmer gives *in extenso*; and well he may: for it is a singularly elegant and happy production.

The Sháh is, of course, taken to Woolwich: then to the Italian Opera, of which we read—

تو کیا دیکھتے ہیں کہ سات سو پریزاد گلاندام مہرچہرہ
زُهرهجبین—ماهتابان و خورشید درخشان اونپہ شیدا ہي ¹—
هرایک پري پرهلے زمرّد اور مروارید اور الماس ٹکے لگلے
هوے ضیاے گیاس ہیں ایسا معلوم ہوتا تھا ² کہ هزاروں ماهتاب

---

¹ A hemistich, of course, in *hazaj.*
² So lithographed clearly.

نکلے ہیں—جوجو راگ اور سَوانگ اور کرتب اور تماشے

دکھلائے کہ بادشاہ اور ہمراہی حیران ہوگئے اِلہی یہ

خواب ہے اور یہ سپچ سپچ کے آدمزاد ہیں یا پریوں کا اکھاڑا

اُترا ہے—خصوصاً جب پریاں تارکے زور سے مثل طائروں کے

اڑتیاں تِھیں یکایک بادشاہ اور سب ہمراہی کی زبان سے

بے بے کی صدا بلند ہوئی—اگر شمہ اوس کا بیان لکھوں تو قلم

بشکن سیاہی ریز کاغذ سوز دم درکش کا عالم ہوا—[1]

The Sháh goes to Portsmouth, and to Windsor a
second time for the review, where—

توپخانۂ رعدنہیب برق نشاں نے ایسی صاعقہ باری اور

آتش افشانی دکھلائی کہ دریا دریا لشکر مانند بحر کے جنبش

میں آگیا—اور توپہلے رعدخروش اژدھاپیکر نے صورت

رَستخیز کی نُمایاں کر دی—[2]

---

[1] Another hemistich in *hazaj*—'*it would be a case of break-pen, spill-ink, burn-paper, shut-up!*'

[2] No one need be told of the purport of *similes* drawn from the *roz-i ḳiyamat* or *roz-i rastakhez*, as Ḥáfiẓ calls it. Palmer's *ṣúrat namáyán kar dí* follows, no doubt, expressions like *ṣúratnamá shudan*, &c.

The Sháh does the lions of the City—visits the Tower, the Bank, the 'Times' Office, &c—all of which Palmer describes with remarkable terseness and vividness. Subsequently he is taken to the Albert Hall, to hear his praises sung by choruses of men and women, of men alone, and women alone. I give Palmer's Persian translation of the chorus of men and women—

مُبارک مُبارک سلامت شها

مبارک مبارک سلامت شها

بهبین آمد از ملکِ ایران زمین

شهُ نامور باجلالِ مبین

بهدَورِش خلائق گرفته هجوم

صدای خوشی خاست هر سُو عموم

چه خُلقی که از دستِ فَیضانِ شاه

زِ عقل و زِ دانش شود روبراه[1]

---

[1] The *Ta'rifát* defines one *'akl* (= *dánish*) thus—*al-'aklu bi'lmala-kati huwa'l'ilm &c*; and *malaka*, according to the same book, is 'an acquired, permanent, mental habit' = *'ádat wa khulk*. Palmer has, therefore, authority for the combination *khulk az 'akl*, at all events. Translate, taking *rúbaráh shudan* and *dast-i faizán* as seemingly used here on trust—'what a (*fine*) character (*it is*) that is formed of the Sháh's generosity, (*his*) intelligence, and (*his*) knowledge!'

مبارک مبارک سلامت شها

صدای رسیده زِ چرخِ برین

مبارک شها مقدمِ این زمین

جوابی رسیده زِ افلاک باز

مبارک سلامت شهُ بے نیاز

شهُ پارس آمد زِ شکرِ عیان [1]

نه از قصدِ تسخیرِ مُلک و جهان

مگر اینکه حاصل کند نامِ نیک

شود از سخاوت سرانجامِ نیک

گذارد همین تیغِ خود درِ غلاف

که صُلح و امان به زِلاف و گُذاف

بخواهد که مانندِ شاهنشهان

بماند بے نامِ او درجهان

The Sháh next pays a visit to Liverpool, where
he was fitly received, entertained, and toasted by the
Mayor—

[1] My copy being blotted here, reading doubtful.

اعلیٰ حضرت لاڑدان و صاحبان میرے سلامت—میں '

پیالہ صحت اعلیٰ حضرت شاہنشاہ کا جو نسلاً بعد نسلٍ

خاقان الخواقین و شاہنشاہِ قدیم و پاستان کے ' ہیں ہمارے

مُلک میں تشریفِ شریف لئے اور معزز اور مُمتاز فرمایا

اور پایۂ اتحاد فیمابین دولتین انگلند و ایران کے واسطے دوام کے

پُختہ اور مضبوط کیا دولت و ثروت و عمر و حشمتِ

شاہنشاہ یوماً فیوماً

From Liverpool he proceeds to Manchester;
thence to the Duke of Sutherland's at Trentham,
where he first encounters the bagpipe. Palmer com-
pares it with the ' *snake-charming* ' (*sámp pakaṛne ko*)
pipe of the *madárí log*—

---

[1] The lithographer makes no doubt about the sentence beginning
with *maiŋ*; so that the verb—*lekar pítá húŋ*, or the like—must have
been left out.

[2] Kaikáwus or Kaikhusrú would be pre-eminently *sháhansháh*, though
the title was by no means restricted to great potentates, as is well known.
Among the ' *Turkomans* ' (*turkán*) the terms *beglarbeg*, *khánkhánán*,
and *khákánu'lkhawákín* conveyed much the same idea. Jingíz Khán
would be an eminent example of this. *Ibn Khallikán* (*sub al'ikhshíd*)
gives the titles of divers sovereigns, assigning that of *khákán* to the
Turkomans alone. Observe, however, the *Kashf—khákán bádsháh-i
turkán wa bádsháh-i chín har dú bádsháh ki dar zamín-i turkistán
buzurgtar búd.* After *ke* some such word as *aulád*, *gharáne*, &c *se*
may be supplied.

مگر صرف فرق یہ ہي کہ بیگچہآپس کي آواز زیادہتر

شیرین اور بلند ہوتي ہي—جب وہ باجہ بجنے لگا تو

حضرت ملکہ معظمہ بحروبر ہفت کشور کے فرزند اور

مہاراجہ دلیپ سنگھ بہادر اوسکے سُر پر ناچے اور زمین

پر کرچ دھرکر پنتیرے دکھلاۓ¹—بادشاہ باغباغ ہوگۓ پھر وہ

مداري بادشاہ کے پاس آیا اور ایک بوتل برانڈي کي کھولي اور

سوڈا واتر ڈالکر ایک بڑے گلاس مین بیرکر حضرت بادشاہ

کے ہاتھ مین دیا—شاہ حیران ہوۓ کہ اِسکے کیا معنے

ہین—عرض کیا یہ پیالہ محبت کا ہي—بادشاہ نے فرمایا کہ

یہ سب سمجھے نہ پیا جاویگا—کہا البتہ دو ایک گھونٹ

—حضرت نے دونون ہاتھون گلاس پکڑکر دو چار گھونٹ

نوشجان فرمائے اور مُسکراکر کہا تو رسم ادا ہو گئي—

سب لوگ کِھلکھلاکر ہنس پڑے

There were magnificent fire-works at Trentham;
one set-piece, a '*fire-ball*' (*átashín golá*), is finely
described—

---

¹ In allusion to a 'sword-dance,' no doubt.

پائین باغ سے ایک آتشین گولا سُرخ جلتا چمکتا

بھڑکتا دھمکتا لَہلَہاتا تڑپتا ایک بڑے تالاب میں گِرا—

اور پھر نِکلکر کئی ہزار فُٹ اوپر اوٹھا اور اوسمیں سے

دو دیو آتشین نِکلے اور باہم مثل رُستم اور اِسفندیار کے

خوب لڑے اور لڑتے لڑتے جب اونکے پیٹ پھٹے تو دو

نِہنگانِ جنگی نِکلے اور وہ خوب لڑے اور جب اونکے سر

کٹ گئے اور دھڑ رہ گئے تو ہزاروں سانپ آسمان سے مثل

شُعلے کے نمودار ہوکر باہمدیگر[1] دوسرے کو مارتے کھاتے

نگلتے اور طرح بطرح کے کیڑے مکوڑے بِچھو طیور ٹِڈی سے

لیکر تا عقاب ظاہر ہوئے—

The Shâh enquired of the Prince next day—how much a year the Duke had ; and, on being told he had 'four krores,' exclaimed—

جو ایسا زبردست اور باثروت ہمسر کوئی امیر ہماری

سلطت میں ہوتا اسکا قتل ضرور تھا—

Of the Crystal Palace, to which the Shâh paid two visits, Palmer says—

[1] This is a little *berabt.*

شیش محل کے برابر دنیا میں کوئی جگہ نہیں ہے —
سب ایرانی اور شاہ اور خلائق کہتے تھے کہ البتہ یہ جادو ہے
طلسم ہے یا نظربند کر دی ہے —

On the second visit to the Palace, the Sháh went *incognito*—'*without crown, sword, or jewels*' (*táj aur shamshír aur jawáhir ke baghair*), with only a few attendants. He mingled freely with the 'shilling-crowd' and was mistaken for one of his own retinue—

بادشاہ سے خود بذریعہ مترجم جو فرانسیسی
زبان جانتا تھا پوچھا کہ تم کو بادشاہ کی سرکار میں کون
عہدہ ہے — بادشاہ نے فرمایا خدمتگارِ خاص اور معتمد
علیہ اور چند ہمراہیوں نے کہا کہ بادشاہ ان پر بہت
اعتماد رکھتے ہیں — صدہا ملِقا دخترانِ فرنگ نے
اشتیاق گرمجوشی اور لمسِ اناملِ فیض شوامل[1] ظاہر کیا
— اکثروں کو اعلیٰ حضرت نے سرافراز فرمایا[2] —

---

[1] A plural, no doubt, of *shámila* = '*something comprehensive in its reach.*' This stylist compound (not uncommon) rigidly means—'*whose reaches are bounty's.*'

[2] 'Kissed them,' I presume.

On the occasion of the Sháh's attendants visiting Syed at Fulham Place, they met Palmer himself : both are invited by them to meet the Sháh at the Palace—

اِس کمترین کو اور سیدِ ممدوح کو یہ پیامِ شاهي سُنایا کہ بادشاہ نے تم دونوں صورتوں کو طلب فرمایا هي —

میرے ساتھ چلے — همنے کہا خلافِ رائے سُلطان رائ جُستن + زِ خونِ خویش باید دست شُستن — کیا مضایقہ الامر فوق الادب —

To Buckingham Palace they accordingly repaired, and found the '*Sháh-i Jálim*,' as Palmer calls him, inspecting St. Thomas' and Bethlehem. On his return, they were duly presented—

مؤدِب سینہ پر هاتھ رکھکر آداب بجائے — سیّد کا حال پوچھا

A brief conversation with Syed ensues, and Palmer is requested to come forward—

پھر حال اِس بےپروبال کا پوچھا اور فرمایا نزد بیا — کُجا فارسي و عربي یاد گرفتي؟ — فارسي از سیّد عبد اللہ

و عربي از عربان دراينجا و هم در عرب رفته آموختم—فرمايا

كه من شُنيده ام تو شاعرِ فارسي هستي—اين هيچمدان

كم كم ميگويد ذِ لاتي سماعتِ بندگانِ اَعلىٰ حضرت[1]—

بهت هنسے—بعده پوچها اين كارِ مدرس از طرفِ كيست؟

—مين نے كہا فدوي خاص مدرّس از طرفِ ملكهٔ معظمهٔ

انگلند است و اين عهده مُختصّ از طرفِ ملكهٔ مايان

است—چند تلامذه ميداري؟—بالفعل همه به اوطانِ

خود رفته اند كه ايامِ تعطيل اند[2]—اَعلىٰ حضرت نهايت

خنده پيشاني سے هنس هنس كے كلام فرمانے رهے اور ذرا غرور

اور نخوت كا نام نہيں—اور صورت سے آثارِ سُلطاني و رعبِ

قہرماني اور ظهورِ مكرمتِ ظلِّ سُبحاني پديدار تهے سُبحانَ

اللّٰه كيا كہنا هي—هم لوگ مُرخص هوئے تو روزنامچه نگار

نے همارے نام اور نشان درجِ نامچه كئے اور دستخط

اوس مين درج كروائے

---

[1] Palmer's answers, if not pointed, are adroit.

[2] '*Afterwards* (*the Sháh*) *enquired*—" *Whose Professor are you?*" I replied, " *I am the Queen's* own *Professor, my office being a special one of our Queen's.*" " *How many pupils have you?*" " *At present they have all gone down, it being vacation-time.*"'

The Shah's questions & P's answers
reported in Persian

Both Syed and Palmer accompanied the Shâh
and party in the visit paid to Madame Tussaud's,
where a sumptuous repast was prepared.   The Shâh,
being due elsewhere, left his attendants (including
Palmer) to partake of the feast—

راقم شریک ملازمانِ شاهي کے بطورِ مُترجِم وهين
ٹهرگیا—علی الصباح بڑے مداح شراب کے تهے ک.
آبِ حیات تهي—ذرا بهي دردِ سریا خلل[1] نهین کیا—
اور کیوں نَ هو ایک ایک بوتل شامپین دس دس
روپے کي تهي اور ایک سو بوتل نوشجان هو گئین

On July 5th the Shâh left London.   Palmer
follows his movements for six more columns.   But
enough—more than enough, indeed—has been given
of this wonderful article to demonstrate the skill and
perseverance of the author.

There is no need to pursue the examination of
Palmer's works any further : *frater est prioris posterior
liber.*   One thing, however, seems to me to demand a
little emphasis, and that is Palmer's power both of
speaking and of writing a scholarlike type of practical
modern Arabic : by this he is best and widest known.
His power of *speaking* is well attested by evidence

---

[1] '*A megrim.*'

accessible to all : of that power, of course, no actual
exemplars can be given.   But, at the instance of the
Spanish saying—*hablen cartas y callen barbas*, I will
put on record that which is now the best available
exemplar of the powers mentioned, viz. a group of
Arabic letters in the practical familiar style, penned
sine ullâ solennitate, so to speak.

The three last Oriental letters I ever received
from Palmer were of this character—written, indeed,
in so easy a style that he 'who runs may read.' These
letters are dated December 1877 and January 1878,
and treat of matters of interest to both, not of a
private or confidential nature.   I have myself *vocalised*
Palmer's words, to assist my readers ; but, of course,
though very careful about his *nuḳaṭ*, Palmer left *iḍbâṭ*
and *i'râb* to his correspondents.

The *first* letter comes from 'Lansdowne Hotel,
Bournemouth.'   In it Palmer attributes his neglect
of writing me to the state of his wife's health, who
had been delivered of a son, and was then confined
to her bed, suffering from incurable phthisis.   He
then describes a very flattering testimonial he had
written for me, and expresses his earnest wish that
I may be appointed his colleague at Oxford :--

ش كانون الأوّل سنــــــــه ١٨٧٧

مولايَ و ملاذي و سيّدي و أُستاذي لا عدمته[1]—بعدَ
ابلاغِكم اشواقٍ توأديّة و تحيّاتٍ ذكيّة اعرِض أنّني اليوم
تشرّفتُ بمرسومِكم الكريم وصِرتُ به قريرَ العين وامّا عدمُ
مُكاتبتي جنابَكم في أثناء هذه المدّة الطويلة فسببُه اشغالُ
بالي بانواعِ البلايا اوّلُها وآخِرُها صحّةُ قرينتي العزيزة فانّها
كانت مريضةً جدًّا جدًّا ثمّ عوفيت ثمّ وُلِدَ لنا مولودٌ ثمّ عادَ
مرضُها الّذي هُوَ مرضُ الرّئتين وها هِيَ الآنَ لازِمةٌ مضجِعها ولا
يبقى أملٌ في شِفائها وهِيَ تغييرةُ السِّنِّ مُطيعةُ[2] الاخلاقِ
جميلةُ الصورةِ كريمةُ السّيرةِ ولكنني استغفرُ اللهَ ان أُكلّف
خاطرَكم العزيزَ بشَرحِ حُزني وارجوكم العفوَ—وامّا المادّةُ
المذكورةِ في مكتوبِكم اعني طلبَكم عُهدةَ التدريسِ العربيّ
في اوكسفُرد فطيّةَ تجدون[3] مكتوبٌ من عند ابينا[4] قد وصل

---

[1] '*May I not lose him,*' instead of the more logical *lá a'damaní faḍlahu.*

[2] Palmer slipped and wrote *muṭá'a,* but recalled and corrected.

[3] Supply here *wa hiya,* I suppose. Of the word *ṭíyat* I shall speak presently.

[4] Name omitted for obvious reasons.

لي قبلَ يومَين او ثلاثةِ اَيام نداءِيكم عند مُطالعتِهِ كتبتُ الي
القسيس الموصوفِ فوراً و مَدَحتُ عِلمَكم الجليل لاسِيَّما
بالعربية

و قُلتُ إني لا اعرِفُ شخصًا مِن اَبناء وطَني اجدَرَ
بهذه العهدة مِن حضرتِكم وإنَّني لم اَرَ احد الآنكليزيِّين
الَّذي معرِفتُهُ اللسانَ العربيَّ و الادَب الشرقيَّ مثلَ معرِفتِكم
إياَّه و اَني احسَبُ جنابَكم مِن اعلمِ العُلماء و اَفضلِ الفُضلآء
وكدّدتُهم¹ تأكيدًا جدّاً في تقريرِكم وإمتثالاً لأمرِكم قد كتبتُ
سطوراً ايضًا في هذا المعني تجدونها في جوفِ هذا المغلَّف
و ارجو اَنها تُؤيد جنابَكم في طلَبِكم هذه العهدةَ
الجليلة لأنَّه كُلَّ ما ذكرتُ مِن مَدائحِ حضرتِكم قد كتبتُهُ
مِن صميمِ الفُؤاد و غايةِ رجايَ أنَّكم تصيروا مُصاحِبي في
العهدة المذكورة—و المرجو مِن مكارِمكم اَن تحفَظوا كتاب
القسيس الموصوفِ ولا تعرِّفوا احدًا بِما قالهُ—و آللهُ تعالي
يُديم وجودَكم الشريفَ طوالَ المَدى و الدُعا—الداعي ادورد
هنري پالمر

¹ Palmer wrote اكدتهم inadvertently.

The *second* letter is dated from the 'Royal Hotel, Bristol,' to which place Palmer had gone to preside at the 'Local Examination.' In it he expresses his readiness to write at once—*apropos* of a notice he had just seen in the 'Times'—respecting certain (contemplated) changes in the character of the Lord Almoner's Chair. He again adverts to his wife's alarming illness, forbidding the faintest hope, sure to end fatally. Then he proceeds to answer a question I had asked in my last—'whether he cared for good cigars?' I had had a few boxes sent me as a (supposed) present; and, being no smoker, I proposed to send them on to him. The letter ends with a few words descriptive of a 'Local Examination' room :—

١٨ مِن شهرِ كانون الأول

سيدي و حبيبي العزيز ادامَ اللهُ تعالي بقاهُ—غِبَّ إهداءِ اوفرِ السلام اعرِض تشرّفتُ اليومَ بمكتوبِكم الشريف وامّا ما اشرتم اليه مِن تنبيهِ رئيسِنا عن تبديلِ صورة الكُرسيّ المَدرسيّ في قمبرج فعلي الرأس و العَين و سوفَ أكاتِبهُ في ذلكَ الخصوصِ مِن دُونِ تأخيرٍ وامّا السّاعةُ فمُناسِبة و مُباركة لأنّه يتوجدُ[1] في صحيفةِ التَّيمِس الصّادِرة

---

[1] So Palmer for يُوجَدُ often.

اليومَ خبرٌ من كمبرج يُشيرُ الي ذلكَ ايضًا—ثم مِن شأنِ

المِسكينةِ زوجتي فحالُها لا تَتغَيَّر و داعيكم لا ازالُ في

الخوف و القلَق جزاكم اللهُ علي تسليَتِكم عبدكم خيرًا

ولكنني لا أراها الَّا في أُردَى حالٍ يومًا فيومًا و امّا الامَلُ

فمضمَحِلٌّ و امّا يومُ الرجا فقد صارَ ليلَ الدجى و ربّما١

ستمكثُ في قيدِ الحيوةِ شهرًا او شهرين فامّا فوقَ ذلكَ

فلا أظنُّ أن يلبَثَ الحينُ و قد صدقَ مَن قال

فلا تَبْعَدْ فكلُّ فتًى سيأتي

عليه الموتُ يطرُقُ أو يُغادي

و علي اللهِ توكُّلي ونِعْمَ الوكيلُ٢—وامّا ما شرحتُموه

في خصوص شربي الدُخان و حُبّي السِكاراتِ الطيّبة فأنا

أشكرُ فضلكم كُلَّ الشُكرِ وجنابُكم اكرمُ المُكرمين ولكنَّ الصحيحَ

انّي لا اشرَبُ السِكاراتِ الّا قليلًا بل اشرَبُ الحِيرونَاتِ

اَلْمَنِيلِّيَاتِ ١ فِي بَعْضِ ٱلْأَوْقَاتِ وَ ٱلْبَيْبِهِ ٢ فِي اكْثَرِهَا وَ عَلَى كُلِّ

حَالٍ حَاشَا أَنْ اثْقُلَ عَلَى حَضْرَتِكُمْ وَ أَتَطَفَّلَ فِي إِحْسَانِكُمْ

وَأَنَا لَا أُرِيدُ شَيْئًا اَلَّا دَوَامَ ٱلْمَحَبَّةِ وَ ٱلْاِخْلَاصِ مَا بَيْنَ الطَّرَفَيْنِ —

وَقَدْ كَتَبْتُ هٰذَا الْمَكْتُوبَ فِي غَايَةِ مَا يَكُونُ مِنَ ٱلْعَجَلَةِ فِي وَسَطِ

مَحَلِّ الْإِمْتِحَانِ وَالنَّاسُ يُصَدِّعُونِي بِٱلسُّؤَالَاتِ ٱلْمُضْحِكَة

وَ يُطَيِّرُونَ عَقْلِي بِوَاهِيَاتِهِمْ وَ كَثْرَةِ اصْوَاتِهِمْ —وَاللهُ الْمَسْؤُولُ أَنْ

يُدِيمَ وُجُودَكُمُ الشَّرِيفَ طُولَ الْمَدَى فِي ارْغَدِ عَيْشٍ وَ اسْعَدِ

حَظٍّ وَ الدُّعَا—الدَّاعِي بِٱلْخَيْرِ ادورد هنري پالمر—

The *third* letter comes from ' Hamilton Rise, Bournemouth,' where Palmer was lodging with his dying wife. He thanks me for the cigars which I had sent him, and bespeaks consideration for his ' domestic troubles ' :—

٣ كانون الثاني سـنـ ٧٨

سَيِّدِي وَ حَبِيبِي ٱلْعَزِيزِ ادَامَ اللهُ تَعَالَى بَقَاءُ—غِبَّ

اهْدَاءَ اوْفَرِ السَّلَامِ وَ التَّحِيَّاتِ ٱلْمَعْرُوضِ انِّي أُهَنِّئُكُمْ بِالعِيدِ

السَّعِيدِ وَ العَامِ الجَدِيدِ جَعَلَهُ اللهُ مُبَارَكًا لَكُمْ وَ لِكُلِّ مَنْ يَلُونُ

---

¹ ' *Manilla cheroots.*'   ² ' *Paper.*'

بكم ١ ثمَّ إنَّ صباحَ يوم تأريخهِ ورَدَ اليَّ التُّحفةُ النفيسةُ ٱلتي

أنعمتُم عليَّ داعيكم بتقديمِها فصيَّرتني ممنونًا جدًّا جدًّا

مرهونًا لِمنّتِكم و الحقيقةُ انّي مُستحيي لِعجزي عن إظهارِ

شكري لهذه النعمةِ الجليلة مع عدَمِ استحقاقي بها و امَّا

كتابةٌ مكتوبٌ يليقُ بفضلِكم فلا اقدرُ علي ذلكِ لا سيّما و أنا

في حالٍ يُشغلني عن كل فكرٍ سليم و سببُ ذلكَ أنَّني

قد طلبتُ من لندن طبيبًا حاذقًا فقال مثلَ ما قال طبيبُ

البلَد أن قرينتي العزيزة مُشرِفة علي الموت لا شكَّ—

و أرجوكم عدَم المواخذة—والله يُديم وجودَكم الشريف طولَ

المَدي في العَيش الرغيد و الحظّ السعيد و الدُّعا—مُحِبّكم

ٱلمُخلِص ادورد هنري پالمر—

The three preceding Arabic letters, which I leave
to speak for themselves, were the last *Oriental* letters
I ever received from Palmer. I only wish I had
space and time to give my own letters in correspondence, if only to contrast my own shade with Palmer's
light.

---

[1] ' *merry Christmas and happy New Year to you and yours.*'

The year 1878 must have been a sad and trying [1]
one for Palmer—his wife lay *in extremis,* his youngest
child (a boy) was dead, he himself was struggling
with asthma and congestion of the lungs, and (what
must have been a crushing blow for him) "his very
dear friend" Ḥussún had left him for ever. "This
sort of thing," pleaded Palmer in an English letter,
"does not tend to make one a good correspondent."
No doubt it did not, in one sense ; but, it was sure
to force him to seek solace from his Arabic or Persian
Muse, and, from that point of view, it made him a very
good correspondent indeed. In the English letters he
wrote me Palmer often seemed ill at ease. He would,
under the influence of strong emotion or for the
purpose of criticism, plunge abruptly into Arabic or
Persian, prose or verse. Thus, to the English words

[1] Fancy a man being so deeply distressed and so mentally distracted
as to have written on *the back of an envelope* :—

إنَّ بعد ختامِ لِفافَني هذه قد آنشتَّ للمِسكينةِ

قَرينتي عِرقُ دمٍ وها أنا حارسٌ مضجِعِها و اللهُ يعلم

بالعاقبةِ—أَليسَ هذا مِن داهياتِ الدهرِ—والناس بقولِ

الشاعرِ—

وإن لم يمُتْ بالسَيفِ مات بغيرِهِ

تنوعتِ الاسبابُ والموتُ واحدُ

just quoted, he straightway tacked the beautiful
couplets :—

لَيْتَ شِعرِي هل كَفَى ما قد جَرَي

مُذ جَرَي ما قد كَفَى مِن مُقْلَتِي

قد بَرَي اعظمُ حُزنٍ اعظُمِي

و فَنَى جسمِيَ حاشا اصغرِيْ ¹

Again, on another occasion, wishing to criticise
my use of *ṭiyat*, Palmer thrust into the middle of an
English letter—

وامّا استمالُ جنابِكم لفظةَ طِيّةٍ في نميقتِكم آلانيقة فهو

عين آلصوابِ و المولَّدون يستعمِلونها دائماً بمعني ضِمن

آلمكتوب يشيرون بها الي مضمونِ آلكتاب و الي كلِّ شيْ

ملفوف في المغلَّف ايضاً فلا بأسَ بايرادِكم اِيّاها محلَّ

الجُملةِ آلفارسية گذارش اين است او غيرِ ذلك من هذا

القبيل——

¹ ‘ *Would that I knew whether sufficed what has flowed—*
Since (the time when) there flowed what has sufficed—from my eyes !
The biggest of sorrows has wasted my bones,
And (all) my body, except heart and tongue, is worn out.’

The last hemistich I have pointed as Palmer pointed it.

It was easier and pleasanter, no doubt, for Palmer to say this in Arabic than in English, inasmuch as a Persian or Arabic form of expression for every phase of feeling and every subject of criticism dwelt in his mind, whence it struggled, hardly ever in vain, to get out.

After 1879 I was not long in finding out that the time had gone by when Palmer was swift and eager to break a lance with me on any point of scholarship suggested. His first wife died: the old state of things passed away. Soon after this he married again, left Cambridge altogether, and plunged into the vortex of newspaper-work. In a letter dated April 20, 1880, he writes—"I am tired of residence and of giving elementary lectures, which after all are no part of a Professor's duty. After this term I shall give up the extra stipend the University gives me on condition of my residing so many weeks in a term, in order that I may be free and get time to work at something better than teaching boys the Persian alphabet." For nine months after this I heard nothing of him, excepting that he had overworked himself, had been very ill, and was more determined than ever "never again to teach alphabets to boys." A few months later he answered a query of mine respecting a point of Arabic criticism, after considerable delay, not in his ancient style, but curtly and kindly, as much as to say—'there you are, don't bother me.' He sent me but a sheet of letter paper, where he would have sent a foolscap at least in old times. At the close of 1881 I was forced to ask him a question respecting the Persian *Akhtar* which I knew he alone could answer. But no answer ever came to that question. It was lost sight of, no doubt, under a superincumbent mass of work.

I did not know of his journey to Egypt last summer: I heard he had been consulted by the Government, that was all. Not till I read it in the 'Times' of a date in the middle of August, did I know that he was in the Desert, and that fears were really entertained for his safety. I knew Palmer to be a man of consummate tact and resource, and I could not conceive any disadvantage he could possibly labour under, excepting, perhaps, a little (Syrian) roughness of accent. As the terrible details of his murder were gradually unfolded in the daily papers, I felt inexpressibly shocked. And all I can do now is to deeply lament his loss and loyally cherish his memory. In him England loses her *greatest* Oriental linguist and *readiest* Oriental scholar, a man of superior genius and resource, whose devotion to his country's cause led him to attempt to rule a sea of passions which the wild wind of bigotry had lashed into fury. If he failed, he paid the penalty of failure with his life ; and it may be said of him, as Arnold said of Flaminius, " he served his country well : and if the Wady Sudr witnessed his rashness, it also contains his honourable remains."

APPENDIX II.

TUMULO SUPERADDITE CARMEN.

षर कारकाग्म्रा ईरपावततोतजिया

मद्रजिपृगयोभटज्यौ ॥ करिग्म्राप

वकाजकमीश्र वकाक पतावके

सायगयौ फ़िरि त्यौ ॥ बुयिमा

वब द्रीबभवावजबावव दावरटयौ

वभिरबैदमबयौ ॥ परदेषमेजा

द्रमस्थौभरिकैपरकाजकोपाम

रषह्मबयौ ॐ ॥

RAMPAL SINGH.

تاريخ فوت المعلّم ادورد هنرى فالمر

لمغفوري قضيّة مصر

١ اِذَا اَمَرَ ٱلْقَضَا اَمْرًا قَضِيًّا

مَضَى مَا لَمْ يَكُنْ يَدْرِي مَضِيَّا

٢ فَكَمْ مِنْ سَمْعٍ اَضْحَى مِنَ ٱلصَّمَّ

وَ كَمْ مِنْ مُبْصِرٍ اَمْسَى عَمِيَّا

٣ سَهَا ٱلْنِحْرِيرُ عَنْ مَعْلُومٍ عِلْمُهْ

رَاَى ٱلْقِطْمِيرَ قِنْطَارًا رَبِيَّا

٤ وَ سَمَّى ٱلْسَمَّ تِرْيَاقًا فَرُوقَا

وَ ظَنَّ ٱلْحَنْظَلَ رُطَبًا جَنِيًّا

٥ مَشَى مَشْيَ ٱلْغَوَافِلِ فِي ٱلْسَوَافِلِ

وَ لَوْ فِي ٱلْعَقْلِ كَانَ فَتًى عَلِيّاً

٦ كَذا مَثَلُ اللَّذي تَعَمَّلَ قِطَّهُ

قَصِيُّ مَالِهِ جُعِلَ دَنِيَّا

٧ وَصِنْهُ حِكايَةُ مِصْرَ وَفاتِحِيها

كَأَنَّكَ كُنْتَ عَنْ قَصْدِي حَفِيَّا

٨ فَإِنْ أَرَّخْتَ عامَ حَرْبِ عُرابِي

وَأَمْرَ الْإِنْكِليسِ الْقَيْصَرِ يا

٩ فَقُلْ إِدْوَرْد هِنْرِي فَالْمَرَ حِيفٌ

كَمِصْرَ وَصُبْحَهُ أَمْسَى عَشِيَّا

١٨٨٢

قاله الميرزا محمّد باقر البواناتي

الملقب بابراهيم جان معطر

مترجم الاغنية القيصرية تعريبًا و

تعبيرًا و تفريسًا و تهنيد

٣ دسمبر سنة ١٨٨٢   المقيم في دارِ السِّلْم لَنْدَن

مرثيه در حقِ شيخ عبدالله الانكليزى المقتول بغدر
المشهور بيروفسور پالمر

شيخ عبداللّه قيدك چرخِ ظالم الامان
نوله بو غمدن دوكرسه اشكِ خون پير و جوان

٢ قيلدى سيفِ حيفِ ايله مصرِ جهاندن ارتحال
پالمرى تيهِ فنادن اوله جنت آشيان

٣ اى ستارهٔ درخشانِ ظرافت بيلمدم
اولمينجه سن كه اختر زيرِ خاك اولور نهان

٤ فارسينك فارسِ ميدانى اى شيخ العرب
مجلسِ اهلِ هنرده شمعِ شعشعه فشان

٥ ايلدك سيروا فى الارضه قبطى آسا انقياد
هند اولوردى وطن وش اكا اولسيدك روان

٦ انكليزه ويردك ازهارِ زُهَير ايله بَيَا
كوشدارِ امرِ رحمن ايدك اَتلُوَ القرآن

٧ حقه‌بازيده يكانه رسمِ فننده فريد
آفرين دانش فضيلت حيف سحّارِ زمان

٨ مرغزارِ خلده اول عنقاى قافِ علم اوچه
ايدى دنيا كلشننده بلبلِ شيرين زبان

٩ زندكى ويردى حيانه چشمهٔ عرفانيله
شمدى جانا وه دريغا تركِ عالم قيلدى جان

١٠ سن سرشكِ خون ايله يازدك بو غمِ تاريخنى
كيتدى روح الدهر بيزدن ناله قيل كون و مكان (١٢٩٩)

١ صاحب والا گهر ادورد هنري پالمر

حاوي فضل و بلاغت جامع علم و هنر

٢ منشئ انشاء دانش مفتي فتواي عقل

نا قل احكا م مسند مخبر اصل الخبر

٣ ناظم اقليم نظم و فا رس ميدان نثر

نا طق منطوق منطق ماهر فن جفر

٤ مثل او درمصر وروم و پا رس و هند و انكلند

عا قلان دهررا شاخصيكم آمد درنظر

٥ مسطر منشور اوكزچشم باشد ملتقي

عقد پروين خو انمش ياكويمش سلك گهر

٦ نقطهٔ خط سطورش نقشهٔ مژگان حسن

چشمهٔ بين السطو دش چشمهٔ نور بصر

٧ حرف لفظش در صفا آئینهٔ معنی نما

معنیش تفسیر بیضا فی الدجی ضوء القمر

٨ نکتهها ی مجملش چون نافهٔ مشک ختن

نقطهها ي اسودش از چشم آهو شوخ تر

٩ رشحهٔ کلک مطیرش هست آب زند کي

مزرع حسن مضامین میشود زان سبز وتر

١٠ وصف تحویرش نباشدحد امکان بلیغ

زانکه حسنش بیشتر با شد بیا نم مختصر

١١ یا الهی تا بود دوران این کردون بود

سا غرعشرت بد ست و تاج اجلا لش بسر

١٢ بینهٔ ز رپیش رویش بادغرق بحر رشک

سنبل تر پیش موی وي بآب نژوم تر

١٣ ختم کیدم برد عاو ثبت کیدم مبرخود

تا شود اشعار مهرم از نگا هش بیرهور

By SEYED HASSAN, *poetically surnamed* BALIGH.

تاريخ فوت ادورد هنرى پالمر صاحب

عالَم از علمست و حُبِّ علم حَبِّ عالَم است۵

غالِم این حُبّ و حبّ و علم و عالَم آدم است۵

چون مُحیط صغیر عالَم قطر علم آدمی است ۵

تنگ گردد عالَمت گرآدمِ عالِم کمست ۵

تا بشُد اِدورد هنرى پالمر تاریخ گفت ۵

حُبّ و علم از عالم ارشُد کارِ عالَم دَرهَم است

۱ ۸ ۸ ۲

گفتهٔ میرزا محمد باقر بوانا ئی ملقب
بابا ابراهیم جان معطر مترجم
عربي بو عبری و فاسي و
هندی سرودِ قیصری
۲۴ نومبر سنه ۱۸۸۲   مقیم دار السلام لندن

The Death of the Sheikh Abdullah.

THE blood-red dawn rolls westward ; crag and steep
　Welcome the splendid day with purple glow :
Through the dim gorges shape and outline creep,
　And deeper seem the black depths far below.

Earth hath no wilder place, her lands among ;
　Here is no cool green spot, no pleasant thing :
No shade of lordly bough, no sweet birds' song,
　No gracious meadows, and no flowers of spring.

The eagle builds his eyrie on these peaks ;
　Below, the jackal and hyena prowl :
No gentle creature here her pasture seeks,
　But fiery serpents lurk, and vulture foul.

I see a figure, where the rock sinks sheer
　Into a gorge too deep for noontide sun ;
Above, the sky of morning pure and clear—
　Others are there, but I see only one.

In Syrian robes, like some old warrior free,
　After fierce fight a captive, so he stands,
Gazing his last—sweet are the skies to see,
　And sweet the sunshine breaking o'er the lands.

Then, while the light of wrath prophetic fills
　His awful eyes, he hurls among his foes—
Wild echoes ringing round the 'frighted hills—
　A flaming prophecy of helpless woes.

Yea ; like a Hebrew Prophet doth he tell
　　Of swift revenge and death and women's moan ;
And stricken babes and burning pains of hell—
　　Then each man's traitor heart fell cold as stone.

And through their strong limbs fearful tremblings crept,
　　And brown cheeks paled, and down dropped every head ;
Then, with a last fierce prophecy he leaped.
　.　　.　　.　　.　　.　　.　　.
　My God ! Abdullah—Palmer—art thou dead ?

W. B.

Miro pal.

KÀNA shundom tu ghias
　　Adūr' o pāni vrī,
Ne pendom mé sā dūro
　　O jāben astis sī.

Kanà shūndom tu vīas
　　Pash-jindo tem adré,
Né pendom dovo sī o tem
　　Te kekéno jindé.

Tu jindes sār i jibia
　　O manush astis pen,
Kennā shyan tu rak'sa
　　Sā kekkenī jinden.

Sī kūshtoben 'dré mériben
　　Adovo astis sī
Awer, kennā tu latchdé lis
　　Tu lias moro 'vrī.

CHARLES G. LELAND.

My brother.

Now when I heard that thou wert gone
  Afar across the sea,
I little thought how very far
  That journey was to be.

And when I heard that thou wouldst tread
  In half-known lands alone,
I little thought thy footsteps sped
  Unto the all unknown.

I knew how soon to every tongue
  Thy tongue was quickly turned,
Now if thou speakest 'tis in that
  Which mortal never learned.

There may be happiness in death
  As many sing or say,
But oh ! in finding happiness
  Thou'st taken ours away.

C. G. L.

Il nous manque un convive—il nous manque un ami,
Qui dort d'un long sommeil sous un rocher sublime :
Ton fanatisme aveugle, ô sauvage ennemi,
Avait-il donc besoin d'une telle victime ?

Mais assez—essuyons nos pleurs à ce banquet,
Que souvent égaya son fin et doux sourire ;
Sur son vaste tombeau déposons un bouquet,
Et n'oublions jamais qu'il est mort pour l'Empire !

W. H. P.

Man hat ihn gesucht in der Tiefe,
  Den grossen, edlen Held,
Als ob er ganz ruhig nur schliefe,
  Verborgen vor aller Welt.

Sein Tod enthüllt die Grösse seiner Seele,
  Er ruft : Elendes Volk, ihr dürft nicht tödten mich ;
Mög' Unglück, Tod and Hölle euch erwarten,
  Mein Körper stirbt, doch meine Seele rächet sich.

Er war die Wahrheit !
  Was sein Mund versprochen wird gescheh'n :
Wenn nicht durch Menschenhand gerächt,
  Die Mörder werden ungestraft nicht geh'n.

Und in der Tiefe sucht man ihn ?
  Blickt hinauf in die Höhen !
In der Tiefe findet ihr vermodertes Gebein :
  Nur hoch erhaben, dort oben könnt ihr ihnsehen.

Zu niedrig ist die arme Erde,
Ein kleines, nur geringes Feld :
Er ging hinauf,
O, trau're Weib,
Erkenn' ihn, Welt !

Palmer emlikine.

Mint a tudomung aar s' harádnur vértancyn
Müködésed tenén lelted düsö haládotat.
Forrów nenetets louhádad es barútid siratauk
Mig a muysúk s' harúd dusö bajnokbun büsr-kilkedner.

A. V.

Or fra di noi è steso il velo nero!
  E a te le mani, fuor dal cieco lato,
Inutili porgiam.   E quel mistero,
    Le tue angoscie ed il crudel fato,
                    Restiam a piangere!

E tu sapendo più di noi, tanto!
  Che ora pur t' è noto il sommo arcano—
Ci puoi sorridere, o Caro Santo,
    Ma noi, benchè lo piangere fia vano,
                    Restiam a piangere!

Benigno Core!   Tu non tornerai
  Allor·che torneranno i Vincitori!
Fia duro lo sfogar i nostri guai,
    E pien le mani degli offerti allori,
                    Starem a piangere!

Che al par di lor, tu se' pur degno—e quanto!
  D' un Vincitor i lauri e le palme,   .
Ben lo sappiam.   Perdonaci intanto
    Lo spargere le gloriose salme
                    Col nostro piangere!

Non fia per sempre!   Ciascun la sua croce
  Ha da portar.   Tu, con coraggio tanto!—
Ci sembra udirti, in lontana voce,
    Sclamar, ' Amici! non mi son compianto :
                    Non tanto piangere!'

                                        F. L.

Wspomnicnie Edwarda Palmera.

SPÓJRZ ! tam w arabskie pustynie,
Tam wsród dzikicgo manowca,
Tam gdzic w skarach oko ginie
Widze z Albionu wędrowca !

Napnód gna go żądza wiedzy,
Swej ojczyżnie sruźyé spieszy,
Zdala od wizianej miedzy,
W posród Beduinów rseszy.

Tajniki wszystkie ict mory,
I ict mętne strony ducha,
On zrozumicé jert gotony
On je bada, zbiera, srucha.

Gdy Anglia perna zachwytu,
Czeka na to zrote żniwo :
Naraz pasmo jego bytu
Rwie sie, ienne to presdżiwo.

Ze zdradnej Araba ręki
Gdy mąz ten dzielny umiera,
Spieizmy dzielié jego meki
Spseizmy ezcié imie *Palmera* !

Gdyly więcej takich synów
Rosrona niwie ojczyzny,
W posród gęstych ict mewnynów
Narodu z nikry by blizny !

E. D. J.

Paryż, Styczeń, 1882.

¡ Hombre insepulto ! este, á cada paso
Dijo la gente, es un dolor estrecho !
Mas yo le repliqué : '¿ Tiene ello acaso
Otro sepulcro que mi amante pecho ? '

E. M. S.

גַּם הוּא אָמַר

אֱדֹוְרָךְ הִנְרִי פָּלְמָר אִם מֵת
אָמְרוּ לְשֻׁנַת אוֹנוֹ:
" מִי שֶׁ'רְצוֹנוֹ בְּמָנָת
יֵשׁ חַיִּים בִּרְצוֹנוֹ:"

מ". ב". א". נ". מ".

תְּמָרִים הֵנִיעוּ רֹאשׁ עַל צַדִּיק כִּתָּמָר
נָשִׁים יָמִים בַּלֵּילוֹת עַל שֵׁם לֵילוֹת בַּיָּמִים

A. M.

'*Ipse Deus, simul atque volam, me solvet.*'

Sæva Arabum qua tesqua patent, et inhospita passim
  Stant juga, sanguineo nascitur orbe dies ;
Jam quoque ferali velamine longior umbra
  Culmine de summo dum cadit, ima tegit.
Lux funesta nitet ; tria, quæ peregrina notavit,
  En capita in letum ducit acerbus Arabs.

Captorum alter habet phaleras alterque Britannas :
Haud facies patrium dedecet illa sagum.
Tertius imbellem Syrium mentitur Eoä
Veste ; sed intrepido discrepat ista viro.
Indignatur atrox animus per barbara tolli
Tela ; sed exitium vir petit ipse sibi.
Vertice præcipiti cava qui supereminet ingens
Est scopulus ; celsa despicit arce solum.
Rupis in extremo jam margine constitit heros ;
Mox Arabas propriis devovet ille deis.
At furias metuunt patrias ulturaque cædem
Numina, et auditas turba cruenta preces.
Inde valere jubet socios, et torvus in altum
Prosilit : ut rapido turbine noster abest.
Ferrea saxa silent ; nec vallibus ingruit horror :
Inque polo liquidum lucet, ut ante, jubar.
At tibi quidquid erat cari, te corda tuorum
Teque sodalitium plorat, adempte, tuum.

S. L.

IN MEMORIAM E. H. P.

Οἴχει δὴ, φιλ' ἑταῖρε, διαμπερὲς, ἀιγίλιπος δὲ
Πέτρου ἄπο ῥιφθεὶς κεῖσαι ὑπὸ πρόποδι.
Οὔνεκ' ἀφ' ἡμετέρης στρατίης, παρὰ χεύμασι Νείλου
Μαρναμένης, Συρίων βάρβαρον εἶργες ῎Αρη.
Τοιγὰρ ἀπὸ κρημνοῦ πήδημ' ἀλίαστον ὄρουσας
'Εχθρῶν ἐν γαίῃ, λευγαλέῳ θανάτῳ,
Σαυτῷ μὲν κλέος ἦρου ἀμυνόμενος περὶ πάτρας,
Τοῖς δὲ φίλοις ἔλιπες δάκρυα κιὶ στοναχὰς.
Μοῖρ' ὀλόη, φιλέεις οὕτω τὰ πέρισσα καθαιρεῖν
Οὐδὲν ἐν ἀνθρώποις ἐσθλὸν ἐῶσα μένειν.

A. S.

APPENDIX III.

WORKS OF EDWARD HENRY PALMER.

WORKS OF EDWARD HENRY PALMER.

Poems of Behá ed Dín Zoheir of Egypt. With a Metrical Translation, Notes, and Introduction, by E. H. Palmer. Crown 4to. Vol. I., Arabic Text, 1876; Vol. II., English Translation, 1877. Cambridge University Press.

Oriental Mysticism: Theosophy of the Persians. 12mo. 1867. Bell & Daldy.

Desert of the Exodus. Forty Years' Wanderings. 2 vols. 8vo. 1871. Bell & Daldy.

History of Jerusalem, the City of Herod and Saladin. By Walter Besant and E. H. Palmer. Crown 8vo. 1871. Bentley.

Catalogue of Arabic, Persian, and Turkish MSS. in Trin. Coll., Camb. 8vo. 1871. Bell & Daldy.

Grammar of the Arabic Language. 8vo. 1877. W. H. Allen & Co.

Outlines of Scripture Geography. 12mo. 1874. Society for Promoting Christian Knowledge.

History of the Jewish Nation from the Earliest Times. Post 8vo. 1874. Society for Promoting Christian Knowledge.

English Gipsy Songs in Romany. With Metrical English Trans. by C. G. Leland, E. H. Palmer, and Janet Tuckey. Post 8vo. 1875. Trübner & Co.

Song of the Reed and other Pieces. Post 8vo. 1876. Trübner & Co.

A Concise Dictionary of the Persian Language. Square 16mo. 1876. Trübner & Co.

Lyrical Songs, Idylls, and Epigrams of John Ludvig Runeberg, done into English by Eirikr Magnusson and E. H. Palmer. Fcp. 8vo. 1878. Kegan Paul & Co.

Haroun Alraschid, Caliph of Bagdad. Crown 8vo. 1880. M. Ward & Co.

Sacred Books of the East. Vols. VI. and IX., 'The Qur'ân.' Translated by E. H. Palmer. 2 vols. 8vo. 1880. Clarendon Press.

Arabic Manual, Grammar, Reading Lessons, Exercises, &c. 12mo. 1881. W. H. Allen & Co.

Survey of Western Palestine. Arabic and English Name Lists, collected during the Survey by Lieutenants Condor and Kitchener, R.E. Translated and explained by E. H. Palmer. 4to. 1881. Palestine Exploration Fund.

Simplified Grammar of Hindustani, Persian, and Arabic. 8vo. 1882. Trübner & Co.

Poems of Hafiz of Shiraz. Translated from the Persian into English Verse, by E. H. Palmer. 1 vol. 8vo. Trübner & Co.

A Concise English and Persian Dictionary. Square 16mo. Trübner & Co.

LONDON : PRINTED BY
SPOTTISWOODE AND CO., NEW-STREET SQUARE
AND PARLIAMENT STREET

MR. MURRAY'S LIST.

The GOLDEN CHERSONESE and the WAY THITHER.
A Narrative of Travels in the Straits Settlements. By ISABELLA
BIRD (Mrs. BISHOP). With Maps and 16 Illustrations. Crown
8vo. 14*s*.

WALKS in the REGIONS of SCIENCE and FAITH :
A Series of Essays. By HARVEY GOODWIN, D.D., Lord Bishop
of Carlisle. Crown 8vo. 7*s*. 6*d*.

MEXICO TO-DAY ; a Country with a Great Future,
and a Glance at the Prehistoric Remains and Antiquities of the
Montezumas. By THOMAS UNETT BROCKLEHURST. With Map,
17 Coloured Plates, and 37 Wood Engravings from Sketches by
the Author. Medium 8vo. 21*s*.

DISSERTATIONS on EARLY LAW and CUSTOM.
Chiefly Selected from Lectures delivered at Oxford. By Sir
HENRY S. MAINE, Author of 'Ancient Law,' &c. 8vo. 12*s*.

The PARTHENON : An Essay on the Mode in which
Light was admitted into Greek and Roman Temples. By JAMES
FERGUSSON, C.I.E., F.R.S. With Illustrations. 4to. 21*s*.

WORSHIP and ORDER. By the Right Hon. A. J. B.
BERESFORD HOPE, M.P., Author of 'Worship in the Church of
England,' &c. 8vo. 9*s*.

A JOURNAL of a LADY'S TRAVELS ROUND the
WORLD : including Visits to Japan, Thibet, Yarkand, Kashmir,
Java, the Straits of Malacca, Vancouver's Island, &c. By F. D.
BRIDGES. With Illustrations from Sketches by the Author.
Crown 8vo. 15*s*.

JAMES NASMYTH, Engineer and Inventor of the Steam
Hammer. An Autobiography. Edited by SAMUEL SMILES,
LL.D. With Portrait etched by Rajon, and 90 Illustrations.
Crown 8vo. 16*s*.

RECOLLECTIONS of ARTHUR PENRHYN STAN-
LEY. Lectures delivered in Edinburgh in November 1882. By
G. GRANVILLE BRADLEY, D.D., Dean of Westminster. Crown
8vo. 3*s*. 6*d*.

The RISE and GROWTH of the LAW of NATIONS.
As Established by General Usage and by Treaties. From the
Earliest Time to the Treaty of Utrecht. By JOHN HOSACK,
Barrister-at-Law, of the Middle Temple. 8vo. 12*s*.

RAPHAEL : HIS LIFE and WORKS ; with Particular
Reference to recently Discovered Records, and an Exhaustive
Study of Extant Drawings and Pictures. By J. A. CROWE and
G. B. CAVALCASELLE. Vol. I. 8vo. 15*s*.

[*Continued.*

JAMES and PHILIP VAN ARTEVELD. Two
Remarkable Episodes in the History of Flanders. With a
Description of the State of Society in Flanders in the 14th
Century. By James Hutton. Crown 8vo. 10s. 6d.

SUNNY LANDS and SEAS : a Cruise Round the World
in the S.S. 'Ceylon.' Being Notes made during a Five Months'
Tour in India, the Straits Settlements, Manila, China, Japan, the
Sandwich Islands, and California. By Hugh Wilkinson,
Barrister-at-Law. With Illustrations. 8vo. 12s.

LIFE of JONATHAN SWIFT, DEAN of ST.
PATRICK'S, DUBLIN. By Henry Craik, M.A., late
Scholar and Snell Exhibitioner, Balliol College, Oxford.
Portrait. 8vo. 18s.

RECREATIONS and STUDIES of a COUNTRY
CLERGYMAN of the LAST CENTURY. Being Selections
from the Correspondence of Thomas Twining, M.A., sometime
Fellow of Sidney Sussex College. Crown 8vo. 9s.

GREECE. Pictorial, Descriptive, and Historical. By
Christopher Wordsworth, D.D., Bishop of Lincoln. New
and Revised Edition. Edited by H. F. Tozer, M.A., Tutor
of Exeter College, Oxford. With 400 Illustrations of Scenery,
Architecture, and Fine Arts. Royal 8vo. 31s. 6d.

METHOD in ALMSGIVING. A Handbook for Helpers.
By M. W. Moggridge, Hon. Secretary of the St. James's and
Soho Charity Organisation Society. Post 8vo. 3s. 6d.

The ART of DINING ; or, Gastronomy and Gastronomers.
By A. Hayward, Q.C. A New Edition. Post 8vo. 2s.

ASIATIC STUDIES—RELIGIOUS and SOCIAL. By
Sir Alfred C. Lyall, K.C.B. 8vo. 12s.

A POPULAR EDITION of the LIFE of DAVID
LIVINGSTONE. Founded on his Unpublished Journals and
Correspondence. By W. G. Blaikie, D.D. New Edition.
Portrait and Map. Post 8vo. 6s.

SIBERIA in ASIA. A Visit to the Valley of the Yenesay
in East Siberia. With Description of the Natural History,
Migration of Birds, &c. By Henry Seebohm, F.R.G.S. With
Map and 60 Illustrations. Crown 8vo. 14s.

A POPULAR EDITION of the LIFE of a SCOTCH
NATURALIST (Thomas Edward). By Samuel Smiles,
LL.D. Uniform with 'Self-Help.' New Edition. Portrait and
Illustrations. Post 8vo. 6s.

[*Continued.*

The LIFE of SAMUEL WILBERFORCE, D.D., late
Bishop of Oxford and Winchester. With Extracts from his Diaries
and Correspondence. With Portraits and Woodcuts. 3 vols. 8vo.
15*s.* each.
> Vol. I. Edited by the late Canon ASHWELL. 2nd Edition.
> 1805-1848.
> Vol. II. Edited by his Son, R. G. WILBERFORCE. 1848-1860.
> Vol. III. Edited by R. G. WILBERFORCE. 2nd Edition.
> 1861-1873.

The STUDENT'S MANUAL of the GEOGRAPHY and
PHYSIOLOGY of BRITISH INDIA. By GEORGE SMITH,
LL.D., Author of the 'Life of Dr. Wilson, Dr. Duff,' &c. Maps.
Post 8vo. 7*s.* 6*d.*

MEN and EVENTS of MY TIME in INDIA. 1847 to
1880. By Sir RICHARD TEMPLE, Bart., Author of 'India in
1880.' 8vo. 16*s.*

A JOURNEY to the WHITE SEA, and the KOLA
PENINSULA. By EDWARD RAE, Author of 'The Country of
the Moors.' With Maps, Etchings, and Woodcuts. Crown 8vo. 15*s.*

LAND of the MIDNIGHT SUN. Summer and Winter
Journeys through Sweden, Norway, Lapland, and Northern Finland. By P. B. DU CHAILLU. Map and 235 Illustrations.
2 vols. 8vo. 36*s.*

LETTERS and JOURNALS of SIR WILLIAM GOMM.
The Helder Expedition—Copenhagen—The Walcheren Expe-
dition—The Peninsula—Waterloo, &c. 1799-1815. Edited by
F. C. CARR GOMM. Portraits. 8vo. 12*s.*

LIFE and WORKS of ALBERT DÜRER. By MORIZ
THAUSING. Edited by F. A. EATON, M.A., Secretary of the
Royal Academy. Illustrations. 2 vols. Medium 8vo. 42*s.*

LIFE and WORKS of MICHAEL ANGELO. Including
Inedited Documents from the Buonarroti Archives. By C. HEATH
WILSON. Illustrations. 8vo. 15*s.*

LIFE, WORKS, and TIMES of TITIAN. With some
Account of his Family. By J. A. CROWE and G. B. CAVAL-
CASELLE. Illustrations. 2 vols. 8vo. 21*s.*

The BEDOUINS of the EUPHRATES VALLEY. By
Lady ANNE BLUNT. With some Account of the Arabs and
their Horses. Illustrations. 2 vols. Crown 8vo. 24*s.*

A PILGRIMAGE to NEJD, the Cradle of the Arab Race,
and a Visit to the Court of the Arab Emir. By Lady ANNE
BLUNT. Illustrations. 2 vols. Post 8vo. 24*s.*

JOHN MURRAY, Albemarle Street.
F F

CABINET EDITIONS OF STANDARD WORKS.

BYRON'S (LORD) POETICAL WORKS. Illustrations.
10 vols. Small 8vo. 30s.

BYRON'S (LORD) LETTERS and JOURNALS. With
Notices of his Life. By THOMAS MOORE. Illustrations. 6 vols.
Small 8vo. 18s.

DERBY'S (LORD) ILIAD of HOMER. Rendered
into English Blank Verse. Portrait. 2 vols. Post 8vo. 10s.

GROTE'S HISTORY of GREECE. From the Earliest
Period to the close of the Generation Contemporary with Alexander
the Great. Portrait and Plans. 12 vols. Post 8vo. 6s. each.

HALLAM'S HISTORICAL WORKS. Portrait. 10 vols.
Post 8vo. 4s. each.
> HISTORY of ENGLAND. 3 vols.
> EUROPE during the MIDDLE AGES. 3 vols.
> LITERARY HISTORY of EUROPE. 4 vols.

MILMAN'S HISTORICAL WORKS. 15 vols. Post
8vo. 6s. each.
> HISTORY of the JEWS. 3 vols.
> HISTORY of EARLY CHRISTIANITY. 3 vols.
> HISTORY of LATIN CHRISTIANITY. 9 vols.

**MOTLEY'S HISTORY of the UNITED NETHER-
LANDS.** From the Death of William the Silent to the Twelve
Years' Truce. 1584-1609. Portraits. 4 vols. Post 8vo. 24s.

**MOTLEY'S LIFE and DEATH of JOHN of BARNE-
VELD.** With a View of the Primary Causes of 'The Thirty
Years' War.' Illustrations. 2 vols. Post 8vo. 12s.

**NAPIER'S ENGLISH BATTLES and SIEGES of the
PENINSULAR WAR.** Portrait. Crown 8vo. 9s.

**ROBERTSON'S HISTORY of the CHRISTIAN
CHURCH.** From the Apostolic Age to the Reformation, 1547.
8 vols. Post 8vo. 6s. each.

SMILES'S LIVES of the ENGINEERS. From the
Earliest Times to the Death of the Stephensons. Portraits and
Woodcuts. 5 vols. Crown 8vo. 7s. 6d. each.
> VERMUYDEN, MYDDELTON, PERRY, BRINDLEY.
> SMEATON and RENNIE.
> METCALFE and TELFORD.
> BOULTON and WATT.
> GEORGE and ROBERT STEPHENSON.

STANHOPE'S (EARL) HISTORY of ENGLAND,
from the Reign of Queen Anne to the Peace of Versailles,
1701-83. Portrait. 9 vols. Post 8vo. 5s. each.

JOHN MURRAY, Albemarle Street.

www.ingramcontent.com/pod-product-compliance
Lightning Source LLC
Chambersburg PA
CBHW030937110726
47900CB00004B/1034